THE
FORBIDDEN
TEMPLE

Patrick Woodhead has been professionally exploring for the last eight
years. He has scaled unclimbed mountains in Kyrgyzstan, Tibet and
Antarctica, kayaked through the unchartered tributaries in the Amazon
and skied over 4,000 km across Antarctica. He is also the founder of
White Desert (www.whitedesert.com), the first luxury safari company
in Antarctica and divides his time between London and South Africa.

THE
FORBIDDEN
TEMPLE

PATRICK
WOODHEAD

arrow books

This paperback edition published by Arrow Books 2010

10 9 8 7 6 5 4

First published in Great Britain in 2009 as *The Cloud Maker* by
Preface Publishing

Arrow Books
20 Vauxhall Bridge Road
London SW1V 2SA

An imprint of The Random House Group Limited

www.randomhouse.co.uk

Addresses for companies within The Random House Group Limited
can be found at www.randomhouse.co.uk

The Random House Group Limited Reg. No. 954009

A CIP catalogue record for this book is available from the British Library

ISBN 978 0 09957 112 4

The Random House Group Limited supports The Forest Stewardship Council
(FSC®), the leading international forest certification organisation. Our books
carrying the FSC label are printed on FSC® certified paper. FSC is the only
forest certification scheme endorsed by the leading environmental organisations,
including Greenpeace. Our paper procurement policy can be found at
www.randomhouse.co.uk/environment

MIX
Paper from
responsible sources
FSC® C016897

Typeset in Electra LH Regular by Palimpsest Book Production Limited,
Grangemouth, Stirlingshire
Printed and bound by CPI Group (UK) Ltd, Croydon, CR0 4YY

For Mike,
Inspiration and friendship in equal measure

'Tides rise. Red waters grow higher. Like islands we vanish one by one, enveloped by the darkness. We must have the courage to evolve, grow stronger. To understand that the losses will be justified, the balance met. Only through fighting for what we believe, can we be truly free.'

Prologue

Just before the bend, he stopped.

The noise he'd heard was like an animal crashing through the bamboo thickets and, thinking it might be just that, the young novice monk halted in his tracks. Then he heard sharp voices barking out orders in Mandarin. Veering off the path, he dropped low behind a dense thicket, his face only inches from the frozen ground.

A few seconds later, four uniformed soldiers burst on to the path, rifles slung over their shoulders. They were talking fast, gesticulating with swift stabbing movements at something higher up the valley.

Rega could see a pair of battered military boots just in front of him, tiny crystals of snow frosting the muddy laces. A few more steps and they would be on him. He could hear the soldier's breathing and the sticky sounds of his mouth working as he chewed on tobacco.

'*Zai Nar!*' shouted another voice, further away, and the boots paused for a moment and then crunched off in the other direction. Rega let out a ragged breath, but his relief turned to horror as he realised what had just happened.

One of the soldiers must have looked back across the interlocking valleys and seen – framed through a gap in the trees like a keyhole –

1

what was meant to have stayed hidden in the jungle of the gorge for several more centuries.

Moments later there were more shouts, and soon dozens of pairs of boots came tramping past where he lay.

It was over. They had found them.

All winter, in the icy basin of the Tsangpo gorge, the monks had waited. As the snows began to melt and the rhododendrons pushed their way through the layers of frost, they knew their time had come. Soon the days would lengthen and the Doshong-La would become passable again. The seasons were changing, and with them their fate.

For months they had heard stories – whispered, terrible stories – filtering through from the outside world. Then, two weeks ago, a pair of snow-covered porters had stumbled into the monastery. Exhausted, they had risked everything to climb through the night and relay the news: on the opposite side of the colossal mountain peaks, they had seen the unmistakable tents of a Chinese patrol.

It was obvious what they had come for – there was no other reason to be sitting at the bottom of one of the fiercest mountain passes in Tibet. Someone must have tipped them off. Now they were just waiting for the end of the winter snowstorms.

As the hours passed, the young novice Rega remained perfectly still. The habitually smooth skin across his forehead was furrowed in confusion and his wide, brown eyes stared blankly out across the darkening gorge. He was naturally thin and wiry and even under his thick, winter tunic, he could feel the cold seeping up from the ground. His arms were folded tight across his chest, trying to stave off the chill, and his legs felt numb.

At first he was unsure what the flicker of light was. Maybe his mind was playing tricks on him after the long hours of cold and fear. But it continued, bigger now, a ball of orange which seemed to grow by the minute, shooting high into the night sky.

The idea was so inconceivable that it was a while before Rega fully understood what he was seeing. Long tongues of fire, fanned and bolstered by the wind, were spreading out across the great timbers of the monastery roof. Even against the dark night sky, he could make out the smoke twisting upwards, the ashes billowing in the heat.

Dragging himself upright, Rega staggered forward, mesmerised by the flames. He had to see what was happening. He had to see it with his own eyes.

Snow scattered from overhanging leaves as he pushed his way through the undergrowth. His breath was coming shorter now from the climb, until at last, he stumbled into a clearing and saw the main façade of the monastery. Raising his arm to shield his face from the sudden wall of heat, he squinted at the devastation. The doors of the great library hung askew from massive hinges, their timbers charred and crumbling. Beyond, at the edge of the vaulted room, a towering mass of books was rapidly being engulfed by a wall of blue flame.

Rega moved farther on, away from the heat, his felt boots passing soundlessly over the stone paving. So far he hadn't seen a single person, either soldier or monk.

Then he began to hear it: a thin, keening sound rising above the crackle of the fire.

Squatting behind one of the huge wooden columns that surrounded the main courtyard, Rega then saw dim silhouettes moving between the shadows. Most of the monks stood round the edges of the court-yard while in the centre, about thirty of the eldest or most infirm stood together, herded into a tight cluster like cattle.

Chinese soldiers stood in front of them, their black uniforms melting into the night.

About ten yards from the main entrance to the courtyard, a young novice monk had been blindfolded. He stood facing a blank section of wall, shoulders hunched. Rega looked more closely and saw a rifle hanging loosely from his hands, the muzzle hovering only an inch or so above the ground.

Suddenly the soldiers around him started shouting, thrusting their rifles into the air like clenched fists.

'Shoot! Shoot!'

As the novice took a pace backwards, struggling to raise the barrel of the rifle towards the blank wall, two of the soldiers grabbed one of the older monks from the huddle in the centre and pushed him forward. Invisible to the novice, the old monk was now in front of him, his face only a few feet from the gun barrel.

A high-pitched wail rose and echoed around the courtyard as the other monks bore witness to the scene.

'Shoot! Shoot!' shouted the soldiers once again. The novice paused, bewildered by the noise.

One of the soldiers closed in on him. He moved with the swagger of authority, his sleeves rolled up past his elbows. Epaulettes with gold insignia flashed in the firelight as he went to stand directly behind the novice. Rega could see that he was whispering something. Then the rifle cracked and the novice was sent staggering back, knocking into the officer behind him.

There was silence. The wail of the monks halted as the body of the old monk slumped on to the courtyard's flagstones, his legs crumpling beneath him.

The bewildered silence was suddenly pierced by further shots, but this time it was the other soldiers, firing their rifles into the air and cheering.

The officer moved round in front of the novice and, taking the rifle from him, patted his shoulder reassuringly. The boy's knees sagged and the officer reached forward to support him. For a moment they stood locked together, two figures set apart from the others.

Then, with practised ease, the officer swivelled the rifle in his hands and slammed the bolt action shut once again. Without turning to look at the huddled group of old monks, he shouted, 'Next!'

Rega watched, his mouth dry with horror as another man was shunted forward from the group. Why the old ones? Were they simply too much of a burden to take back over the mountain pass? Or was he witnessing an example of the senseless violence they had all heard was accompanying this so-called 'Cultural Revolution'?

In the far corner of the courtyard he suddenly heard the sound of women screaming. It had to be the two nuns that had arrived as emissaries from Namzong nunnery. The temple doors were flung open and, through the gloom, he could see what a small group of soldiers was doing inside. For a moment he watched, revulsion rising like bile in his throat. Then a sudden surge of adrenaline unlocked the paralysis in his legs. He must get away from this place, get out, tell others.

As Rega went to turn away, he felt a sudden push from behind. The blow sent him sprawling forward on to the flagstones and Rega twisted round in time to see the grinning face of a soldier stepping out from the shadows.

He was a big man, with a jowly face and dark, gleeful eyes. He grabbed the neck of Rega's tunic and pulled him up with one arm so that their faces were almost touching. The stink of stale tobacco was sharp on his breath.

'You like watching?' The fillings in his teeth gleamed in the dark. 'We can fix that.'

Spinning Rega's wiry body round, he slammed his knee into his back and pinned him to the floor, pressing the side of his face against the flagstones. Rega felt his mind empty. He didn't say a word, but just stared past the columns of the courtyard at the flames leaping up to swallow the roof of the library. The blue and orange tongues of fire were iridescent against the black sky.

Above him, the soldier had untied the sling from his rifle and was quickly looping it into two knots, a few inches apart. He drew the sling in front of Rega's face so that there was a knot in front of each eye socket. There was a pause, then Rega screamed as his whole head was yanked backwards with a violent jerk. The soldier twisted the sling round like a tourniquet, tightening the pressure with each turn.

Rega clawed behind him with useless hands, the scream dying on his lips. His cheeks tightened, trying to resist the immense pressure as the knots burrowed deeper and deeper into his skull. With another half-turn, the knots sank further still until his eyeballs imploded, a viscous, cloudy liquid streaming down his cheeks.

Rega let out a gurgling sound as he went limp on the floor.

Those beautiful, burning rooftops were the last thing he'd ever see.

Chapter 1

20 April 2005

It was six in the morning and dawn had just broken over the roof of the world. Tawny fingers of light filtered down past the jagged peaks of the Himalayas, lending a luminous glow to the orange tents staked down on the dark scree.

Luca Matthews unzipped his tent and, still in his thermal underwear, stepped out into the freezing mountain air. He was tall with a powerful back that stretched the fabric of his thermals as he unfolded himself from the tent. Scruffy, dark-blond hair fell across a face that was deeply tanned by the intense mountain sun. Only his eyes were ringed with paler patches from where he had been wearing his glacier goggles.

For a few moments he stood there, sipping coffee from a tin mug and savouring the feeling of being the first up. He only ever needed a few hours' sleep each night and often found the morning's silence one of the rare moments in the day when he felt truly calm. As he breathed in the tingling air, the heat from his mug eased the swelling in his knuckles. Peeling some dead skin off the pads of his left hand, he ran his finger gingerly over a cut that stretched all the way back to his wrist, and shook his head. Bloody climbing injuries. They just never seemed to heal in the dry mountain air.

Grabbing a sheepskin coat that he had bought for a few hundred rupees from one of the market stalls in Kathmandu, he weaved past the smouldering remains of the campfire, balanced his mug carefully on a rock, and urinated. When he was younger, his father had impressed upon him the importance of having a good view when taking a piss. Little did Luca know then it would turn out to be one of the only things that he and the old bastard would agree on.

Crooking his neck to one side, Luca yawned and massaged a shoulder blade. After five days of lugging provisions up to base camp, the straps of his rucksack had bitten deep into his back. No doubt about it, this was the most thankless part of the climb: effort without technique or reward, encouraged only by the sight of an occasional peak piercing the blanket of cloud overhead.

Hopping on to another boulder, he sat down and wrapped his arms round his legs, drawing his knees up under his chin in his habitual pose. His eyes followed the incline of the mountain as it curved up for two or three miles before hitting the first glacier, a snub nose of pitted ice gleaming brilliantly in the morning light. Beyond it, range after range of mountains extended back to the horizon, their pinnacles reaching high enough to be whipped by the ferocious winds of the earth's Gulf Stream.

Two and a half thousand metres above him, the summit ridge finally came into view; the last stretch of ground between him and the top of Makalu, the fifth highest mountain on earth and Luca's second eight-thousand-metre peak.

Normally the sight would have given him a jolt of pure excitement but this morning Luca felt distinctly unsettled, a jittery unease that seemed to seep from his stomach into his bones. Flicking the rest of his coffee on to the ground, he watched it steam for a moment before striding back to the tents.

Getting to that ridge was going to be the most dangerous part of the climb.

*   *   *

'You planning on sleeping the whole day, princess?' Luca called, banging on the frame of one of the tents.

The snoring inside stopped and there was a shuffling noise, then the sound of a throat being cleared.

'Christ, that has to be one of the worst sleeps I've ever had. My damn Therma-rest deflated halfway through the night.'

Luca grinned. 'How about some coffee to celebrate your good mood?'

More shuffling, then the tent's zip peeled open to reveal the square-jawed face of Bill Taylor. A few days' worth of stubble darkened his chin, and his normally amused-looking pale blue eyes were puffy from lack of sleep. Above his sunburned forehead, thinning hair stuck straight up from his head as if he'd just received some kind of electrical shock.

'I'll stick to tea, thanks, mate,' he said, the words swallowed up by another cavernous yawn. 'It beats me how you mainline that filthy stuff.'

Luca leaned down to put the saucepan of water on the tiny portable stove and turned the nozzle. A gentle roaring sound filled the campsite. He watched Bill slowly unfurl his large frame from inside his sleeping bag.

'You look like shit,' Luca said softly. 'You sure you're up to starting the climb today?'

'Are you kidding? I'll be fine.'

Bill stretched his arms high above his head before lumbering over to the same rock as Luca had done to relieve himself. 'But I'm relying on you to have found us the perfect route up.'

Luca's eyes shifted back to the mountain face, his jaw clenching.

'It's quite simple on the first section, pretty much all the way up to where we'll set up camp two. After that, there's the long stretch through that vertical ice field. Of course, that's going to be more hairy. But once we make it on to the summit ridge, it's no more than two hours to the top.'

Bill had wandered back and now crouched down beside him, his gaze also fixed on the mountain. Luca handed him a mug and poured in some boiling water. As Bill took the steaming tea their eyes met for a second and, before he had even opened his mouth, Luca knew what he was going to say.

'Piece of piss.'

Luca grinned.

An hour and forty-five minutes later, they were on their way.

Chapter 2

They had been climbing for nine hours with barely a word exchanged. The dull ache of exhausted muscles made their movements clumsy and unco-ordinated.

Luca led up a long, curving arête, plodding through the deep snow and breaking trail. From his waist harness, two eight-millimetre climbing ropes trailed down, snaking over the snow and outcrops of ice to where Bill was climbing, fifty feet below. They had been taking it in turns to lead, but as the hours passed the sinking snow had sapped every ounce of their strength. Both moved at the same unrelenting pace, an ice axe held loosely in their leading hand.

Trying to steady his breathing, Luca forced himself to slow his movements as he kicked down in the snow: once . . . twice . . . Only on the third attempt did he manage to stamp down enough powder to step forward. But every few minutes he would puncture through the crust, sinking down past his thighs. At the sudden jarring, his heavy rucksack would wrench him off-balance, jerking his body round painfully and Bill would simply wait, unable to help, while Luca wasted yet more energy trying to right himself again.

The morning's clear skies had been replaced by a thick belt of dark cloud that loomed over the higher reaches of the mountain. With this came a strong wind that funnelled up the ridge and both climbers were forced to crook their necks to one side, sheltering under their hooded Gore-Tex jackets.

Just up ahead, the ridge hit the main vertical wall of ice that they had seen from base camp. They needed to camp further back from the wall, far enough away from falling rocks and ice. Checking his watch, Luca swung off his rucksack and began untying the shovel strapped to the back. As he began digging, Bill slowly closed up the remaining distance, arriving out of breath and leaning his hands on his knees, while he recovered.

'What do you think of that cloud?' he asked, breathing still laboured. 'The forecasts said it was going to get worse tomorrow.'

Luca paused, a shovelful of snow sliding to the ground. He lifted his goggles off his face and wiped the sweat out of his eyes.

'It'll pass,' he said, and carried on digging.

Bill nodded. He had climbed with Luca long enough to know not to question him about the weather. Whatever the forecast said, somehow Luca always seemed to get it right. It had become a standard joke between them. Whenever Luca lay down, everyone thought it was going to rain.

Unstrapping his own shovel, Bill started digging alongside him. In thirty minutes they had completed the snow hole and soon both of them were lying exhausted in their sleeping bags inside it, the soft roar of the MSR stove blocking out the noise of the outside world.

As soon as day broke, Luca punched through the thin wall of snow by his sleeping bag, letting the fierce morning light flood in. Cold air rushed through the gap, dispelling the stale air from the previous night. It had been a long, fitful night, neither man sleeping properly from the altitude.

Bill unzipped his sleeping bag and sat up, groaning as a headache split along the back of his skull. He stayed still, waiting for the pain to pass, while Luca shuffled forward, keeping his head bent under the low ceiling of snow. Reaching into the top of his rucksack, he handed across one of the granola bars and the tube of condensed milk. Sugar was the only way to get a climber's body moving again in the morning.

'Pass the water will you?' Bill muttered, gesturing to the plastic bottle by the stove. 'Must have got dehydrated during the night.'

'Headache?'

'Bitch of a one.'

After a few mouthfuls of water, Bill turned to look through the open hole in the snow, inspecting the sky outside.

'You were right about one thing at least.'

'The weather's not the problem,' Luca replied, stuffing his gear into his rucksack. 'It's the ice field. Did you hear the rocks coming down during the night?'

Bill nodded. Every few hours throughout the night, they had heard rocks ricocheting down the face and smacking into the hard ice of the glacier below. Both had woken with a start each time it had happened, but there was nothing to be said. They knew it was the most dangerous part of climbing Makalu's western pillar.

They packed up in silence, methodically going through the process of striking camp, their minds on the climb ahead. They were over six and a half thousand metres up already and the ice wall was going to require some serious technical climbing. No more easy snow ridges or easy retreats.

'You've planned the route,' Bill said, his eyes flicking over Luca's face. 'Why don't you lead today?'

Luca could hear the edge in Bill's voice, but didn't look up from clipping the straps on his rucksack. They both knew the lead climber would be more exposed up there. 'Sure,' he said, hoping the nonchalance in his voice didn't sound forced. 'No worries.'

Twenty minutes later they stood out on the ridge, feeling the warmth of the morning sun. Luca had uncoiled the ropes and passed two of the ends over to Bill. He, in turn, swung a heavy sling filled with friends, ice screws and nuts off his shoulder and handed it over to Luca, who begun clipping them into his harness in a well-practised and deliberate order.

'Never met anyone so anal about where they clip their hardware,' Bill noted.

'You know how it is – the higher up we get, the more stupid we become. At least this way, I know where everything is.'

Despite the dull ache in his head, Bill smiled. Back home, Luca's flat was one of the most disorganised places he had ever set foot in, surfaces covered with unopened mail and abandoned clothes. Yet out here in the mountains he seemed to undergo a complete character transformation: exact, thoughtful, with no cut corners or laziness.

'I'll belay you up there,' Luca said, pointing forty feet above their heads to a black outcrop of rock clinging to the vertical ice. Then, with a quick nod to check Bill was ready, he moved forward along the ridge, adjusting the length of the leaches on his ice axes.

Moving up on to the wall so that his hips were almost pressing against it, Luca kicked in his crampons, sending tiny shards of ice tumbling below. With fluid, rhythmic movements, he hammered in his ice axes, working his way higher with each step and taking care to keep his front points balanced on the natural shape of the ice, rather than always kicking new steps. He didn't look up, minutely absorbed in what was in front of him.

He knew he had to compartmentalise the climb. Had to focus on the first pitch, then the second. Nothing more. Thinking ahead to the summit ridge was just too far away. Above him, the cliff continued vertically for another thousand metres.

Hours passed – the same movements, the same rhythm. The sun slowly travelled across the sky, switching their shadows from right to left as they reflected off the polished ice. Both men moved silently upwards, just a few words exchanged as they handed over the hardware at the end of each pitch.

Luca dug his axes in and spread his legs wider, adjusting his balance. He unhooked an ice screw from his belt and wound it into a smooth patch of ice just by his shoulder. Clipping the rope through the carabineer, he leaned back against it, dropping his weight into the seat of his harness and relieving the intense pressure on his calves. Then he wound in a second screw, clipped in and peered down between his legs.

Following the line of the ropes, he could see Bill fighting his way up. That was the way he climbed when he got tired, always fighting. He would hammer his axes in, spraying ice everywhere, using strength not skill to move himself higher.

Somewhere off to the right, Luca heard a noise and a small collection of rocks, some the size of a man's head, came clattering down the cliff-face. They were far enough away not to be any danger, but the sight of them bouncing off the granite wall in puffs of dust was unnerving. Even rocks that size would splinter straight through their helmets.

Luca saw Bill tilt his head up to watch the rock-fall and for a moment their gazes met. Neither said a word. Playing these kinds of odds was a choice they never spoke about.

Sending a cloud of frosted breath out into the air before him, Luca looked up, allowing himself a rare moment to check their progress. They had been climbing fast and were nearly two-thirds of the way up the face. A few more hours and they would be under the summit ridge.

As the afternoon dragged on, he felt the pace starting to slow even further. He could hear himself grunt each time he pulled his body upwards and his forearms felt swollen and numb. There was a strange, cramping spasm in his right leg that he knew wasn't from the cold. He wondered, almost clinically, how much longer his body could bear it.

Longer, he knew, than Bill's could. Over the course of the last few hours, as Luca had tried to move forward, the ropes would often snap taut at his waist, jerking him to a standstill. He would wait for a minute, allowing Bill to catch his breath, but when he tried to press on, they still wouldn't budge.

Fifty feet below, Bill could feel sweat mingling with the thin veil of ice across his face before running down into his eyes. Beneath his jacket, his chest rose up and down in ragged bursts and, whenever he stopped to try and steady his breathing, he was hit by a protracted bout of coughing which left him feeling even shakier. He tried to kick in his crampons and get a better grip, but his legs felt wooden and unresponsive, his front points just scraping over the smooth ice. In each hand, the axes felt unbearably heavy, and as he swung against the wall he knew his movements were becoming increasingly desperate.

He stopped again, bracing himself for another fit of coughing. Looking up through his fogged goggles, he could see the outline of Luca waiting above.

'You all right?'

As the words floated down to him, Bill went to respond, but another bout of coughing tore through him. After nearly a minute it finally subsided, leaving Bill panting for breath. He tilted his head back and, clenching his jaw in anticipation of the pain, yelled out a single word.

'Rest.'

Even from the distance, Luca could hear the strain in Bill's voice – you didn't climb for seven years with someone without being able to instantly gauge their level of discomfort. Judging by the jerky rhythm of the last hour or so, Luca guessed that Bill was now running on empty.

About twenty feet above his head, Luca had spied an outcrop of rock that might be big enough for the two of them to sit on. He had been working his way towards it for the last half-hour. Waiting for enough slack in the rope, he climbed the last few feet and, with trembling arms, hauled himself over the lip. With his back wedged against the ice and his legs dangling over the edge, he heaved back on the rope to take some strain off Bill.

'Fifty feet more,' he yelled down. 'We've got our own private balcony up here.'

For hours Luca had had his nose pressed against the mirror of ice, totally absorbed in the climb. Now he sat back in the sunshine, blinking at the world that was spread out beneath him.

Every view was different and no matter how much he climbed, the experience of having a new perspective was always breathtaking. As the sheer scale of the surroundings came into focus, his personal struggle with the mountain seemed to fade, shrinking him to what he was: a tiny human, clinging to a giant aberration of land.

Except that this time the aberration had a strange sense of order to it.

Luca squinted in the bright light, trying to take it all in. To his right stood a ring of snow-capped mountains, flawlessly aligned. His eyes followed the peaks as they curved round in a perfect circle. It was the symmetry that was so extraordinary, as if they had been positioned with a pair of compasses. At the centre lay a blanket of cloud, impenetrably thick.

As he watched, the cloud started to shift. It began to part slowly, changing and reforming, before something began to take shape at its centre. Luca felt his grip slacken slightly on the rope as he leaned forward involuntarily.

Light poured in through the gash in the clouds, illuminating one side, then the next. As the shape beneath finally broke free of its swirling cover, Luca realised that he was staring at a pyramid so perfectly proportioned it had to be man-made.

Except that it couldn't be. Surely. What else could be in the middle of the Himalayas except a mountain? Looking out across the horizon, he realised it was smaller than the surrounding peaks, but only fractionally. That would make it nearly seven thousand metres high. Absurd to think that humans could build anything so big.

A trembling hand appeared over the ledge beside him.

For a split second Luca just stared at it, his thoughts still on the pyramid mountain. Then, shaking himself awake, he lunged forward to grab Bill's wrist. He pulled as hard as he could while Bill struggled to gain purchase, his crampons clawing over the dark rock. Long seconds passed before he managed to worm his way far enough on to the ledge. Then he collapsed, flat on his back, the only sound the heaving of his chest.

'Mate, are you OK?'

Even behind his goggles, Luca could see the sick exhaustion in Bill's eyes. He looked pale and utterly spent, as if each hour's climb had gradually leached a little more colour from his blood.

'You OK?' Luca repeated, automatically gathering up the last few coils of rope. Already he felt his gaze being drawn back to the pyramid. 'You've got to check out this mountain, Bill. I've never seen anything like it.'

Bill opened his mouth to answer, but was suddenly hit by another bout of hacking coughs. Luca turned back in time to see his head loll to one side, a string of bloody spittle stretching from his lips. The lack of oxygen in his blood had started to turn his lips mauve.

'Shit,' said Luca softly, and then as he saw Bill slowly close his eyes, he raised his voice.

'Bill . . . you have to stay awake.'

Bill remained motionless, his eyes shut tight.

The throbbing in his head was unbearable, even the smallest movement threatened to split his temples, paralysing him with pain. For hours he had tried to fight it, but now even his vision was starting to blur.

'Head is killing me,' he managed. 'The altitude . . . we're climbing too fast.'

'How bad is it?'

It took Bill a few seconds to muster the energy to speak. When he did it came out as little more than a murmur.

'I can't see so well.'

Luca swore before turning and looking up the sheer wall of ice.

The summit ridge was no more than half an hour's climb above them. The weather was absolutely perfect – low winds, good visibility. This expedition had been months in the planning, and now here they were in the perfect position – the mountain was offering itself on a plate. For the last few hours he had known he was going to have to make a choice, have to decide what mattered most. As he stared up at the summit he realised with absolute certainty that it was within his reach, was his for the taking.

'Bill, listen. I'm going to tie you to the ledge just here, only for an hour or so, and go for the summit. You'll be all right, I promise.'

Somewhere in his exhausted brain, Bill processed these words. He raised his head to speak then another bout of coughing convulsed through him, his chest rising and falling like a fish thrown on to dry land.

After a moment his body went limp and he slowly turned his head aside to spit a thick globule of phlegm on to the nearby rock.

'You . . . can't leave,' he hissed.

He opened his eyes, squinting through the pain.

'Don't . . . fucking . . . leave,' he repeated.

Bill tried to focus through the fog of his thoughts. He had to stay awake, had to fight the crippling lethargy. The seconds stretched. He felt his consciousness dip and the darkness drag at him. For the longest time, nothing happened. All he could hear was the noise of his own chest, heaving up and down. There was nothing except the blackness clouding the edges of his vision, slowly sinking in on him.

'Luca . . . please.'

Bill's voice was nothing more than a pathetic murmur, his last thoughts fading on his swollen lips. Then, somewhere through the haze, he saw Luca's silhouette move closer until he was standing directly overhead. Bill felt a hand on the front of his climbing harness and his body being hoisted forward towards the edge of the cliff.

He reached up, trying to grab on to Luca's arm. He was balanced right over the long drop of the cliff beneath.

When Luca finally spoke, frustration thickened his voice.

'Come on. Let's get the hell out of here.'

Chapter 3

There was no natural light, only a collection of squat candles connected by long rivulets of syrupy wax. From their flames came a low aureole of light, illuminating the outline of five seats carved directly into the stone walls.

The seats were arranged in a semi-circle, following the natural shape of the chamber. All but the middle one was occupied by a cross-legged figure dressed in highly ornate robes. The fabrics were all dyed in rich contrasting colours and wrapped in complex folds so that only the right arm of the figure remained bare.

On the other side of the circular chamber, a small collection of personal effects had been laid out neatly on the stone floor. There were five of each item, prayer wheels, beads and miniature golden bells, stretching away from the candlelight.

One of the figures leaned back, pulling aside the yellow cowl that covered his face.

'The divinations were correct,' he said in a voice cracked by age. 'The boy has been found.'

The others turned to look at him, their elderly faces creased in surprise.

'You are certain of this?'

'I am.'

Another of the monks leaned forward in his seat, arranging his red robes around him.

'How did you find him so soon after His Holiness passed away?'

The monk in the yellow robe smiled. 'It was indeed a marvellous thing. The smoke from the cremation blew south-west, confirming exactly what the Tshangpa oracle said. After only a month of searching, we found the boy in a small village called Tingkye.'

'A month?' another monk interrupted dubiously. 'How can *he* be found in only a month?'

'If the divinations are correct, you should do nothing but rejoice that we have found him so fast.'

'And the boy – what is he like?' asked another, slightly younger monk, his green robes glinting in the candlelight as he leaned forward eagerly to address the others.

'He is only nine years old, a peasant with no learning or education. Yet as soon as I cast eyes on him, I saw he possessed a spirit that was identical to his predecessor's. When I showed him the personal effects, he did not hesitate for a moment. He chose His Holiness's personal prayer wheel, then the golden bell that he only used in his private chamber. Presented with five different prayer beads, he cast his hands over each before settling on the one that can only be used by His Holiness – the beads made of jade and silver that are the mark of Shigatse. The boy took them into his pocket and then looked at me curiously, saying, "These are mine. Where did you find them?"'

As the old monk finished speaking the other three bowed their heads in awe. The search could take years, even decades, and yet in only a few weeks the boy had been found.

Eventually one of them raised his head.

'And what of the golden urn?'

'It was he who was chosen. With each trial, it soon became clear to me that he did not even know he was being tested. The movements came to him naturally, as if he were following a dream he had already experienced. Such things could not have been taught.'

There was another long pause as each monk considered the significance of what they had been told. Then the younger one in the green robes glanced round the semi-circle, his eyes bright.

'We must inform Shigatse that their new leader has been found.'

The monk in the red robes shook his head abruptly, sending shadows flickering across the chamber's walls.

'No. We must tell no one. The boy's identity must be concealed at all costs. If such news were ever to leave this room, there are many more powerful than us who would seek to control him. We must act quickly, brothers, or suffer a terrible fate.'

He turned his head slowly so that his gaze fell on each of them in turn.

'This is the most important secret we will ever have to keep,' he said, raising his finger towards the ceiling of the chamber. 'The very fate of Tibet now depends on us.'

Chapter 4

The climb down was relatively easy.

Luca began by using the ropes to lower Bill down from the ledge, but almost as soon as they started the descent, he began to feel better. The profound lethargy that had crippled him further up the mountain dissipated with each new lungful of thicker air. As the hours passed, and they abseiled quickly downhill, strength seeped back into each tired muscle.

Soon he was climbing down at almost the same pace as Luca. By the time the pair of them reached the lower slopes where they had built the snow hole, the only ill effect that remained was an occasional rasping cough.

Bill's mood, however, had darkened. He knew that what he had experienced up there were the first signs of a full-blown pulmonary oedema. Both he and Luca had witnessed it once before on the north buttresses of Mont Blanc. A solo climber had got himself stranded high on the mountain, cut off by the darkness and high winds. Bill and Luca had turned back earlier that afternoon and reached the safety of the Cosmiques refuge, nestled on the ridge above the towering pinnacle of the Aiguille du Midi.

Throughout the night, the sounds of the dying climber crackled through on their radio.

At first he just coughed, but after a while he began breathing with a slow, laboured gurgling sound as his lungs filled with liquid. By the time the helicopter arrived at daybreak, he had slipped into a coma.

A day later, when they had made it down to Chamonix village, they found out he had died on the way to hospital – drowned on his own body fluid.

The incident was replaying itself in Bill's mind as they trudged along a narrow ridge in silence. Suddenly, without warning, he stopped and dug his ice axe into the snow. He lifted his goggles up on to his sunburned forehead and turned to face Luca, eyes squinting against the harsh sunlight.

'You were going to just leave me up there!'

Luca stopped and the rope between them sagged, paying out in a small arc.

'Not for long, mate. We were just below the summit . . . maybe twenty minutes or so. I thought I could bag it quickly and come back for you.'

'Don't bullshit me. We weren't that close.'

Luca began coiling off the slack in the rope automatically.

'This isn't the time to do this,' he said quietly. 'We're both knackered from the climb and we've got another couple of hours to camp one.'

Bill picked up his ice axe, shifting the weight of his rucksack. Then he stood looking down the ridge as if weighing up his words.

'Tell me, Luca, is that how it played out on Everest?'

The placatory expression on Luca's face instantly wiped off and his grey eyes became as expressionless as polished marble. Unclipping his pack, he let it slip to the ground, trying to control a sudden surge of anger. But colour had appeared in blotches on his cheeks and when he spoke his voice was barely more than a hiss.

'Don't ever say that again. You know exactly what happened.'

After a pause Bill shrugged and went to trudge past him, but this time Luca remained where he stood, barring the way.

'I'm serious, Bill. Don't ever say that again. You know what it cost me.'

'Then how could you even think about leaving me up there? Didn't you learn your lesson?'

'Learn my lesson? Jesus Christ, Bill! Did you ever stop to consider that maybe I wasn't thinking straight up there either? Altitude hits everyone a different way. I thought we were right under the summit.'

'It shouldn't even have crossed your mind . . .'

'Enough of this shit!' Luca interrupted, raising his hand. Gathering up his rucksack, he started trudging down the ridge, then stopped a few paces farther on and turned back.

'I've just spent the last four hours babysitting you down that cliff. If it weren't for me, you'd still be fucking up there!'

For a few moments more they stared at each other in mutual recrimination, the heat of the argument threatening to boil over. Then Luca suddenly swung round and continued walking, his gloved hands clenched into fists by his sides.

It took them two weeks to get back home, a procession of clambering aboard planes and dismounting trains throughout Tibet, Nepal, and eventually England.

During the journey, the subject of the climb had been broached, but not resolved. Both of them had ended up apologising for what they had said on the mountain, and both had nominally forgiven the other for all that had been said. But it was as if a shadow had fallen over them, a lurking feeling of distrust that had never before been part of their friendship. They still bantered together but it had become stilted and hesitant, as if their time on Makalu was something to be ashamed of, rather than a near victory over one of the world's hardest peaks.

Now they stood stiffly on the platform by the Heathrow Express, their brightly coloured rucksacks and tanned faces drawing some curious glances from passing commuters.

The normal ritual was for the two men to go to the Windsor Castle together for a celebratory pint before they split off in their different directions, but this time it was tacitly understood that this was not going to happen.

'Well, here we are again,' said Luca, attempting to sound cheerful. 'Your missus will be pleased to see you're back in one piece. You can tell her it's my fault we're late again.'

'Yeah, well . . . maybe,' said Bill, smiling awkwardly.

Luca stuck out his hand and they gave each other a perfunctory handshake.

'I'll see you around then,' Bill said, and for a second his habitually cheerful expression flickered, revealing the bleakness beneath. Then he set his jaw and, grasping the straps of his rucksack, turned and disappeared quickly into the sea of commuters.

Luca stood looking after him, part of him wanting to call out. He had had two long weeks to come up with something to break the ice between them. It was just a matter of apologising again for what had happened up there on the ridge, acknowledging that he'd screwed up. He'd never seen Bill lose his temper before, and knew how hurt he must still be.

But somehow the words stuck in his throat. That mention of Everest had cut deep and over the time spent travelling back, fermented into a hard bitterness that he just couldn't seem to shrug off. Hoisting his rucksack off the grimy concrete floor, Luca walked towards the gaudy lighting of a café populated by commuters drinking lattes and leafing through the morning papers. Scraping back one of the metal chairs, he ordered a double espresso from the waitress, his eyes wandering idly across the ant-like hordes thronging the platforms, and fixing upon the triangular glass ceiling of the old Victorian train station.

The prism of light slowly bled through into an image of the pyramid mountain. It had been haunting him ever since the climb down. It was there whenever he closed his eyes; in the cloudscape as he'd stared out of the plane windows, in the distant skyline as the train rumbled into the city centre. Several times on the journey back he had opened his mouth to talk to Bill about it, but whatever it was that was hanging in the air between them had prevented him from saying anything more.

He could picture it now as if he were still sitting on that ledge: one face gleaming in the sunshine, edges looking like they had been filed straight then dusted with ice and snow. It was better proportioned even than the Matterhorn, like a child's drawing of the perfect mountain.

Each time Luca thought about it he kicked himself for not having taken a photo. But by the time he had pulled Bill off the ledge the cloud had rolled back in, and not even the ring of mountains surrounding it was visible. Like his chance of reaching the summit, there had been only the briefest of windows. And thanks to Bill, he had missed both opportunities.

Someone brushed past him in a mackintosh wet from the rain, spilling some of his coffee on to the table. As Luca swore and scrambled for some paper napkins, he heard his train being announced over the Tannoy. He should really get on it – do what Bill was doing and go home. Take a long hot bath, empty his clothes into the laundry basket, and banish all thoughts of fantasy mountains.

The only problem was that he felt like doing exactly the opposite. And there was only one person he knew who would understand.

Breaking into a genuine smile for the first time in a couple of weeks, Luca tossed a couple of pounds on to the table, shouldered his rucksack, and set off in the direction of a phone-box.

Chapter 5

From a distance, the only indication of the two military jeeps was the dense cloud of dust trailing behind them. The two vehicles bounced over the pitted road in close convoy, engines revving high to cope with the altitude.

Second Lieutenant Chen Zhi had been squashed uncomfortably on the battered passenger seat for three hours. His olive green military uniform was grey with dust and he sat awkwardly, his heavy frame listing over and forward as if trying to see something just below the jeep's outside wing mirror. In truth, all he was trying to do was relieve some of the mounting pressure from being jammed in the same position for so long. His lower back ached, and with each new pothole he could feel his whole body jar from the contact.

As he stared out through the windscreen Chen was caught between willing the journey over and the dread of what he knew was waiting for him at the other end. The front wheel bounced over a hole again, connecting with the wheel arch of the jeep and sending everything on the dashboard flying into the air. Chen looked across at the driver, amazed by how many potholes he was actually hitting, but remained silent. The noise from the strained engine was too loud for him to speak.

Instead, he reached into the top pocket of his shirt and pulled out a leather wallet. Behind his own picture and official military ID was a strip of four photos taken in a train station booth in Lhasa. The picture showed his ten-year-old son sitting on his mother's knee, with Chen himself kneeling behind them awkwardly in civilian clothes. His son was trying to wriggle free, while his wife looked over her shoulder as if to ask for his help. He wondered why he'd always liked this photo so much. Perhaps it was because it felt real and spontaneous – a lifetime away from what he had now become.

The photos had been taken four years ago, before he had even joined the service.

Amongst everything that had changed, the one constant was that on the rare weekends when he had some time off, he still took his son past that same train station on his way to play Mah Jong. The other men never said anything about the youngster tagging along. Then again, it was hardly as if anyone would have dared. They all knew Chen was in the Public Security Bureau now – and PSB were untouchable.

He sensed a new movement and turned to see the driver craning his neck forward over the steering wheel. Hammering the gearstick hard into third, the jeep jumped forward as the engine took the brunt of the braking and their speed slowed. Up ahead, a small outcrop of houses stood baking in the midday sun.

They pulled up behind the lead jeep. Chen could see the other soldiers quickly leave their vehicles and fan out across the tiny village square. All of them brandished rifles on their shoulders. The locals melted back into doorways, their eyes wide.

Chen watched through the streaked glass of the windshield. Despite the long hours and the stifling heat of the jeep, all he wanted to do was stay where he was.

Beijing must have known how much he would hate this. It was always like that. Always a test. And once he opened the door, he knew he would have to go through with it. The die would be cast.

There was a tentative rapping on the window and Chen swivelled in his seat to see a man standing only a few inches from the glass.

With a flick of his wrist, Chen motioned him to back off and then, with a heavy sigh, pulled on the door handle.

Outside the air was maddeningly hot. Everything was caked in dust: houses, vehicles, people. Everything was grey, and still as the grave.

Straightening his back so that he brought himself up to his full height, Chen motioned for the man to come closer. He was not Tibetan. Indian perhaps, or a mixture of the two, with fast, shifting eyes that like a fly never seemed to settle on anything for more than a moment. His teeth were badly worn, the discoloured roots visible behind crooked stumps.

'Where is he?' Chen asked, staring down at him.

'Money first,' the man said, rubbing his fingers together slowly. Chen reached into his back pocket and pulled out a small wad of fifty-yuan notes held together by elastic bands. He tossed the money over, keeping his distance.

The man took his time, creasing back the corner of each note as he counted. Eventually he simply pointed to an unremarkable house set back from the central square.

'You're certain?'

'Certain,' the man replied in a low voice. 'I have been watching.'

Chen signalled to the soldiers with a couple of fast jabs of his hand and they fell in behind him. As they walked the few paces to the house, he could already feel the sweat prickling up in the small of his back and armpits. He marched on, reaching the battered wooden door in just a few strides and slamming it open.

At first all he could see was blackness.

Thin shards of light pierced through the uneven woodwork of the house and eventually he could make out a tiny living area: central fire, a few pots and pans, and a couple of low wooden stools. From round the corner, a young woman in a dirty apron suddenly appeared and screamed with shock at the sight of the soldiers. Chen motioned again and two of his men moved forward quickly, dragging her out through the doorway.

Stooping under the low ceiling, Chen moved through the house and located two further rooms. In the second, a boy was sitting cross-legged on the floor. As Chen stepped into the room, the boy's startled brown eyes followed his every movement.

He was wiry and dirty, his face streaked with mud. Despite his age there was a certain calmness to the way he stared, as if in the battle between confusion and fear, he had not yet decided between the two.

He remained seated, his chin tilted upwards as he took in the entirety of the man looming over him.

'What is your name?' Chen said in Tibetan, feeling the words fall from his mouth.

'Gedhun,' the boy replied quietly.

At this response Chen shut his eyes for a moment, blocking out the world. When he opened them again, the boy was still staring at him.

'Come here,' Chen said, gesturing with his hands.

The young boy stood and took a hesitant step forward across the room, his small hands balled nervously into fists.

'Everything will be OK,' Chen heard himself saying. 'Shut your eyes.'

He was looking at those hands, trying not to think of his own son.

'Go on,' he said again. 'Shut your eyes.'

The boy squeezed them shut and as the lids closed a couple of tears rolled down his dusty cheeks, leaving two clean tracks.

His lips were still moving in prayer when the bullet came. With a deafening crack, his small body was thrown back across the room, slamming into the far wall before sliding down into a pile of disjointed limbs.

The dying noise of the shot left an eerie stillness behind it. Chen sagged to his knees, trying to fight against the suffocating feeling that seemed to cramp his entire abdomen.

It wasn't imaginary – suddenly he couldn't breathe. The air just wouldn't pass into his lungs. He clawed at his shirt collar, desperately trying to loosen his tie. Lurching forward on to his feet, he stumbled out through the living area, toppling a pot resting on the corner of the fire. He heard it crash to the ground just as he arrived outside and into the terrible heat.

They were all there, staring at him. They fixed him with their vacant, stupid gazes, as he pushed past them towards the jeeps. He leaned against one of the cars, finally dragging the dry air deep into his lungs. Pulling open the door, he frantically tried to find the cigarette pack he had seen earlier which belonged to the driver. It was jammed under his seat, by the door. Chen broke open the pack and put a cigarette to his lips then tried to inhale. It didn't work. He tried again, sucking hard on the filter.

Why was it not working?

It was the sergeant who grabbed his shaking hands, holding them still for a moment as he brought a light to the cigarette. Chen inhaled deeply, once, twice, and then a third time in quick succession. Eventually he let out a long, ragged breath, sending a plume of smoke skywards.

'Get the body. Beijing will want to see it,' he managed. 'And get those fucking people away from the house.'

The sergeant nodded curtly and then ran off towards the house, barking orders. Chen watched him go then silently moved around behind the two stationary jeeps, into the shade of one of the nearby houses. He inhaled on the cigarette again then leaned forward, his hands on his knees, and vomited.

Chapter 6

'I don't hear from you for three months. Then you turn up out of the blue with a rucksack full of dirty clothes and want me to dig up some old satellite maps . . . Now, why doesn't that surprise me?'

Luca smiled, resting his hands on the arms of his leather chair. He still remembered the days when he used to be genuinely terrified of Jack Milton's craggy face and withering gaze. As a boy he'd sat in this study, in this same sagging armchair, and felt the weight of the long silences that seemed to be part of every conversation he had with his uncle.

For the young Luca, Jack's prematurely lined face and shaking hands had always been just another sign of his strange otherwordliness. He was a professor of geology at Cambridge University and somehow different from everyone else. Everything about him was unpredictable, often erratic and confused. It was only as an adult that Luca saw these idiosyncrasies for what they really were – the signs of an ex-alcoholic who had strayed too close to the edge before purging himself of his addiction. Now he drank endless cups of coffee, channelling his compulsive drive into the minutiae of the rocks he studied.

The study hadn't changed in all those years and was still crammed with books. Wooden shelves honeycombed the walls right up to the ceiling, so that the uppermost volumes threatened to shower down amidst a cloud of dust. At shoulder height, some of the books were pushed aside to make room for selections of rock samples, stacked in small piles and having long since lost their identifying labels.

'You're the only person I know who really gives a shit,' Luca said, dunking a biscuit into his coffee.

'Well it's good to know I'm top of a long list,' Jack laughed, creasing the deep-set lines at the corners of his eyes. 'So go on, tell me everything. Makalu must have been quite something.'

There was a pause. As his nephew remained silent, Jack stopped smiling.

'Is something up?'

'Everything's fine. Except Bill got altitude sickness and we missed the summit by a couple of hours. We sort of fell out on the way back down and I'm not sure we're on speaking terms right now.'

'Oh, I am sorry,' said Jack softly. 'I know how much time you two put into it. But I'm sure you'll sort out things with Bill. You've been friends far too long to fall out for long.'

'Yeah, I suppose so.'

'Come on, Luca. Nothing can have been said that can't be taken back.'

Luca shrugged. 'Is it all right if we don't talk about this?'

'Sorry, I didn't mean to push,' Jack said, his brow creasing further as he took another gulp of coffee. 'So are you going to tell me some more about this pyramid mountain?'

Luca's face slowly lit up, a smile forming at the edge of his lips.

'I wish you had been there, Jack. It was incredible. And set in the middle of a stunning ring of mountains. Have you ever heard mention of it?'

'No,' Jack said, standing up and walking over to his desk. 'After you called, I dug everything we have on the area east of Makalu from the departmental library. Took me a while to find these and blow the dust off them. Not exactly the world's most sought-after documents.'

He carried the maps over to the low table and knelt down. Fishing out his reading glasses from his breast pocket, he held the first map up to the light.

'This one's about six months old – the most recent.'

He pulled it a little closer and studied the grid references, drawing a finger over the contours of the Himalayas. He stopped suddenly and prodded. 'There's Makalu.'

Luca moved round the table so that they were shoulder to shoulder and peered more closely at the markings. The map showed a vast swathe of the Himalayas, with swirling currents of cloud bending round the massive peaks and valleys.

'I'm guessing it would be forty kilometres or so east of that,' said Luca. 'Somewhere over here.'

Simultaneously their eyes swept over the map until they alighted on a small cluster of peaks, bent round in a perfect circle.

'That's them!' Luca said, feeling a strange lift of excitement. Part of him hadn't expected them to exist at all.

'It's strikingly symmetrical, I'll admit,' said Jack, adjusting his reading glasses and leaning forward to examine the formation more closely. 'But you say the most interesting mountain was the one in the middle? All I can see is cloud.'

'It was right in the centre, Jack. It sounds odd, I know, but it was like a kind of a pyramid, perfectly proportioned, as if someone had been up there with a chisel. I only caught a glimpse of it when I was high enough on Makalu.'

'A pyramid-shaped mountain,' repeated Jack, immersing himself in the twisted contours of the map. He had studied maps all his working life and was able to interpret the graphite markings as if staring down on each peak for real. 'If it's anywhere near the same height as the others in that range then that would make it nearly seven thousand metres high – which, as you know, would make the Matterhorn look like a molehill.'

Luca nodded. Between the ring of mountains, all he could see was a thick belt of cloud twisting in between the peaks. He leaned closer, searching for the slightest sign of the pyramid mountain. There was nothing.

'Any other maps of the region?'

'Sure,' said his uncle. 'We have nine or ten of these satellite images, going back a few years. One every six months or so.'

Together, they lifted the first map off the table and laid it on the floor. Luca quickly bent over the next one, his face furrowed in concentration. Jack glanced over at his nephew, feeling a flicker of concern to see that light in his eyes. It was no accident that whenever Luca worried him the most, it was when he reminded Jack of himself. It was not something he would ever put into words, but he was pretty sure his nephew had inherited the same dark, addictive streak.

'Shit!' said Luca as he traced his finger across the region. 'Still cloud.'

They went through each of the maps in turn. Discarded, the massive sheaves of paper covered most of the study floor, their edges curled up like giant scrolls.

'Always the same: cloud covering the entire region. How is this possible?' Luca said eventually, staring directly at Jack. 'There's not a single break in any of these images.'

Seeing his frustration, Jack sighed. Wincing slightly as his knees cracked, he began gathering the maps off the floor.

'You have to understand that some mountains create their own weather systems. They reach so high into the atmosphere that they actually change the weather around them. In this particular case, they create a lot of cloud.'

Luca had heard the theory before. The great summits of the Himalayas could cause moisture in the atmosphere to condense around them and collect along their massive flanks. The invariable result: cloud.

'But why can't the satellite penetrate the cloud? Can't you switch to infra-red or something and see through all that kind of stuff?'

Jack lifted an eyebrow.

'Sure. If you change bandwidths, you can cut through any weather you like. The military do it all the time. But who the hell is going to pay hundreds of thousands of pounds for something like that in the middle of the Himalayas? The Geology Department can barely afford to get me out of this damn office once a year, let alone source material like that.'

He paused before adding, 'And even if we had the money, the Chinese and Indian Governments get very touchy about satellite imagery along their borders. We wouldn't even get a response if we tried to go through official channels.'

'What about other maps? Is there anything else we could try?'

'That's everything we've got. Look, you've got to understand that this is an area the size of Spain and vast sections of it remain almost completely unmapped. This is one of the last untouched regions on the entire planet. You, more than most, know what it's like out there. There's nothing as far as you can see: no people, no animals, just snow and rock. And it's only us tired old geologists who get excited about that. Everyone else just sticks to the glamorous peaks, like Everest and K2 – and, of course, Makalu.'

Luca acknowledged the dig. Jack was right. Few but geologists cared about the smaller, less well-known mountains. He looked across the last map, at the vast tracts of peaks it depicted and marvelled at how much of the Himalayas remained totally unexplored. Like the human brain, the majority was uncharted territory.

Jack stood up and gingerly lowered himself back into his armchair.

'So, Prodigal Son. Dare I ask if you've called your father since you've been back?'

Luca frowned. 'I just got in a few hours ago, Jack, give me a break. I'll go and see him some time in the next few days.'

His uncle started to say something but Luca broke in.

'You are going to spare me the lecture, aren't you, Jack?' he said with a slight edge to his voice. 'If I'd wanted that, I would have gone straight home.'

Jack shrugged and drank some more coffee.

'Well, I'm hardly one to give advice on family matters. Especially with your father. I blew that a long time ago.'

'Come on, Jack, I'm here to talk about this mountain,' said Luca. 'If the pyramid is as perfect as I remember it, it could be one of the most exciting things anyone's discovered for years. Surely there's some way of tracking down more information about the area?'

Jack nodded. Leaning forward in his chair, he scrawled a couple of names on the back of a used envelope.

'There are a couple of ways I can think of, but both are long shots so I wouldn't get your hopes up. There's a Department of Asian Studies somewhere around the back of the Fitzwilliam Museum. There should be someone there who can point us in the right direction . . . and help us find someone who specialises in Tibetan geography or something similar. But your best bet will be the University Library. You should see if any of the early British explorers went near that region. Their accounts are usually pretty detailed.'

He paused, then after a moment's thought, added, 'Try around the eighteen hundreds, during the time of the "Great Game". That's when the British were paranoid about the Russians invading India and sent lots of spies up into the border regions. They mapped it all covertly, measuring distances by counting their own steps.'

He leaned over and took a swig from the dregs of his coffee, considering the idea of walking the breadth of the Himalayas while counting every single step.

When his gaze swung back up, it seemed to include Luca.

'Crazy bastards,' he said softly.

Chapter 7

Behind the vast, grey-brick façade of Cambridge's University Library lies centuries' worth of learning. Over seven million books, manuscripts and maps are contained in this giant edifice, the most precious being stored in the great tower which sticks up above the main structure like a factory chimney. Casting a long shadow over all who enter, it is a solemn reminder of the sheer weight of knowledge stacked inside.

Luca halted in front of the imposing entrance, fishing out Jack's pass from the back pocket of his jeans. It was here, if anywhere, that he would find a reference to the pyramid mountain.

Following a group of students through the main lobby, he walked up echoing stone steps that smelled of floor wax into the index room. Row after row of worn, faded drawers lined the room, each containing ranks of neatly numbered and annotated cards.

Luca pulled out a few at random, not having a clue where to start. There were no signs or explanations as to how it all worked, just thousands of seemingly identical cards. What was it about high-brow institutions that made them still persist with such archaic systems? What was wrong with using a damn computer? Was it some sort of initiation test, to keep the unworthy philistines at bay? Here he was, in one of the greatest libraries in the world, and he couldn't find a single book.

A couple of girls stood a few feet away from him, hugging books to their chests. One of them had hazel eyes in a round, pretty face. He caught her eye.

'I don't suppose you could give me a hand?' he asked. 'I'm completely lost.'

'Sure,' she answered, moving round and looking down at the drawer he'd pulled out. 'What are you looking for?'

'Well, that's the problem, really,' he said, smiling apologetically. 'It's not exactly specific . . .'

Fifteen minutes later they had drawn a blank, and it was obvious from the strained smile on the girl's face that she was regretting having agreed to help in the first place.

'Look, I really think you'd better talk to a librarian,' she said, flicking back her hair impatiently. 'They take a while to pin down but, like I said, they really know their stuff. Sorry, but I have to run to a supervision . . .'

Twenty minutes later, Luca was leaning over the issue desk with a distinctly less attractive woman. She wore bracelets that jangled each time she flicked through the long line of reference cards, and an overpowering perfume that hung in the air between them like a cloud. But despite it all, she obviously knew her stuff.

'OK, so that's seven books that cover the region,' she said briskly. 'Five of them we have here, the other two you'll have to call up from the basement.' She gave Luca a disparaging glance, taking in his suntan and faded sweatshirt. 'Would it be simpler if I ordered them for you myself? I'll get you a photocopying card while I'm at it.'

Finding a spare desk, Luca was soon hunched over a pile of books in the hushed, cavernous reading room. The librarian had cross-referenced nearby villages and landmarks, pulling out any books by or about explorers who had ventured anywhere near the region in the last hundred years.

For the next few hours he worked steadily through them, occasionally making notes in the small Moleskine pad that he and Bill always took with them on expeditions.

It proved to be frustrating work. None of the explorers had got much farther than the Indian border and Luca had skimmed through three of the books, his pen poised, before one scruffy-looking volume began to show more promise.

In his introduction, the author, Frederick Bailey, a British officer serving in India at the beginning of the twentieth century, described how he had decided to enter Tibet illegally, heading north over the Himalayas in search of a 'mighty river gorge'. On first inspection of the hand-drawn map at the front of the book, Luca immediately realised that Bailey's seemingly random route put him about fifty kilometres east of Makalu.

The prose was typically Edwardian, slightly pompous and emotionally stilted, but within a few pages Luca had been sucked into Bailey's account. In 1913 he and another officer called Morshead had worked their way up and across the Indo-Tibetan border to reach a fabled waterfall in the heart of a river gorge. The journey sounded difficult as well as clandestine. There were jungles with trees a hundred feet high, mountain passes and murderous Abor tribesmen to negotiate. Luca was amused at the classic British stoicism and how they kept stiffening their upper lip to 'muddle their way through'.

After escaping from one village under a hail of arrows and spears, the pair recouped in the dense jungle. Morshead had been hit no less than eleven times, with Bailey's only further comment on this being a terse: *'What a sanguine reminder it was of how hard it is to kill a man in sound health.'*

Luca's smile faded suddenly. God, what had happened to explorers nowadays? One dose of malaria, or a toe lost to frostbite, and they called in the helicopters. In the old days, explorers would disappear from the face of the earth for years. And they literally did disappear. They weren't calling in every five minutes from a satellite phone or updating their website with the latest news. These men struck off into the wilderness, alone and utterly cut off from the rest of the world. They pioneered the trails. They drew the maps.

Somehow life today had become so tepid. It took such an effort to actually get away from anything familiar that escape itself became the point of the expedition, rather than any discovery that might arise from it.

Something was catching the corner of his eye. Luca looked up to see that his mobile was flashing silently on the desk. Picking it up, he saw that it was his father calling. With a sigh, he put it down again. He must have heard the news that he was back – either that or it was a lucky guess. Then again, his father always did have a sixth sense for that kind of thing.

Turning his phone face downwards, Luca exhaled before looking down at the book again.

Despite a tantalising reference to 'that vast, unmapped region east of Makalu', there seemed to be nothing out of the ordinary about the mountains Bailey and his companion had gone hiking through. A few pages later, Luca was skimming through the explorers' experiences with a more benign tribe, the Monpa, when he nearly missed a brief diary extract:

The local Monpa describe the Tsangpo river gorge as a 'beyul'. After much vague discussion with the chief, we discovered this term to mean some sort of highly sacred sanctuary, but from what it was impossible to discern. On further discussion we were told that there are many such sanctuaries throughout Tibet, hidden in the most in-accessible regions.

We enquired as to the whereabouts of these other sacred places and only after much cajoling (and nearly half our supply of

*expedition gin) did the little fellow let on.
Drawing a picture of a lotus flower in the dirt,
he described a group of mountains, formed
into a circle. At their centre, another mountain, which is supposedly the gateway to some
sacred place.*

*Rather amusingly, when asked where the
ring of mountains was, he replied that it had
been made invisible by a great sorcerer. He
claimed that one had to use the wisdom from
a book called the Kalak Tantra to see inside
it, but as with all these things, the Tibetan
villagers' penchant for the mystic is seemingly
endless. It really is quite impossible to get
things clear.*

*We decided to stick to the matter in hand
and concentrate on getting into our own river
gorge 'beyul'.*

Luca looked up from the page, his mouth suddenly dry. These were *his* mountains. They had to be.

So what did Bailey mean that they had been 'made invisible by a great sorcerer'?

One thing Luca knew about Tibetans was that they loved anything supernatural. To them, gods literally roamed the heights and demons lived in the valleys. Almost every occurrence, even simple things such as bad weather or failing crops, was explained as an act of magic and sorcery.

Luca looked up through one of the long windows at the moody English sky. White clouds shrouded the tops of the city's spires. Cloud . . . that was it! Within this context, the chief's assertions about a great sorcerer having cast a spell over the mountains made perfect sense.

The clouds themselves had rendered the centre of the mountain ring invisible, just as they had on the satellite map.

Standing up, Luca shuffled the books into a neat stack and then made his way over to the photocopying machine.

There was more to this than he had first thought. He could feel it.

Chapter 8

Two monks stood on the roof of Tashilhunpo Monastery, their heads bowed in sorrow.

Usually the rarified mountain light reflected off the golden rooftops, making it unbearably hot and bright. But today was different. Dark cloud had rolled in from the east, blanketing the sky and threatening rain.

Below them, the city of Shigatse stretched across the plains. Squat, white houses sprawled out from the central hub of the monastery in chaotic tentacles, blurred together by the grey light. The people on the streets moved with a heavy listlessness brought on by the humidity. Rain was uncommon this high on the plateau and it was as if the whole city was holding its breath, waiting for the skies to finally break.

'Jigme, we must always remember our duty and never give up hope,' said the taller of the monks, resting a consoling hand on his shoulder. 'The Gelugpas from Lhasa will have some idea of how to proceed.'

'How to proceed?' echoed the other monk bitterly. 'The eleventh Panchen Lama has been murdered before he even reached Shigatse. And he was just a boy. Just a boy! Now nothing will stop the Chinese . . .'

He brought his hands to his mouth, as if the words themselves could somehow inflict further damage. Above them, the first specks of rain hit the ramparts of the monastery roof, congealing in the layers of dust.

'It is inevitable,' admitted the taller monk. 'The Chinese will install their own candidate and crown him on the first day of June in the solar calendar, at the Linka Festival. But still, we must trust in the will of Buddha and never give up hope.'

As the rain began to quicken, both monks remained where they stood. Drops splashed on to their heavy robes and shaved heads, beading down the sides of their faces like tears. Both felt too exhausted to move, as if the rain somehow reflected the way the whole world was feeling.

It had all happened so suddenly. They had both presumed since the death of their former leader that it would take years for his reincarnation to be found. Yet, without their even knowing that the search had officially begun, news had come through that the young boy had been murdered, shot before he had even stepped out of his village.

With the Dalai Lama in permanent exile in Dharamsala, the Panchen Lama, the Bodhisattva of Wisdom, was the practical ruler of the country. It was under his decree that the Tibetan people were governed and the rule of law maintained. Now the same question ran through both men's minds as it had done all morning: how could Tibet protect itself from the Chinese if their next leader was to be one of them?

A soft rumbling announced a motorcade of vehicles pulling into the monastery's main entrance. Three stretch saloon Mercedes with blacked-out windows slowly eased their way across the drive's ancient flagstones. They crunched to a halt before the main entrance. As soon as they caught sight of the cars, the two monks turned soundlessly and hurried down the spiral staircase that led from the roof into the courtyard below.

They arrived, breathless, just as the last of a large group of dignitaries exited the cars.

'We are honoured by your visit,' said the taller monk, bowing low. 'You bring solace in difficult times.'

He stepped back as a very old man in a vast yellow hat and red robes moved ahead of his entourage, a wooden cane gripped in his hand. The Head Lama of the Gelugpa sect briefly nodded a greeting to them both before allowing himself to be ushered into the main hall of Tashilhunpo Monastery, where a multitude of novices were preparing tea and refreshments on a long wooden table.

'Get rid of these people,' he said, glancing around at the bustling young monks. 'What I have to say is for your ears alone.'

'Of course, your Holiness,' said the shorter of the monks, shooting a sideways glance at his companion. Snapping his fingers several times, the commotion in the room quickly died. The novices disappeared through the hall's many exits. When the last door had been shut quietly behind them the old Lama leaned forward, his neck craned under the weight of his immense yellow hat.

'Come closer,' he breathed.

The two monks moved forward obediently, sinking down on one knee so that their heads were almost touching.

'All is not as it seems,' the old Lama whispered, his eyes fixed warily on the main door to the hall. 'We got to the village first and moved the boy.'

Both kneeling men lifted their heads and stared directly at the old monk, their faces brimming with a mixture of scepticism and wonder. Then, as he slowly nodded in affirmation, tears of relief welled up in their eyes.

'But who was it who was killed?'

'It was the boy's younger brother. An innocent,' the old man replied. 'We pray for him in his next life.'

As both men went to stand up, the Lama's arms shot out, pressing them back down on to their knees with surprising strength.

'You are the custodians of this temple until he returns. I have known both of you since birth and understand that you would never betray the truth.' His piercing eyes dwelled on each of them for a moment. 'We must act as if the boy is lost and ensure the Chinese believe they have had their victory. But when the time is right, you must both be ready to receive him in Shigaste and return him to his rightful place.'

'But where is he?'

A smile flashed across the Lama's wizened face.

'He is finally beyond their reach.'

Chapter 9

Driving into Guildford city centre, Luca looked up through the windscreen at the leaden sky. It was the dead colour that only ever seemed to settle across the damp Surrey countryside. The sun lacked the strength to differentiate between the buildings and sky, so that the drab concrete buildings bled into the skyline like a half-finished painting.

Pulling into the car park in the battered white Toyota Land Cruiser he had inherited when he was seventeen, Luca felt a familiar sense of claustrophobia wash over him. It was always the same whenever he looked up at this particular office block, a feeling that had failed to diminish over the years. He stepped out of the car, slipping on his suit jacket and folding the collar up against the drizzle. Fumbling for a moment with the top button of his white shirt, he adjusted his tie, hating the feeling of constraint. It felt as if there were two hands encircling his neck, waiting to squeeze.

He signed in with reception, taking the lift up to the eighth floor where his father's company was based. The soft draught of the air conditioning greeted him as he walked through the heavy, glass-panelled doors and into the reception.

It had only been two and a half weeks since he had felt a fresh mountain wind across his face every time he stepped out of the tent, but already it seemed half a century ago. By this time in the morning – 8.30 a.m. – he would have been up for hours, watching the morning sun filter across the snow-clad peaks. But here in England he felt he was sealed away from the outside world – as if nature were something to be feared and carefully excluded.

'Hi, Luca.'

He looked up to see one of the office juniors standing by the entrance to the kitchen. He was holding a small plastic cup brimming with some viscous brown liquid that could equally have been coffee or tea.

'Your father sent me to tell you he wants to see you.'

'Already?' Luca said, his voice dropping into a mutter. 'For Christ's sake.'

Stepping into his own glass-walled office, he began leafing through the stack of papers on his desk, shunting them into two piles. Almost all of them were out of date orders for the four-wheel-drive vehicles the company exported around the world. Cold-calling and making sales came easily to Luca; it was the paperwork he detested so much.

After tapping on his door, Luca stepped inside his father's office to see him seated behind his large, leather-topped desk, speaking on the phone. He was bending forward, peering down at a document, so that the thinning hair combed carefully across the crown of his head was clearly visible. When he looked up, Luca saw eyes of the same grey as his own, but dark-ringed from age and years of working late. He nodded briefly at his son and raised a finger, gesturing for Luca to keep quiet as he continued his call.

Luca leaned against the door, not wanting to venture further into the room. It hadn't changed in all the years his father had occupied it: the same cabinets with the same collectibles neatly displayed on top and dusted once a week. Various awards and certificates for exporting still hung on the far wall by the window, while below them were a couple of photograph frames with their backs to him.

Luca didn't need to see the pictures. They were all too familiar to him. The larger of the two was a formal family portrait: his mother with her hand on her husband's shoulder, while he as a teenager –

the only son and great white hope – smiled up at them, basking in their approval.

That was before he broke it to them that he was going to dedicate his twenties to climbing; that he would work hard for the company while he was in the country and draw a small wage, but long-term he wasn't cut out for the family business.

Despite the many conversations they had had to this effect, his father still hadn't accepted this decision. He tried hard to change his son's mind and regularly pulled guilt trips on him about the cost of his education and how he was depending on Luca to take over the family business. The word 'family' was always stressed, dragged out and emphasised, as if he didn't know who his parents actually were.

At twenty-seven years old, he knew he should have broken away from it all a long time ago, but the truth was he found it impossible to find project work that was flexible enough to pay him the minute he was back in the country. And so the uncomfortable status quo went on between father and son, bonded by guilt and mutual dependency, both seeing the relationship as a means to different ends.

As his father continued talking, Luca's gaze moved to the windows where rain was splattering down the long length of the glass. The minutes passed; three, four, five. His father showed no sign of ending his conversation. He had twisted round and was now concealed behind the wide back of his swivel chair. All Luca could hear was the occasional sound as he sucked in the air between his teeth or the odd grunt of agreement.

Then the chair came swinging round again and, without even making eye contact, his father clicked his fingers, pointing to the seat on the other side of his desk. Luca sat down as directed, a joyless smile on his lips. His father had always had a special talent for making him feel humiliated before they had even exchanged a word.

As the phone was finally returned to its cradle, his father leaned back in his chair and eyed Luca above his glasses.

'So you're back,' he said with a brief smile.

'Yeah. Got in on Thursday.'

'Good. And, did you reach the top?'

Luca shook his head.

'No. We missed the summit by a couple of hours. We had a few issues on the ice wall, but the real problem was that Bill got hit with altitude sickness just after we passed seven thousand metres. All the same, it was one hell of a climb. If it hadn't been for that, we'd definitely have made it.' Involuntarily, he felt his face break into a wide smile. 'You know how much I love it up there, Dad.'

His father looked away as if he had said something mildly offensive.

'Well, don't tell your mother that. You put her through hell every time you go off on one of your damn' fool adventures. She worries herself sick.'

Luca's smile turned brittle.

'Come on, Dad, you don't need to get like this every time I mention climbing.'

There was a long pause while his father took off his glasses and inspected one arm thoughtfully.

'Look, Luca, your mother and I have been speaking about a few things while you were away. I think perhaps I made a mistake putting you in domestic sales. I thought it would suit you because of the way you are, but the reality is it doesn't challenge you enough. So I've come up with something else I think you might like. A promotion, let's call it.'

Luca's heart sank in his chest as he looked at the expression on his father's face. He could toughen himself up to deal with the undercurrents of disappointment and disapproval, but when his father tried to be nice, that was the worst. That was when he really did feel like an ungrateful jerk.

'Look, I know you don't like being cooped up in this office, so the idea is to send you to some of the places where the market is starting to open up a bit. Dubai and Manila, for example. You can set up meetings with potential clients . . . form your own relationships. You'd be good at that. And you'd get all the perks, you know. Five star hotels, a driver for the days when you're there. We know you love travelling . . .'

Luca shifted uncomfortably in his chair. 'Look, Dad, it's not that I don't appreciate you trying to help me out. And I know that there are people next door who'd queue up for that kind of posting. But I've already tried to tell you, this isn't what I want to do long-term.' He spread his hands apologetically. 'I'm just not a car salesman.'

His father's face darkened instantly. 'Don't be such a bloody snob, Luca,' he snapped. 'There's only so long you can persist with this expensive hobby of yours. Soon enough the sponsorship will dry up, especially if you keep on failing on expeditions like this last one. Your mother and I had thought that after the whole Everest débâcle, you would have seen sense and packed the whole thing in. But, well . . .'

Luca's jaw clenched as he stared back at his father.

'You've never even bothered to listen to my side of the story.'

'I hardly think I need to! It was splashed all over the papers before you even got back. I read quite enough without needing to hear any more of the sordid details. I mean, your mother even had some of her friends . . .'

He didn't finish his sentence but instead leaned forward across the desk, his thumbs buckling beneath his weight.

'I shouldn't have to spell this out, Luca, but we have the family name to consider.'

Luca remained motionless, desperately resisting the urge to fight back. Family name? Christ, his father could be such a prick.

'I know finding your path in life is difficult,' he continued, his voice becoming abstract as if he were dealing with one of the office juniors. 'But you're not so young any more, and there's only so long you can keep living by your wits and not assuming real responsibilities.'

Luca closed his eyes briefly before taking a deep breath and dragging himself up from his chair. Sometimes he could hardly believe they were related.

At the doorway, he managed a faint smile. 'Maybe you're right, Dad. Give me a while to think about the job. And I'll call Mum too, let her know I'm back safe and that we've had this chat. Meanwhile, I've got a cracking headache. If you don't mind, I'm going to take all my work back home today, to catch up. I'll get more done there anyway, without any distractions.'

His father looked at him for a moment, before nodding uncertainly. 'OK. Well, let me know. Good to have you back, Luca.'

'Thanks, Dad.'

He turned and walked out of the office, the effort of smiling making his face ache. As he entered his own small office, he slammed the door shut and stood in the centre of the room, the anger surging through him. After all these years, how could his own father understand so little about what made Luca tick?

His eyes settled on his desk, the paperwork stacked in two crooked piles. With a sudden sweep of his arm, he sent them flying against the long bank of windows, papers fluttering down like leaves. They settled across the thick carpet, a mass of densely printed forms and Post-it notes, edges stirring in the steady draught from the air conditioning.

This is not the way it's going to be, Luca said to himself, his eyes screwed tight as if in prayer.

This is not it.

Chapter 10

The Director General of the Public Security Bureau in Beijing slammed his hand down on his desk, making his aide jump.

'How can this have happened?' he seethed. 'I was told our intelligence was a hundred per cent.'

The aide looked down at the carpet nervously, waiting for the storm to pass. He was a short, compact man, with a neat chin and eyebrows that slanted at sharp angles. He stood in silence, hating the fact that he always had to deliver the bad news.

'If I may, sir, our sources tell us that the brothers were very similar-looking. There might only have been a year or so between them.'

'That's no excuse!' the Director General shouted, slamming his fist down on the desk once again. 'If word of this gets out, it'll destabilise the entire damn' province!'

The aide thought quickly. He knew from experience that when the Director didn't have someone to punish directly, the blame was more likely to fall on him.

'Sir, I believe it was Second Lieutenant Chen who was the cause of the mistaken identity. Please instruct me on how you intend to deal with his inexcusable error?'

The Director General breathed out slowly, bringing his right hand up to his heavily lined forehead and smoothing back his grey hair. Despite his age, he still had a thick shock of it that was peppered with dark streaks, and his high-arched nose gave him a hawkish appearance accentuated by his sharp eyes.

Suddenly he stood up and paced over to the window. He poked one long finger through the slats of the closed blinds, looking out at the multitude of people thronging the streets far below.

The aide waited in silence as the seconds passed, watching the tension set his superior's hunched shoulders together. Eventually the Director swung around again, his face rigid with determination.

'Call Captain Zhu Yanlei.'

'Sir?' The aide looked startled.

'You heard me. Call Zhu. I want him standing here in three minutes.'

The aide walked quickly over to the phone and dialled the three-digit internal number. He knew it by heart – Zhu was someone with whom he had had protracted dealings in the past. In fact, if there was anyone in this office he feared more than the Director, it was Captain Zhu.

Two years ago he had been told to reassign Zhu from the field to an office job, based a few floors below where they were now standing. Despite his always having achieved results, it appeared that even by the PSB's standards, Zhu's methods were too much to stomach. The aide still remembered the case files he had studied with photos of the state of some of Zhu's 'interviewees'. The images had haunted him for over a week, giving him a nervous cramp in his bowels, and that was just after a few HR discussions with the man.

After he had made the call, they both sat in silence as the second hand ticked around on the wall clock. Sweat had started to flow freely from the aide's armpits and down the sides of his body when there was a soft knock on the door.

'Come in,' said the Director General, pulling himself to his feet again.

He looked at the man who walked in, remembering, with a sudden chill, how effeminate he always seemed.

He was pale, even for a Chinese, with black hair combed away from his forehead and swept over in a neat side parting. The hair around his ears and the back of his neck had been cropped so short that the white skin of his scalp was visible underneath. His face was oval, with a delicate jawline and thin, pursed lips that were nearly the same colour as his skin. It looked as if all the blood had drained out of them.

Zhu was dressed in an immaculately pressed uniform which hung from his narrow shoulders in perfect vertical lines. He didn't salute or make any gesture of greeting, but merely stood rigid in the centre of the room with one hand folded over the other, while the gold epaulettes of his captain's insignia stood out in proud horizontal streaks across his shoulders. As the Director began speaking, outlining the events of the last twenty-four hours, Zhu remained absolutely still, not a single twitch from his entire body betraying his air of composure.

The aide found himself leaning forward slightly, trying to see past Zhu's silver wire-framed glasses and into his eyes. He remembered them from before: the blank stare, the wide, black pupils.

The Director finished. After a brief silence Zhu finally moved, unclasping his hands and placing them behind his back. The movement caught the aide's eye and something nagged at the back of his mind. He had heard a rumour from one of the other aides on the sixth floor . . . what was it about Zhu's right hand?

'So your man murdered the wrong brother?' Zhu said, his voice soft, almost pleasant.

The Director nodded. 'Yes, exactly, and if it ever got out that an attempt had been made on the eleventh Panchen Lama's life, there would be a full-scale revolt across Tibet. We need you to contain this.'

Zhu didn't answer. The Director continued, his tone becoming unusually conciliatory, 'I will obviously have you reinstated on the active list, with whatever team you deem necessary to carry out the operation.'

Zhu smoothed his side parting. He was clearly in no hurry to make a rejoinder and instead seemed to look around him for the first time, taking in the large rectangular coffee table, the solid wood desk and the hard, high-backed chairs. As his gaze fell on the aide, he gave a tiny smile of satisfaction that made the aide's mouth go dry. Zhu's reversal of fortune was obviously pleasing him hugely, and no wonder – from being struck off the Ops list, he now had the Director General of the PSB practically begging him to clean up his mess.

'I would like the lieutenant who failed in his mission to be on my team,' he said finally.

The Director shrugged. 'I cannot imagine he will be of much use, but if that's what you wish . . .' he gave a nod in the direction of the aide '. . . consider it done.'

Zhu nodded. 'And how long do I have to complete the mission?'

'There are seven weeks until the Linka Festival and we need to be absolutely confident that this matter is resolved by then. You are booked on a flight to Chengdu tonight, with a connection to Lhasa the following morning. I am granting you the same dispensation as previously. You are free to use whatever methods you deem appropriate.'

He shot a sideways glance at the aide before looking Zhu straight in the eye.

'But, Captain, there's no need to . . . complicate matters. You are required to contain this situation and ensure that it remains secret. We need you to find the boy. That is all.'

'Find?' replied Zhu in a tone of mild surprise, hands still clasped behind his back.

The Director looked down at his desk, averting his eyes for the first time. When he spoke, his voice was little more than a whisper.

'Kill,' he said simply.

Zhu's lips curled slightly into a smile.

'I'll be back within a month.'

Chapter 11

Tossing his car keys into the empty fruit bowl, Luca pulled some dirty clothes off the bed and lay down. He stared up at the ceiling and breathed out, attempting to exhale all the staleness he'd felt since first walking into his father's office.

He had left the building almost immediately after their conversation, shaking his head as he had gathered up the scattered papers from the floor. As he walked out of the lift a small group of colleagues were standing at the entrance, clutching take-away cups of coffee and shaking their umbrellas. Luca had dredged up a smile as they clapped him on the back and asked him about the trip. Then, pleading a bad headache, he'd escaped to his car.

Now he exhaled again, feeling the tension slowly seep out of him. He glanced across his small flat towards the tiny open-plan kitchen in the corner. By the cluttered sink was a huge stack of mail. He had scanned through it all when he first got back, looking for any hand-written envelopes. The rest, he knew, would just be an assortment of bills or endless offers for broadband or the latest mobile phone.

Christ, there was just so much of it.

They had only been away five weeks. Five weeks. Such a brief amount of time, yet the rest of the world had been churning away at such a pace it made him feel he had been away for years. At some point today he should file it all away, write letters, send cheques.

Raising himself off the bed, Luca walked over to the kitchen and stood by the mail. Then, with a sudden angry movement, he gathered up all the envelopes in both hands and rammed them into the lowest kitchen drawer.

Screw it. It could wait some more.

Glancing at his watch, he took a bottle of Coke out of the fridge and levered the top off using the sideboard. Taking a few gulps he then sat down to make some work calls. For a couple of hours he worked steadily through the emails and phone messages, hating the sound of his own voice as he grovelled to the string of customers he had neglected.

He felt so tired, so drained of energy, yet it was only midday and he'd done nothing more strenuous than travel a few miles up and down a motorway in a car. Out in the mountains, he could climb for hours on huge vertical pitches, swinging his axe in again and again. Then, after no more than a few hours' sleep, he could do it all again, day after day, even at high altitude. But here he felt perpetually out of breath: choking on the dense, petrol-fumed air, jolted by the barging shoulders of commuters on the streets. It made him feel like an old man.

As he worked his eyes would occasionally flicker over to the stack of papers lying by the side of his bed in the adjacent room. Most of them were photocopies from the library book that had mentioned that ring of mountains. At the bottom, larger than the rest, was the folded satellite map that Jack had given him. He had looked at it several times over the last few days, and each time he did, his thoughts went straight to Bill.

He should ring his friend. Get back in contact. They had already let this argument fester for too long, and besides, he couldn't feel any worse than he did right now.

Luca was just about to pick up the phone again when a text came through. It was from Jack Milton, asking if a package had arrived.

After dialling his uncle's number and resting the phone under his ear, Luca strode over to the kitchen drawer and sifted through the contents. Nothing. As the phone continued ringing, he opened the front door of his flat and went into the communal hall to look through today's mail. There was a brown cylindrical tube, taped up with thick sellotape and slightly crushed from being pushed through the letterbox.

'Jack. It's Luca.'

There was a clunking sound, then a soft cursing as Jack caught the edge of his coffee cup on the desk.

'Hey, Luca, how are you? Did you get the package I sent?'

'Yeah. It's right here. Hold on a second.'

Ripping open the cylinder, Luca pulled out a large photocopied sheet of paper that was curled in on itself. Clamping the phone to his shoulder, he spread it out on the kitchen counter, using the empty bottle of Coke to hold down one edge. A beautifully detailed pen-and-ink drawing filled the entire piece of A3 paper. It had been rather clumsily photocopied, so that the bottom right-hand corner was missing, but as Luca realised what he was looking at, he felt his pulse quicken. A disbelieving smile crept across his face.

'Holy shit, Jack! Where the hell did you find this?'

'I thought you'd like it,' he replied, a smile in his voice. 'After you mentioned the word *beyul*, I did a little bit of research myself. That scroll is just the half of it.'

The picture showed eight snow-capped mountains forming a perfect circle, and at its centre another mountain shaped like a pyramid. The artistry of the original work must have been spectacular. The detail was meticulous, every inch crowded with finely inked images and complex symbols.

In the centre, at the very summit of the pyramid, a priest was depicted, staring out from the page with the otherworldly detachment of someone deep in meditation. In his open hand was a symbol: a circle with eight points merging into a central triangle.

'It's called a *thangka*,' Jack continued. 'They were originally teaching scrolls, drawn by Tibetan Buddhist monks and passed on from monastery to monastery. And I found your pyramid mountain when I was looking though the *Mahayana Sutras*.'

'The what?'

'It's a philosophical doctrine adopted by a certain sect of Buddhists. I was put on to it by one of the lecturers here in Cambridge, but they said the real people to talk to were from the Asian Studies Department.'

Luca's voice rose in pitch. 'But that pyramid is exactly what I saw from Makulu. This proves that the mountain actually exists!'

Jack laughed. 'As a scholar, I can assure you that it doesn't *prove* anything. You'll need to find a few other corroborating sources before you can claim that.'

'But Bailey's book in the library,' said Luca excitedly, his eyes falling on the photocopies stacked by his bed, 'it mentioned that the pyramid mountain was in one of these *beyuls*.'

'Again, that's anecdotal. But you're right, it is beginning to get interesting. Listen to what I discovered in the *Sutras*.' Jack paused, trying to find the right place in his notes. 'So, according to this, the ring of mountains is supposed to depict the eight-fold path of a lotus flower. And then, right in the centre, is this mythical kingdom.' He paused again as he tried to decipher his own spidery handwriting. 'It's called *Shambhala*.'

'A mythical kingdom?'

'Apparently so. It's a place where the Lamas have moved on to some kind of higher spiritual plane. You know, total enlightenment and all that.'

Jack reached out one shaking hand and picked up his mug of coffee. Kingdoms of total enlightenment – Jesus, he could do with a bit of that around here.

'What do you think this means?' asked Luca.

'Like I said, it might not be anything more than coincidence, but I thought it would give you a bit of a boost. I know how you get when you come back from a trip.'

Luca traced his fingers over the picture, his eyes fixed on the focal point. A ring of mountains with a pyramid at the centre . . . It just seemed incredible.

'Thanks, Jack. That's the best news I've had all day.'

'Pleasure. And, in the meantime, I'll send you this *Mahayana* book and you can read up about it for yourself. If you are serious about finding out some more, then I'll make a few more enquiries and see if I can't arrange a meeting or two.'

Putting the phone down, Luca walked over to his bedside table and fished out the folded satellite map. With a handful of drawing pins and a thick black marker pen in his left hand, he unfolded it and pinned it up on the patch of wallpaper at the end of his bed. He then wrote a single word in the bottom right hand corner.

BEYUL?

Chapter 12

His face was old as only a Tibetan face can be.

Lines cross-hatched their way across its leathery surface, like a paper bag that had been crumpled into a ball and hastily smoothed out. His dark brown eyes were set deep in their sockets, staring out from beneath long, straggling eyebrows. Around his body were wrapped thick red robes, but years of exposure to dirt and sunlight had faded them to almost the same colour as the ground.

The old monk sat on a pile of earth a few hundred yards from the entrance to Menkom village, but rarely turned from his vigil to look back at the thatched houses. Although a few thin wisps of smoke still trailed out from the chimneys into the cobalt sky, the village was almost completely still. It had been ravaged by disease for over a month, ever since the traders had come.

The first to fall ill were the old men, disappearing from their usual place by the side of the road. Then it spread: to young children, women, and finally the men working out in the fields. In just a few weeks, the once lively village had become ghostly and withdrawn.

Most people remained indoors, lying fever-ridden on the wooden floors of their homes, while outside cattle ambled through the streets untended. Small, black pigs poked their noses through piles of rubbish in the stream and chickens nested in the thatch rooftops. No stones were thrown at them, no voice raised to scare them away.

As the old monk watched, something distant on the pathway seemed to move then became stationary again. He got slowly to his feet, leaving his prayer wheel lying at his side, and squinted down on to the bare earth slopes of the lower valleys. Haloed by the late afternoon sun, he could just see a small cloud of dust hovering above a black shape. It was hazy, little more than a smudge merging into the horizon.

Gradually, the shape began to separate into its component parts: first, the outline of a yak's great arching horns, then came the silhouettes of people following behind. Through the dust came a second yak, then another, until he could see an entire caravan of men and beasts toiling up the valley at a steady pace.

It was them. It had to be.

Finally the first of the yaks drew level with him, the heavy brass bell around its neck clanking with each step. Its huge flanks were dread locked with dust and dried mud, and on the arch of its withers heavy saddlebags were roped tight. As the mighty beast snorted, long strands of saliva oozed from its nose, beading with the dust from the pathway.

From somewhere near the back of the line, a voice called out above the noise. Amidst a ragged cacophony of bells the row of animals came to a juddering halt. With clothes stained grey from travel, a figure slipped off the back of one of the yaks and approached the monk. As a filthy cloth was pulled away from the figure's face the monk found himself looking at the dark suntanned cheeks and green eyes of a young woman clearly exhausted from her journey.

'*Tashi delek*, venerable father,' she said, bowing her head to reveal long, black hair that was matted with dust. 'We are looking for the gatekeeper.'

The old monk nodded, an unaccustomed smile creasing his face even further.

'*Tashi delek*,' he replied, in a voice hoarse from disuse. 'I am he.'

With that he reached forward, clasping her hands in his and bringing them towards his heart. 'I did not expect to see you until the solstice.

But it is wonderful indeed that you have arrived safely. Our guide is ready to escort you when you have gathered your strength. He is a climber from your own country and has been looking forward to meeting you for many weeks now.'

The young woman smiled briefly in thanks before grasping the monk's hands tighter. 'Sir, I know you have not yet been informed of this, but there is someone I need to take with me.'

The monk's expression clouded over and he began shaking his head before she had even finished speaking. 'I know how precious you are to our order, but that will not be possible. The guide can take only one person at a time. Only one. And, as you know, only the chosen may go.'

The woman looked down at the ground for a moment. When she raised her head again, her green eyes were bright with determination.

'He *has* been chosen, and must be taken first. It is vital that your guide should leave with him immediately. In the meantime, I will wait in the village until the guide returns to escort me. You must trust me, venerable father, he is more important than I.'

She had barely finished speaking when there was a scuffling sound from behind the herders and a small boy of about nine years old raced up to the woman and slipped his hand trustingly in hers. He had ragged dark hair and bright brown eyes, although the whites were bloodshot from dust and fatigue. He was wearing an oversized sheepskin coat, tied at the middle by a piece of knotted rope. Looking first at the woman, he then turned his gaze on the monk and asked in a voice that was clear and calm: 'Is this the place?'

The woman smiled down at him, one hand resting on his shoulder.

'Not yet,' she said. 'But we're not far now.'

Chapter 13

The brass plaque said PROF. SALLY TANG, ASIAN STUDIES. Jack caught a glimpse of his reflection in the shiny metal, and running a hand briefly through his hair, gently rapped on the door.

'Come in!'

As he entered Sally Tang came out from behind her paper-covered desk, shifting her reading glasses on to the top of her head. She was even more petite than he remembered, with a smart beige jacket hanging off her tiny frame and long brown boots that were little bigger than a child's.

'Jack.' Sally shook his hand warmly. She tucked a lock of her jet black bob behind one ear and studied him, her fine-boned face angled to one side like a bird's. 'You look well. Much better than in Kathmandu. Sit down, please.'

Jack smiled, settling himself into a burgundy leather armchair in front of her desk.

'I hope you don't mind my usurping your meeting with Robert,' she continued. 'I heard him mention that someone was coming into the department to talk to him about *beyuls*, and when I found out it was you, I couldn't resist cutting in.' She perched herself on the front of her desk. 'But I must say, Jack, spiritual myth is a bit out of your usual line, isn't it? As I recall, you were never interested in anything much unless it was as solid as a rock.'

'Even dinosaurs like me can evolve, Sally – and if I didn't have such a lousy memory these days, I would have come straight to you rather than cold-calling Professor Harris. But, of course, you're right. It's actually my nephew who's become interested in the subject.' Jack glanced at his watch and frowned. 'He's late as usual, but I hope that nice secretary . . . what's her name?'

'Emily.'

'I hope Emily will send him our way. Meanwhile I should probably give you the background. Don't suppose there's any chance of a cup of coffee . . .'

Five minutes later they were both sitting in armchairs by the bay window, nursing mugs of coffee. It was now three years since they had met, by chance, on a flight out to Nepal. Sally had been waiting for her visa into Tibet, on her way to a relative's wedding, and Jack had been on one of his geology field trips, acclimatising before going further up into the mountains. Having established their common link of the university, they had met up for dinner at her hotel, arguing good-naturedly about their different perspectives on Asia and comparing notes on academic life over cups of chrysanthemum tea.

Now they chatted easily for a while, catching up on the last few years. Sally's astute brown eyes hardened momentarily when Jack mentioned the pyramid mountain. But as he went on to describe the other discoveries they had made about the secret system of *beyuls*, she began to smile again.

'Well, you have got yourselves in over your heads, haven't you? And no wonder. A geologist and an adventurer, trying to tackle the esoteric myths of Buddhism. Now the first thing I should tell you is—' She broke off as the phone buzzed on her desk and, with a frown, went to pick it up. 'Yes, yes. Send him through.'

A few moments later Luca walked in, wearing jeans and a yellow T-shirt with 'Easily Distracted' written across it. He smiled in a practised way, pushing his fringe of blond hair back from his face.

'I'm sorry I'm late,' he said, glancing at Jack before directing the full wattage of his smile at the tiny Tibetan woman. 'I'm afraid I didn't inherit the punctuality gene in the family.'

Sally shook his hand in greeting, then glanced down at his T-shirt. 'I suppose I should try and get to the point as soon as possible. Pull up a chair, Luca. I was just about to explain to Jack why you shouldn't believe in fairytales.'

Luca hung a soft leather satchel over the back of his chair and settled down, his expression instantly focused.

'Go on.'

Sally spread her hands. 'Well, Jack has been telling me about your adventures in Tibet and your interest in *beyuls*. It's a fascinating area of Buddhist folklore, no doubt about that, but I'm afraid that's all it is: folklore.'

Luca frowned and leaned forward, resting his chin on one fist. 'But the books all say the same thing, and they're pretty specific: that *beyuls* are sanctuaries of total enlightenment, the most holy places in all Tibet. And they say there are twenty-one of them, situated in the most remote areas of the country.'

Sally sighed. 'Believe me, you're not the first person to be seduced by the idea of *beyuls*. But just listen to what you are saying – sanctuaries of total enlightenment. Doesn't that sound like a myth to you?'

As Luca went to object, she raised one eyebrow and fixed him with a pitying gaze that was usually reserved for her first-year students. There was a pause before she continued speaking, her voice softening a little.

'Think of it this way: the *beyul* myth could be equated to the search for the Holy Grail. As any psychologist worth their salt will tell you, people love a seemingly impossible quest. It brings up all sorts of atavistic feelings: that somehow they are special and will defeat the odds.'

'So you're saying these places don't really exist?' said Jack, sounding disappointed. 'They're just figments of someone's imagination.'

Sally smiled, shifting her tiny frame more upright in the armchair so that her feet dangled a few inches above the ground.

'It all depends on your point of view. I'm not saying there isn't any truth to them. I'm just saying such truths aren't literal, and certainly not to the extent that you can prove them by sight or touch.'

Jack nodded. 'You're talking about metaphors, right? Well, they're certainly common enough in religious belief.'

'Metaphors?' Luca exhaled impatiently. 'Guys, you've completely lost me. Metaphors for what? I don't even understand what *beyuls* are exactly. Sanctuaries keep on being mentioned – but sanctuaries from what?'

'Oh, the usual sort of thing . . . darkness, evil, all that sort of stuff,' Sally answered, turning her face towards the window. '*Beyuls* are a central theme in the many apocalyptic myths of Tibet. It's similar to Biblical prophecy: when the end comes, and the world is consumed by chaos, the Lamas will lead the common people to these *beyuls* and, once there, they will find the wisdom and enlightenment necessary to weather the storm.'

Jack cleared his throat. 'So there's no truth to the idea that they contain priceless treasures?'

Sally Tang laughed, switching her gaze from one expectant face to the other. 'Well, only in as much as every good fairytale features a hidden treasure. The myths certainly do refer to immense treasures, of infinite value. But, boys – have you any idea how many hapless fortune hunters have wasted their whole lives looking for such hidden treasures and vast riches? It's like those endless quests for Shangri-La. They went off, searching vast mountain ranges or hacking their way into mighty river gorges . . .'

'And what did they find?' This time it was Luca who spoke.

'They found what you would expect to find in such places – rivers and mountains. They went on wild goose chases, mistaking ancient Tibetan legends for literal truth.'

Luca leaned forward in his chair. 'So there never were any treasures?'

'That is exactly what I am saying,' Tang answered impatiently. 'There was nothing but myth. The fortune hunters found no empirical evidence at all.'

As she spoke, Luca reached behind him and, picking up his satchel, slipped open the buckles. Inside was the rolled photocopy of Jack's *thangka*, which he'd unpinned from his wall to show her: the pyramid mountain lay at the centre of the picture, surrounded by its circular range of mountains.

'No evidence at all?' he repeated, staring at her quizzically. 'So how do you explain the fact that I saw these mountains, exactly as they're drawn here? Well, minus the squatting monk.'

The professor sighed at Luca's stubborn line of questioning.

'I grant you that some of the stories go into detail about the twenty-first or "mountain" *beyul*. It is supposed to be the most enlightened out of all the *beyuls*, a kind of heaven on earth, if you will. It's often described or illustrated just as it has been here – a pyramid-shaped mountain with a strange ring of mountains that protect it. But, of course, the genesis of most legend and myth lies in reality. No doubt the concept of the holiest of *beyuls* arose because there was this peculiarly symmetrical rock formation – and that may well have been what you saw.' Her eyes rested for a moment on Luca's bare, tanned arms, folded across his chest. 'But if you're thinking of haring off to Tibet in search of the holiest of *beyuls*, then I'd urge you, as a friend of your uncle's and also a responsible adult, to reconsider.'

She flicked a sidelong glance at Jack before turning back to Luca, her bright eyes suddenly very serious. 'Over the years many Westerners – often those who were dissatisfied with their own daily lives – have become obsessed with these *beyuls*. As a result, a lot of them died very lonely deaths in some of the farthest reaches of Tibet.'

Jack looked over at his nephew who was now staring out of the bay window, apparently lost in thought. 'Luca? Are you with us?'

He nodded silently.

'I'm sorry to disappoint you, really I am,' said Sally, cocking her head to one side again. 'Though from my own selfish point of view, I have to admit I'm delighted by the outcome of your curiosity. I have had the pleasure of meeting you, Luca, not to mention getting back in touch with Jack here. Now, if you'll excuse me, I have a meeting at eleven o'clock. But what do you say about the three of us making a date . . .'

'So what about the *Kalak Tantra*?' he said softly.

'The what?' said Jack.

'Sally knows what I'm talking about.'

Jack looked from one face to the other, noting the determined expression on Luca's and the fact that the smile had frozen on Sally's. 'Now you've lost me. Can someone fill me in?'

'The *Kalak Tantra*,' Luca said, his eyes challenging Sally, 'was discovered in the last years of the nineteenth century. It appears to be a sort of road map, showing the location of every single one of the *beyuls*. Apparently the *Tantra* gave a set of rules, a precise code, that had to be adhered to if you wanted to get into them. It listed the entrances, the routes in, even what time of year the journey should be made.' Luca clapped his hands together enthusiastically. 'It gave you everything you needed actually to get into one of these places!'

Sally gave a curt nod, her eyes following Luca's every movement.

'Some Westerners have even said they have seen parts of the *Tantra*,' he added, opening his hands out flat as if he were holding a copy of the book in his hands.

For a moment Sally remained motionless, then she looked over at Jack and grinned. 'No one can accuse your nephew of lacking determination,' she said, her expression slowly melting into its habitual stare. 'But if you'd read a bit more of the *Mahayana Sutras* and not just the first couple of chapters, you'd have discovered that no one has even seen a complete copy of the *Tantra*. Minute fragments of it do exist – a few vague words here, a cryptic sentence there. But more often than not, the claims are wildly exaggerated. Parts of the *"Tantra"* are even sold to a few gullible tourists as they walk round the Bakhor in Lhasa. It's not that different from Christians buying splinters of the "True" Cross.'

She tucked a strand of hair neatly behind her ear, looking over at Jack again.

'Listen, I wish we could carry on talking.' She glanced at her watch, which looked huge on her tiny wrist. 'But I have a meeting that can't wait . . .'

'Of course.' He stood up and stretched. 'Sally, you've been wonderful. I'll drop you an email and we can work out a plan to meet again.'

'Thanks, Professor.' Luca stood up, flashing her another smile as he swung his satchel over his shoulder. 'That was fascinating.'

The two men walked down the corridor in silence, Jack shooting glances of concern at his nephew as they descended a flight of stone stairs and came out into the building's open quadrangle.

'I know it's a blow,' said Jack finally as they steered around the neatly mown circle of grass. 'But Sally's a smart woman, and if she tells you it's a fool's errand . . . .'

'I don't trust her,' said Luca abruptly.

Jack looked incredulous. 'Don't be ridiculous! She may not have told you what you wanted to hear, but Sally Tang is a—'

'I thought we were going to see a Professor Harris, anyway?'

'Yes, well, I forgot this was Sally's department. When she heard that it was me making enquiries, she arranged for us to see her instead.'

Luca shook his head. 'She's holding something back, I'm sure of it.'

Jack sighed and shrugged. 'OK, well, I'm sorry for you. You won't find a better mind or anyone willing to give you more time. Now, how do you feel about finding a café? I'm gasping for a coffee . . .'

As the men ducked under a stone arch, went past the porters' lodge and into the street beyond, Professor Tang retreated from the bay window where she had been watching them. She bit her bottom lip, trying to decide.

It had been years since she had had any official duties in this arena, and part of her wanted to do Jack a favour and overlook the matter – categorise it as low risk. But there was something about the younger man that had worried her. For all his lazy charm he was very focused, and he had obviously chanced on pieces of information that would fan his interest. She doubted that she had deterred him for a second. If anything, judging from that handsome, brash face that was obviously used to getting its own way – she'd probably only succeeded in arousing his curiosity all the more.

Having reached a decision, Sally opened the lowest drawer in her desk and pulled out a battered, leather-bound address book. She flicked through the pages until her finger was resting under the number she sought. A few moments later she waited as the crackly connection was routed, via Beijing, direct to the Lhasa office of the PSB.

Chapter 14

Cathy watched as Bill loosened his tie with two fingers and kicked off his shoes. He put his feet up on the coffee table with a sigh.

'Really, I'm fine,' he said. 'It's just been another bitch of a day at the office.' Stretching his arms above his head, he yawned. 'Everything's fine.'

His wife perched on the arm of the sofa opposite, fingering the buttons on a cushion. Her shoulder-length hair was pulled back into a ponytail from a quietly pretty face and she was wearing one of Bill's huge knitted jumpers, her hands lost in the long sleeves.

'You keep saying "fine" but you haven't been yourself since you've got back. I can tell something's wrong. Why won't you just tell me?'

'Because there's nothing worse than coming back from a long day at the office and being asked if you're all right, over and over again,' Bill snapped. He closed his eyes and sank a little deeper in the sofa, wiggling his toes in his socks. 'It's exhausting.'

Cathy took a deep breath. 'Then why don't you seem to notice when Ella and Hal are talking to you? Or me, for that matter.' She hesitated, biting her lip, and continued, 'I know it can be a bit of an anti-climax after these trips, but you've always seemed so pleased to see us before. This time . . . well, it's like we're barely here.'

'That's not true,' protested Bill. 'Of course I'm happy to be back with you and the kids.'

There was a brief silence. The TV flickered mutely, announcing the beginning of the seven o'clock news. Bill reached for the volume on the remote, then gave a yelp as Cathy jumped up and snatched it from him. The picture shrank to a dot as she flicked the power switch.

'Enough, Bill. Something happened up that mountain, and seeing as I'm the person you've chosen to spend your life with, I think I have a right to know about it.'

Bill sighed and rubbed his eyes. He looked up, wincing to see her expression.

'Look, I haven't wanted to talk about this because I know what you think about Luca sometimes, and, well, he's . . . my friend.' Bill paused for a moment and slowly shook his head. 'But since he hasn't even called me or made any attempt to set things right . . .'

'What did he do?' Cathy interrupted, her voice steely.

Bill sighed and looked down at his large hands for a moment before speaking. 'You know when I got altitude sickness? I think Luca was planning on leaving me up there.'

Cathy's eyes widened. 'What? He *what*?'

Bill flapped his hands as if trying to put out a fire. 'Look, it didn't happen so don't make a big thing out of it. But he said something about going for the summit and leaving me on the ledge. You know, it's hard to be sure what the hell *did* happen up there. I wasn't exactly thinking straight.' Then he turned his head, looking back towards the blank television screen. 'The strange thing is that part of me wishes he had gone for the summit. Then I wouldn't have to feel so damn' guilty, like the whole thing is unfinished business because I got ill.'

'Jesus, I always knew he was selfish but I never thought he'd go *that* far. The man ought to be locked up!'

'Come on, Cath, you know you can't judge what happens up there from the safety of our living room. It was just the heat of the moment and funny things can happen to your brain at altitude.

77

Besides, he didn't actually do it. And he was the one who got me down.'

'But this isn't a one-off. Luca has a track record. Everybody knows he walked past those people dying on Everest.'

Bill looked up accusingly. 'That's just what the bloody tabloids said, Cath, and you know it. Luca was trying to get the hell off the mountain. He didn't even know those guys were up there.'

'That's what he told you.'

'Yeah, that's what he told me, and I believe him. I know Luca's always had a hard side to him, but he'd never go that far.'

Cathy looked over at her husband. Bill looked pale and strained. He had dropped a few pounds, and there were shadows under his eyes from the restless nights he'd been having. Moving to sit down beside him, she leaned forward impulsively to give him a hug. As she rested her chin on his shoulder, her glance strayed to the framed photo of Luca and Bill standing at the summit of the Eiger. Their goggles were up around their foreheads and grins split their faces. It had been a speed ascent of the north face and the whole climb had gone without a hitch.

'Well, at least you know you'll never climb with him again.'

Bill remained silent.

Cathy pulled back and looked him in the eye. 'Bill, please tell me you aren't going to climb with him again? Look, we all know what Luca is like. The kids love him, and he's sweet with me. Probably, underneath it all, his heart is in the right place. But in the end, Luca is out there for Luca. That's not someone you can rely on.'

A lock of hair had escaped her ponytail. She pushed it back impatiently.

'Besides, we have a deal, right? Some good, uninterrupted family time.' She reached for his hand, her voice growing more determined. 'Right, my love?'

The phone rang, making them both jump. Bill let go of her hand with a strained smile, crossing the room to pick up the receiver.

'Hello,' he said. 'Yes . . . Oh, it's you.'

He turned so that his broad back was to his wife. Cathy felt her heart begin to thump.

'Fine, and you?'

There was a long silence before Bill spoke again.

'Right. Well, that's good of you, maybe some time later this week.' He paused again and listened for a few minutes. 'I see. OK, well, how about twenty minutes then? The Windsor Castle.'

He put down the receiver and turned back to face Cathy. She felt her heart sink as she saw the new light that had appeared in his eyes.

'Talk of the devil. Luca wants to speak to me, face to face. To apologise.' Bill started walking towards the door, picking his jacket off the coat-hook as he passed. 'I said I'd meet him for a quick pint.'

Cathy looked down at her hands, realising they had started to tremble. 'Don't go,' she said quietly.

Bill was in the middle of sliding his arm into his jacket. He looked round at her in surprise.

'Why on earth not? We need to sort this out.'

'Because I don't believe for a minute he'd be apologising unless he's got something else up his sleeve. And I can't bear the thought of him persuading you to go on another trip. I just can't bear it.'

'My love, I'm going for a pint with the man. That's it.' Walking over to the sofa, he kissed her briefly.

'I'll be back in an hour,' he said. 'In plenty of time to help put the kids to bed.'

Three hours later, Cathy lay curled up in bed, pretending to sleep. As Bill crept into the bedroom she smelled the smoke from the pub on his clothes, heard the unevenness to his tread.

'Cathy,' he whispered as he sat down on the edge of the mattress, pulling off his boots. 'Cathy love, are you awake?'

Even before he reached out to switch on the bedside lamp, she heard it in his voice. He was going away again.

Every instinct screamed inside of her. This time something bad would come of it.

Chapter 15

Two dust-streaked jeeps cut through the north-east outskirts of Lhasa, moving fast. After turning down a long, pitted cement drive, they halted in front of the complex's iron gates and security passes were handed over. A moment later there was a clunking sound as old electric motors fired up and the massive gates slowly pulled back on their hinges.

Past the long line of garrison buildings, the jeeps rounded a smaller, prefabricated block and came to a halt once more. As the engines died, Second Lieutenant Chen quickly stepped out, squinting against the streaming wind. He stood for a moment in silence, surveying the drab, military buildings and the desolate landscape. Then he jumped slightly as he noticed Captain Zhu had appeared by his shoulder.

'Drapchi Prison, sir,' Chen shouted above the noise of the wind.

'What are these outer buildings?' Zhu asked, seemingly indifferent to the dust blowing across his face.

'The northern five are for ordinary criminals. The other two house the re-education centres.'

Zhu nodded, then turned and started walking towards the door of the smaller building. Within a couple of strides Chen had caught up with him, but was careful not to get too close. He towered above the captain, taking one stride for each of his two, and was very aware of how his size could upset his superiors. It had happened before, when he had first graduated from the Academy. After everything he had heard about Zhu's reputation, he wasn't about to make the same mistake twice.

As they crossed the few remaining yards, Chen averted his gaze from Drapchi's windswept exterior. It had always been a hellish place, but he knew that the external appearance was nothing compared to what lay directly beneath. Mile upon mile of subterranean passages, built during the 1960s by the prisoners themselves, stretched out across the entire complex. There were hundreds of cells, each one an exact replica of the next and all kept in perpetual darkness. Electric lighting was only permitted in the interrogation rooms.

But it wasn't so much the dark that got to Chen, nor even the occasional sound of a prisoner's screams. It was the smell. He had never experienced anything like it. It was as if the stench of panicked humans had been rubbed into every one of the bare concrete walls.

Despite the heat Chen shivered slightly, thinking back to his dreadful mistake over the boy. When he'd first heard the news, he was terrified what they would do to him, but by some miracle he'd been allowed to stay on the mission. He didn't doubt, however, that his life was hanging by a thread. Beijing wasn't famous for second chances, let alone third.

A guard with a pale, bloated face was there to meet them at the entrance. He carried a flashlight, and his blinking eyes seemed pained by the daylight. He gestured them inside and down a wide, circular staircase with an iron-bar security door at the bottom. After he'd signalled into a room beyond, the door was buzzed open and their slow procession began down the first of many corridors.

Chen could feel that the temperature had already dropped. In only a few metres the heat and wind from outside had been replaced by a chill that seemed to seep through from the sheer weight of the concrete all around them. As the guard marched off down the corridor, his flashlight cut a narrow beam of light across the walls and floor. Every few steps they passed the silhouette of a cell door or an interlocking corridor, before it faded back again into the shadows.

As the guard turned, shining his light round to check on them all, Chen suddenly caught sight of Zhu. His features were bleached white by the beam. He had a handkerchief pressed to his nose, but Chen could see the top half of it was wrinkled in disgust. Obviously the smell was getting to him too.

They were approaching the yellow glow of a ceiling light and the corridor widened into a room. At first it was hard to see much, then various shapes began to take form. Towards the back of the room was a heavy wooden bench with thick strapping and several buckets of water lined up on top of it. Further to the left was a rickety metal chair with a figure slumped forward in it, his shaven head almost touching his knees and his face concealed from view.

As the guard switched off his flashlight, a second figure stepped out from the shadows. He was small and gaunt looking, with wide eyes that stared vacantly ahead. He was wearing a cheap plastic cooking apron and long rubber gloves that stretched past his elbows like medieval gauntlets. Approaching the guard, he handed him a clip-board and, without even registering the others, walked past into the dark corridor and was gone.

The guard swivelled the clipboard round and read the name of the prisoner aloud.

'Jigme Sangpo. A monk from Tashilhunpo Monastery,' he said, his voice as wavering as his eyes.

The figure in the chair did not lift its head.

Zhu stepped forward into the room, his left arm outstretched for the clipboard.

'I know who he is, idiot.'

Tilting the pages towards the light, he scanned the notes that had been kept during the prisoner's interrogation. It had been going on for just over three days, with successively stronger tortures being intro-duced every few hours. They had got nothing from the early phases, but as Zhu had already guessed from seeing the water and the plastic gloves, the electro-shock treatment had brought better results.

He moved closer to the figure on the chair. He crouched down and slowly tilted the man's face up from his knees. There were jagged burn marks lacerating his cheeks, stretching right across his face from where the copper wire had been attached. As their eyes met, Zhu could see that the prisoner's were dull and bloodshot from long hours of pain. He had both his arms folded into his lap, with his hands resting over his groin. That was where they would have done the most damage, Zhu thought, especially to a monk.

After so many hours, all the monk had said was that 'two climbers had been brought in from Nepal' to move the Panchen Lama. That was it. Nothing more.

Zhu looked into his eyes, searching for the slightest trace of emotion. That must be all he knew. No one could resist this kind of treatment, and he had already held out for an impressive length of time. Once broken, it was rare for a prisoner to hold back. They usually said anything to get the electric shocks to stop.

'You must not feel bad about what you have told us,' he whispered, moving close but careful not to touch the monk. 'You have done your duty and we are grateful for it.'

The prisoner stared blankly at this new apparition before him, his mind clouded by the hours of pain and endless questions. In the half-light, the man's black pupils seemed to expand, obscuring any trace of the true colour of his eyes. Those black circles were boring into him. He could smell the man's aftershave and the subtle aroma of his freshly washed face.

'You have done well,' he said.

Tears welled up in the corners of the monk's eyes, streaking through the dirt on his cheeks. He had betrayed the boy, betrayed his entire religion. His single consolation was that he only knew a couple of the minor details of the escape, and so had had little to tell. But however little it was, the fact remained – he had told the Chinese.

Captain Zhu stood up, his eyes moving from Chen to the guard.

'Move him up to the day cells in the main complex.'

'But, sir, political prisoners are . . .'

The guard's voice broke off as he saw the expression on the visitor's face darken. For a moment Zhu remained quiet, allowing silence to fill the room. The guard straightened up, wishing he had kept his mouth shut and growing more and more uncomfortable as the moments passed.

Eventually Zhu handed him back the clipboard.

'This is no ordinary monk but one of the High Lamas of the Gelugpa sect,' he said, in an icy voice. 'You will treat him with the respect he deserves. Now, see to it that he is washed and has a good meal.'

As the guard quickly pulled himself up into a salute and moved forward towards the prisoner, Zhu grabbed the flashlight from his hand.

'And return his prayer wheel and beads,' he added.

Zhu signalled to Chen and they moved back down the dark corridor. As Chen fell into step behind him, his eyes following the beam of light passing over the floor ahead, he felt a strange sense of elation. Even after prisoners had given everything, named everyone involved in a suspected plot and many more besides, they were usually left to rot down here. There were no court proceedings, no appeals or transfers. The cell doors were simply slammed shut and the matter closed for all but the unfortunate soul within.

But today was different. Zhu had given a simple order and now the monk was being transferred. Just like that.

As they followed the line of the corridor, Chen's expression softened. He had heard of the Captain's reputation and, like everyone else, found his presence in the office unnerving. But when it came down to it, there was obviously more to this man than any of them had suspected.

He cleared his throat, picking his words carefully.

'Do you think the information will be helpful, sir?'

Zhu continued walking, but after a moment replied over his shoulder.

'It's vague, but it might be useful when cross-checked with something else.'

'Yes, sir.'

They reached the iron security gate at the foot of the main stairwell. Zhu reached up and banged the end of the flashlight against the metal a couple of times, the noise quickly muffled by the concrete walls. From the annexe behind, another guard buzzed them through and they climbed up the wide circular staircase in silence, pausing only by the door to the outside. Chen turned towards Zhu, having mustered the courage to say something more.

'I think you did the right thing, sir.'

Zhu looked at him, his expression unreadable.

'I mean, transferring the monk up to the surface,' Chen continued, his voice beginning to falter. 'He had told us everything he knew already. It was as good to let him go.'

Zhu seemed to be nodding slowly as Chen spoke. Then he reached out with his left hand and slowly turned the handle on the door.

'Every man's last day should be a good one,' he said as he stepped out into the light.

Chapter 16

Eight days after their meeting in the Windsor Castle, Bill and Luca arrived in Kathmandu airport with five large duffel bags of climbing equipment and dried food. Stepping out of the terminal, they stood blinking for a moment in the brilliant sunlight, taking in the sheer chaos that is Nepal's greatest city.

Billows of pungent smoke rose from the grills of food vendors, while beggar children darted through the heavy traffic, scanning the backs of taxis for the pallid faces of newly arrived tourists. Every so often there was a grinding of gears as a car swerved to avoid a cow, lying placidly in the middle of the road with the confidence of a lifetime of Hindu privilege. Amidst the incredible clamour, soldiers in pale blue uniform lined the streets, waving their truncheons and blowing their whistles at largely indifferent locals.

Signalling to the nearest in a long line of decrepit taxis, Bill and Luca loaded their bags, using some spare rope to tie down the boot of the car. The car's engine stuttered, and then they were heading for the narrow streets of the Thamel district.

Luca leaned his head out of the open window, the hot air whipping across his face. The fumes, the noise, even the piles of rubbish rotting in the alleyways, somehow felt like a release from the stifling claustrophobia of the last few weeks.

One thing he was sure of – there was no turning back now.

Then he remembered his parents' faces as he'd told them he was going back out to Tibet so soon after the last trip. Luca had steeled himself for anger rather than abject disappointment, and flinched at the memory.

'You know you can't come back and work here again,' his father had said, grey-faced, and ignoring the warning hand his wife laid on his shoulder. 'It makes a mockery of the other employees if you're just hopping in and out whenever you feel like it.'

'Yeah, I know that, Dad,' Luca had told him. 'But this mountain, if we find it, would be a huge deal in the mountaineering world. It could set me up on the lecture circuit, let me do this as much as I like.'

'And Bill?' interjected his mother.

'He doesn't see himself making a career out of it. His wife . . . well, I won't go into details but he's seeing this as a last hurrah – a way to go out with a bang before he quits climbing altogether. If it works out, it'll be the climb of our lives.'

After a while he had got up to go. As he had kissed his mother goodbye, he'd noticed she was trying to hold back the tears and his father remained stiff-backed as Luca had hugged him goodbye.

Poor sod, he thought now as he looked out at the blurry chaos of Kathmandu. All his father had ever wanted was a son to be proud of. The problem was that the word meant such different things to each of them.

Away from the crowds, the car had picked up speed. Luca looked up above the ramshackle buildings and their bundles of defunct telephone wire to where he could just make out the foothills of the Himalayas beyond. The grassy slopes gave no indication of the extreme conditions that lay just a few thousand feet further up there, he knew that life would stall and dwindle: the cold peaks stretched up into the highest reaches of the sky, even bordering the stratosphere.

That was where they were going. Up and into a world that so few people truly understood. As Luca stared up at the peaks, Bill reached forward and tapped his shoulder.

'We're cutting it fine on getting our visas, aren't we?'

'Don't worry, I've emailed Sonam. It's all fixed.'

'You're sure about that?' Bill's forehead creased in concern. He'd been anxious since they left, and for good reason. Cathy had been absolutely furious when she had found out they were off again and had refused to speak to him for two whole days. It had only been the promise that this would be his last expedition that had finally made her relent. Despite everything she had said when they parted, Bill knew only too well what this was costing his marriage.

'Really, it's all sorted. Look, Bill, I know it was a hard decision, but this is going to be the best trip we've ever done. You made the right choice.'

Bill was attempting to return his smile when the exhaust backfired suddenly and the taxi lurched to a halt outside the steps of the Chinese Embassy. Luca walked round the back of the car and came up to Bill's open window.

'You stay here and keep an eye on our bags.'

'What am I, a sodding Labrador?' he protested. 'Why do I have to stay in the car?'

Luca grinned. 'Just give me your passport.'

With an obvious show of reluctance, Bill dug into his rucksack and pulled out a cellophane bag with his passport inside. He handed it out through the car window.

'Cheers,' Luca said. 'Now, try not to chew on the upholstery.'

The chill of the air conditioning gave the interior of the embassy an instant sense of calm, like walking into a church. One of the swarming officials asked Luca to wait in a side room and he sat down, enjoying the respite from the heat outside. Folding one leg over the other he picked up one of the discarded newspapers and began leafing through it, looking at the pictures.

Ten minutes later the door opened and a tall, smartly dressed Nepalese man approached, his shoes tapping against the polished floor. He had shiny black hair and large, lugubrious eyes set in a gentle face. Luca smiled as he recognised Sonam.

'*Namaste,* my friend,' Luca said warmly. 'How are you, Sonam?'

'Very good, Mr Matthews, it is good to have you back so soon.'

'How did it go with the visas?'

'I will show you.' Sonam rummaged around in the small leather briefcase he was holding and produced two sheaves of paper. The Chinese governmental seal was stamped boldly at the head of each.

'I have just finished getting you and your companion on a group visa for Tibet. I was unsure what occupation to fill in and so therefore have put "employee".' He gave Luca a sideways glance. 'I hope this is satisfactory?'

Luca grinned. 'You're a genius, Sonam. That's brilliantly vague.'

He nodded. 'There is, however, a small problem. This permit is only valid in two weeks' time. We have had many restrictions on numbers entering Tibet and, I am regretting to say, there are no sooner visas available.'

Luca's smile dimmed.

'Two weeks? You're kidding me?'

Sonam shook his head gravely. 'And the permits will only allow you on the standard route back to Nepal. Each night, you must be checking with the local police station, right up until the Friendship Bridge.'

Luca stared at the sheaves of paper, his thoughts racing. The expedition was supposed to last four weeks in total. Even that was more than Bill could afford. If Luca told him they would have to kick their heels in Kathmandu for another fortnight, Bill would be on the first plane home.

'We've got to get round this, Sonam. This is Kathmandu. Everything has its price.'

'This is indeed Kathmandu, Mr Matthews,' Sonam said, a note of anxiety in his voice, 'but we are standing in the middle of the Chinese Embassy. They would take my licence if they thought I was trying to bribe . . .'

'OK, let's be calm about this,' Luca interjected, leading him by the arm over to a corner of the waiting room. 'Use one of the touts out in Thamel to get the permits for you. They're all bloody crooks anyway.'

'Mr Matthews,' Sonam said, eyes widening and looking even more worried, 'it is not that I don't want to help. It is just . . .'

Luca raised his hands, gesturing for Sonam to calm down again. One of the officials glanced over at them from behind the large marble desk at the back of the main room.

'Look, Sonam,' Luca said, lowering his voice further. 'You know as well as I do that if I go and pay off one of the touts, they'll fleece me for every damn dollar I have. I know what a big favour this is, but we just can't wait two weeks.'

Sonam's eyes darted nervously to the security guard standing by the main entrance. His expression became grave, a deep vertical crease furrowing his forehead. He inhaled slowly before eventually nodding his head.

'I will see what can be done,' he said softly. 'But it will be more expensive.'

'Thank you, Sonam.'

Luca reached into his trouser pocket, surreptitiously pulling out a tight wad of notes wrapped together with a twisted elastic band. The notes were torn and filthy, having passed through thousands of different hands on their journey through the markets. Taking Sonam's arm, Luca gently placed the bundle in the palm of his hand.

'There should be plenty there. Whatever you don't use, you can keep.'

Sonam's cheeks instantly flushed bright red and he fumbled a few times before managing to hide the money in the side pocket of his suit jacket.

'When I said I would help, I did not mean you should be handing me money in the middle of the Embassy!' he hissed, shooting another worried glance at the security guard by the door. 'Let us leave now and I will send news later.'

Out on the steps of the building, Luca offered him his hand. 'Don't worry, Sonam, this will all work out fine.'

Sonam slowly shook his head. 'Mr Matthews, I just hope you are not getting yourself into trouble. The Chinese are not to be played with like this. The consequences can be most serious.' Buttoning his jacket, he nodded curtly before walking down the steps and starting back in the direction of Thamel.

Luca watched him dodge round a cow lying in the gutter and then turned his gaze back across the street. A gaggle of grubby children had collected around the taxi. Bill was leaning out of the window, in the middle of folding a piece of scrap paper into a leaping frog. Luca walked up to the car and lifted one of the children out of the way.

'Excuse me,' he said to the child's curious, upturned face. 'Bill, we're done. Let's get out of here.'

He signalled to the taxi driver and the car rattled into life. Bill quickly handed the half finished frog to one of the young girls then reached into his pocket to produce a bundle of filthy rupee notes. At the sight of the money, the children all started shouting. Thin brown arms shot through the window and he started cramming notes into each open hand. The children's excited faces pressed against the glass of the driver's door and only stopped pushing forward when Bill leaned back and turned out his pockets to show that they were empty.

'No more, no more,' he shouted, and put his hands together in the traditional Nepalese salute. 'Namaste!'

As the taxi pulled away to join the main flow of the traffic, the children all put their hands together, their echoing cries of 'Namaste!' soon drowned out by the noise of a car backfiring somewhere down the street.

'Good way to start a riot,' Luca said, looking over his shoulder at his friend.

'I know, but the little buggers have to eat, don't they?'

There was silence as they both turned to stare out of their respective windows. As they passed under the mass of overhead banners and edged further into the narrow, crowded streets of Thamel, Luca thought back to Sonam again and wondered if he had done the right thing. If there were two things that kept the city of Kathmandu moving, they were bribery and gossip. The problem was that one tended to lead to the other.

'Everything OK with the permits?' Bill asked, leaning forward between the front seats.

'No worries,' Luca said, flashing him a reassuring smile. 'Picking them up later at the hotel.'

'Great. So no problems at all?'

'Like I said, everything's sorted.'

Luca bent forward and rummaged in a small leather bag at his feet. He picked out a rolled up piece of photocopied paper, a little battered round the edges. Swivelling round, he handed it over to Bill so that it partly uncurled, showing the corner of a pyramid-shaped mountain, intricately illustrated.

'Let's go for a pint at Sam's. There are a few other things you should know about this mountain.'

Chapter 17

It is said that a giant ogress lies under the land of Tibet, held hostage by some rather clever urban planning. Like Gulliver and his Lilliputian captors, temples were constructed over the giant's limbs, pinning her to the earth and preventing her from wreaking devastation throughout the holy land.

Over the heart of the beast was built the Jokhang – greatest of all the Buddhist temples.

Having ditched their bags at a hostel and taken showers, Luca and Bill now stood looking through a crack in the Jokhang's huge, gilded doors. In the chalky evening light, the gentle sound of chanting rolled around the temple.

Both men watched mesmerised as men, women and children brought their hands together above their heads and, with eyes screwed tight shut and hands clasped together, lay flat on the ground, extending their arms towards the Buddha within. Without order or symmetry they stood up and repeated the process, again and again, for hours at a time. To prevent them from wearing down the skin on their hands, small bits of cardboard were tied around their palms. Like a million crickets rubbing their back legs together, a rasping noise bounced and echoed off the stone walls.

'Amazing,' murmured Bill. 'To have such belief.'

'Isn't it?' agreed Luca, his eyes following the constant flow of movement.

He looked up to where thousands of lines of criss-crossing prayer flags fluttered in the breeze high above them. They were tied from building to building, across lamp-posts and guttering, any place where they might catch the wind. Each patch of coloured cloth was emblazoned with Buddhist *sutras* and pictures of wind horses. As the fabric flapped in the breeze, the horses were said to be carrying the prayers up into the heavens.

Luca counted five colours to the flags, and checked again. He knew of the four sects of Tibetan Buddhism, each one with their own distinct colour, but had never heard of blue representing one of the orders. Perhaps it was another sect that had previously existed and had now fallen by the wayside. Or maybe there was a whole other strand of Buddhism out there he had simply never heard of. He shook his head. He had always found the enormous scope of Tibetan religion bewildering.

Walking away from the great doors of the temple, the men passed round its back, following hundreds of others along the well-trodden pilgrimage trail of the Barkor. The buildings to either side were high, hemming in the narrow streets with walls made from thick blocks of ancient stone, whitewashed in the traditional Tibetan style. Market stalls lined every inch of the streets, cluttered to overflowing. Everything was for sale, from army surplus military jackets to yak-bone prayer wheels, old Tibetan scrolls to plastic cutlery sets.

The vendors stood behind their tiny stalls, sipping yak-butter tea and occasionally heckling one of the passing devotees. There were hundreds of pilgrims, moving in a steady flow around the temple. Each held a prayer wheel of varying size. The top half of the wheel was attached to weighted beads that were spun round in a constant cycle to release a series of holy words written within. Some hung nearly a metre long, requiring a support hanging from the owner's belt and great circular arm movements to get the momentum going.

Bill and Luca were passing the first of the market stalls when three small children, dirty and with cardboard still strapped to their hands, approached. Giggling and talking rapidly amongst themselves, one of them walked up to Luca and pulled on his arm. He crouched down, smiling.

'Hello, guys.'

One whispered something to the next who hesitated for a second before leaning forward and gently pulling the blond hair on Luca's forearm. He looked amazed to discover it was actually attached.

'Of course . . . Tibetans don't have any body hair,' Luca said, glancing up at Bill, before turning back to face the children. 'If you think that's bad, kids, look at this.' And, leaning forward, he pulled down the top of his T-shirt to reveal a patch of hair at the centre of his chest. The children squealed in delighted horror and retreated backwards, hugging each other. The same boy who had made the original discovery stepped forward again and pointed at Luca.

'*Po*,' he said simply, then ran off to the temple doors closely followed by his friends, all shrieking with laughter. Bill and Luca looked at each other blankly.

'Any guesses?'

'Not a clue,' said Bill, before they moved off again, strolling past the remaining market stalls. From behind each came shouts of 'Cheapie! Cheapie!' as yak-bone dominoes, jade necklaces and ceremonial knives were thrust in front of them with encouraging grins.

'So what are we going to do about our visas?' Bill asked, as they gravitated towards one of the stalls at random. 'I thought you said you had it covered?'

'I had the *border* covered,' Luca corrected, 'but we're just going to have to figure something out for heading further east.'

'You know what they're like, Luca. Once an area goes on the restricted list, there's no way in hell they'll change our permits. And if we do try and leave, they'll definitely assign us one of those idiot interpreters who'll do nothing more than spy on us the whole time.'

'We'll find a way,' Luca said absent-mindedly, shaking his head as a vendor pressed on him what looked to be a human skull emblazoned with a silver swastika. He turned the skull over in his hands slowly, running a finger over the tiny indentations where the brain had been.

'Listen, Luca, I'm serious,' Bill said, taking him by the wrist. 'I'm not about to waste three weeks kicking my heels in Lhasa, waiting for a bit of paper. I don't have time for this.'

'Neither do I, but I've already arranged . . .'

As he tried to speak, the vendor had moved round to the front of the stall, beaming a well-practised smile. She started listing prices enthusiastically, using her right hand to count the numbers off, bartering herself down from an outrageous starting point without Bill or Luca having said a word. Eventually, Luca spoke a few words of his limited Tibetan to her and she slowly retreated behind the stall, her expression instantly darkening.

They moved off again, back into the flow of human traffic.

'What I was trying to say is that I've already arranged a meeting with René,' Luca explained. 'He'll be able to think of something. He always does.'

Bill stopped in his tracks. 'René? You're serious?'

'Why not?'

'Because he is a disaster waiting to happen and I don't think we should have anything to do with the man! How the hell he hasn't been kicked out of Lhasa yet, God only knows.'

'Yeah, but if there's one person who knows how to get visas and deal with the bastard Chinese roadblocks, it's him.'

Turning down one of the side streets, Luca headed in the opposite direction from the main temple and away from the Tibetan quarter.

'Come on,' he said, quickening his pace. 'Or we won't get a table.'

A few hundred yards later they found themselves on Lhasa's main high street. The wide strip was flanked with modern shops, the fluorescent signs and electric lighting clearly marking the transition from the Tibetan quarter into the rest of the city run by the Chinese.

Dusty cranes towered over half-finished buildings in every direction, and at the end of the high street they could see the golden roof of the Dalai Lama's former residence, the Potala.

Up on its hill and carved into the living rock, the palace of a thousand rooms remained aloof from the urban development below, its vertiginous walls shielding it from the hasty expansion all around. But what was clear to see was that, the 'peaceful liberation' by the Chinese had not just been an external assault on the city of Lhasa and its temples. Inside, the pulse of the Dalai Lama's former residence was slowly fading.

The Chinese had forbidden monks from worshipping in the temple. Its hollow rooms and deserted corridors were now bereft of their presence. Stone steps, worn in the middle from centuries of footsteps, were now barely used. The deserted shell of the building conveyed little of the teeming life that had once made its chambers, murals and thousands of figures of the Buddha seem to actually breathe. Now, the Potala stood silently at the end of the high street and was little more than an empty shell – a tourist attraction for anyone but Tibetans.

At the end of the street, Bill and Luca passed rows of shop windows with new posters glued on top, showing a picture of a pale Chinese man, about twenty years old and with a shaven head. He stared out impassively, his expression neither welcoming nor hostile. Thick bold characters were printed below. By the sheer number of posters visible, it was obviously important news.

Luca bent forward, peering at the newly pasted posters. At the bottom of every one was a single sentence printed in English: *His Holiness the eleventh Panchen Lama's inauguration, 1 June 2005.*

'Looks like we're going to miss the big event,' Luca said, pointing to the date.

'He doesn't look very Tibetan to me,' Bill said, frowning slightly.

'Well, whoever he is, with the Dalai Lama gone, he's going to be the man in charge.' Luca glanced up from the poster. Twenty yards along he spotted the turning he'd been looking for.

'Hey, that's the one,' he said, slapping Bill's shoulder.

Leaving the poster, they cut down the street and within a few paces the shining stores and paved roads gave way to mud tracks and ramshackle houses. Following the trail a bit farther, they threaded through a maze of twisting back streets and, after a few dead ends, came across the familiar open porch of a wood-built restaurant. Bill looked at Luca, anxiety creeping back into his face.

'Let's just get in and out as fast as we can.'

Luca turned to reassure him before going through the doorway.

'Relax, Bill. It's just René. Trust me on this.'

Bill grimaced, shaking his head as he followed his friend inside into the din of the restaurant. Trusting Luca was exactly what his wife had warned him not to do.

Chapter 18

The restaurant was brightly lit and packed with tourists. Waiters in traditional Tibetan dress wound their way around tables serving momos and yak burgers. Misplaced as it was down a dusty side street in Lhasa, it also felt surreally suspended between cultures.

As soon as Luca and Bill stepped into the room, they could hear René. He had a deep, booming voice that was usually accompanied, as it was now, by a string of expletives. A tour operator who had been working in Lhasa for nearly eight years, René, with his stubbled, red face, swollen midriff and crumpled clothes, made it clear how oblivious – or blind – he was to the subtleties of Eastern culture.

Right now he appeared to be delivering a monologue to a meek-looking tourist sitting at one of the tables on the far side of the room. As René's vast belly quivered only inches away from the man's face, it looked extremely likely he was regretting having asked a question in the first place. Fragments of the restaurant owner's impassioned diatribe floated across the room, culminating in René pointing a thick digit directly at the man's nose and bemoaning 'every one of the dull-witted layabouts who passes through Lhasa these days'.

Luca started to laugh. Catching sight of him across the room, René did a double-take and then bellowed across the rows of tables: 'What do you think you're laughing at, you skinny Englishman?'

The patrons curled their toes and sank lower in their seats, anticipating yet another outburst.

'At you, you old bastard!' Luca shouted back as René began to scythe his way through the seated diners, jolting some into their plates and scaring others into hurriedly scraping forward their chairs.

Beaming at them with bloodshot eyes, René pulled them both into a bearlike hug before slapping them on the back several times and herding them over to a table near the rear of the restaurant. Once they were settled with a shot of cheap brandy in front of them, Luca spoke.

'So how are things going, René? Still battling bureaucracy?'

René rolled his eyes and slugged back the contents of the shot glass.

'Nothing changes. Nothing ever fucking changes,' he replied gruffly. 'The Chinese build and build, but it's still the same old shit. The agencies refuse to talk to one another, and God forbid they should actually make a decision. If they pass the buck, they take no responsibility. So they always pass the buck.'

He refilled his own small glass, adding a little more to Bill's and Luca's, despite the fact that they hadn't touched their drinks yet.

'It's all about keeping you off balance,' René continued, obviously warming to one of his favourite subjects. 'They keep you bouncing between agencies, make sure you're disorientated all the time, so you don't even know who to ask any more. That's how they like it.'

'How do you cope with doing business like that?' asked Bill.

'Hah! Business . . . I don't know – I really don't. Sometimes I wish we would all just get kicked out of the country so we could create another Tibet somewhere else.'

Distracted by something, René fell silent for a moment and Luca followed his gaze towards a table in the far corner of the restaurant, raised on a small platform by the window. Two soldiers were seated there in silence, waiting for their food. One of them was strikingly large for a Chinese, his black shirt stretched across a powerful chest; the other was slim-built and almost effeminate, with pale, fine features and oiled black hair. Even across the smoky restaurant, they could see that the smaller of the two men seemed to be eyeing the crowds of people around him disdainfully.

René reached out, catching the arm of one of the waiters scurrying from table to table.

'Make those two by the window wait for their food, and see to it that they get the wrong order,' he said.

The waiter blinked in confusion but, knowing enough not to argue with his employer, promptly retreated to the kitchens to relay the order.

Luca shook his head slowly in a mixture of disbelief and admiration. Few people would deliberately tangle with Chinese officers. He put his hand on René's wrist, speaking quietly.

'We're leaving in the next few days for the area east of Makalu and we've only got the standard permits. Can you help us out?'

'Going back to finish off Makalu, eh? I tell you, you boys have got real balls to be climbing those kinds of mountains. Not like most of the tourists round here who bugger off round Kailash for a few days, then go home and write a book about it.'

Grabbing the glass in front of him, René downed the contents and returned it to the table, smacking his lips loudly. He sniffed, switching his gaze to a table of three noisy diners who had evidently just arrived in Tibet. They all had neatly pressed clothes and sharp haircuts, and were laughing to themselves about something the waiter had mispronounced.

'Hear that, you lot?' René bellowed across at them. 'Which one of you fucking idiots is writing a book then?'

As the restaurant fell silent all three of the people at the table looked round, confused by the question. René glowered at them a moment longer, then shaking his jowly, unshaven face he turned back to Bill and Luca again. The dull murmur of the restaurant slowly continued.

'That should stop them pestering the waiters for a while,' René said with satisfaction.

Bill looked across at him, wondering how on earth he managed to keep any customers.

'René,' Luca reminded him, 'the permits?'

'Oh, yes,' he replied. 'You know, I'm not even sure which agency to ask any more . . . the TMA, Foreign Office . . . who knows? As I said, they try to keep you off-kilter. I did hear something recently, though. One Westerner managed to get permission to go down to the border and do some climbing, and where do you think he got his papers? The Forestry Commission! Can you imagine that? The bloody Forestry Commission.'

He tilted his head back and let out a low groan.

'I came to Tibet nearly a decade ago as a botanist,' he continued. 'In those days the scientists on the other side of the fence would help you out. You know, apply for permits for you and lend a hand. But now . . . Christ, it's always such a mess . . .'

Bill and Luca both remained silent as he trailed off, waiting for René to return to the subject. Eventually, he seemed to remember they were waiting for his advice.

'Look, if you two are serious about it, you're just going to have to peel off the standard route to Nepal and head east without anyone knowing. The Tibetans won't care where you're going, as long as you keep feeding them enough dollars, and I should be able to cover you from this end.'

'And if we get caught venturing off without permits?' broke in Bill.

'Who's going to check our permits?' said Luca, waving his hand impatiently and downing his own shot of brandy. He winced and René looked on approvingly, refilling his glass as he set it back down on the table. 'We're going to be halfway up a bloody mountain.'

Bill sat forward in his seat, his voice terse. 'I think it might be sensible to have an idea of what we're up against before gallivanting off into a restricted area. And how the hell are we going to shake off the interpreter? They don't let you leave without one.'

'We'll just have to give him the slip. Get up early,' Luca replied.

'That's it, sneak off early? That's the plan?' Bill said, shaking his head. 'You are kidding me, right?'

Luca raised his hands defensively.

'Come on, Bill, it's not like we haven't done worse before. And like he said, René will be able to smooth things over from this end.' Turning to look at him, Luca saw René lean back in his chair, the glass of brandy clutched loosely in one hand and resting on top of his belly. 'That's right, isn't it?'

René seemed to drift reluctantly back to the present. He looked at them with eyes glazed from brandy. 'You should be all right,' he said eventually. 'You're not going anywhere too politically sensitive. It's the tour operator who gets all their . . . attention. I'll fix up some documents for you and they'll get you where you need to go.'

They sat for a moment in silence, all appreciating the risk he was taking.

'You know what I say? Screw 'em. After all the years of this shit, being thrown out would probably be a weight off my mind.'

'Thank you, René,' said Luca.

'Yes, thank you,' added Bill.

René nodded, signalling that the matter was now closed.

Scraping back his chair, Luca got to his feet.

'Back in a second,' he said, winding round the crowded tables and heading for the toilets.

On his way back into the main room, he stopped. The slim Chinese officer from the table by the window was standing in his way, polishing the lenses of his glasses with a cloth held in one hand. He kept the other in one of his pockets.

Luca stood still for a moment, waiting for him to move, and after a few seconds, coughed politely. The man slowly finished wiping the lenses, apparently in no hurry to get out of the way. Finally putting his glasses back on, he turned to look at Luca.

His eyes had unusually wide black pupils which seemed to obscure most of the irises. They made for a curiously blank expression. There was something about the way he stared straight through him that made the back of Luca's neck tingle.

'Excuse me,' he said, using one of his few phrases of Mandarin, and ducked past, shaking his head.

Bill and René were engrossed in conversation when he got back to the table.

'You really are an ignorant brute, aren't you?' René said, smiling at Bill. 'The swastika is a Buddhist symbol intended to bring good luck. You see it painted on doorways and religious artefacts every-where around here. Hitler just twisted it round a little, like he did with everything else.'

'But painted on a human skull?' Bill asked as Luca shuffled on to the bench seat beside him.

René snorted. 'Don't they teach you anything these days? The guys here don't look at death the same way Westerners do. Think about it. What are the Tibetans supposed to do with dead bodies? Bury them? Hah! You try digging six feet down with the kind of perma-frost they get up here on the plateau. You'd be all fucking day!'

He gulped down another shot of brandy, signalling with his glass for Luca to do the same. Luca hammered it back, shutting his eyes as the taste of the alcohol hit him, and then grinning broadly.

'And for that matter, you can't cremate bodies either,' René continued, wiping his mouth with the back of his hand. 'There are bugger all trees up at this altitude and any decent wood is used for making stuff they need, not stuff they want to get rid of.' He lowered his voice dramatically. 'You know what they do instead?'

Both of them shook their heads.

'They take long knives and slice the bodies into small pieces . . . bones, cartilage, muscle . . . everything gets hacked off the corpse. Then they let the vultures pick clean the skeleton and feed the pieces of flesh to the dogs.'

Bill choked on a sip of brandy and then shook his head, turning a little green. 'That's disgusting.'

'Makes perfect sense to me,' countered René cheerfully. 'It's called a sky burial, which sounds very peaceful and spiritual when, as with everything in Tibet, the reality is a little more bloody. The only bit of refinement about the whole thing is the flowers. It's one of the few places where you get any decent varieties of *Cousinia* – gorgeous colours and actually rather rare. Pressed quite a few of them in my time.' He paused for a second indulgently. 'Anyway, the upshot is that lots of the leftover body parts get used for tools, musical instruments, all sorts of stuff. The head you saw was probably part of a drum, or possibly a drinking bowl.'

He remained silent for a moment, allowing this gruesome image to sink in.

'Why not? If it can hold slopping brains in there, it should be able to cope with brandy!'

Nearby, some of the diners put down their knives and forks abruptly. Luca and Bill noticed their squeamish stares and started smiling.

René's own red face creased into laughter, and before his belly had stopped shaking he was reaching for the brandy again. He held the bottle poised in his hand for a moment, face suddenly serious.

'Whatever you're up to this time, boys, good luck to you. If it means taking some risks, I'm willing to back you. Tibet's a country that needs more people with courage.' He began to refill their glasses, glancing sideways towards the two officers over by the window. A sudden melancholy tinged his smile. 'And this is where I find mine!'

Raising their glasses together, they all downed the shot. Luca and Bill winced. René burped dramatically.

'Just one more thing,' Luca said, as the heat of the brandy spread through them. 'What's a *po*?'

For a moment René frowned in concentration. Then he scratched the back of his head with his sausage fingers.

'I'm pretty sure it means monkey,' he said. 'Why?'

Chapter 19

'Wake up, Babu.'

The man looked down at the boy sleeping in his arms. The child's head was nestled into his chest, so that all that was visible was a mop of tousled hair that swung back and forth in time with his step.

'Wake up now, Babu. It's time.'

He gently shook his arms and the boy gave a soft murmur. A moment later he tilted his neck back and yawned, his mouth stretching wide like a bear cub waking from a deep sleep. His eyes fluttered open; once, twice, then remained wide for a moment longer, trying to focus on the weather-beaten face of the man who was carrying him. He was staring straight ahead, eyes fixed on a faint glimmer of light in the distance. With each laboured breath frosted air appeared from his lips, slowly dissipating into the night sky as they moved forward.

The moon shone over the mountain peaks, bleaching out all colour from the path they had been following for hours. The guide was tired now, his steps slow and deliberate. Beads of sweat collected on his forehead, running freely down his dark skin before disappearing into his glistening black beard. He was hardened to the long climbs and endless trails of his native Nepal, but the weight of the rucksack on his back and the boy in his arms had taken its toll. The light in the distance was all that was keeping him going now.

As they continued forward, step by step, the boy swivelled his head within the man's arms, watching the lights in the distance grow stronger. They climbed the mountain in two blurred vertical channels of fire. The boy's hand instinctively went into the pocket of his sheepskin jacket, clutching the string of ornate prayer beads within. He worked them through his fingers one by one, the worn jade comforting to the touch.

Eventually the path grew wider, the scree on the ground becoming more compacted and worn from use. Large rocks had been moved out of the way and lay stacked along its edges in neat piles. The man stopped, letting Babu slip to the ground so that he was standing on his own feet and clasped his small hand in his. Before them, wide stone steps opened out, signifying the beginning of a vast stairway that led up into the blackness of the mountain.

The guide exhaled deeply, an exhausted smile appearing on his lips.

'Well done, Babu. We've made it.'

The child tilted his head back so that their eyes met. He smiled.

'I won't forget you what you did for me,' he said, his voice sounding older than his years.

The man simply nodded and swung his rucksack off his back. Reaching into one of the side pockets, he pulled out a small object wrapped in cloth. He unwound the fabric to reveal a delicate brass bell, the metal a dull gold in the moonlight.

'Let them know we are home.'

Babu took the bell and swung it before him, so that a high-pitched chime cut through the still air. There was silence, man and boy waiting expectantly. Then suddenly, the sound of a vast horn answered from somewhere far above – a deep hollow note that seemed to resonate through every rock and stone on the mountainside. Babu squeezed the man's hand fearfully. Returning the pressure gently, the man led them forward on to the first of the mighty stone steps.

As the two figures walked up, streaks of light began to separate into individual flames. Drawing level with the first of the burning torches, Babu noticed the silhouette of a figure seated behind it on the ground. Light from the flame played across the contours of his face, revealing a young man of possibly twenty years old, his hair shaved off and his head tilted backwards. His eyes were shut tight and he seemed oblivious to their passing.

Babu gazed around him, craning his neck to take in every detail. Behind each torch sat a figure in an identical pose, hundreds of them, all dressed in striking cornflower blue robes that were wound around their bodies so that only their right arms were exposed. The staircase stretched on and on and behind each torch was another blue-clad figure. As they climbed, flames crackled in the soft breeze, shooting off sparks which spiralled up into the night sky.

Then came the sound of singing. At first it was soft, barely audible, the pitch meandering between bass and tenor. Then more voices joined in, one building upon another, until the sound was flooding the mountainside in a beautiful, rolling chant.

Slowly Babu became aware of shapes looming out of the darkness. There were buildings, vast, sheer-walled buildings, ashen from the moonlight and stretching back into the mountain. As he pieced each impression together, trying to see where they began and finished, he felt a sudden jolt on his arm. His guide had come to an abrupt halt. They were standing at the top of the stairway which had opened out into a courtyard. A long line of trees cut through its centre while open braziers of burning logs were standing under archways in the surrounding walls.

Only a few feet ahead of them stood two monks, separate from the massed ranks of the others, both waiting with their hands clasped together in greeting. The smell of incense hung heavy in the air.

The guide bowed low before them.

'*Namaste*, venerable fathers,' he said. 'I request sanctuary for one who has been chosen.'

'Why does he seek us?' replied one of the monks, his voice hollow and rasping. He was ancient, with a thin, angular face bleached white by age. As he spoke, his eyes stared blindly in the direction of the guide.

'Because yours is the true path.'

'What will he do with our truth?'

'He will serve the will of Buddha.'

After a respectful pause the second of the monks moved forward. He was younger, in his mid-fifties, and his lips were turning upward in the beginnings of a warm smile.

'*Tashi delek*, old friend,' he said, standing before the guide. 'You must be tired from the journey.' Then, turning to Babu who stood staring up at him, 'Welcome, child. The Abbot has requested that you go to him immediately.'

The monk reached out his hand, taking hold of Babu's and made to lead him away, but the boy recoiled, clutching on to the leg of his guide. The man crouched down so that his face was level with the boy's.

'You must go with Dorje. He will protect you from now on. I can't stay with you any longer, I have to go back to the village to guide your friend.'

'But who are they?' asked Babu, his voice high-pitched and frightened.

'They are . . . friends,' replied the guide, unclasping the boy's hand and gently pushing him forward. 'Go with them.'

As the monk before them gave a short bow and turned to lead Babu through one of the archways in the courtyard behind, his elder colleague reached out a hand and stopped them.

'This boy is not of age,' he hissed.

'I know.'

'And what of the initiation?' the older man continued, lowering his voice even further. 'He must go before the Council.'

'Not this one, Rega. I represent the Abbot on this.'

Babu gazed up at the old monk who stood blocking their way. His young face grew serious as it studied the strange milky irises that seemed to stare down at him from damaged eye sockets. Then he smiled, childish innocence flooding his face as he reached out and plucked the edge of the monk's blue robe.

'Don't be upset, father. I will not be here long.'

Chapter 20

23 May 2005

A caravan of three yaks and four men toiled slowly across the dry Tibetan hills. The animals set the pace, a lumbering gait that varied little whether the trail led up or down. They followed the slow course of a muddy brown river with patches of green vegetation and stunted, windblown trees on its banks. The trees offered some shade against the midday heat but soon the path twisted again, up and away from the river, into the open plateau beyond.

Away to the south, Bill and Luca caught their first proper glimpses of the Himalayas. The snow-capped summits tore through a low bank of cloud like a jagged case of knives. Even from the distance, they looked colossal and forbidding.

Bringing up the rear of the caravan were two Tibetan yak drivers, Jigmi and Soa. They wore thick sheepskin jackets and felt boots that had been repaired so many times that the original fabric was almost completely lost to stitching. Between them they maintained a constant soundtrack, alternately yelling encouragement to the animals or, if they strayed a pace or two away from the pathway, hurling small pebbles at their woolly flanks.

Each day the group left before dawn and only stopped on the rare occasions when the trail branched. The yaks would jangle to a halt, awaiting further instruction, while Bill and Luca gulped down some iodised water, thankful for the break. At the back of the line, Jigmi and Soa barely drank or rested, seemingly oblivious to the sun and heat.

When they first set off from the road at Tingkye, they had passed a new village every few hours. Each was bustling and affluent, with whitewashed houses adorned with ornate, brightly coloured windowsills. On the flat roofs the women bundled cut hay, while out in the terraced fields the men worked the land. Clouds of dust hovered over entire villages, the hay a brilliant yellow in the sunlight.

But soon the villages became smaller and more sporadic. The houses shrank to little more than shacks with rickety wooden planks for walls and loose thatch on the roofs. Cooking smoke rose from each, billowing out through cracks in the walls into the cloudless sky. The smaller villages seemed to be almost deserted except for a few children and the occasional lethargic dog staked out in the shade of a tree. Sometimes they would pass without even being noticed. Only a couple of brief months remained before the season changed and everyone able to work was out in the fields.

After three days of walking and camping on the side of the trail, they finally reached the top of a high spur. Luca stood on a large boulder, clicking off photographs from a battered Canon camera. He knew that Bill never took one on any of their expeditions. When he'd once asked why, his friend had tapped the side of his head, saying that he preferred to store it all there rather than rely on bundles of shiny paper that would fade over the years. Luca's eyebrows had shot up in amazement at such an old-fashioned sensibility, and eventually the two men had had to agree to differ.

Satisfied with the photographs, Luca reached inside his rucksack to unfold a map, while Bill weaved around the back of one of the yaks to stand beside him. Luca could see the first in a long line of mountains stretching away ahead of them. Mist clung to their foothills as if it had been belched out from folds in the ground, and the summits bent round to the north-east like the spine of a slumbering dinosaur.

All around them there was a sense of peace, as if time had slowed down and the world was finally breathing again in its own natural rhythm.

'That's them,' said Luca softly. 'That's what we're here for.'

Bill looked down at the map, then squinted across at the ring of mountains.

'Jesus! They're stunning. How high do you think they are?'

'Probably somewhere just over six. If this is halfway correct, we'll soon cross over the Jongsang-la and start descending to a few more villages at the base of these mountains. From the looks of it, there are three in total.'

Luca's mouth moved as he practised saying the name of the first village on the map. Then, pointing his finger down across the valley, he shouted, 'Rawok-tso' to the nearer of the two yak herders. The man had his knee up against the side of the leading beast, tightening the rope that stretched underneath its belly. Looking up at Luca, he nodded his head and with his free hand pointed in the same direction.

'Rawok-tso,' he said, and gave the rope an almighty tug.

Over the next two days they followed the same path, twisting through the foothills of the mountains. Luca remained silent almost the entire time, eyes scanning every fissure and turn of the range ahead. From time to time he would click his tongue with frustration and stride out, pressing the yak-herders to quicken the pace and only calling a halt to the day's march long after the sun had set.

As the hours and days wore on, his mood darkened. By the time the others emerged from their tents in the morning, he would have sloshed the remains of his coffee on to a nearby rock and be striking camp, ready to leave.

Bill knew exactly what was getting to him. So far they had not seen a single, workable route through the circular range. Their flanks rose up like the sides of a fortress, unbroken for mile after mile, with only occasional gullies carving through them. Originally Luca had thought that these gullies would lead them up to the higher ground, but each was steep and covered in loose scree. As the sun passed across the sky, warming the mountainsides, rocks come clattering down the face. Hemmed in by the walls of the gullies, they smacked into the lower slopes with terrifying speed and regularity. The noise echoed across to where they stood motionless, listening to the reverberations. Jigmi and Soa would mutter darkly to each other, but neither Bill nor Luca said a word – each rockfall a constant reminder of the dangers that lay ahead.

While Luca grew ever more agitated, Bill withdrew into himself, keeping to the back of the caravan. He seldom looked up at the mountains, keeping his focus locked on the pathway where he took the journey a step at a time. Only around the campfire in the evening did the two friends engage in any real conversation, with Luca complaining about the lack of possible routes while Bill tried to stifle his own growing sense of apprehension.

As they curled into their sleeping bags each night, Luca could see Bill hunched over, his broad back concealing the small moleskin journal he always brought with him. He knew it was Bill's way of dealing with being apart from Cathy, and in all their expeditions together he had not once asked him what he was writing. It had always been like that – Bill recounting every last detail, categorising and processing his thoughts in neatly handwritten sentences.

At the last village they'd passed, Luca had used his phrase book and limited Tibetan to try and get some more information from the locals. After a somewhat torturous exchange, punctuated by hand movements and confused silences, it became apparent that the locals had never crossed the mountains and knew of no paths that did, either in winter or summer. When Luca pointed to the summits and gestured as to whether they had ever been climbed, the farmer questioned had only given a confused smile, as if querying why anyone should want to go to the top of a mountain anyway.

But as they began to move off towards the next village, the farmer had grabbed Jigmi by the shoulder, his face creased in worry. They spoke for some time, with Soa soon becoming embroiled in the conversation. Both of the herders looked equally disturbed.

Eventually Luca broke in, signalling to Jigmi to explain to him. He tried, speaking slowly with hand gestures, while Luca struggled to make some sense of it all with the aid of his phrase book.

'What's he on about?' Bill asked.

Luca thumbed swiftly through the pages. 'Not sure, but that farmer is obviously putting the fear of God into him.'

Finding the right page, Luca looked for a word and repeated it slowly to Jigmi who nodded vigorously, looking relieved.

'They're saying there is an illness up in the next village,' Luca explained. 'I'm not sure what.'

Bill frowned. 'If the farmer's reaction is anything to go by, it could be pretty serious.'

Luca repeated the word again. All three men nodded, with the farmer pointing down the path for extra emphasis. After a pause, Luca turned back to Bill and shrugged.

'Look, these people are very superstitious,' he said. 'They probably think it's some kind of sign. It doesn't mean the illness is deadly or anything.'

'You reckon? Take a look at the man,' Bill replied, his own eyes fixed on the farmer's face. 'I don't know about you, but I'm not walking right into the middle of a disease-ridden village if I can help it.'

Luca sighed, looking out past the few shacks to the mountains beyond. His eyes followed their jagged outlines meeting the horizon.

'I've seen no route through in all the time we've been following this path. We've got to go on to see if there's a way up past the next village. Every range has a chink in its armour somewhere, and I bet you this one is just around the corner.'

Bill shook his head.

'Haven't you been listening to what this guy is trying to tell us? It's not safe.'

'So what are our choices? We either press on and hope everyone's had their flu jab, or we cancel the whole damn trip. I don't know about you, mate, but I for one have come way too far to turn back now.'

As Luca started to shoulder his rucksack, avoiding eye contact, Bill remained fixed in thought, his expression tense. Then his shoulders seemed to relax and he looked up at Luca with a resigned smile.

'Screw it,' he said softly. 'You're right, we can't turn back now. We've come too far.'

They both turned to see the herders still engrossed in conversation with the farmer who seemed to be even more panicked than before. He gestured erratically with his hands, his voice raised. Jigmi and Soa looked on, their worried eyes following his every movement.

Bill watched them for a moment before turning back to Luca.

'I'm in. But I think they're going to be less of a pushover.'

Chapter 21

A fax rolled off the coffee-stained machine and on to the floor of the Public Security Bureau's headquarters in Lhasa. Less than a minute later the blurry printout was retrieved, placed into a standard, government-issue file and set before the eyes of Captain Zhu.

He read the missive then leaned back in his chair, using his left hand only to light a thin cigarette. As he inhaled the smoke, letting the remainder curl up into the sunlight, he smoothed the side parting of his hair. His eyes ranged over the small, smoke-stained office he had requisitioned before resting on a faded poster taped to the far wall. Snow-clad mountains were wrapped round in a panoramic display with the morning light just touching the summit of each one. There were other such pictures like this around the office – peasants leading yaks through the ploughed terraces, nomads camped on the edge of crystal blue lakes. Hard to believe, but that was what the rest of Tibet was really like. It was like something out of the Dark Ages.

On the way back from Drapchi Prison their convoy had passed rows and rows of diggers and cranes. All around them, men and machines hammered away in construction sites with clouds of dust clinging to the sides of iron girders and scaffolding rigs. New mobile phone towers had shot up and there was a frenetic energy to the now sprawling city of Lhasa. It was hard to imagine that barely a mile out of the city everything changed. The wide highways faded into dust tracks and the mighty new glass buildings were little more than empty shells, lit only by sporadic electricity.

Zhu had insisted on driving back through the Tibetan quarter. On receiving the order, Chen immediately radioed ahead and two armoured cars were sent to meet them near the entrance to the Jokhang. As they approached, the atmosphere had immediately changed inside the jeeps. The soldiers straightened in their seats, pulling the magazines off their AK-47 rifles to check the first round.

As they beeped their horns, edging through the narrow streets thick with people, Zhu watched hundreds of Tibetans going about their day. The market was brimming with activity: hawkers calling their prices, old men playing dice on the side of the road, and the endless procession of devotees circumnavigating the holy Temple. Each turned to stare as the Chinese vehicles pushed their way through, the soldier in the passenger seat leaning right out of the rolled-down window and shouting for them to make way.

Through the thin glass, Chen and Zhu absorbed the undisguised hatred in the onlookers' stares. As their car passed, silence spread through the market. Some vendors stood still, their chins raised defiantly, while others craned their necks, hoping to get a better view of their oppressors.

'In the riot last week they burned the local police station by the Potala,' Chen whispered. 'The crowds are still pretty worked up about our reprisals.'

'Interesting,' murmured Zhu.

From the maps, he knew that they were trespassing on the last enclave of Tibetan culture in Lhasa. The rest had been bulldozed to make way for new buildings, but the kilometre square area around the Jokhang was the last of the old city. And, judging by the grim determination on their faces, the Tibetans obviously meant to keep it.

Zhu smiled before leaning back in his seat. He had wanted to see it for himself – that simmering rage. He wanted to know what would happen if news of the threat to the Panchen Lama ever got out into the open. Now he knew how thin the famous philosophy of peace was stretched in his opponent. This fight was going to be more interesting than he had thought.

Catching his smile, Chen shivered. He had seen enough of his new boss by now to guess what was giving him pleasure.

They had been working side by side for only forty-eight hours, yet Chen was already starting to understand more than he would have liked about him. He knew enough not to speak unless spoken to and would spend long hours in silence, simply waiting for the next order.

Now he stood in front of Zhu's desk back at headquarters, watching those pale, blank features knitted in concentration over a file.

'Sir, I have just received a report that two Westerners have not checked in with the local station at Nyemo.'

Zhu raised his left hand and Chen slid the paper across the desk.

'They were on a tourist visa, sir, heading down the standard trekking route to Nepal. But I also discovered that they were here only a month ago, and on that occasion received special climbing permits. I thought I should bring this to your attention because they left their interpreter here in Lhasa.'

'Left?'

'Yes, sir. They apparently departed early in the morning in a Land Cruiser, leaving him waiting at the bus station.'

Zhu studied the expression on Chen's thickset face, the mixture of deference and dogged determination. He knew that Chen had been working late into each night, carefully combing through every scrap of information that might be related to their mission. There were dark rings under his eyes and his hair was still ruffled at the back of his head. He was obviously terrified of falling behind or putting a foot wrong. Zhu had come in early that morning and noted, with some satisfaction, that he had been sleeping in one of the empty cells downstairs.

'So where are they?' Zhu asked.

'I am not sure, sir. We don't have that information yet.'

Zhu stared at him before extinguishing his cigarette on the side of the glass ashtray, twisting the stub round until every trace of its glowing head was black.

'Was I not clear enough about what happened last time? Your incompetence cost your superior officer dearly.'

Chen stared fixedly at the square of carpet in front of the desk, keeping his legs tense to stop them from shaking.

'I will not make the same mistake now that I am in command,' continued Zhu. 'Don't ever come to me with incomplete reports again.'

'Yes, sir. I apologise, sir.'

'Do you at least know which travel agent sanctioned their permits?'

'Jagged Travel, sir. The owner is listed as one René Falkus.'

Zhu nodded.

'Get my car. We're paying him a visit.'

Chapter 22

With every step they closed in on the disease-ridden village.

It was late afternoon and a muted orange light cast long shadows below the ridges on the path. To the right, the cliffs rose up from the ground in a massive, unbroken wall. Beyond they could see the streaks of white as glaciers carved down from the summits of the mountains.

They had been going since before dawn and both Bill and Luca had sore feet from their La Sportiva 'Evo' mountaineering boots. The rigid soles and padded insulation were more suited to ice climbing than trekking and both were counting the hours until they could take them off for another night's rest.

A hundred yards behind where they walked, Jigmi and Soa called out to the line of lumbering beasts slowly wending its way along the path. From their hunched shoulders and moody stares, it looked as if the herders were also tired, but they had been like that all day. Even after the promise of an extra fifty dollars each, it had taken Luca nearly an hour to persuade them to continue.

'Look, over there,' he said to Bill, pointing to the ridge ahead of them. Faint wisps of smoke were rising up into the harsh blue sky. 'That must be the next village.'

Bill looked up and gave a strained smile. He was looking forward to a rest, but the thought of what they might find at the village had been worrying him for the last few hours. He could still picture the look the farmer had given them as they had left the last village and wondered how Luca had managed to persuade him to ignore such a desperate warning.

Luca came to a sudden stop, his boots crunching on the pathway. Just ahead, a bedraggled monk sat in the lotus position on a small pile of stones. In his right hand a prayer wheel spun in continuous motion, the movement seeming to pass through his entire body. He rocked back and forth, a low chant coming from his lips. His face looked like unpolished mahogany, cross-hatched with lines, and his watery eyes stared out to nothing in particular.

The last of the evening's light filtered down over the far mountain ridge to where he sat, illuminating his filthy red robes. As Bill and Luca stared at the monk, the yaks ambled up behind them, coming to a disjointed halt with a soft clanging of bells.

Luca took a pace forward and, crouching down, gave the traditional Tibetan greeting.

'*Tashi delek*,' he said, then, pointing to the village ahead, 'Menkom?'

The old monk continued swaying backwards and forwards, seemingly unaware that he was even being spoken to.

'Menkom?' Luca repeated, a little louder, waving one hand in front of the monk's eyes.

There was not a flicker of recognition. Luca shrugged and glanced back at Bill. 'He looks a bit thin. Maybe he wants some food or something? Pass me one of the chocolate bars, will you?'

As Bill dug into his rucksack and offered a brightly wrapped chocolate bar, the monk seemed to wake up and focus on the two men, waving the chocolate away with a sweep of his hand and pointing to the far ridge.

'What do you think he wants?' said Luca.

Bill followed the direction of the pointing finger to where the orange sun had sunk halfway behind the mountain ridge. When he turned back to face Luca, a smile was playing on his lips.

'You know, I think the old guy just wants us to get out of his sun.'

Both men backed off a few paces and as the orange light washed over him again, the old monk nodded contentedly before settling back into his solitary chanting.

Bill looked over at Luca, and laughed softly.

'Ever get the feeling we're a touch behind these guys?'

After pitching their tents on a flat patch of ground a little further on from the monk, they walked up to the village in search of water. The farmer's warning loomed in Bill's mind once again, and he felt a prickle of fear creep up his spine.

The village was nothing more than a collection of twenty or so shacks, built beside a small stream. Each building was raised on stilts above the hard earth, with uneven steps leading up to a single door. The doorframes provided the only touches of decoration, with symbols drawn across them in faded red and yellow paint.

Everything was so still that they assumed the place must be deserted. Bill looked over at Luca, his face relaxing into a smile.

'Maybe the farmer thought it was haunted,' he said with relief. 'A kind of ghost village or something.'

But Luca shook his head, his expression tense.

'Look,' he said, pointing at a shack further up the stream.

As soon as they spotted one figure they seemed to be everywhere, camouflaged by their dirty rags against the porches where they were sitting. Pitifully thin people sat listlessly on the steps: men with skeletal faces and children on their mothers' laps, bodies barely more than a heap of bones. The only sound was the occasional bout of coughing. As Bill and Luca approached, hollow eyes followed their progress with a mixture of apathy and hunger.

'Jesus Christ,' muttered Luca, raising his hand to cover his mouth. 'What the hell happened here?'

Bill shook his head, looking down the line of shacks to where another movement had caught his eye. A couple of mangy dogs were picking their way through the piles of rubbish by the banks of the stream, the lines of their ribs clearly visible.

'I don't know, but I don't like being here one bit,' he whispered. 'This place looks more like a morgue than a village.'

As he spoke he looked over to the nearest of the shacks where a small girl was lying in the shadow of the roof. Strands of matted black hair covered her face, but aside from the shallow rising of her chest, she was completely still.

Bill moved over and crouched down beside her. As he came close, her eyes flickered slightly and then were still, seemingly oblivious to the shock of seeing a white man standing above her. Sweat beaded her skin, and the fevered beating of a pulse was visible between her angular collar bones.

'It's probably not a good idea to get too close,' Luca said from behind him. 'Let's get on with finding the well and use the purification pump back in camp.'

Bill didn't answer, his thoughts drifting as he imagined his own daughter in the same situation – wearing nothing more than a dirty dress, with bare feet and no one to feed her. He wondered if this girl's parents had already died from the sickness and if so, why someone else had not taken her in so that she at least had someone with her during the final few days of her life. She seemed so unwanted and alone – a life just left to slowly flicker out.

Behind him, Luca was still speaking.

'I reckon it must be something like typhoid or cholera. We've had both those jabs so I'm pretty sure we're in no danger . . .'

Without hesitating, Bill scooped his hands under the little girl's body and lifted her into his arms. Luca gave a shout of alarm, but Bill ignored him. She was as light as feather, no heavier than his daughter despite the fact that she was probably twice her age.

'We'll get the antibiotics from our medical kit,' he whispered to her. 'They'll clear you up in a few days.'

Luca shook his head.

'You can't do that, mate. You have to put her down.' He moved closer. 'There's a whole village suffering here and we've only packed a few courses of antibiotics. We might well need them ourselves.'

Bill's forehead wrinkled in disbelief.

'Tell me you're not serious?' he said. 'Come on, we can help this little girl. We're stronger than she is.'

Luca looked skywards, closing his eyes briefly.

'It's not that I don't want to help her, but we can't go round doling out medicine. That's not what we are here for. We've got a tiny medical kit and only two or three courses of antibiotics. What happens if one of us needs them?'

'I don't give a shit if we need them,' Bill countered, his voice rising. 'I'm prepared to take that risk.'

'Yeah? Well, I'm not. You can't do this, mate. Think about it.'

There was a silence as both men stared each other out.

'Look, we've been here before,' said Luca, more gently. 'There are always children or women whose lives could be saved by some drug that only costs a tenner. It's horrible, I know, but it's also the reality of being out here in Tibet. It's not for us to start handing out drugs just because it makes us feel better.'

He paused, staring down at the little girl in Bill's arms.

'For Christ's sake, I *want* to give her the drugs just as much as you do, but it just doesn't make sense. Who are we to decide who gets them and who doesn't? Why not the women so they can look after the children, or some of the younger guys so they can work the fields?'

Bill didn't answer.

'Come on, mate. I know it's shit, but we've got to be practical here.'

There was a long silence before Bill eventually turned and very carefully laid the girl down on the step where she had been lying. He stared at her for a while before reaching into the breast pocket of his jacket and curling her hand round a crumpled chocolate bar.

'I'm sorry,' he whispered, then stood up, squaring his shoulders. As he looked at Luca, his eyes hardened.

'Come on then. Let's get that fucking water.'

Luca nodded grimly, his grey eyes fixed on Bill's. Then, together, they marched up the track, their boots crunching over the rocky ground.

Chapter 23

When they woke up the next morning, the herders were gone.

For the first time on the expedition Bill was the first to rise, immediately taking in the smouldering remains of the campfire and the baggage dumped in a pile beside it. He swore, then slapped his hand against the fly-sheet of Luca's tent.

'OK, OK.' Luca emerged with tousled hair, rubbing his eyes. 'What's the problem?'

Bill simply pointed to the baggage and for a moment Luca craned his neck round, looking for the herders.

'Oh, shit.'

Wearing only his thermal long johns, he walked barefoot across the dusty ground to the pile of heavy bags. Crouching down, he unzipped each one to double-check its contents. Without his top on, the alabaster white of his torso contrasted against the dark tan of his forearms and face. From the last week of being on the trail, he had lost a few pounds in weight and now looked lithe and wiry. His wide shoulders cut down in a 'V' towards his narrow waist and as he crouched on the ground, with his body coiled over the bags, the entire line of his ribs was visible down his back.

Picking up one of the two wooden boxes that lay to either side of the fire, Luca prised open the top. Both boxes had a few broken slats.

from days of being strapped to the yaks, but the supplies were still carefully packed within.

'At least they left the food and our gear.'

'Yeah,' said Bill. 'But we're stuffed if we don't find a route up from here. There's no way we can carry on with everything ourselves. How many days' food do you think we have left?'

Luca shifted the boxes to one side and looked from bag to bag again, his frown deepening. 'I don't know, but we can't afford to waste any more time. We've got to find a way up that rock-face. I'll go up this morning and see whether there's anything that will work. Are you okay staying here and sorting through the gear?'

Bill nodded. Twenty minutes later he was building up the fire as Luca tightened the laces on his climbing boots and, without another word, left in the direction of the mountains, his shoulders hunched with fresh determination.

He spent most of the day pacing up and down the base, scanning every inch of the mountains' curving flanks. There was something about the cliff-face that was bothering him. No matter which angle he viewed it from, he couldn't quite visualise the way ahead. The cliff itself was a vertical drop of about eight hundred metres with long, ragged cracks running down its entire length. It was solid granite and would hold their protection well, but it was the route itself that looked almost impossible. It was a maze of overhangs and long sections of perfectly smooth rock.

From time to time his vision blurred and for a few moments it would seem as if the rock itself was changing shape. But then he would blink again and it would change back, so that he was left looking at smooth, unpassable sections of rock.

By the time he got back to camp it was late afternoon and his eyes were aching.

There was no sign of Bill. A small fire made from clods of dried yak dung smouldered away by the tent and neat coils of rope were laid out over the fly-sheet. Resting on one of the bags were bundles of nuts and friends, while the carabineers had been clipped by size on to slings.

Luca grabbed the battered kettle and shook it, feeling water slosh around inside before balancing it on the corner of the fire. For a moment he looked back at the mountains, his eyes searching for a route. There must be a way through. There just must be.

As he was taking the first sip of his coffee, he heard a commotion coming from over the ridge. With his mug still in his hand, he walked up the path to the first of the village shacks.

Bill was standing there, a rucksack open at his feet and about twenty villagers huddled around him. They had obviously dragged themselves from their huts and stood, some swaying from weakness, with their hands outstretched. Shaking his head, Luca threw his coffee onto the ground and sprinted the remaining distance.

'Luca,' Bill exclaimed, his cheek flushing with guilt.

Luca took in the emaciated figures crowded around him. 'Tell me you haven't . . . ?'

'I couldn't stand by and let it happen.'

Luca began to say something then fell silent, shaking his head in disbelief. He couldn't exactly get the antibiotics back again. The damage had been done.

'Great,' he said sourly. 'Really fucking great.'

'I'm sorry,' Bill said again. 'I spent all day trying to stop myself but I just couldn't stand the idea of us sitting healthily in our camp . . .'

Luca looked at the villagers gathered around them with their hopeful smiles. They held their medicine carefully in the palms of their hands, nodding their heads and giving thanks to these strange newcomers and their gift of healing.

'But we only had a few courses,' he sighed. 'What the hell are you giving the rest of these guys?'

Bill gave a sheepish shrug and looked away.

'Just a few painkillers. Everyone saw me give the antibiotics out, so I had to give them something. It's all I could think of and . . . well, it won't do them any harm.'

As he spoke, another hand stretched out from the crowd. Bill dutifully doled out two small white pills, finishing the bottle, when a movement from the far side of the village caught Luca's eye. A figure was striding towards them.

The figure was tall, with two straight curtains of very dark hair framing its face. In contrast to the shuffling forms of the villagers, the woman moved with the vigour of full health, the hem of her dirt-stained tunic billowing out behind her.

'Who the hell . . .?' Luca murmured as she approached the edge of the crowd.

She stopped and even beneath the grey scarf that was tied like a surgeon's mask across her face, the men could tell that she was furious. Strong dark eyebrows were angled low over green eyes that blazed with hostility. She stared from Bill to Luca, then back again. Around them, the crowd fell silent.

Raising her right arm, the woman yanked the scarf down to the neckline of her tunic revealing high cheekbones that cut down to lips pressed together in disdain.

'What the hell do you think you are doing?' she asked in English and with only the lightest trace of an accent. Jerking her chin up, she gestured to the bottle Bill was holding.

'Give me that.'

Bill's mouth dropped open in surprise as he handed over the empty plastic bottle.

'You speak English.'

Ignoring him, she glanced at the bottle's label before looking up again, eyes shining with anger.

'Nurofen,' she said. 'You have got to be kidding me. Have you any idea how irresponsible that is?'

'I just thought . . .'

'No. You didn't think,' the woman cut in. 'This village is riddled with cholera, and here you are handing out painkillers! Don't you understand, these people actually believe your Western drugs will cure them? All you're doing is abusing their ignorance.'

'Hold on a second,' Luca interrupted, pulling himself together. 'Bill's already handed out all our courses of antibiotics – stuff we now don't have for ourselves. He couldn't handle disappointing the others so had to give them something.'

The woman gave him a scornful glance. Then, turning to the assembled group of villagers, she spoke quickly in Tibetan, her voice low and emphatic. After a few moments the villagers began to look from her to Bill and Luca, their faces uncertain. As she continued speaking, they started to shake their heads and back off a pace or two, jealously guarding the white pills.

'Of course they don't believe me, why would they?' the woman said, exhaling in frustration. 'You've given them hope, and that's the first they've had of it in a long time. But why do I get the feeling you won't be around to pick up the pieces when they realise the drugs don't work?'

'Look, we didn't mean any harm,' Bill protested, his hands raised defensively.

'That's what you all say . . .' she began, then drifted into silence, shaking her head in disgust. She let the empty bottle fall from her hand and Luca and Bill watched as it rolled a few centimetres on the ground before sticking on a patch of mud. Pulling the scarf back across her mouth, she gave them a final, withering glance before heading back towards the far end of the village. As she left, the crowd started to disperse, a few people staring down at the empty bottle before retreating to the wooden stoops of their homes.

'Jesus,' Luca said, his eyes wide. 'Where the hell did she come from?'

'I have no idea,' said Bill, 'but now I really do feel like an idiot.'

Luca turned to see his friend staring down at the empty bottle, his shoulders slumped.

'You were only trying to help. Don't take it to heart. At least a couple of them will be saved by the antibiotics.'

'Yeah, but . . .'

As Bill raised his head, the beginnings of a smile crept across Luca's face.

'I'll tell you one thing, though. We're sure as shit not getting a dinner date out of this.'

Slowly Bill's expression eased, the tension starting to drain from his face. He glanced back at the hut the woman had entered.

'Who do you think she is? I mean, she barely even had an accent.'

'Beats me,' said Luca. 'Maybe she's an aid worker or something. She looked more Nepalese than Tibetan to me. Wherever she's from, I get the feeling she wasn't too impressed.'

'Yeah, well, I was only trying to help,' Bill muttered. Straightening his shoulders, he turned back towards their campsite.

After a final, curious glance towards the woman's hut, Luca followed.

Chapter 24

'Who is it?'

There was no reply, only repeated knocking, mechanical and incessant.

'For the love of God, stop that infernal racket!'

With more than his characteristic lack of agility, René lumbered across the empty restaurant in the direction of the front door. He winced as he blundered through a shaft of sunlight, breaking through from the curtains, and gingerly rubbed his temples.

With years of experiencing biblically proportioned hangovers, he knew that an ice pack and a stiff dose of Paracetamol should just about see him through the day. Both, however, were kept in the kitchen which lay in the opposite direction from which he was currently headed. Reason enough for him to ignore the interruption altogether. Only the interminable knocking had galvanised him into any sort of action.

As he unbolted and swung open the door, René mustered what remained of his strength.

'What the hell do you think . . . ?'

He stopped abruptly, eyes slowly focussing on the silent figures in front of him. Three silhouettes stood in line on his doorstep, haloed by the harsh morning light. René squinted at them, feeling his headache double in size. Without a word, the leading two soldiers pushed past him and into the restaurant.

'An unexpected pleasure,' René said, stumbling back a couple of paces.

A third man stepped over the threshold. He was smaller than the other two. As he walked further into the room, René could see his face was delicate, almost feminine, with no trace of stubble. Only the harsh line of his thin lips offset the fragility of his features.

Captain Zhu looked René up and down, his eyes hardening in disgust. He took in the checked shirt that had been hastily pulled on before René answered the door, displaying stains from the previous evening's festivities. Above its collar, René's jowly cheeks were blurred by a couple of days' worth of stubble and his hair was still flattened by his pillow.

Zhu pulled a chair out from under a table and seated himself. Across the room, the two other soldiers were standing to attention. One of them, the massive one with the thickset neck and shoulders, moved a step closer. René recognised them from the other night. He'd sent them the wrong food.

Swallowing a couple of times, René tried to get some moisture back into his mouth.

'Foreign Office visa and permits,' demanded Chen in his broken English.

'For Christ's sake, I've been in Lhasa for eight years,' René protested, folding his arms across his barrel chest.

'Foreign Office visa and permits,' Chen repeated tonelessly.

'OK, OK. Keep your shirt on.'

René backed away towards the stairs, and, bracing himself for the pain he was about to inflict on his own head, shouted up for one of his staff to come down with the necessary paperwork. A moment or two later a Tibetan girl came cautiously down the wooden steps. She was tall and gangly and, like most teenagers who have only recently developed out of childhood, awkward with her height. Her shoulder-length hair was tied back in a simple ponytail, framing a shy face set with large, brown eyes. As she handed a file over to her employer, she darted nervous glances at the restaurant's unwelcome visitors.

'Thanks, Anu,' René said quietly, noticing that the seated soldier was following her every move. 'Why don't you go back up to the office and wait for me there?'

He turned to Chen.

'You'll find all the necessary permits in here. Knock yourself out.'

Chen frowned as he tried to understand what was meant by this last phrase. René smiled. Using slang was one of his favourite ways of confusing officials. Chen skimmed through the paperwork, then laid the file down on the table.

'We need all paperwork,' he said, tripping over the pronunciation. 'All permit issued.'

'You're investigating me? Why?' René said, surprise outweighing his annoyance. There was silence and he stared past Chen's size-able frame, directing his question to the seated officer beyond. Despite his silence, there was air of authority about him. From the sidelong glances this huge brute in front of René was directing at the man, it seemed that even he was scared of him. One thing René knew about living in Lhasa was that you always had to speak to the man in charge.

'Look, I had a full investigation by the CMA only four months ago,' he said to Zhu, in a more reasonable tone. 'All the permits I issue are above board. You can just get the report off them.'

Zhu slowly raised himself to his feet and lit a cigarette with his left hand.

'But we are not the CMA,' he said in his precise English. 'And from the dossier we already have on you, Mr Falkus, it would appear that you would do well to give us your full co-operation. You wouldn't want to be deported over something so trivial as a wrongly issued permit, now would you?'

'Deported?' René challenged. 'What the hell are you talking about? No one's deporting me.'

Zhu gave the briefest of smiles, it flickered on and off like a lighter running low on fuel.

'Well, let us start by reviewing the permits for the two Westerners who were recently travelling to Nepal.'

He motioned to Chen who opened a file he had been holding and read out the names,

'Luca Matthews. Bill Taylor.'

'How do you say in your country?' Zhu said, glancing back at René. 'Ring any bells?'

For a moment René was caught by surprise, then his expression darkened and he glowered at the other man with undisguised hatred. He was just about to shout a protest, trying to bluff his way out of the situation, when he suddenly stopped, catching himself before a word had escaped his lips. He'd suddenly realised what the epaulettes on the officer's jacket actually signified.

René quickly glanced away and stared down at the floor, his mind reeling.

How the hell had he missed them when the soldiers first walked in? Everyone knew that gold and black insignia. This man was PSB. And a full captain at that.

'I'm sure there's just been some confusion here,' he said eventually. 'They were just standard tourist permits. Nothing more than that.'

'Well, your "standard" tourists have not yet reached Shigatse. In fact, they seem to have disappeared completely. They even left without their interpreter,' Zhu said, inhaling on his cigarette and blowing the smoke across the table. Then, without looking at René, he spoke again, his voice soft, almost conversational.

'Where are they?'

'I'm not sure . . .'

'Where are they?' he repeated, his tone unwavering.

René stood in the centre of the room, staring down at his bare feet. His toes were balled up against the cold flooring. For some reason, having no shoes on was making him feel horribly exposed.

Why the hell was a full captain of the secret police asking him questions about something so banal as a permit? Had the boys been telling him the truth or were they up to something more than just climbing Makalu?

'Maybe their truck broke down and they've been held up a few days. These things happen.'

'That could be the case,' Zhu replied, unblinking. 'Yes, maybe that's it. The truck.'

There was another silence and René tried to work out what to say next, but found his mind struggling to keep up. If only he weren't so damn' hung over.

'So why are these two particular foreigners back in Tibet after only a month?'

The change of direction in his questioning caught René completely off-guard. Christ, they had been fast. The amount of paperwork these guys had to wade through, it normally took them weeks to put all the pieces together.

'I don't know why they came back,' he said, shrugging his bear-like shoulders. 'Maybe they like it here.'

Zhu stared at him, their eyes meeting. A split second later René broke the gaze, looking away to the window.

This seedy expat was holding something back, Zhu was sure of it. Two foreigner climbers back within a month to the same godforsaken area, and now they had suddenly disappeared. The monk at Drapchi had said that it was climbers from Nepal who had come to rescue the Panchen Lama, and the Westerners had arrived from Kathmandu and were last seen heading south-east. That would put them near Tingkye.

Even if the location were a coincidence, the timing could not be. Back now, at the very same time that the boy had been spirited away.

Zhu stood up from his chair, and addressed Chen.

'Have him dress properly and take him into the station for questioning.'

René glared at the slight, precise figure before him, rage finally triumphing over his hangover.

'I am a Foreign National. I have rights,' he said through gritted teeth. 'We both know it. You can't touch me.'

'I think you might be surprised what we can do,' Zhu said, and with the tip of his shoe delicately stubbed out his cigarette on the wooden floor, leaving a small circular burn mark. For a moment his eyes turned upwards, slowly taking in his surroundings as if for the first time.

'By the way, nice place you've got here.'

Chapter 25

The chill of the night drew in quickly and a multitude of stars appeared across the black sky. Bill and Luca lay close to the campfire, away from the direction in which the wind was blowing its smoke. Their feet were right up against the embers, almost burning the soles of their boots, as they watched the boil-in-the-bag rations begin to simmer in the small aluminium cooking pot.

'You go back to the village and ask if you want to,' Bill said again. 'She must think I'm a complete idiot for handing out the antibiotics.'

Luca grinned and leaned his head back in his clasped hands. 'I'm just as guilty as you by association. Besides, women seem to like you. It's that trustworthy face of yours. Fools 'em every time. Take Cathy, for instance . . .'

At the mention of his wife's name, the smile faded from Bill's face. He stared into the glowing embers, his expression clouding over. Luca sat forward again.

'Sorry, mate, I shouldn't have brought that up. And for the record, about the antibiotics, I've been thinking about it and . . .'

He stopped mid-sentence. From somewhere in the darkness came the crunch of stones on the path. Both men sat up straight as the old monk they had seen at the entrance to the village came slowly into view, his red robes glowing in the firelight. He raised a hand in greeting, emitting some guttural syllables that neither of them could understand. His right hand was extended behind him and it took a second for Bill and Luca to realise that he was leading someone out from the shadows.

The woman from the village stepped into the light.

After a moment's surprise, Bill and Luca both scrambled to their feet.

'Hello,' Luca said hesitantly.

Without answering, the woman moved around the fire, her green eyes switching from Luca to Bill as if assessing them both. Suddenly the old monk started talking again, his voice thick and rasping.

The woman waited until he had finished, then nodded.

'My friend wants to introduce himself. He is Gyaltso Choedon of the Gelugpa sect.' She paused before adding, 'And I'm Shara.' A smile crept across her lips, transforming her face. 'I'm sorry we got off to such a bad start this afternoon.'

Luca grinned. 'Don't worry about it. We were just saying the same thing.' He offered his hand. 'I'm Luca. This is Bill.'

By the time Bill had reached across to shake her hand, the old monk had sat down by the fire and was shuffling forward, warming his hands against the flames. As they joined him, his dark eyes glinted slightly as he stared from one man to the other. His face was set in a crooked smile and he seemed strangely pleased with himself; a different man entirely from the one who had ignored them on the pathway.

Luca nodded respectfully to him before turning to Shara.

'So, I'm guessing from your English that you're not from this village?'

'No,' she said simply. 'And I imagine you're not either?'

Luca glanced over at Bill who was staring at her from across the flames. 'Yeah, we're pretty far from home. We're both from England originally, but we've been to Tibet a few times before. I don't think either of us has ever come across anyone who speaks such fluent English as you, especially as far out in the sticks as this.'

'"In the sticks?"' repeated Shara quizzically, then laughed. 'You see, my English is not as good as you think.'

'I'm sorry, I meant, remote, far away from towns or cities.'

'I see,' said Shara. '"In the sticks". Yes, I suppose we are.' She glanced over at the monk who smiled at her approvingly. 'Well, originally I come from Nepal, but I grew up at an English school in Dharmasala in Northern India. I used to work there on . . . translations. With such a mixed society, many of us spoke several different languages.'

'And how did you end up out here?' Luca continued.

'I work in medicine and am part of a team that tours through the most remote villages in Tibet offering help where we can,' Shara replied quickly. Then her eyes flicked towards Bill. 'As you can see from today, there are many who need us.'

Luca nodded slowly, as Shara leant forward towards him.

'And what about you? Why are you out here, in the sticks?'

'We're climbers,' Luca replied, a trace of pride creeping into his voice. 'We're here for a few weeks to try and climb one or two of the mountains on the other side of the valley.'

'But these mountains aren't famous or particularly high. Why *here* exactly?'

'Well, I guess it started a couple of months ago. We were high on another mountain and spotted this range. From all the maps, it looked as if none of them had been climbed and so we came out here to try some first ascents.' He shifted forward a little, his expression suddenly less casual. 'I've actually been trying to find out if they really are unclimbed from a few of the villagers, but my Tibetan's not exactly great.'

'No one has climbed these summits . . .' Shara began, but before she could say any more the old monk started speaking again, his voice louder and more insistent than before. Shara turned and spoke to him for a few minutes. He seemed to be pressing her on some point, repeating the same phrase over and over again, and tugging on the sleeve of her tunic as he spoke.

Bill and Luca shot each other glances before Shara turned back to them.

'Gyaltso wants me to tell you about a proposition he has for you.

He says that if you want to climb these mountains, he will show you a way up through the rock-face.'

Luca sat bolt upright, almost leaning into the fire in his excitement. 'You're serious? He really knows a way up the face?' As Shara made to answer, he added, 'Ask him about the first section of rock, Shara. It's a gulley that we're missing, isn't it?'

Bill also was watching her intently.

'Is there something further on from the village? Something we haven't seen yet?' he asked.

Shara raised her hands. 'I'm sorry, I don't know the way myself, but Gyaltso would be able to show you. If you agree, of course.'

Luca had levered himself up so that he was on his knees.

'There's really a way?' he said incredulously, staring over at the monk in excitement. 'I've been over and over that face all day and I couldn't see a thing.'

'Shara, how does an old monk from the Gelugpa sect know the way up a technical rock face?' Bill said suddenly. 'And if there really is a route, then surely that means the mountains have already been climbed?'

'I said the summits had never been climbed. The lower slopes have. And to answer your question, when he was younger Gyaltso used to go up there every summer, searching for rare herbs. That's how he knows of a route.'

'Rare herbs?' Bill repeated. 'Didn't think there would be many of those on an icy glacier . . .'

'Certain lichens grow on the rocks at these altitudes,' Shara replied, her face tilted towards the fire. 'There are many ingredients from the mountains used in our traditional remedies. But, of course, now that he is getting frail, Gyaltso looks to me to continue his work.'

'You? You're going up into the mountains?' Bill asked, glancing at her slight figure.

'Yes.'

'By yourself?'

Shara sighed, continuing to stare into the fire.

'No. There was a guide here at the village who was due to lead me, but he has fallen sick, like everyone else.'

The old monk's watery eyes had been switching back and forth between them the whole time. He fidgeted forward, pulling on Shara's sleeve once again, asking for a translation. They spoke quickly, then she turned to Bill and Luca once more.

'He wants to know if you accept the condition.'

'Yeah, of course we do,' Luca said. 'I want to see this route he's discovered.'

'Hold on a second,' Bill said. 'What condition? You just said he would show us the way up the rock-face.'

Shara pushed her hair back from her eyes and for the first time her confidence seemed to slip.

'The condition is you'd have to take me with you.'

As the men glanced at each other, Shara laid a hand on the monk's arm. Then she looked up at Bill and Luca. 'I realise it's a lot to ask, but the herbs I am looking for are very precious and would mean we can start treating some more of the people here at this village. All you have to do is get me past the rock-face. After that, I will leave you to go for your summits.'

'You've got a deal,' Luca said, the excitement rising through his voice. He turned, looking at Bill for confirmation, but Bill remained silent. There was a pause as everyone including the old monk waited for him to speak.

'Can you give us some time to think about it?' Bill said eventually. 'It's late and with the herders gone, we're going to have to think about how we're going to sort the rest of the expedition.'

'Of course,' Shara replied. Then, climbing to her feet, she helped the old monk to his.

'We shall leave you in peace. Good night, gentlemen.'

With a brief bow, they retreated from the light of the fire and back up the pathway towards the silent village.

*   *   *

Stoking some more dried yak dung on to the flames, Luca stared at Bill, who hadn't said a word since the visitors had left.

'I don't get your problem with all this,' exclaimed Luca. 'This is the best bit of luck we've had since getting here.'

Bill only grunted softly and continued staring into the fire. Luca waited for a moment, then exhaled in frustration.

'We're being offered a route up and you've barely said a word. What is it with you?'

Bill's eyes connected with Luca's as he shifted his weight up onto his elbows.

'Something's not right about all of this,' he said, shaking his head. 'I can't put my finger on it exactly, but it just all sounds too easy.'

'Too easy? Jesus, Bill, will you stop worrying for once? Let's just go with it and see what happens. Worst case – the old monk doesn't have a clue how to get up the rock-face and we're back to square one.' He stared across at Bill, studying his closed expression. 'Is this about earlier today? She was pretty harsh about the antibiotics but . . .'

'I don't give a shit about the antibiotics. It's this whole situation. We're looking for a route up and suddenly, here she is, all smiles and bargains. Bit of a change from earlier this afternoon.'

Luca thought for a second, then the corners of his mouth curled into a smile. 'You know what I reckon it is? I reckon you're just pissed off because an attractive girl came out of the middle of nowhere and tore a strip off you.'

Bill didn't rise to the comment but instead went back to staring into the embers of the fire. Luca inhaled deeply, knowing all too well how stubborn his friend could be.

'Why don't you just give her the benefit of the doubt? And besides, if she gets to collect those herbs then she'll be able to help the villagers. You heard what she said. You'll be getting what you wanted all along.'

The frown on Bill's forehead gradually softened.

'Come on mate,' Luca continued, 'With the herders gone, its not like we've got a whole load of other options at the moment.'

For a long while Bill didn't speak. When he finally looked up from the fire, his eyes connected with Luca's, but they seemed to be looking right through him.

'I don't know what to think,' he said. 'But right now, I guess you're right. She's all we've got.'

Chapter 26

The four of them stood with their heads bent back, eyes following the old monk's grubby forefinger as it traced a line down the sheer wall of rock.

In the misty morning light, the buttress of the mountain resembled the knuckles of a giant's fist, scoured with cracks and fissures, seemingly impenetrable. But as the monk's finger traced a line down the rock face, Luca's vision blurred as it had done the day before and he suddenly realised what the old man was trying to show them.

'Well, I'll be damned,' he muttered under his breath.

'What is it?' asked Bill, standing just behind him.

'That crack he's pointing to . . . look at it again.' Luca cocked his head to one side as his eyes swept up along the contour of the rock-face. What had appeared to be a large crack running from the base to halfway up the rock-face was, in fact, a narrow ledge. Like staring at the inkblots of a Rorschach test, Luca's eyes suddenly reversed their focus and what had simply been a fissure in the rock, now became something wide enough for a human to stand on.

Bill shook his head. 'I can't see it.'

'You have to kind of unfocus your eyes,' Luca answered distractedly.

After a few moments, Bill began to smile. 'Jesus, yes. I see it now.'

Luca shook his head in disbelief, turning to where the old monk stood.

'How the hell did you find that?'

The old man smiled then looked pointedly over at Shara who stood staring up at the cliff-face, her expression unreadable.

Luca turned back to the cliff. Even with the ledge, it was still going to be one hell of a climb. Not for the first time since last night, he wondered if they would be able to keep their side of the bargain. After they had decided to accept the monk's condition, the four of them had talked more over breakfast that morning. They were to get Shara above the cliff and on to the flat of the glacier beyond. Once there, they would set up a base camp from which they could tackle some of the nearby peaks and she, in turn, would be able to collect her herbs. A week later, they would all descend together.

As Luca stood there, staring up at the route, he felt a tap on his shoulder. Bill motioned for him to step away from the others and the pair of them moved closer to the cliff. Opening their rucksacks, they began laying out ropes and hardware on the ground in neat piles.

'I'm still not sure about this at all,' said Bill in a low voice. 'Are you buying this whole rare herb thing? We've been up in the mountains a thousand times and nothing grows at that altitude.'

Luca shrugged, squatting down to count the pile of climbing bolts.

'Maybe it's possible you get lichen or something up there. Who knows?'

'It just doesn't make any sense. I got the feeling last night that the whole charm offensive happened because the old fella had forced her into making a deal with us.' Bill scratched the side of his face distractedly. 'I wonder why that would be?'

Luca stopped counting and looked at him impatiently.

'Bill, the bottom line is that I really don't care what she is doing up there. All that matters is that we've been shown a route up and we're one step closer to finding the pyramid mountain.'

'Yeah, but I don't see the connection between . . .'

Luca stood up, pulling two climbing harnesses from the rucksack. He looked at the deep frown lines running across his friend's forehead.

'Come on, mate. Give it a rest. We came here for the pyramid mountain. That's all that matters. In a few days' time, we'll have found a route through these mountains and be standing at its base.'

He handed a harness across to Bill.

'Piece of piss,' he said, the beginnings of a smile on his face.

Bill stared down at the harness for a moment before reaching forward and taking it. He went to say something more, but Luca swivelled away from him, staring out towards the distant mountains. Low on the horizon, faint wisps of cloud were gathering on the peaks.

'We should get moving,' he said. Then raising his voice to include Shara and Gyaltso, 'We need to be on top of this cliff before the wind picks up.'

Shara took in the crisp morning air and clear skies. She cast a doubtful look towards Bill.

'Trust him on this,' Bill confirmed. 'The weather is the one thing Luca always gets right.'

'The one thing?' queried Shara, an eyebrow raised.

While Bill and Luca finished preparing the ropes, the old monk led Shara away and started talking to her. They kept their backs to the men as they looked out at the mountains. Luca was in the middle of uncoiling two of the eight-millimetre ropes when he glanced over and noticed the old monk reach into the small satchel slung across his shoulder. He pulled out something wrapped in a piece of cloth. Luca only saw it for a split second before Shara slid it quickly into her own bag.

She put a hand on the old monk's arm, seeming to reassure him about something, before walking over to where Luca was standing.

'Are we ready?' she asked.

'Yeah, we're ready.'

He studied her for a moment, impressed by how calm she appeared before the climb. She stood with her hands on her hips, the strong bones of her face emphasised by the way her hair had been pulled back in a ponytail. Her green eyes were levelled at him in a look that was both confident and challenging. Instead of the dirty tunic of the previous evening, she wore a thick cream jumper with a high neck. It was pulled tight around her waist by a leather belt while the felt boots she was wearing were laced with twine, in similar fashion to the herders' but of much better quality.

A green canvas bag with metal clasps and padded shoulder straps lay by her feet. Earlier that morning he had seen her pack a thick sheepskin jacket and several pairs of tightly knitted woollen gloves. Looking down at the bag, he wondered what it was that the old monk had given her.

'It's going to be a hard climb and you should travel the lightest,' Luca said. 'Why don't you put some of your stuff in my pack and I'll carry it for you?'

Shara gave him a quick smile. 'I should be all right. It's not too heavy,' she said, raising the bag a little to test it.

'Up to you,' said Luca.

Bill walked up to them with a loose bundle of slings in his hand.

'We didn't have a spare harness,' he said to Shara, 'so I've rigged this up for you. It's not pretty, but it'll hold.'

Luca swung the ropes round, tying off two figure-of-eight knots into his own harness and then signalled to Bill to start belaying him. He was about to move on to the narrow ledge and begin climbing, when the old monk stepped up to the cliff-face and approached him. Luca stood in silence as he old man placed gnarled hands on his cheeks and began mumbling a long stream of rolling syllables. Resisting the urge to pull his head free, Luca waited until he had finished, feeling awkward with the sudden solemnity of the situation.

'A blessing,' Shara explained, as the old man turned and did the same to Bill. With Shara he bent forward so that their foreheads were touching and with his eyes firmly closed, repeated a silent prayer, his lips moving slowly with unspoken words.

When the old monk had finally backed away, Luca nodded to him, smiling faintly.

'Don't worry. We'll take good care of her.'

With that, he glanced across at Bill and moved forward on to the ledge, keeping his hips close to the rock and the top half of his body arched out, so he could see higher up. Shara watched the ropes slowly paying out to where Luca climbed in a steady rhythm, only pausing every five metres or so to clip in one of the bolts that hung in a great bunch of twisted metal from his harness. In what seemed like just a couple of minutes he was fifty feet above where they stood, his movements fluid and precise. There was an absolute confidence to the way he climbed, each grip of his hand deliberate, each foothold instinctive and self-assured.

Pausing again, he jammed down two bolts about a metre apart into an open crack in the rock. Offsetting the angle, he clipped a carabineer through each point and ran through a sling, twisting it back on itself with a flick of his wrist. Clipping the climbing ropes into a third carabineer, he screwed the locking gate closed and finally put his weight back into the seat of his harness, secure.

'OK,' he shouted down the face. Bill tied Shara into the same rope and then motioned her forward. He counted out ten more metres before tying himself in.

'Just take the exact same route,' he said. 'And whatever happens, don't look down.'

Shara moved methodically, keeping her focus on the wall ahead and trying to ignore the fact that her legs felt wooden and her heart was beating in her throat. Despite appearing confident in front of the others, as soon as she started climbing higher she realised that there was no more pretending. This was it. Along the actual ledge, the going was not too bad and although much slower than Luca, her feet moved upwards in a near-constant flow. Every few metres, the ropes ahead of her would gently tug at her waist as Luca pulled in the slack from above.

As she reached fifty feet above the ground, the ledge naturally sheared off, leaving an exposed patch of perfectly smooth rock.

Shara stopped, feeling for a handhold higher up the cliff. There was nothing above or below – just smooth, unbroken rock. All she could think to do was to press her body flat against the cliff and edge her way higher, but without a decent grip her balance felt tenuous, as if the slightest breeze would send her toppling over the edge. She'd watched Luca climbing this part from the ground. He hadn't even hesitated.

Looking across the gap, Shara could see where the ledge continued. It was only a metre or so away. All she had to do was lean out.

She felt her breath quicken and shallow as the sweat collected across her forehead. She tried to move, tried to force her heavy, unresponsive legs forward, but every instinct screamed out for her to stay where she was.

'Come on,' she murmured to herself. 'Come on. Just one step . . .'

Slowly closing her eyes, Shara inhaled deeply. She could hear the ragged exhale of her own breath, but forced herself to breathe deeper and deeper, calming her nerves. Then her eyes flicked open and, with a sudden lurch, she pushed out across the drop. The side of the cliff yawned out below her and, for a second, she looked down, seeing the hazy outline of the ground. As her foot connected with the opposite side of the ledge, the toe of her right foot slid on a loose pebble lying near the edge. Suddenly, she was tumbling backwards, her knee banging sharply against the cliff and her hands clawing at the bare rock.

There was a split second of weightlessness and Shara just stared in horror as the cliff seemed to move away from her. Before she had time to even cry out, there was a huge jolt as the ropes snapped tight, forcing the air from her lungs. The straps from her sling harness dug viciously into her waist and kidneys, while the heavy bag on her shoulders yanked her whole body backwards, pulling her off balance. Everything went still. There was silence, except for the slow creaking of the ropes.

'You OK?'

Luca's voice wafted down to her.

Shara tried to shout back but her mouth was completely dry. As she fought to steady her breathing, her body slowly spun round on the end of the ropes, facing her towards the distant mountains. Using her hips, she swung her weight round again, fighting to get her feet flat against the rock. After a few moments they finally connected.

Shara swallowed a few times more, trying to get some moisture into her mouth.

'Fine,' she shouted, feeling her lungs bursting from the effort.

A moment later the ropes tugged upwards and, inch by inch, Luca slowly hoisted her the couple of metres back towards the ledge. Shara reached forward, gripping on to the rock and taking her weight out of her harness, feeling disorientated by the lack of support from the ropes.

Edging her way along once more, she rounded a corner of the cliff to see Luca, hanging in the seat of his harness, coiling in the slack rope. As their eyes met, a smile flashed across his face before he reached out one hand. For a moment, Shara's eyes flitted from the rock to his outstretched fingers, gauging the distance. Then, with a lunge forward, she grabbed on to his wrist. The movement was clumsy but he was able to switch his grip and hold her tight, drawing her towards him.

Shara clung to his shoulders, a wave of relief washing over her at the contact, at the sudden feeling of being secure. Before she had even looked down, he had clipped her into the same two anchor points as himself and was gently pushing her back into her harness.

'You OK?' he said softly. He'd seen the same wide-eyed look many times before.

Shara exhaled, pushing back strands of hair from her clammy face.

'I had no idea it was going to be like this,' she said. Then after a pause while she tried to steady her breathing, 'This probably isn't what you want to hear, but I really hate heights.'

Luca laughed out loud.

'Fine time to tell me.'

Despite herself, Shara found herself smiling.

'I know. I'm sorry.'

'Don't worry, you're doing great,' he said.

Shara shook her head slowly, her voice barely more than a whisper. 'I've always been dreading this part of the journey.'

'Part of the journey?' Luca asked, turning to look at her. 'What do you mean?'

She shook her head again.

'I'm just going to be a lot happier when we reach the top, that's all.'

After a moment, he nodded thoughtfully. 'Well, it looks like the ledge gets broader up there and the going gets easier. We're going to have to move fast, though, if we want to stay ahead of the weather.'

He gave another tug on the rope and, moments later, Bill's face appeared round the edge of the cliff.

For another four hours they continued climbing. Bill and Luca took it in turns to lead, while Shara stayed in between. Bill remained silent for most of the climb, taking the sling full of hardware from Luca as they switched leads and pressing on up the ledge without a word. He climbed fast, pulling impatiently at the rope to Shara's harness and forcing her to keep pace. But as the ledge became easier, she began to climb with more confidence. The crippling sense of fear she had felt at the beginning was now forgotten, replaced by a strange sense of exhilaration.

Finally, she came out on to the top of the cliff and staggered like a drunk over to where Luca stood, pulling the rope through a belay.

'That was incredible,' she said, flopping down on the flat rock.

Luca's eyes switched from staring at the far mountains and he smiled down at her.

'That was one hell of a first climb. You should be proud of yourself.'

Shara gave a tired but happy smile. Beyond where Luca stood, she could see the high summits of the mountains encircling them like an immense amphitheatre, their peaks stretching up thousands of metres into the sky. Glaciers streamed down from their summits, converging on the lower slopes. Not far from where they were, she could see the snub nose of the nearest one, rising up like a pitted barricade.

Moments later, Bill appeared above the cliff edge. He walked straight past where Shara was sitting and up to Luca.

'Great climb, huh?' Luca said, smiling.

Bill seemed not to have heard him. 'We need to get moving to the shelter higher up,' he said. 'The wind's picking up fast, like you said.'

Shara got to her feet and walked up to where they were standing. She had been so absorbed in the climb she hadn't even noticed the changing weather. The ghostly clouds they had seen that morning now streamed across the sky, muting the afternoon light. They had obviously been climbing in the lee of the wind for all this time, but now they were exposed to its full force and she could feel it rip through her heavy jumper. Reaching into her pack, she put on the sheepskin jacket, using her leather belt to pull it tight around her body and buttoning it high up under her chin. The jacket also had a hood lined with soft wool and fringed with long, black fur that she pulled up to protect her face.

'Let's get moving,' Luca said, coiling the slack rope across his shoulder in equal lengths. 'We've got to get to the far side to be out of the wind. You OK with that, Shara?'

She looked pale and tired, but without another word swung her pack on to her shoulders, ready to leave. Luca smiled again, amazed by how different she seemed from the angry and aloof girl they had first met in the village. Bill had been completely wrong about her, he was sure of it.

'I'm ready.'

Within seconds she was roped up between the two of them and together they trudged off towards the start of the snowline like convicts in a chain gang.

With each minute that passed, the wind grew steadily in strength. Funnelled by the adjacent peaks, it rampaged down the mountainside, picking up loose snow from the glacier floor and hurtling past them. Squinting against the swirling air, Luca leaned into it, concentrating on the route ahead. They had to reach the shelter of the higher ground.

As he marched forward, tugging at the rope, Shara struggled to keep pace. She panted in the thin air as huge, swirling belts of cloud rolled across the sky, blurring out the horizon. The ground had become a great flowing blanket of driven snow, with the wind streaming across the hardened ice, until all they could do was bend lower still against the maelstrom.

Luca trudged forward without checking his stride. All around them, the noise of the wind grew and grew, until it became a shrieking sound that made the sides of their Gore-Tex hoods clatter at deafening volume.

Hours passed and the strength of the wind only increased. It was relentless, the streaming snow eddying round their faces and condensing on their raw cheeks. Snow forced its way past their hats and neck gaiters, trickling down their bodies like sand and making them shiver from cold.

They had been going for three hours when suddenly the rope at Luca's waist snapped tight. He waited for a moment, bracing himself against the wind, then stepped forward once again. It remained fixed. Behind him, he could see the blurry outline of Shara. She was bent forward, her hands on her knees.

As he trudged back along the rope towards her, Bill appeared out of the gloom. For a moment they stood in silence as the snow quickly covered the coils of rope at their feet. Shara was still bent double, struggling to breathe in the rushing air. Frost layered her face and her heavy jacket hood was caked in snow. She was shaking violently from the cold, her arms hugging her body to stay warm.

Luca pulled her upright, staring into her eyes. They were glassy, her eyelashes frosted at the end.

'Hold on,' he shouted to her. 'We're stopping here.'

Bill swung off his rucksack, pulling out the tent and poles. With heads bent low, they knelt on the hard snow, staking down the main body of the tent while the fabric flapped and twisted in the wind. Bill had his right glove off, the end clamped between his teeth, as he used his bare fingers to work the poles through the fabric sleeves.

'OK,' he shouted, holding one of the ends tight. As Luca put tension on the pole, the end slipped past the attachment at the corner of the tent, digging down into the snow beneath. With the snow half-blinding him, Bill hadn't seen what had happened and Luca pushed harder, digging the pole down deeper into the snow.

Suddenly it flexed then gave a brittle snap.

Luca looked up to see the main support for the tent buckling to one side.

'Shit!' he shouted, banging his fist against the snow.

He flung his end to one side and crawled across the billowing fabric to where Bill crouched on the opposite side. For a moment they knelt in silence, heads only inches apart, as they tried to work out what to do.

'Back to the rock-face?' Bill shouted.

'Too dangerous.'

Luca then squinted across to where Shara stood.

'We don't have much time. You stay with her. I saw some over-hangs in the rock west of here. Before the weather closed in.'

'OK,' Bill shouted back. Balling up the tent fabric with both hands, he trudged round to Shara who was still standing, arms clamped around her body. Wrapping the fabric around her to shield her from the worst of the wind, he pushed her down on his rucksack. Then he put one arm around her shoulders and with his spare hand tried to brush some of the caked snow away from her face.

Reaching into his jacket pocket, Luca pulled out his GPS and waited for the satellites to triangulate. Finally he got a clean signal and took a waypoint of their position. With a final glance at Shara, he shouldered his pack and marched off.

Seconds later he was lost to the blizzard.

Chapter 27

The strip light flickered, its pallid glow picking up the curls of smoke from Captain Zhu's dying cigarette.

The green walls were pockmarked with patches of raw cement and there were no windows, only a decrepit metal fan bolted to the far corner of the room, one of its three blades missing. A plastic table, which had evidently been left out in the rain for many years, stood unsteadily in the centre, exuding a dank smell of mould.

Of the two chairs that stood to either side of it, one supported the considerable bulk of René Falkus. Squeezed in between the plastic armrests, his body filled every part of the chair, forcing him to sit unnaturally upright, thick thighs locked together as if the need for modesty far outweighed that of comfort.

Across the table, Zhu had one leg folded over the other as he delicately stubbed out what remained of a cigarette. They had been locked in the same position for almost an hour, Zhu asking questions while René tried to answer with as little detail as possible, the pounding in his temples only exacerbated by the remnants of his hangover.

Leaning back in his chair, Zhu allowed his eyes to settle on one of the stains on René's shirt.

'I understand that you feel some loyalty to your friends, but is it worth risking everything you own to protect them from something that is simply inevitable? You must know by now that we will find them.'

'I've already told you,' René said tiredly. 'They're just on the standard route.'

'Tell me where they are.'

René shrugged and looked down at the table.

'I don't know where they are.'

'You will lose everything you have worked for,' Zhu continued, his voice suddenly softening, as if he personally would regret such an outcome. 'Your restaurant, your bar, everything. All we need to know is where they went.'

'One phone call to the Foreign Office and we'll soon see what you can do to my restaurant,' René countered. 'I have rights and you know it.'

Zhu's expression looked thoughtful for a moment. 'Of course, your rights . . . The problem is, I don't think there are too many lawyers inside Drapchi Prison.'

A muscle flickered in René's cheek. He had heard the stories. The miles of underground cells. The darkness.

There was a pause as he steeled himself, choosing his next words very carefully. He had been in Lhasa for a long time, and had learned how to deal with the Chinese. But somehow this newcomer was different. There was something about him that turned the stomach. Something that made René think that the worst thing he could do was to show any fear. Clenching his jaw, he looked straight into the captain's eyes.

'Either charge me with something or get me the hell out of here. Enough of this bullshit.'

Zhu didn't respond. Instead he leaned forward, picking up the silver lighter lying on the table. Using his thumb, he sparked it then snapped the lid shut again. He did this several times before leaning back in his chair again, leaving the flame burning.

'You still have no idea what I could do to you, do you?' he said. 'I can take your livelihood, just like that.'

As he said the word, he snapped the lighter shut. René dragged up a smile, the effort clearly costing him.

'Yeah? Then what else have I got to lose?' he said, squaring his shoulders across the table.

For the first time that afternoon a smile of genuine pleasure crossed Zhu's face. He uncoiled himself from the chair and stepped over to the bolted metal door. He knocked twice and it swung back on its hinges.

'Everyone has something more to lose, Mr Falkus,' he said, and walked out into the corridor beyond.

René sat waiting in the dank cell, unable to make out the curt orders Zhu was giving outside. Sweat gathered on his upper lip and with a sweep of his tongue he licked it off. As Zhu's footsteps softly receded down the hallway, a new silence fell. Despite the fact that he was craving a cigarette, something prevented René from leaning forward and taking one from the open packet that had been left on the table. Instead, he just sat there, listening to the hum of the fluorescent lighting.

A moment later the door burst open and three burly soldiers dressed in military fatigues rushed in. They shunted the table to one side, grabbing hold of René by his shirt collar and lifting him bodily from the chair. It happened so fast that he barely had time to shout out before one of the soldiers had kicked the chair from under him, sending it spinning to the far corner of the room.

They half-carried, half-dragged him down the corridor, his feet skidding along the smooth concrete floor.

'Get your hands off me, you bastards . . .' he started when one of the soldiers elbowed him right across his jaw. René howled in pain. The soldier raised his arm to strike again.

They pulled and shoved him down another corridor, and then another. Finally, with a fierce yank on his hair, they pulled him to an abrupt halt. One of the soldiers pointed to some wire mesh set at waist-height in the wall in front of him.

The mesh area was about the same size as a brick and René had to stoop to peer in. Through the cross-hatching of wire he could see a cell identical to the one he had just been in. A table stood in the centre and, to the left, two figures in profile.

René could feel his breath quicken and his heart start to beat faster.

Please God, no. Anything but that.

One of the figures was hunched over the table, her dark hair obscuring most of her face. Her gangly legs were clamped together at the knees and her upper half had been stripped bare. With only her crossed arms, she tried to cover her small, adolescent breasts. Even through the wire mesh, René could see that Anu's hands were shaking.

The man next to her was a soldier. René didn't recognise him, but he was wearing the same fatigues as the three who had just dragged him from the cell. He had a broad back which stretched the fabric of his military-issue shirt, and his hair had been shaved almost to the skin of his squat head.

As René stared in disbelief, one of the man's coarse hands reached down to unbuckle his belt, while the other moved across and grabbed Anu's slender leg. She flinched violently, her large brown eyes fixed on some unseen part of the floor.

'Oh, God,' repeated René in a whisper, feeling his stomach contract and the bile rise in his throat. 'Please. No.'

Despite the hair spilling across her face, René could still see the line of tears on Anu's cheeks. The soldier moved closer still, leaning his whole body forward so that his face was only an inch from hers. His right hand had begun kneading the inside of her thigh, moving deliberately higher with each turn.

René's mouth went dry as he stumbled backwards. He reached out to steady himself on the wall behind when the soldier to his right shunted him off balance, sending him sprawling to the ground. René hit the stone floor hard, knocking the wind out of himself and gasping for air. Clambering to his knees, he raised his arms to steady himself when the soldiers descended on him once again. They hoisted him up in one movement and pushed him back along the corridor.

Then came Anu's scream, a high-pitch sound that wavered and abruptly ended.

René squeezed his eyes shut, imaging the soldier's beefy hand being clamped over her mouth. Zhu would be waiting for him in the interrogation room. He turned back towards it, all the strength drained from his legs.

The same sentence kept drumming over and over in his head: 'Everyone has something more to lose'.

God help him, so did little Anu.

Chapter 28

Wind scorched across the mountainside, whipping the loose fabric of the tent's fly-sheet into a frenzy of movement that clattered like gunfire. Shara and Bill sat huddled together, rocking backwards and forwards in a vain effort to stay warm. They had draped the sleeping bags over their thighs. Snow collected in the folds like piles of icing sugar.

'Come on, Luca. Come on,' Bill muttered under his breath. The wind buffeted against his hunched shoulders, slowly stripping away the last vestiges of warmth. By his side, Shara's whole body convulsed from cold. Her lips looked waxy, with a bruised tinge to them, and her eyes were squeezed tight against the blowing snow.

Bill reached up, pulling the fly-sheet a little higher above her shoulders. He knew there was precious little time left before she became fully hypothermic. The misgivings he had been feeling about her were suspended, replaced by an urge to protect her from the terrible cold.

'He's not coming back, is he?'

The words sounded slurred, dropping out of Shara's numb lips.

'He'll be back.'

As she closed her eyes again, Bill twisted his neck round in the direction Luca had taken. The horizon was just a blur of streaming snow with no distinction between ground and sky.

'Please God, let him come back,' he murmured, fighting to stop his own body from shaking.

At first, Shara barely registered the arm lifting her off the ground. Then she tried to stand but her legs buckled underneath her and Luca had to force her arm over his shoulder and take her full weight.

'Let's go,' he yelled across at Bill, who uncurled himself and staggered to his feet.

With his other hand, Luca grabbed Shara's canvas bag and began half-pushing, half-dragging her through the snow. They trudged off in the direction he had come, heads held low against the storm. Every few steps Shara's knees would give way and Luca grunted from the effort of keeping her off the ground. A little further on, he stopped. Taking his GPS from his pocket, he peered down at the small, grey screen, damp from snow. Then, a few seconds later, they were on the move again, following a slightly different bearing.

Shara was beginning to slip from Luca's grasp, her body a dead weight on his shoulder, when a huge wall of rock suddenly loomed over them. Luca followed its course, running his gloved hand along the side before stopping twenty paces later and swinging off his rucksack. Bending low, he pushed it under an overhang of rock.

Checking that Bill could see him, he flattened himself against the ground and slithered underneath, pulling Shara down with him by one arm.

Inside, it was dark and perfectly quiet.

After the incredible noise of the blizzard, the sheer absence of sound felt disorientating, as if he had just lost one of his senses. From inside his jacket pocket, Luca pulled out a small, plastic lighter and with numb fingers, managed to spark the flint and hold his thumb down on the gas.

A bubble of light swelled inside the cave.

It was much bigger than he had thought, almost high enough to stand up in. A strong, acrid smell hung in the air. Wriggling forward, he made space for Shara and half-dragged her through the opening. Pulling her deeper into the cave, he propped her up against the side and wiped some of the snow off her face. She was trembling violently, her cheeks ghostly pale.

'I can't . . . I can't . . .'

'It's OK,' said Luca. 'We're safe. Everything's going to be OK.'

Tears trembled on her lashes but didn't spill. Shara just stared ahead with a stunned expression as Luca reached into the top section of his rucksack and pulled out a miniature Petzel head-torch. He squeezed the elastic band over his forehead and thumbed the switch across, filling the cave with the white light from the high-powered LEDs. He then pulled out his own sleeping bag, tucking it around Shara's legs.

'I'm going to get the stove going,' he said, just as a rucksack was flung through the gap and came crashing down on the floor beside them.

Bill hauled himself under the lip, before collapsing inside. After a moment's stillness he turned, plugging his rucksack back into the entrance and sealing out some of the wind.

Luca crawled forward on his hands and knees, pulling out the metal MSR Whisperlite stove and laying it carefully on the bare rock. With shaking hands, he pumped the plastic top, injecting the fuel into the line, and sparked the lighter underneath. After a few tries, the fuel caught with an orange flame and faint trails of black smoke belched out from the top. There was a popping sound as the stove tried to draw through the fuel, then all went silent again.

'Shit,' Luca said, blowing on his fingers to try and warm them up. He pumped the stove again, trying to inject more fuel into the line, and ignited the lighter once more. The flame leaped up, then faded into smoke.

'Try mine,' Bill said, swivelling round and undoing one of the straps on his rucksack. A second later he turned back with the stove and two spare fuel bottles in his hands. Luca didn't look up but with thumb and forefinger unscrewed the bottom nut on his stove, opening up the fuel value completely. He sparked the lighter and with a sudden 'whoosh' the stove ignited, filling the cave with its gentle roaring and sending yellow light dancing into the farthest shadows.

Ten minutes later they were all gripping mugs of hot tea, quietly watching the steam curl upward by the wide beams of Bill and Luca's head-torches. Shara was tucked further back into the cave, cocooned in her sleeping bag, her arms and head just visible above the thick down feathers. Her cheeks had regained some colour, but her face still looked drawn and exhausted.

'Thank you,' she said softly, staring directly ahead. Bill and Luca looked across at her.

'I wouldn't have made it out there without you both . . .' She stopped, choking on her words, and huddled deeper into the sleeping bag to hide her tears.

'You did well out there,' Bill said, blowing on to the surface of his tea. 'That was some nasty weather.' He looked at her sympathetically for the first time since they had set off that morning. He understood all too well how the hours of strain and fear could catch you by the throat. There was always a point on any expedition when you got emotional, and so far Shara had shown nothing but self-control.

He took a noisy sip of his tea, then grinned.

'Luckily we have Luca here who, in a storm, in the middle of God-knows-where, still manages to come up with this place. It's better than the bloody Ritz, mate.'

'Yeah. We were lucky. It would have been impossible to dig a snow hole out there in that wind.'

Bill nodded slowly. If it had just been Luca and him, they would probably have made it through till dawn by toughing it out. But with Shara in tow it was a different story. They both knew that if they hadn't found the shelter of this cave, the cold would have probably killed her.

Luca fell silent, absent-mindedly stirring a packet of dehydrated food into the saucepan before glancing towards the back of the cave.

'I think there's a draught coming in from over there,' he said, leaving the saucepan and pulling the lighter from his jacket pocket. The flame leaped up, then pulled sideways as the airflow drew across it.

'There must be another entrance somewhere farther back . . .'

He got to his feet and was starting to edge his way towards the back of the cave, his head bent low against the ceiling, when the food started bubbling by his feet. Curbing his curiosity, he knelt back down and began carefully spooning it out into three small plastic bowls. As he handed one to Shara she tried to decline, feeling too tired to eat, but Luca pressed it into her hands.

'Eat it. It tastes horrible, but it'll do you good.'

Bill was spooning his into his mouth without comment. Within a few minutes he had finished and, with a yawn, was settling deeper into his sleeping bag.

'You know, as hotel rooms go this one's not bad, but you might have chosen somewhere that smelled better,' he said, sniffing the air a few times.

'I was a little pushed for time,' Luca replied, his eyes flicking to the back of the cave again. He sat with his shoulders bent forward, as if the wind was still blowing behind him.

Bill sniffed again.

'What *is* that smell?'

'Whatever it is, you're going to have to live with it. I'm not going back outside to find somewhere else.'

Luca gently took the bowl from Shara. She had only eaten half, but her eyes were already starting to close.

'You'll feel better in the morning,' he said to her. 'I'm sure the storm will have blown itself out by then.'

Chapter 29

Luca's eyes jerked open. Something had changed.

He blinked, trying to adjust them to the darkness.

A noise must have woken him, but it was pitch black in the cave and he couldn't even make out the shapes of the others in their sleeping bags, lying just a few feet away. With nothing to focus on, he lay still and listened, feeling the hairs stand up on his arms.

There was a scraping sound, the quiet shuffle of something soft brushing across rock. Luca steadied his breathing, wondering if it could be one of the others moving in their sleep, but the noise was definitely coming from farther back in the cave.

More silence. Then a long, deep inhalation.

The sound was suspicious, purposeful; a sense probing an unfamiliar aroma as it filtered across the still, dark cave. Luca froze, his mind fogged from sleep as he tried to understand what was happening. Then, suddenly, he felt a grip on his arm, making his whole body go rigid with fear. He saw the dark outline of a figure bending over him, then felt the soft brush of long hair against his cheek.

'It's a bear.'

He heard Shara's voice, so soft it was almost inaudible. She was very close, her lips brushing against his ear as she breathed the words to him. He could smell the aroma of her skin and feel her cheek pressing against his.

'Get out of here,' she whispered.

As Luca moved forward, there was a faint rustle from his sleeping bag and he felt Shara's hand squeeze his arm harder. She moved away silently as Luca woke Bill, who was sleeping just beside him.

On their hands and knees and blinded by darkness, Bill and Luca silently pulled themselves out of their sleeping bags. They had been sleeping with most of their clothes on already, but needed their boots and jackets if they were to make it in the storm outside. As they fumbled across the hard rock, every soft scrape of their boots or rustle of clothing seemed to betray their presence, the noises echoing across the dead silence of the cave. Luca's leg brushed over the nylon of his sleeping bag, prompting another long, inquisitive sniff from the back of the cave.

As he crawled forward, Luca realised that Shara was now waiting by the entrance. He came up next to her, seeing her face in the murky light filtering through from the storm outside. She was already fully dressed and ready to leave, her sheepskin jacket buttoned up and her rucksack at her feet. How had she managed to get ready so fast?

Then came a deep growling. At first it was a soft sound, almost gentle, a guttural note that rolled around the rock walls. Within seconds, however, it had gathered in strength, only moments away from becoming a roar.

Luca pushed aside the rucksack blocking the entrance, sending a soft swirl of white noise into the cave as the space was unplugged. Then, grabbing Shara by the shoulder of her jacket, he pulled her forward. Without looking back, she slid out under the overhang. Luca could feel Bill's presence right behind him and pulled him forward to follow her out. As he did so, he adjusted his balance, moving his right foot just a few centimetres to the left and his boot connected with the saucepan resting on the stove. For a split second there was silence, then came a sickening crash as the metal clattered down on to the rocky floor.

The growling exploded into a roar.

Luca felt a rush of air from behind and instinctively threw himself headlong into the opening. Misjudging the distance, he smacked his head on the roof of the overhang, but somehow the main bulk of his body got through. Clutching his forehead, he rolled out on to the snow and into the terrifying intensity of the storm outside.

The wind was so loud that it whipped painfully across his body, the loose spindrift almost blinding him. As he got to his feet, staggering away from the cave, Luca's cheeks burned in the freezing air. He had sprinted twenty or so paces before he suddenly stopped, his heart hammering in his chest. Bill! Bill was still in the cave.

Swivelling round, he tried to see into the darkness and could just make out a silhouette, grey and blurry against the dark rock. It was Bill, trying to force his way out of the opening. His body was only half out, his bare palms scrabbling in the snow as he tried to lever himself forward. As Luca watched, paralysed with shock, a horrible scream escaped Bill's lips and his body arched upwards. Then, suddenly, he was out, rolling down the bank of snow towards Luca.

It was only then that something in Luca unlocked and he ran forward, grabbing Bill by his shoulder and hoisting him up on to his feet. Together they ploughed through the snow away from the cave, staggering in the deep powder as the wind whipped across their faces.

A hundred yards on, they collapsed on to their knees, lungs burning.

'You all right?' Luca shouted.

Bill didn't answer, his eyes wide. He was breathing in shallow, erratic bursts.

'You all right?' Luca shouted again, grabbing Bill by the collar of his jacket and forcing him to look up.

For a moment Bill just stared open-mouthed, as if he didn't know who Luca was. Then he nodded slowly, his whole body trembling from the surge of adrenaline.

'It didn't get me,' he panted. 'Just clipped the back of my legs, that's all.'

His breathing started to slow.

'I'm OK,' he panted, his mouth dry. 'I'm OK.'

Luca's head slumped forward in relief, resting on Bill's chest. He slowly shook his head.

'What the fuck was that?' he said, his voice ragged from emotion.

Bill didn't answer, but as Luca stared down at the ground, past Bill's climbing boots, he noticed a small cloud of black fanning out slowly into the snow. For a moment he stared at it, confused as to what it was.

'You're bleeding,' he shouted finally. 'Jesus Christ!'

Forcing him into a sitting position, he grabbed the back of Bill's thighs, running his hands down each leg. They felt warm, and the palm of his hand was sticky with blood. The back of Bill's Gore-Tex trousers had been shredded by a raking claw marks and there was a long strip of flesh hanging loose from the main stem of one leg.

Bill's breathing slowed as the adrenaline ebbed from his body. He stared at Luca.

'How bad is it?'

'We need to stop the bleeding.'

Looking up through the rushing snow, he caught sight of a dim silhouette coming towards them, battling the wind and snow. A moment later Shara stood over them, her arms wrapped across her body for warmth. She had her canvas bag over one shoulder and Bill's half-filled rucksack over the other. She stared down at them, the fierce wind tugging at her hair.

'Bill's bleeding. Can you help?' Luca shouted up at her. Shara immediately bent down, pushing the rucksacks to one side and feeling Bill's legs for damage. After a moment, she looked directly into his eyes.

'You're going to be OK,' she said, battling to be heard above the storm. 'You just have to try and relax while I bandage this.'

She turned to Luca.

'Have you still got that torch?'

Luca stared at her blankly. He had left his rucksack back in the cave. Then, his hand shot to the breast pocket of his Gore-Tex jacket – his head torch and lighter were still inside. Fumbling with the zip, he pulled out the torch and flicked the switch with his thumb, before handing it across to Shara.

Then he sat down on the snow behind Bill, shielding him from the worst of the wind.

Shara took a small folding knife from her jacket. Opening the two sides of her heavy sheepskin, she started cutting strips from the bottom of her jumper and tying them around Bill's legs. Luca had his arms around Bill's back, hugging him tight and rubbing his shoulders to generate heat. Wind and snow swept round them, covering their outstretched legs. Every few seconds, Shara would stop working and clamp her hands under her armpits to stave off the biting cold.

'You're going to be all right, mate,' Luca whispered into Bill's ear. His jaw was clenched, his bare hands curled into fists against the pain and the cold.

Now that the adrenaline had passed, the cold seemed to have a terrifying new strength. It was obvious that none of them would last much longer. Neither Bill nor Luca had managed to find their fleece hats or insulated gloves in the cave. Shara was the only one who was fully dressed.

'We've got to go, Shara,' Luca shouted across the noise of the wind. 'Otherwise we're going to freeze to death out here.'

She had finished tying the last of the makeshift bandages. The bleeding had slowed and she leaned over towards Luca, her expression set.

'The cuts aren't too deep, the problem is the skin around them. It's already starting to swell from infection. If that was a bear, the infection is likely to come on fast.'

'We've got to reach the rock-face on the other side of the glacier. Get out of this wind,' he said. 'We'll worry about the infection later.'

Shara looked down at Bill's swelling leg.

'No. We need to sterilise the wound now, then give him antibiotics.'

Luca shook his head. 'For Christ's sake, Shara. We're in a blizzard
in the middle of the Himalayas! And you know we don't have any
antibiotics left.'

She closed her eyes, her expression agonised.

'Come on, we're going,' shouted Luca. He started dragging Bill to
his feet. 'The rock-face is our only hope.'

Shara didn't answer but stared into the wind, her hair billowing
out behind her.

'Get moving!' Luca shouted. 'We've got to reach the rocks.'

She shook her head. 'There's another place.'

'What? Up here? What do you mean?'

Shara didn't answer, but instead began muttering something to
herself, shaking her head slowly. As Luca stared at her, waiting for an
answer, Bill rocked forward, trying to get to his feet. He grabbed on
to Luca's arm and Luca turned, hoisting him vertical.

'Can you walk?'

Bill hobbled forward a few paces in the streaming wind and nodded
hesitantly. 'Yeah. I can make it. Shara, what place are you taking about?'

'For God's sake, Bill. There is no place,' Luca shouted, his voice
raised in desperation.

Ignoring him, Bill moved closer towards her. 'Is there really a place,
Shara?'

She nodded. 'Please, there's no time to explain. Just follow me.'

Reaching down and opening her bag, she pulled out the object
wrapped in cloth that Luca had seen the old monk hand to
her. Holding it in one hand, she swung her canvas bag back over her
shoulder again and handed Bill's rucksack to Luca. A moment later
she was marching forward, disappearing into the white of the storm.

For a second, Luca and Bill looked at each other. Then Bill grabbed
Luca's arm and began limping in the direction she had gone, his face
set with determination.

Chapter 30

Zhu was waiting, one leg crossed elegantly over the other, when the soldiers bundled René back in.

Two of them then moved to either side of the door, guarding it, while the third bolted it shut from the outside. René was left standing by the wall, his large frame slumped as if the strings of a marionette had been cut. His jaw was already beginning to ache and he could feel his lip had split at one corner. There was the taste of blood in his mouth and a bruised imprint on his neck where the soldier's hand had been.

'Please, Mr Falkus, take a seat,' Zhu said slowly, gesticulating to the other side of the cell where the chair remained on its side.

René hesitated. Taking a couple of paces forward, he righted it and gingerly lowered himself down.

'She's just a kid . . .' he began in a hoarse whisper.

Zhu didn't answer, but instead glanced at the two soldiers by the door and nodded for them to leave. When it had shut behind them, he smiled at René.

'The gentlemen you've just met,' he began, 'are from a special division of the army that I have commandeered. For all that, I'm afraid they're not exactly what we might call "refined". I myself once had the privilege of being interrogated by them.'

Still smiling, he took his right arm from where it normally remained behind his back and started rolling up the long shirtsleeve.

'Nothing more than country boys, bored and frustrated,' he continued. 'Having said that, they do perform their tasks with a certain . . . creativity.'

René stared at the hand Zhu was now resting on the table. It seemed completely normal, slender and pale like his other one, except for one difference. Where the nails on his left hand were neatly manicured into little white moons, the fingers on this one looked longer and somehow inhuman. René blinked, his mouth going dry. Each nail had been pulled out, one by one.

The fingers had obviously long since healed but the nails had never grown back, leaving stretched skin rounding the end of each finger. The skin was redder in colour and perfectly smooth, as if his hand were facing palm upward. Zhu began slowly drumming them on the table while René's eyes darted from one finger to the next.

'I believe Anu's interrogation has only just begun,' he continued. 'So I suggest you start talking. It's your choice, of course, but if you're quick, I might even be able to intervene and put an end to the whole thing. Otherwise, who knows how long it will last or what else they will think of to do with her once they have had their fun?'

René looked up from Zhu's hand, his jaw clenched.

'Please,' he said. 'Just let her go and I'll tell you everything.'

Zhu fished out a pen and notebook from the breast pocket of his jacket. 'Then, let's start.'

'They're just . . . a couple of kids,' René stuttered. 'They do these climbing expeditions all over the place. A few nights ago they turned up in my restaurant asking about permits to get down south. They're trying to climb a mountain near the border called Makalu. That's all they are – climbers.'

He was speaking with his hands outstretched in front of him, pleading for Zhu to believe him.

'Climbers,' he repeated.

René nodded, desperate. He had to get the captain to believe him. He had to get Anu's interrogation to stop.

'So where did your "climbers" leave the main road?'

'I can't remember exactly,' René said, frantically trawling through his memory. 'It was a little town south of Shigatse. I had some yaks waiting there to take them further into the mountains.'

'Its name?'

'What?' he said, confused. Why was the captain pressing him so hard on such a small point? Surely he should be more concerned about where they were now? But he had to stop the soldiers. He had to think. Even now they might be . . .

'Tingkye,' he said suddenly, clicking his fingers. 'That's the place. Tingkye.'

Zhu nodded, his expression blank. Then he bent forward, scribbling a brief note in the pad.

'What do these climbers look like?'

As René gave descriptions and explained what little else he knew about Bill and Luca, Zhu felt an inward surge of satisfaction. He had been right all along. These were the two foreigners the monk had been referring to at Drapchi. They had to be. With the mention of Tingkye as well, there was no way this could be a coincidence.

Nearly fifty years ago, a couple of British soldiers had helped the Dalai Lama escape into India, and now, it seemed, they were doing the same with this boy. They must have got to Tingkye before that idiot Chen and were now moving the child towards the border. They would be attempting to get him across the Himalayas into India.

As René droned on, Zhu thought quickly. He could have the borders tightened along the standard routes, but still, it was an impossible area to control. The Himalayas were just too vast. If they were climbers as this oaf said, they would be able to go almost anywhere. Climbers were the perfect choice for crossing a border unseen.

René finished speaking and the room fell silent. He sat rubbing the corner of his mouth with the back of his hand, blood still trickling down from where his lip had split. Zhu shifted his weight forward and reached into his trouser pocket. He pulled out a white handkerchief, sliding it across the table.

'That's everything you know?' he said, gesturing to the handkerchief.

René picked it up, dabbing at his face.

'Everything. I promise. Now, for the love of God, please stop that interrogation.'

Without taking his eyes from his notepad, Zhu barked out a few orders in Mandarin. One of the guards from outside quickly unbolted the door and stepped inside. Zhu spoke fast, not once looking up as the man saluted and then withdrew.

'Had you told me the truth originally, Mr Falkus, you could have spared her innocence,' Zhu said quietly. 'I am a reasonable person, but you must understand, I will get what I want.'

He stood up, collecting his cigarettes and lighter from the table. He signalled for the guard again then paused for a moment, looking down at René.

'So that's it? You're going to look for them on Makalu?' René asked, his face scarlet with anger and humiliation.

Zhu started to speak, then hesitated. There was something about the way Falkus had asked the question that wasn't right. His tone had been belligerent when it should be broken. What if this disgusting Westerner was smarter than he looked and was sending Zhu on a wild goose chase, feeding him parts of the truth to whet his appetite? He stared down at René's bloated frame, hunched over the plastic table. Zhu needed to be sure he wasn't being played for a fool.

'Pack some warm clothes, Mr Falkus,' he ordered, moving towards the exit. 'We leave tomorrow morning, first thing.'

'What?' René protested. 'Where am I going? You said . . .'

Zhu didn't look back at René as he walked through the door, his right hand slotted back into his pocket.

'You're going to show us where these climbers went, Mr Falkus. Personally.'

Without checking his stride, he set off down the corridor, letting the sound of René's protests fade into the heavy concrete walls.

Chapter 31

Shara was marching purposefully for the other side of the glacier, seemingly unaware of the gap widening between them. In the thickening darkness, they struggled to keep the beam of her torch in sight, grunting from the effort of trudging through the snow.

Bill felt the infected heat burn in his left leg, and pushed down harder on Luca's shoulder for support. Both men struggled to stay balanced in the thick powder. The only consolation was the wind, which had started to taper off as they climbed away from the basin of the glacier. They were no longer in its main path, the higher ground offering some respite.

As the hours passed, the cloud started to disperse. Patches of moonlight shone through on to the snow. From time to time Shara would stop and using the light from the torch, look down at the object she was holding in her hands. Then she would turn back to the mountains as if searching for something through the swirling cloud. It was some time before Luca got a clear enough view to see that she was holding a book, the light catching on its gilded cover.

'Where the hell are we going?' he muttered. 'If she knew her way around here all along, why didn't she say anything before?'

Bill grunted in response, conserving his energy. The fever had started to take hold, and his forehead was burning up.

As Shara strode on, widening the gap to a hundred metres or so,

Luca strained to make out where she was going. He had Bill's head-torch on and peered through the wash of artificial light trying to see which direction she was headed. It looked as if they were being led up the side of a mountain's flank towards some outlying pillars of rock. The pillars were enormous, jutting out from the base of the mountain like a field of ruined temples and stretching on for what looked like at least a kilometre. In the moonlight, it looked like a maze of dead ends, the perfect place to lose your bearings.

Luca stared upwards, the sweat running down his forehead. Even if they made it through the pillars, just beyond them he could see that the rocks fed into a snow gulley that looked impossibly steep. There were being marched into a dead end.

'This is bullshit,' he panted, shifting his grip on Bill's shoulder. 'She's taking the wrong line.'

Tilting his head back, he yelled after her. 'The route's easier down towards the valley.'

A hundred yards further on, Shara was nearing the first of the pillars. As they drew closer, the rocks seemed to grow in dimension, leaning towards them ominously and extending back as far as the eye could see. Shara kept the book out in front of her, its pages illuminated by the beam of the head-torch. At the sound of Luca's voice she turned and waited, her teeth chattering from the cold.

'Where the hell are you going?' Luca said as he and Bill arrived next to her, panting. 'There's no way through there.'

'We have to pass through the Kooms.'

'The what? What are you talking about? And what's with the book?'

'You just have to trust me, Luca. All I can do is give you my word.'

Stepping past them, Shara knelt down on the snow. Pressing her hand against the back of Bill's legs, she felt the heat coming through the bandages. She rolled one higher, pulling it tight, and Bill let out a groan, his legs buckling under him. Luca had to widen his stance to take the extra weight.

As Bill regained his balance, he looked down at Shara.

'How much farther?' he asked, his voice no more than a whisper.

'Not too far now. But we must keep moving. The infection has set in.'

With that, she stepped out towards the first of the outlying rocks, moving towards one in particular. Shining the beam of the torch carefully up the side of the immense slab, she looked back down at the book before shaking her head in frustration.

'What are you looking for?' Luca asked, but Shara only started striding off once again, skirting round the rocks and higher up the mountain on the snowline.

'Wait! For Christ's sake, Shara.'

Ahead of them, the beam of light flashed from side to side, illuminating the towering pinnacles of rock piecemeal. Occasionally Shara would stop to rub her hand against one in particular, brushing away the dust and snow.

Suddenly she stopped by a massive pillar. It was shaped like an obelisk and tilted at a forty-five-degree angle. They watched her run her hand over the entire length of the stone as if searching for something. Then abruptly she stopped, retraced where she had been, and shone the torch on a spot she had been touching. Stumbling up behind her, Luca followed her gaze and saw that three lines had been etched together in a triangle at about knee-height. One side of the triangle was slightly thicker than the other, the whole thing being no bigger than a child's hand.

Shara suddenly turned towards them, the torch beam swinging round with her.

'Follow me,' she said, her voice grim. 'Step *exactly* where I step.'

Without another word, she ducked under the slab of rock, her body melting into the shadow of the Kooms.

The strain on their arms and legs was relentless.

All around them the pillars rose twenty or thirty feet above their heads. Slabs of rock lay broken at different angles, forcing them to turn up and down, right and left, as they weaved their way past each obstacle. Shara's beam of light twisted ahead of them in the darkness, pausing only occasionally as she felt her hand across another rock, then pointing the way through.

Luca looked at the chaos around him. At some point during the mountain's past, the main part of the cliff must have collapsed in on itself in a vast avalanche, carving out pillars of rock and tabular formations that stretched down the entire western side of the slope. The rocks were so crowded that once inside the giant maze, they could see only brief glimpses of the night sky above them. Within minutes of passing the outlying rocks, Luca had lost all sense of direction and simply followed Shara's moving torchlight, using his own to pick their way across the holes in the uneven ground.

As they moved deeper into the rocks, he realised that most of the stones were leaning towards the right, in the direction the avalanche had fallen. The easiest route would have been to follow their line down the slope, but Shara was persistently heading through the more difficult terrain, back up the mountainside.

She clambered from rock to rock, methodically searching for the next mark and only pausing to refer back to the book. Luca and Bill followed behind, crawling on their hands and knees across flat slabs, before slithering through a dark hole and dropping out into a new part of the maze below. With each new obstacle, Luca had to shoulder most of Bill's weight, supporting him under his shoulder when they were vertical or dragging him across by his arms when the route got worse.

Bill's face was etched into a continuous grimace and whenever the underside of his leg caught on a sharp edge of granite he shrieked with pain.

Resting against a nearby rock, Luca looked down at his friend's face in the bubble of light from the headtorch. Bill's jaw was locked rigid as he fought back a sickening wave of nausea and his body slumped forward with exhaustion.

'What is this place?' he said, his voice barely more than a whisper.

'A nightmare,' said Luca, doubling over on to his knees as he tried to catch his breath. 'I've never seen anything like it. I hope you were wrong about her, Bill. We're entirely in her hands.'

They fell silent, watching Shara's torch beam bob along ahead of them. A few moments later it wavered and then switched back to where they stood.

'Be very careful here,' she said, her voice tense. She was perched on top of a high boulder, looking back at them over her shoulder. 'Keep close to the left.'

Luca shook his head, staring up at her with his hands still on his knees. He raised himself, wiping the sweat from his eyes, and watched as she wriggled her way down the other side of the rock, disappearing from view. Luca began to speak, but Bill raised his hand for him to be silent.

'Listen to that,' he said.

Luca froze, his senses straining. There was the sound of running water, bubbling away somewhere beneath them.

'An underground river?'

Bill nodded slowly, wincing again as he pushed himself off the rock and on to his feet.

'Must be the meltwater from the glaciers higher up.'

They staggered forward again, dropping down the other side of the boulder after Shara. Beneath was a flat section that was easier going and they moved side by side, with Bill's arm over Luca's shoulder. Luca was looking up towards Shara, the beam of his torch following his gaze, when Shara suddenly turned back towards them.

'Left!' she shrieked, shining the light at their feet. Just a few inches away from Luca's right boot, the rock sheared off and there was a series of chasms dropping down into the darkness below. They could hear the rush of the water beneath and felt an undercurrent of cold air rising up to meet them.

Luca instinctively leaned left, away from the drop. Together they staggered forward again, nearly losing their balance as they tried to keep their shoulders pressed up against the far wall.

'Jesus Christ,' Luca hissed as they reached the safety of the next boulder. 'This is fucking suicide.'

For another half-hour they followed her lead. The route started to get a little easier now, the spaces between the rocks widening. Finally they rounded a giant boulder and came out in front of the narrow snow gulley that they had seen before from the lower slopes. Shara stopped, knee-deep in snow, staring up towards the top of the ridge.

'We're nearly there,' she whispered. 'One last push.'

Bill tilted his head up towards the slope then shook off Luca's grip, sinking down to the ground.

'It's too much,' he breathed.

Luca stood next to him, bent double and winded by the effort. The relief he'd felt at finally being out of the Kooms quickly evaporated as he ran his eyes up the length of the gulley. It was less steep than he had first thought, but the snow was deep. It stretched up, perfect and unbroken in the moonlight, over five hundred feet above them.

To their left was a near-vertical wall of rock which bent round into the gulley. At the very top, Luca noticed something hanging down over the slope – a snow cornice. From the constant wind whipping up the side of the mountain, the snow there had stacked up into an immense, overhanging slab which could easily trigger an avalanche if it collapsed.

Luca stared at it, trying to focus through his exhaustion. They were hemmed in on both sides by the cliffs. If that cornice went, there would be no escape.

Behind them, the first flecks of dawn had started to blossom over the horizon. The sky was turning grey, a half-light before the sun managed to rise above the mountains and burn off the night's gloom. Dawn would soon be upon them.

'Please, Luca,' Shara said. 'We have to keep moving.'

He didn't answer but only sank down so that he was shoulder to shoulder with Bill, both of them facing the steep gulley. Bill raised his head and, for a moment, they looked at each other.

'Bet you're glad you let me talk you into this expedition,' Luca said.

A flicker of emotion passed across Bill's face. He tried to smile, but it came out more like a grimace. His pale blue eyes slowly passed over Luca's face, taking in the large swelling on his forehead from where he'd dived out of the cave, and the matted hair which clung to his cheeks with sweat.

'You look like shit,' he murmured. There was a moment of silence before Luca's shoulders started to shake. A wave of laughter took hold of them both. Their laughter grew louder, dampening their eyes, before Bill broke into a coughing fit. He curled forward, his body convulsing as it rattled through him. After a while he managed to lean back again and they sat in silence, watching Shara trudge up through the deep snow. She was moving slowly, but as the minutes passed, they could see she was making ground.

'Where are we going?' Luca asked, the elation suddenly evaporating. The euphoria was replaced by a terrible sense of desolation, brought on by the hours of constant strain. He could feel tears welling up in the corners of his eyes and his throat was suddenly tight to the point where he thought he might choke.

'Come on, mate,' Bill managed beside him, his voice little more than a murmur. 'Piece of piss.'

Luca nodded, fighting back the tears. Then, with a sudden surge of energy, he pushed himself off the rock and on to his feet. He offered his hand to Bill.

'You're right. We can do this.'

Bill raised his own hand, lacking the strength to do anything more. Luca grabbed his wrist and was about to wrench him to his feet when he felt the violent trembling of Bill's arm. The fever had taken hold of him completely.

With a desperate shout, Luca yanked him forward, getting his shoulder under Bill's arm again. Side by side, they waded into the gulley, forcing their way higher with each step.

They had trudged on for what seemed like hours when all of a sudden, the first rays of sunlight burst on to the ground in front of them, burnishing the side of the mountain and illuminating Shara's tracks ahead. They kept moving, step after step, each muscle stretched to breaking point.

Luca stared up to the highest point of the ridge and saw that Shara had already reached it. She had stopped moving, her dark hair whipping behind her, and was staring out over the hidden side of the mountain. On they went, Bill groaning now with each step and Luca fighting with every ounce of strength to keep him moving. Every few paces his legs would sink down into the deep snow, so that he had to use his free hand to claw their way along.

The ridge seemed to stay just out of reach, each pace they took getting infinitesimally smaller, each movement costing more energy than they had. Then, with a final shout, they broke free of the slope and collapsed at the top. As Shara came back to check on Bill, her eyes ringed with fatigue, something made Luca pull himself up on to his feet once again and stumble over to where she had been standing. He took a couple of steps forward, swaying on his feet unsteadily, and stared at the view.

At first he couldn't see much at all. The morning sun dazzled his eyes. Then slowly shapes began to take form and he blinked, taking it all in.

'My God,' he whispered, barely able to believe his eyes. 'That's impossible.'

Chapter 32

'Another.'

A glass was slammed down on to the table top. With considerable effort René shifted his bulk forward on his chair, craning his neck so that his eyes were level with the diminutive Tibetan barman's.

'Fill me up, Shamar.'

With laudable strength of character, the barman shook his head. Picking up the half-empty bottle of brandy, he placed it right at the back of the glass shelving over the bar.

'Mr Falkus, I think you drink too much tonight.'

René shook his head wearily. He turned and focussed his bleary eyes on the Westerner sitting across the table from him.

'You see that? I'm not allowed into my own bar and now I can't even get a drink at this shit hole. It's worse than prison.'

He'd started to raise himself to his feet, his bear-like chest expanding in the process, when his companion intervened.

'Come on, Shamar, the man needs a drink.'

From the top pocket of his khaki shirt, he pulled out a wad of grubby notes and peeled off three ten-yuan bills which he placed on the counter. The barman shrugged and turned away to reach for the brandy. 'You drink too much, Mr Falkus,' he repeated. 'I sorry for you.'

René sat down heavily and his friend returned with the bottle.

'Yeah, well, I'm sorry. You're sorry. We're all sorry. Now I have to head off into the mountains to go and help the bastard Chinese find those boys. I've got to lead them right to them. And for what? I'll tell you what. To save what I already fucking owned.'

René's companion poured a shot of brandy into each glass and waited for the rant to continue.

'Have you any idea how much I hate the mountains? Those endless bloody paths and horrible leeches . . . size of your damn' fingers. But what's really going to drive me crazy is having that son-of-a-bitch captain following me every step of the way. He'll be like the worst leech of all, sitting on the underside of my balls.'

René shook his head, suddenly feeling very tired. He had spent two full days awake in the PSB headquarters and even a swift injection of alcohol wasn't doing much to lighten his mood. He had been released for a few hours to prepare his trekking equipment, with Anu being kept in the police cells to ensure he returned. But having made his way home, he had found his restaurant closed, official tape stretched across the front door and a policeman barring his way. Eventually he had phoned an old friend of his in the travel business who'd agreed to lend him some equipment.

'You'd think eight years here would count for something, wouldn't you?' he said, anger suddenly turning to melancholy. 'You'd think it'd give you some security, some foothold. But just like that' – René clicked his fingers – 'they can take it all away. Now I've got to betray the very people I wanted to help.'

'Stop beating yourself up about it, René. It was their decision to go into the restricted area, and you shouldn't have to pay for their mistake.'

'Yeah, I know.' He nodded wearily. 'But I just don't understand why a full bloody captain of the PSB would be dealing with this. It doesn't make any sense.'

'That's what worries me too. Are you sure those boys are on the level?'

'Sure? Who's sure of anything out here?' René said, rubbing the stubble on his chin. He stared across the bar, thinking back to the last time the boys had come into his restaurant. He couldn't quite remember the conversation, but he was sure they were just there for the thrill of climbing. That's all those two were about. So why in hell was a PSB Captain on their trail?

'What about throwing some money around?' his friend suggested. 'You know, make it all go away.'

'Captain Zhu Yanlei is one of those tight-arses from the mainland. Anyone approaching him waving notes wouldn't stand a chance.'

In all the years the two men had been organising expeditions in the Himalayas, they had always been able to buy their way out of trouble. The only bone of contention was how much: officials here had soon got wise to the price nervous capitalists could afford when pushed.

René looked up from his glass and caught the doubtful expression on his friend's face.

'I'm serious. I haven't seen anyone like this guy in Lhasa before. He was something else, but God knows what. He looked at me like I wasn't even human.' René's jaw clenched as he pictured Zhu's face; the ashen skin without even a hint of stubble and the black, unflinching eyes. 'He threatened me with Drapchi.'

'Drapchi? Jesus Christ.'

René nodded, his eyes suddenly very afraid. He thought back to the interrogation; Zhu perched on his plastic chair, the dampness of the cell and the endless wafts of cigarette smoke. He had never felt helplessness like it.

'But first things first,' René's friend continued. 'They've got to find them and from what you've said, that's not going to be so easy.'

'I know. I haven't a clue where they've gone. I got news back from the herders that they didn't go all the way to Makalu, but some pissing little village called Menkom. After that, they just seem to have vanished into thin air. They left nearly three weeks ago. Hardly any food, no porters . . .'

'So where the hell are they?'

'You tell me. But one thing is for sure: I either find them, and hand them over to Zhu, or I lose my restaurant and my employees . . .' René stopped talking, looking down at the table. He hadn't told anyone about Anu yet.

There was a pause as both men reviewed the gravity of his situation. Then, shifting his chair closer to the table, his companion advised him: 'In a place like Tibet, you look after just one person – yourself.' He jerked one thumb towards his chest. 'We're all fucked anyway. It's just a matter of time.' He gave a wry grin and raised his glass. 'Here's to being between a rock and a hard place.'

René reached for his own glass, then paused for a second.

'I'll do whatever they tell me,' he said, turning the glass in his fingers and watching the brandy slosh against its sides. 'But I'm going to make Zhu wish he'd never walked into my restaurant. That much, my friend, I can promise you.'

The two men downed their drinks in one. René wiped his mouth with his sleeve before taking a long drag on his cigarette, blowing the smoke up into the whirling blades of the ceiling fan. He inhaled again, but this time it triggered a coughing fit. His cheeks flushed even redder. After several seconds of convulsing he settled back down again, the unnatural colour draining from his face. The man opposite looked on with interest.

'René, can I ask you a question?'

He nodded.

'Since you're going to the mountains, you ever thought it might be a good idea to quit those damn' things?'

René looked across at his friend, his expression suddenly sober.

'You should know better by now,' he said. 'I'm not a quitter.'

Chapter 33

Luca stared down into the neighbouring valley, his eyes still wide with shock.

Near the top of an immense cliff, a cluster of buildings perched hundreds of feet above the valley floor. They were painted white, punctuated by the hundreds of narrow black windows that dotted their vast, sloping façades. Stairways rose from the lower slopes, hewn out of the same rock as the cliff-face and snaking up through the mass of buildings, interlocking here and there before tracking off in different directions. The focal point of the whole scene was the sheet copper roof of the main building that flashed gold in the morning sun. From its sides, long banners of pale blue silk billowed softly in the breeze.

Shara stood next to him, her eyes moving over each building in turn.

'The Monastery of Geltang,' she said softly. 'I've waited my whole life to see this.'

'It's like a mirage,' Luca said, then turning to her, his voice urgent despite his exhaustion, 'where are we, Shara? What is this place?'

She shook her head. 'All you need to know is that it's a monastery, a safe place where we can get help for Bill. Save your strength. We still have a valley to cross.'

She turned back towards Bill who was lying against a rock. His head had slumped to one side. She knelt down, cupping his chin in her hands.

Bill's eyes were half-closed, their bloodshot whites just visible, and his mouth hung open, spittle collecting at the corners. His hair was slicked down with sweat and his whole body trembled violently. He was in the full grip of the fever now – soon the delirium would start. As she felt down under his thighs to check the makeshift bandages, a watery mixture of blood and pus seeped out across her hand.

'The infection has come on so fast,' she said, tears of guilt pricking her eyes. 'He's lost so much blood . . .'

Bill could see her face above his: the swathe of long black hair, the green eyes wide with concern. Then he heard her voice again, but this time only fragments of what she said made sense. There was a rushing sound, as if she were speaking from behind a waterfall. He heard her say something to Luca. A monastery . . . A valley to cross . . .

'Bill.'

Through the waterfall, he heard his name spoken from a distance, then Luca's face was right before him.

Now his feet were stumbling across a path, his climbing boots dragging over the rocks and kicking up dust. Stones showered down beside them as they descended into the new valley and he could hear the sound of his own breathing filling his head. It was heavy, laboured, blocking everything else out.

Colours swam across his vision: the dull brown of the path, flashes of blue as his head briefly rolled back towards the sky, and then back to the arid land again.

Then came a brilliant white. It was intense, burning out every other colour. He squinted against it, his whole world painfully bright, before realising that it was the sun reflecting off huge marble steps.

He could hear breathing again, louder now. It was Luca, his face pressed right against Bill's as he hauled him up the steps, one at a time.

Then there was a dull crack and Bill felt his head recoil. He lay still, face down on the marble steps, where Luca had missed his footing and fallen. A warm, salty taste filled his mouth. Blackness edged around his vision like spilled ink, growing thicker, closing around him, blotting out the brilliant white.

An image of Cathy came to him then. She was curled up on the sofa in the living room, a blanket over her legs. He was there with her. She was smiling. She was smiling because he was there.

'Come on!'

Luca's voice.

'Come on, Bill! Stay with me. We're nearly there.'

He could hear the edge of panic and wondered why Luca was so upset. Why was he shouting at him?

Another voice. Female. Not Cathy. The swathe of black hair was back again and he felt himself being lifted once more. The stairs. The bleached out white.

To his right, he heard an animal groan as Luca fought with every ounce of strength in his thighs to climb the final few steps into an open courtyard. Luca felt a muscle in his lower back tear and his body buckled to one side, but he kept pumping with his legs, dragging Bill forward.

Luca's eyes were wide, staring straight ahead. There was a manic light to them as the adrenaline disconnected him from all feeling in his body. Every emotion was blocked, bypassed by the single need to reach the top. He had to finish, had to reach the summit. Nothing mattered except reaching the summit.

They came out into a courtyard of grey flagstones, warmed by the sun. A line of wide-leafed trees ran through the centre, each surrounded by a scattering of fallen white and purple blossom. Further back, just visible through some archways, another smaller stairway seemed to lead to a separate complex of buildings.

'Find . . . someone,' Luca panted as he laid Bill down on the flagstones, his breathing so laboured he could barely get the words out. For a moment Shara stood motionless, her mind blank and her eyes dull with exhaustion.

'Shara! Wherever the hell you've taken us . . . get some help!'

She looked at him for a moment, something like fear flickering across her face. Then she seemed to gather herself and nodded, stumbling off towards one of the many archways.

Luca turned back to attend to Bill. He sat with his own legs out straight, resting Bill's head on the top of his thigh. Looking down at his friend's face, he saw the broken nose from where they had fallen on the marble step. Blood crawled down the side of his face like the trails of a spider's web.

'We've made it, mate,' Luca whispered. 'We did it.'

There was not a flicker of response. Bill's head stayed slumped to one side, his eyes closed. Luca shook his shoulder gently.

'Stay awake, Bill. That's all you've got to do. Stay awake for just a few more minutes.'

Luca peered more closely at his friend's face. There wasn't a hint of movement. He bent forward, pressing his ear against Bill's mouth, listening for any sign that he was breathing. Nothing.

'No. No. No,' Luca repeated, panic rising in him as he put two fingers against Bill's throat, pressing down to feel for a pulse. He stared at his fingers, stained with a mixture of blood and dirt, willing them to find a heartbeat. All he could hear was the hammering of his own chest.

Forcing himself to slow his breathing, Luca closed his eyes and concentrated. Gradually, he began to feel the faint flutter coming from Bill's throat. It was so weak it was barely perceptible, running fast and irregular – but it was there.

Luca tilted back his head, breathing out a long sigh of relief, and let his eyes scan the buildings encircling them. There was a stillness to them that made him feel the whole place hadn't seen movement for centuries, and now they were the first to trespass upon it.

Opening directly off the courtyard, the façade of the main building towered over them. Proportioned against the mountains the monastery had been impressive, but only now that he was up close did Luca understand the true scale of his surroundings. Walls reached up, smooth and unbroken, for hundreds of feet above them, cut into the rock of the mountain itself.

Behind him, he heard the sound of footsteps and turned to see a group of three monks following Shara through an archway. Each had a shaven head and wore a long cornflower blue robe that billowed with the speed of their approach. Before Luca had managed to get to his feet, a short man who was plainly the leader came to stand before him, arms folded across his chest.

Shara appeared by his side.

'This is Drang, the aide to Geltang's chief physician. They're going to take Bill to him now.'

Luca looked at him, taking in the raised, twisting scar that ran from the crown of Drang's head all the way down to his left eyebrow, making it droop slightly. He looked to be about forty years old, short and very stocky, with eyes shadowed by a heavy brow. His hair was shaved to stubble, while years spent exposed to the harsh Tibetan sun had turned his skin the colour of hardwood. His right arm was bare, the veins crossing his powerful forearm standing out in jagged lines.

Drang motioned to the two other monks who quickly moved to either side of Bill and hoisted him up by his shoulders and legs. Both strained under his weight, then, adjusting their balance, moved off towards the far stairway.

'Hey, wait!' Luca said, raising one hand. He made to follow, shuffling forward whilst clutching his lower back. But before he could move more than a couple of steps Drang's arm shot out, grabbing the front of his Gore-Tex jacket so that he was stopped dead in his tracks.

'What the hell . . .' Luca said in surprise, staring down at the beefy monk. He was nearly a foot taller than Drang but only half his build, with barely the strength to stand. As Luca reached up to force his hand away, Shara stepped forward, speaking urgently in Tibetan.

A moment later, Drang's fist slowly unclenched, releasing the front of Luca's jacket and he stepped back a pace.

'I'm sorry, Luca. Drang just meant for you to stay out of the way,' Shara explained. 'Time is running out for Bill. We should not disturb them.'

Luca shook his head slowly, his mind fogged by tiredness.

'Is he going to be all right?'

'We'll do everything we can, I promise.' Then, taking Luca by the arm, she led him to the far side of the courtyard with Drang following silently in their wake.

'I know you're worried and have a thousand questions, but we're all exhausted. Drang will lead you to some quarters where you can wash and sleep. I'm going to do the same, but I'll be waiting for you when you wake. I promise I'll answer all your questions then.'

Luca stared at her, the weight of fatigue overwhelming his suspicion. He could feel himself swaying. That final climb, carrying Bill across the valley and up those stairs, had drained every last vestige of strength from his body.

'As soon as you hear any more about Bill . . .'

'I promise to let you know,' Shara said, with a faint smile. 'Bill's a strong man. He'll make it through this.'

They walked up to a thick, wooden door set under one of the courtyard's arches. With a stabbing movement of his hand, Drang motioned for Luca to continue into the shadowed interior of the monastery.

With a final glance at Shara, Luca ducked his head and stepped inside.

As the door closed behind him Shara leaned against one of the vaulted pillars, resting her forehead on the hard stone. Her legs trembled from sheer exhaustion and she felt a wave of nausea pass over her. She stood like this for a moment, trying to muster the strength to move, when suddenly she heard a voice directly behind her.

'What have you done?'

Spinning around, she saw a figure advancing out of the shadows. The silhouette of a man moved towards her like an apparition. Then, as it was illuminated by the full light of day, she saw that the figure was thin and angular, with a body bent from age and robes hanging loose around it. The face was deathly pale except for some patches of brown, sun-damaged skin visible beneath his balding white hair.

'I said, what have you done?'

The eyes . . . there was something wrong with his eyes. Shara found herself staring into milky-white irises. The sockets too were damaged by some long-ago injury. And yet those eyes seemed to stare directly at her, blank but somehow accusing.

'I . . . I . . . don't know what you mean,' she stammered back in Tibetan, feeling herself recoil as the figure moved closer.

'You may have shown courage by taking your brother's place, but you have now disgraced him. And us,' the man hissed, a vein sticking out on the side of his neck as if a worm had been caught under its skin. 'You have brought outsiders to our monastery. You risk everything that we have spent centuries trying to protect!'

'But I had no choice . . . he was going to die.'

'You of all people should know the value of what we have here. If they ever discover . . .' The figure lapsed into silence.

'Gather your strength.' He signalled impatiently for Shara to follow him along one wall of the courtyard, towards another entrance. 'You are going to tell me everything you know.'

Chapter 34

Cloud lay thick across the valley. It covered everything, wrapping around the crooked sides of mountains and smoothing flat the twisted valleys in between. Beyond its reach, Geltang Monastery perched high on its rock-face like a giant eyrie, its sheer walls basking in the warmth of the morning sun.

Behind one of the endless lines of open windows Dorje stared out, his hands clasped behind his back and his eyes half-closed as they squinted against the glare of the sun. His normally placid expression had sharpened. A deep vertical worry line creased the centre of his forehead. He breathed in deeply, nostrils flaring as they drew in cool air from outside, and tried to steady his nerves.

His eyes followed the same line of jagged peaks he had witnessed each morning for the last thirty-six years. But today he looked upon the mountains afresh, each knife-edged ridge and towering summit so magnificent and perfect that he could scarcely believe the beauty of them all. It was only now that he felt such awe. Only now that he knew they were threatened.

Dorje slowly shook his head. Thirty-six years since he had first arrived at Geltang as a young novice monk, and in all that time he had never felt as uncertain as he did right now. Despite all their preparations, despite their every precaution, the impossible had happened: foreigners had finally discovered the monastery.

Swivelling round, he set off down the corridor with un-accustomed haste. Passing the nearest flight of steps, Dorje turned left at the end of the corridor, then right, coming to a halt in front of a heavy gilded door. He raised his hand to knock, then stopped, his head slowly slumping forward until his forehead was resting against the wooden doorframe.

He had to get Rega to agree with him.

Rega and he were equals in the monastery, second only to His Holiness the Abbot. They had ruled every facet of the order for over a decade while the Abbot gradually withdrew into himself, as custom dictated. As his enlightenment became such that he reached the highest levels of the Wheel of Life, so his introspection grew ever-more intense. Now the Abbot was almost never seen outside his quarters, becoming a hermit within his own monastery.

He had been their great leader, the monk who had first begun the long and dangerous process of bringing the treasure to Geltang, and yet now the Abbot so detached from life at the monastery that he had become almost a myth within his own lifetime. As each year passed and the Abbot's concerns grew esoteric, the daily responsibilities of running the monastery had increasingly been delegated to them.

In the present crisis, it was vital that the frayed network of alliances throughout their order be pulled together rather than allowed to splinter apart. A schism would threaten the very heart of all they held secret.

Lifting his chin up and smoothing his robe, Dorje knocked firmly on the door and entered.

The room was badly lit, and it took a moment for his eyes to adjust to the dark. The only source of light was a narrow window in the far corner and the huge, vaulted room seemed to swim in a grey half-light.

Rega sat on a massive wooden chair, raised on a dais in the centre. His angular body slumped back against it, dwarfed by the chair's giant frame. Standing to one side was a second figure, its identity lost in the shadows. It turned at the sound of Dorje's approach and the monk immediately recognised the muscular form of Rega's chief aide, Drang.

Rega looked up, his blind eyes fixing unerringly on the new arrival.

'Dorje,' he said, the word more a fact that a form of greeting.

Dorje gave a brief nod before striding purposefully forward, coming to a halt a few paces away from the chair. He glanced at Drang, standing to one side.

'Leave us,' he said with a wave of dismissal.

For the briefest of moments Drang's eyes fixed on Rega. Then he bowed low, keeping his eyes locked on Dorje, before retreating silently from the room.

'I have come to decide what must be done,' Dorje said, standing with his hands folded in front of him. 'We need to make our recommendation to His Holiness.'

Rega's cowled head slowly tilted to one side.

'You know as well as I do what must be done,' he said, his voice little more than a whisper. 'It is whether you have the courage to make that choice.'

Dorje paused before asking, 'So what would you have us do?'

Rega's hands lay open across his lap as if appealing to the heavens.

'We cannot risk them ever leaving. From this day onward, the Westerners must be forced to stay at Geltang.'

Dorje exhaled slowly, glancing away from Rega's lifeless gaze and staring towards the window and its single shaft of light.

'You know we cannot do that. Not since our order was founded has such a course ever been followed . . .'

'Nor have we ever had such visitors!' Rega suddenly roared, pulling himself to his feet. 'We cannot let them back into the outside world and put at risk everything we have worked for. Others will inevitably follow and I, above anyone else, know the consequences of that.'

'The consequences are not always the same.'

Rega's lip curled in disdain. He stepped off the dais, the movements of his old body fluid and self-assured within his chambers, and stopped only a few inches away from Dorje.

'Look into my broken eyes and tell me that again,' he hissed, throwing the cowl of his robe back so that his whole head was exposed. 'I have suffered experiences you cannot possibly imagine. The last thing these eyes saw was our monks being butchered and the sacred treasure burning. And you dare suggest that the consequences will not be the same?'

Dorje found himself retreating a pace. Then he stiffened his back and replied in a measured voice.

'I think perhaps your judgement on this matter is clouded. They are not Chinese, these men, but simple climbers. And you would do well to remember that, although they did not know it, they were actually the ones who ensured our treasure was delivered safely.'

'They acted unwittingly!' Flecks of spittle shot from Rega's mouth as he spoke. 'Imagine how differently they would have acted if they knew what she was delivering.'

Dorje shrugged his shoulders, his frown line deepening.

'These are uncertain times, but I believe they must serve some purpose in being here. The will of Buddha brought them to our gates. We cannot judge them, nor condemn them, without first understanding why they are here. I understand the suspicion you must feel, given all that you have been through . . .' Dorje's voice trailed off.

'You understand?' Rega sneered. 'You understand what, exactly?'

There was a pause, the tension between them heightened by the absolute quiet in the chamber.

'Do you know why they lined up the older monks?' Rega asked softly.

Dorje was bemused. 'What are you talking about?'

'They lined them up because it was not practical to bring them back over the mountain pass. They would have slowed the soldiers down too much. Instead, a novice was chosen and a gun placed in his hands. Then . . . BANG!' Rega clapped his hands together, the noise echoing loudly. 'The Abbot was shot first. Then they did away with all our most venerable fathers, one by one, while the rest of our order stood by, watching by the light of our own burning monastery.'

Light from the window cut across Rega's face. All the colour had drained from his cheeks.

'But I never saw the others die,' he continued. 'By then I had lost my sight. I just heard the endless cracks of the rifles.'

Dorje looked down at the ground. A well of sickening emotion flooding through him – pity mixed with revulsion at such violence. He had always known that Rega had escaped from one of the earliest *beyuls*, but in all their time together, he had never once heard him speak of it.

'You are right,' Dorje said slowly. 'I cannot imagine what you have been through. I apologise for my presumption.'

Rega brushed off the remark, his expression still harsh.

'Unless you wish to stand by and watch history repeat itself, the foreigners must be forced to remain here. That is the only solution.'

As he spoke there was a rap on the door and Drang quietly stepped inside. He made to approach them but Dorje's hand shot out, gesturing him to wait.

'Even if we agreed to it, how do you propose to detain the Westerners?' he asked, his voice kept low so that only Rega could hear.

Rega leaned closer to him, so Dorje could smell the musty aroma of his robes.

'The Perfect Life. We must force them to take it.'

Dorje's eyes widened in surprise. Before he could speak Rega had signalled for Drang to approach.

'A messenger from the Abbot,' Drang announced.

Behind him a tall boy of about fourteen hesitantly shuffled into the room. The boy's robes clung to his gangly body and he moved awkwardly, as if too tall for his age. He came to a halt a few metres away from the dais and dropped into a low bow. As he pulled himself vertical once again, he reached out his right hand which contained a tightly-rolled scroll. He presented it in the direction of Rega then, realising his mistake, quickly moved his arm so that it was pointing towards Dorje instead.

Dorje gathered himself and moved towards the boy.

'Thank you, Norbu,' he said softly. He knew how flustered the Abbot's aide could become by just the simplest change in his routine. Dorje's eyes quickly scanned the parchment.

'We are to keep the Westerners separate and to observe them. That is the Abbot's decree.'

'But it is for us to advise him,' Rega protested. 'Does he not wish to hear our voice on such a matter? And what of the Council of Elders?'

Dorje didn't answer but simply released the corners of the parchment, allowing it to roll back on itself. He stood lost in thought while Rega began pacing up and down in front of the dais.

'I do not like what has been happening recently,' he proclaimed, his thin fingers balled into fists. 'Strange things have happened that have never been allowed before. Two weeks ago a boy arrived who did not pass our initiation and was not of age, yet he was shown directly to the Abbot's quarters . . . And now this mild treatment of Westerners. Does the Abbot not realise that they could destroy everything?' He pointed to Norbu, standing with his head bowed subserviently. 'You, Abbot's messenger, who was that boy exactly? You are the one charged with looking after him, are you not?'

Norbu's eyes looked to Dorje pleadingly then back to Rega.

'He . . . he is from Lhasa, venerable father,' he answered, stuttering slightly. 'The third son of the Depon family.'

'Indeed. And, tell me, who is his father?'

Norbu's cheeks flooded with colour. He rocked back and forth, shoulders hunched from tension. His lips moved silently as he tried to articulate the sentence and hold back his stammer.

'He is the honourable Gyaltso Depon, second . . . second governor of the city of Lhasa.'

Dorje swept forward, coming between Rega and the boy.

'Enough of this!' he said. 'This boy is just a messenger.' Then his voice became gentler as he put a hand on Norbu's shoulder. 'Go to the Abbot, child, and inform His Holiness that we will honour his request to keep the Westerners separate and observed.'

With obvious relief Norbu scuttled out of the chamber, eyeing Drang warily as he squeezed past him and out of the door.

Dorje inhaled deeply. 'I will set watch on the taller Westerner, you the injured one. I understand that your physicians are working on him now.'

Rega gave a distracted nod.

'Well then,' Dorje continued, 'we shall wait and see what the will of Buddha decrees.' He then turned towards the exit. 'And, Rega, you have every right to be sceptical of foreigners, but we must wait for them to reveal their true natures. We must allow them to show themselves to us, and if they act honourably, if they respect and understand Geltang's true purpose, then perhaps they will make the decision for us.'

Rega remained absolutely still, so that Dorje wondered if he had even heard what had been said.

'We all agree that the Perfect Life is not a decision to be taken lightly,' Dorje added in the face of Rega's silence, then swept out of the room.

Rega waited until the door had closed before pulling his cowl over his head once again. It cast a deep shadow over the top half of his face, leaving only his jutting chin visible beneath. A long time ago he had watched calamitous events unfold in this way, seen so much lost due to the inaction of others.

This time there would be no such mistake.

Chapter 35

Captain Zhu stood at the head of the pathway, watching the trail of soldiers pass beneath him in single file.

The eight soldiers from the SOF unit in Chengdu had arrived before dawn at Gonkar airport on a special charter Ilyushin IL-76 jet. As the vast balloon tyres slowly ground to a halt and the rear of the plane lowered with a hiss of hydraulics, Zhu had watched the soldiers swiftly clamber out and on to the waiting trucks. He didn't need the files he'd been faxed on each one of them to know they were professionals. You could see it from the way they moved.

Over two days of travelling had followed on hard, sun-baked roads. They had then left the trucks and started walking along meandering trails, the soldiers maintaining an unrelenting pace. Each carried an enormous pack, their QBZ-95 assault rifles held loosely in front of them. At the slightest noise, the butt of the rifles instinctively shifted up into their shoulders while their thumb clicked off the safety catch. They would stand perfectly still, eyes scanning their surroundings, bodies tense, as they waited for the all clear. Despite the comparatively easy terrain, it was obvious that none of them was taking anything for granted.

Zhu had commanded this kind of man before: every movement drilled into them by training, every order completed with detached professionalism. For them, the mission objectives changed, but the realities of life in the field was always the same. For hour after hour they marched along in the mountain heat, utterly indifferent to it, while the remainder of the group struggled to keep pace.

Lumbering along at the back, two hundred yards behind the last in line, was the bearish frame of René Falkus. Completely at odds with the military green of the others, he wore thick brown corduroy trousers and a pale blue shirt. A spotted red and white handkerchief was tied round his neck in a vain effort to absorb the rivulets of sweat running down from his hairline, while his chest heaved in the thin mountain air. Already the sun had seared his forehead and cheeks a painful pink and he squinted, eyes half closed, against its harsh light.

René glanced up to see Zhu standing high above the path, watching the line of men move past. For a moment their eyes met before René wiped the sweat from his forehead with the sleeve of his shirt and trudged on. He settled back into his normal pace, his eyes reverting to the spot they had been trained on all day.

Three from the back of the line and marching purposefully ahead was the only member of the team who had been taken from Lhasa, aside from Chen and Zhu himself. And the moment René had stepped up into the truck, he had recognised the same shaven head and thickset neck he had seen in the interrogation room. It was the brute who had raped little Anu. And now here he was, walking along the path, only a few hundred feet ahead.

Since they'd first set out René had found it almost impossible to tear his eyes away from the man. He studied the weathered hands stuffing rations into a rucksack; the jaw moving slackly as the man chewed and spat out tobacco. Even his blank expression drew René's gaze. And yet, each time the man looked up, René found himself avoiding eye contact, like a schoolchild with the class bully.

Later he had learned that the man's name was Xie and that he was nothing to do with the other soldiers. He was a rank private from a conscript division, and at first René had wondered why he was here at all. He looked so disorganised and out of place, nothing more than a thuggish brawler amongst professionals. He shuffled from one task to the next, his beady eyes always fixed on the others, making poor attempts to mimic their movements.

Then it had occurred to René. Zhu had brought him along for his benefit. It was a sick way of controlling him; a daily reminder of little Anu's rape and what else could happen if he refused to help the Chinese.

René looked up ahead to where the route narrowed and the path twisted its way around the side of a colossal mountain range. Above the foothills he could see the beginnings of a sheer-sided rock-face rising up to the snowline. Beyond it, the entire mid-section of the mountain was lost behind a thick layer of cloud.

The soldiers' boots crunched to a halt ahead of him. René stopped, thankful for the rest, and watched as Chen walked back down the line and stopped in front of Zhu. He was holding a military issue map and a GPS in his other hand.

'We are on the outskirts of another village, sir,' he said.

Zhu looked up at the ridge and the smoke curling into the sky.

'Which one?'

'The last, Captain. It's called Menkom.'

They both walked to the front of the line. An old monk was sitting on a mound of earth, basking in the sunshine.

'Ask him if he has seen any Westerners pass this way,' Zhu said, motioning for Chen to translate.

Chen spoke a few words in halting Tibetan but the old monk stayed silent, staring right through him, his prayer wheel spinning with gentle sweeps of his wrist.

'Foreigners,' Chen repeated again, sensing the soldiers pulling up behind him to watch what was going on. 'Have you seen any?'

The monk didn't answer.

Inclining his head so it was only an inch from the old man's ear, Chen whispered in Tibetan, 'Don't make it hard on yourself, old man. I know you understand me.'

There was a faint crunch of gravel as someone shifted their weight from one leg to the next and then the soft, crackling sound of Zhu inhaling on his cigarette. They were all watching him. Waiting for him to do something. Still the monk didn't answer.

Biting down on his bottom lip, Chen swung back his arm and brought the flat of his hand whipping across the old monk's face. The slap sent him rolling back through the dirt, knocking the prayer wheel he had been holding out of his hand.

Zhu took a step forward, idly picking it up, his left hand stroking the line of beads. The old monk stared up at him from the ground, watching him finger his most sacred possession.

'You need to be more persuasive,' Zhu said. 'He doesn't seem to understand.'

For a split second Chen hesitated. Then he moved forward again, grabbing the monk by the front of his tunic and lifting him off his feet. The old man swung in his hands like a rag doll, toes paddling the air as if still trying desperately to connect with the ground.

Chen stared into his eyes, willing him to say something, anything. He knew how far the captain would take this just on a whim.

'For Christ's sake, put him down,' René said, pushing his way to the front of the group. Chen paused, still holding the monk in the air, while Zhu spun round, his black eyes hardening.

'This monk wears a red robe, or what's left of one anyway,' said René. 'That means he's part of the Gelugpa sect and they often take a vow of silence. Even if he wanted to answer, from the look of him he probably lost the power of speech years ago.'

There was a pause as Chen looked at Zhu and Zhu stared at René, trying to assess whether he was telling the truth. René could feel sweat gathering in pools under his arms.

Eventually Zhu gave a brief nod and Chen released his grip on the old monk who crumpled in a heap on the ground.

'Thank you for enlightening us,' Zhu said, with a smile that didn't reach his eyes. He then moved closer, whispering into René's ear, 'Interfere again and I will have one of the soldiers break your legs.'

René stared at the ground as Zhu flicked away his cigarette and without another word, continued up the trail towards the village. The other soldiers hoisted their packs and followed, leaving René standing next to Chen.

'Must have been scary, huh?'

Chen turned, surprised to hear the Westerner speak to him.

'A pacifist the same age as my grandmother. And all you've got is a machine gun.'

As he spoke, René looked directly into Chen's eyes and for the briefest moment, thought he saw a trace of doubt there. He opened his mouth to say something more but Chen grabbed his shoulder, swivelling him round so he faced the village once more.

'Back in line,' he said in broken English, pushing René forward.

Ahead of them Zhu walked on, finally coming to a halt in the central part of the village. His eyes ranged over a few of the villagers lying emaciated and sick in their doorways, unmoved even by the sight of a Chinese patrol.

A stream of water trickled past each house, wending its way around piles of rubbish that had been left to putrify in the mud. Bottles, old bits of rope and plastic bags were scattered over the ground. A few goats and a dog sniffed through the rubbish in front of one of the larger houses. The dog was bone-thin, its ribs visible through its matted coat as it chewed on the end of a splintered bone. As Zhu watched, the dog's jaw widened and it retched. It sniffed a couple of times, then started eating its own vomit.

Zhu approached one of the piles of rubbish, his boots squelching in the soft mud by the stream. He moved slowly, eyes scanning the ground. From his years of experience at the PSB, it was something he did automatically. Rubbish was the one thing everyone forgot to hide. A hundred yards further up he stopped, eyes settling on a small, plastic bottle partially concealed in the dirt. With the tip of his boot, he carefully flipped over the object and peered down at the writing. It was in English – an empty bottle of painkillers.

The Westerners had been here after all.

Zhu allowed himself a brief smile. Along the last stretch of the trail, he had started to worry that they had broken off earlier and headed up the mountains. The sheer walls of rock looked impassable to him, but then again, he didn't pretend to be any kind of mountaineer. But this village was the end of the trail. They must have started climbing from here.

Pulling a white handkerchief from his pocket, Zhu dabbed his forehead. The sun was directly above them now, its glare intensified by the rarefied mountain air. Moving back a few paces towards one of the larger wooden shacks, he stood under its eaves by the front door, his eyes gradually adjusting to the shadow.

A moment later he saw Chen approaching, striding across the open ground.

'Your orders, sir?'

'Set up camp in the lower fields away from this place,' he said, eyes taking in the rest of the houses where a few of the villagers sat languidly on the steps. 'The Westerners were here and somebody saw something. Line up the women by the stream for questioning. And, Lieutenant, don't stop until you find out exactly what they know.'

'Yes, sir. And the rest of the village?'

Zhu paused for a moment in thought, his hands clasped lightly behind his back. He was about to speak when he felt something behind him brush against his right hand. He flinched, spinning round on his heel in alarm.

Lying on the wooden doorstep of the house was a small boy in an oversized shirt that was bleached by dirt and age. He had been tucked behind a decrepit bench by the door and Zhu hadn't even noticed him when he had first come in under the shade. While they had been speaking, he had crawled forward and stretched up to touch the nailless fingers of Zhu's right hand in an effort to get his attention. The boy looked up at him with pleading eyes, his scrawny body ravaged by cholera.

'Help us,' he breathed, his chest working up and down from the effort, making his collar bones stand out under his sunken skin. From the look on his face, it was all too obvious what he was saying. Zhu didn't need a translation.

Zhu stared down at him, frozen by the physical contact. His eyes ran over the boy's small hands, dirtied and grasping as they pulled on his fingers once again, touching the stretched skin on the tips where his nails had once been.

Wrenching his arm free, Zhu stumbled back into the harsh sunlight, his lips curled in revulsion. He frantically wiped his right hand on the side of his trousers, retreating as far from the child as he could.

'Burn the village,' he hissed, wiping his hand one last time and placing it deep in his trouser pocket. He looked across at Chen who stood bewildered by the front step of the house.

'Burn it to the ground.'

Chapter 36

Luca opened his eyes to see the afternoon sun slanting through the open window. For a moment he lay flat on the narrow bunk, staring out vacantly across the small, bare room. Then he exhaled slowly and dragged himself to his feet. Every muscle in his body felt stretched and bruised and there was a dull thumping in his head.

Moving over to a porcelain bowl by the bed, he wet a small cloth and ran it over his face and hands. The palms of his hands were still stained black with dried blood. By the time he wrung out the cloth, the water had turned the colour of rust.

Last night's ordeal was coming back to him in flashes now: Bill's piercing scream by the cave, the burning sensation in his own arms and legs as he'd clambered after Shara. It had taken every ounce of his strength to get them to the monastery, and despite what he sensed must have been a long, deep sleep, he still felt weak and depleted.

Leaving the cloth by the basin, Luca stepped up to the window and took in the view. The monastery seemed just as unreal in the daylight. As he peered straight down from the ledge he saw that the building stretched away beneath him, level after level, to the mountain's base. It looked to be at least two hundred metres high, as if two large cathedrals had been stacked one on top of the other.

On the horizon was a series of interlocking valleys. Each had layers of green terraced fields running round the side of the mountains in narrow bands, like the contours on a map. Luca could just make out the silhouettes of people, planting long rows of crops, their backs hunched as they worked the earth.

'Geltang Monastery.' Luca said the words out loud, as if they would make more sense that way. What was this place? A secret sect of monks, hidden away in the mountains? But if so, what were they all doing here, and how had Shara known about them in the first place?

A knock on the door made him swing round in surprise, causing his back to spasm. Reaching behind him to lean on the bed, he was still cursing softly as the door was unbolted from the outside.

From the shadows of the corridor, a monk appeared in the doorway.

'*Tashi delek*, Mr Matthews. I trust you have slept well?'

The man must have been somewhere between forty and fifty, but it was hard to tell given the perfectly smooth texture of his skin. His head was shaved in the traditional monastic style above gently upward-slanting eyes, and he wore the same cornflower blue robes as Luca had seen on the monks who had taken Bill away. The man extended a hand in greeting, his lips curving into a faint smile.

'My name is Dorje,' he said, his voice gentle and deliberate. 'I am one of the few at Geltang who speak English, and have been instructed to be your guide.'

'Hello,' Luca said, offering his hand. Dorje shook it while studying Luca openly, his expression one of unhurried calm. Luca felt he should say something more to break the silence.

'Your English is very good,' he said finally.

'Thank you, Mr Matthews,' Dorje replied, his smile widening a little. 'Now, if you would please follow me, Miss Shara would like to see you. On the way, perhaps I will have a chance to acquaint you with a little more of our humble monastery.'

With that he set off sedately down the corridor, hands clasped behind his back like a college professor. Luca followed and, despite his aching legs, had to measure his stride to stop himself from stepping on the hem of Dorje's robe. They made their way down the tight corridor, passing flaming yak-butter lamps that had been lit in small alcoves cut into the stone walls.

'Is there any news of Bill?' Luca asked after a while, when it became obvious that Dorje's guided tour was going to be conducted in silence.

'Regrettably, it is too early to tell,' Dorje answered, speaking over his shoulder. 'Your companion was in very poor health when he arrived, but I understand that our physicians have been working on his legs all through the day.'

'But he is going to be OK, isn't he?'

'We must wait, Mr Matthews. We cannot do more than that.'

'Is he at least conscious?' said Luca, his voice rising a little. 'I'd really like to go and see how he's doing.'

Dorje paused by a wooden staircase.

'Miss Shara will be able to give you more information, so I must ask you to wait until then. For my part, I have been told that your companion needs complete rest and that it is impossible for you to see him at this time.'

The way he spoke suggested the matter was gently, but firmly, closed. He continued walking again. After a second Luca shrugged and followed, staring down at the back of his shaved head. A few hundred yards further they passed a wider section of hallway where two young monks were standing, speaking in low whispers. As Luca and Dorje passed, both gave low, respectful bows, but their eyes studied every movement Luca made.

'Can you tell me more about this place, Dorje? What is Geltang exactly?'

Dorje raised one arm, as if gesturing to the entire monastery.

'Geltang is a place of preservation. It is a repository of culture, wisdom and enlightenment.'

Luca nodded, waiting for him to elaborate, but Dorje lapsed into silence again.

'But why has it been built out here in the middle of nowhere?'

'Indeed, I must congratulate you on completing a most arduous journey. It is no small matter to reach our walls. But I am quite certain your training as a mountaineer stood you in good stead.'

'Yeah, it helped,' said Luca impatiently. 'But what about the monastery? Why's it been built so far up in the mountains?'

Dorje smiled apologetically.

'I'm afraid my English is not good enough to answer such questions adequately,' he said. 'Ah, but here we are already – the eastern balcony.'

They rounded a corner and the corridor opened up into a vast terraced area made of huge white marble flagstones and surrounded by gleaming walls. The only splashes of colour on the terrace came from an array of miniature trees and plants, similar to Japanese bonsai, which studded the walls in small, individual alcoves.

At the centre, a stone fountain poured water into a shallow receptacle below. The overflow of water then travelled through an open channel in the ground until it reached the balcony's edge where it fell hundreds of feet down, past the foundations of the monastery and on to the cliffs below.

Spectacular as the balcony was, it was not designed to be introspective. As the water tumbled down like a moving sheet of glass, it drew the eye to the view above it.

Luca's gaze was directed upwards, coming to a halt halfway up the perfect lines of a familiar mountain.

'I don't believe it,' he said, forgetting the stiffness in his legs as he stepped eagerly forward. 'It's actually here.'

Framed by two larger peaks in the foreground, he could see the chiselled outline of the pyramid mountain. There could be no mistake – this was the same mountain he had seen all those weeks ago on Makalu. Despite the summit being concealed by a thick layer of cloud and the lower flanks lost to surrounding foothills, it still looked absolutely magnificent.

'It's unbelievable.'

'Indeed,' Dorje replied softly.

Both men stood gazing at the view. As Luca's eyes traced the sides of the mountain he imagined himself up there, slowly picking a route along the cracks in the rock, gradually working higher until he reached the very top.

'Always cloud,' he muttered to himself before swinging round to face Dorje. 'I looked at so many satellite maps, trying to catch a glimpse of it, but the whole mountain was always covered by cloud.'

'That is its nature,' agreed Dorje. 'Like us, it prefers to remain hidden from the world.'

Luca nodded, turning back to the view. 'Has anyone climbed it?'

Dorje shrugged. 'While collecting herbs or performing similar errands, members of our order have certainly walked across its foothills.'

'And the summit? Has anyone been to the summit?'

Dorje sighed quietly.

'No one has been there. I am afraid we do not share your Western predilection for "conquering" such wondrous feats of nature.'

'Does it even have a name?'

'Name? No. No, Mr Matthews,' Dorje continued, his nose wrinkling a little, as if he had just noticed an unpleasant smell. 'Our mountain does not have a name. Just as climbing it would be an act of quantifying it, or, to put it another way, of being able to measure oneself against it, we believe naming it would have a similar effect. It is enough for us that it is simply there.'

Luca nodded distractedly. He drew his gaze away from the mountain and over the intervening valleys to where they stood. Now that he was here, he could see how similar the landscape was to that shown on the *thangka* Jack had given him. He thought back to the professor at Cambridge too and the comments she had made about the 'mountain *beyul*'. Dorje had said Geltang was a repository of enlightenment . . .

There had to be some kind of a connection.

Turning away from the mountain, Luca glanced over at Dorje.

'Is there a relationship between the mountain and the monastery?' he asked.

Dorje looked startled for an instant, then his expression assumed its habitual calm.

'Mr Matthews, I am just a lowly monk here at Geltang and nothing more than a humble translator. I think it best you talk to someone else more qualified to discuss such matters. But what I can tell you is that the mountain creates moisture. Its sheer presence generates clouds and precipitation, which in turn feed the crops you see in the fields below our monastery. We grow all that is consumed here and it is the mountain that enables our existence. Rare indeed for a place as inhospitable as the Himalayas.'

'I wasn't meaning the crops so much . . . more the religious significance. You said Geltang was a repository, right? Well . . .'

Luca's voice trailed off as Dorje turned away from him towards the entrance to the balcony.

'Ah,' he said, his expression clearing with relief. 'Miss Shara has arrived.'

Despite his growing frustration, Luca felt his pulse quicken as he turned to see Shara crossing the balcony towards them. She had changed from her climbing clothes and now wore blue monastic robes similar to Dorje's.

With uncharacteristic haste, Dorje moved off to greet her, walking round the side of the fountain and bowing low. As Luca watched, he clasped her hand in his and whispered something with an expression of utmost solemnity. After a moment Shara nodded and with a brief smile, came over to greet Luca, leaving Dorje by the fountain.

'It's good to see you,' Luca said, realising how much he meant it. He went to take her hand but Shara hesitated, pulling back from him and crossing her hands in front of her. There was a sudden air of formality about her that made Luca's smile quickly fade.

'Is everything OK?' he asked.

'How is your head?' she said, ignoring the question and studying his forehead where a cut ran back into his hairline.

'Got a hell of a hangover, but I'll be OK. More importantly, have you heard any more about Bill?'

'He's regained consciousness, but is still very weak. Now we have to wait to see how he copes with the secondary infections.'

Luca stared into her eyes. There was a distance there he had never seen before. Even when she had been angry with them in the village, she had at least been directing all her attention on them. Now there was a cool detachment in her manner that seemed so out of place given all they had been through together.

'But he is going to recover,' Luca persisted, dragging his mind back to Bill. 'We made it here in time, didn't we?'

'I don't know, Luca. We're just going to have to wait and see what happens.'

There was silence as her words sank in. Luca shut his eyes, thinking back to what had happened that night in the cave. The thoughts and images were still confused: the terrible silence, the fumbling in the dark, and then, right behind them, that almighty roar. He could remember the feeling of Shara's soft skin as she had pressed her face against his, whispering that a bear was in the cave.

Luca halted, mid-thought, and rewound the images in his mind. There was something about this that wasn't making sense.

'When you woke me in the cave, you were already dressed,' he said, slowly piecing it together. 'You were getting ready to leave, weren't you? You must have been planning to ditch us and head to Geltang on your own.'

Shara began to shake her head. 'Luca . . .'

He glanced across to where Dorje was slowly inspecting the line of plants set into marble alcoves. He looked entirely absorbed in what he was doing, but was easily close enough to hear their conversation. Luca refocused on Shara's face as if for the first time and lowered his voice. 'Bill was right about you. You were hiding something all along.'

Shara sighed and stared down at her hands. When she looked up again, the detachment was gone and her face suddenly showed subtle lines of anxiety and fatigue.

'What I told you was mostly true. The guide due to take me here had fallen sick and I needed your help to get above the rock-face. After that, you're right, I was going to head off alone into the Kooms and come all the way to Geltang. I didn't want to lie to you, Luca, but there is so much more to this than you realise.'

'So why were you coming here in the first place? I mean, what's a woman doing here amongst a load of monks?'

Shara paused, pushing back a strand of hair from her face.

'I was granted exceptional permission to come to Geltang because I was replacing my brother and delivering something.'

'Your brother? What's he got to do with all this? What was he delivering?'

'I can't tell you that. But please, Luca, don't ask any more questions. It's not . . .' she paused again, choosing her words carefully '. . . it's not wise for you to ask too many questions.'

'Come on, Shara. We went through hell up there and now you're telling me not to ask questions!'

'Keep your voice down,' she hissed, casting an eye towards Dorje. She leaned closer. 'Look, it doesn't matter what I was delivering, but please, just do exactly as Dorje says. I beg you.'

Luca looked at her, bewildered by the obvious sincerity in her eyes. Why was she so reluctant to answer any of his questions? They were already at the monastery. Surely the secret was out?

'Geltang is one of the hidden *beyuls*, isn't it?' he said suddenly. 'That's what you're trying to protect.'

Shara's eyes widened in surprise. 'Where did you hear that word?'

'That's what this place is, isn't it? It's one of those sanctuaries?'

'Don't talk about things you don't understand. Never mention that word again.'

Shara was glowering at him, as she had before at the village, then she stepped back a pace and inhaled deeply. The tension seemed to drop from her shoulders as she stared directly at him, her green eyes pleading once again.

'I know how determined you can be, Luca. But this is not something you should get involved with. Just let it go. All you have to do is wait until Bill gets better, then you two can leave and go back to England.'

'I'm only asking you to tell me what the hell is going on. I think I have a right to know.'

Shara was about to speak again when Dorje materialised behind them. He was staring at her and as he stepped closer, she dropped her gaze to the floor.

'It is time for evening prayers,' he said, a terse edge to his voice. 'Miss Shara, I am sure you will be wanting to get back to your quarters to prepare for the service.'

Shara nodded, her eyes catching Luca's for a moment before she moved away around the side of the fountain.

'Wait a second,' he protested, attempting to follow her, but Dorje gently grasped him by the arm, preventing him. Luca looked down in surprise at the mild-looking monk who had managed to stop him in his tracks.

'Mr Matthews, we have our own arrangements to attend to. Please do not concern yourself. You will see Miss Shara in only a few hours, after this evening's meal.'

'But I want to . . .'

Luca's sentence trailed off as he watched Shara stride past the fountain and with a final glance to where they stood, retreat into the inners of the monastery and disappear from view.

'Come, Mr Matthews,' Dorje said cordially, 'the eastern balcony is only one part of the monastery. There is still so much to see.'

For a moment Luca stood still, ignoring Dorje as he motioned for him to follow. Then he looked back towards the pyramid mountain. It was now completely shrouded in cloud.

There was something about this place that didn't add up, and he was going to find out what is was. With or without Shara's help.

Chapter 37

'Is that right?' Luca said, chasing a clump of starchy rice around his bowl.

He was seated at the small wooden table in the corner of his room with Dorje perched opposite. Arranged in a semi-circle before them was a series of white porcelain bowls that had arrived on a tray carried by Dorje. They contained a modest assortment of rice, pulses and vegetables which he'd been picking at half-heartedly for the last half-hour.

Since the trip to the eastern balcony Luca had been locked in his room, pacing restlessly from wall to wall, waiting until dinner and the chance to speak to Shara once again. But as Dorje had just politely explained she wouldn't be joining them this evening after all, nor did he know when she would be next available. Instead he continued with an endless litany of pleasantries while Luca's frustration steadily grew.

'That is indeed right,' Dorje replied. He then paused and inhaled deeply, possibly a prelude to yet another lengthy silence.

'One's duties must come before social visits and I am sure you understand that Miss Shara is most busy with her work. Now, have you eaten enough of the vegetable mo-mos? They are considered something of a delicacy here in Tibet and the ingredients are grown just below our monastery near the . . .'

'I understand that she's busy,' Luca interrupted, laying down his chopsticks. 'You've already told me that. But she said she would be here for dinner and promised to answer some of my questions then. There is so much about this place that doesn't make sense to me.'

Dorje gave a smile brimming with reassurance.

'I am sure Miss Shara will visit you when she is ready. All in good time.'

Luca exhaled in frustration, pushing away what was left of the food. His right hand instinctively reached down to his lower back, massaging the thin line of muscles he'd damaged on the last few steps of the stairway. The angle of the hard-backed chair was making them spasm painfully.

Where was Shara? Why wasn't she here? His desire for some answers pressed on him like a physical need. He felt sure that if he could just talk to her for longer, she would tell him the truth. Dorje had been skirting around it all day, evading every question with half-truths and obscure, rambling explanations.

There was just so much Luca wanted to know. Why had Geltang been carved out of the mountain and hidden away in such an in-accessible part of the Himalayas? Such a feat of engineering must have taken lifetimes to accomplish. And what were all the monks doing here in the first place, cloistered away from the outside world for centuries on end?

The mountain *beyul* – that's what the professor had said. It was the holiest of all the secret *beyuls*; the fulcrum about which the heart of Buddhism turned. Could Geltang really be that place? Could it be the ultimate goal that fortune hunters had been searching for all those years? Shara had certainly seemed defensive enough when he had hazarded the question.

Luca stared across at Dorje as he contentedly sipped his tea. Whatever the truth was, Dorje wasn't about to be the one to tell it. But Shara was different. There was a connection between them, some-thing that had grown out there in the mountains. He had felt it even as she had tried to keep him at a distance this morning on the balcony.

There was something about the look in her eyes when she had told him to do what Dorje said . . . as if she feared for him but was torn by some conflicting loyalty.

Luca stared across the table at Dorje, who was evidently enjoying the silence.

'I want to go and see Bill this evening, Dorje. I want to check that he's all right.'

The monk set down his cup carefully on the table in front of him.

'As you already know, Mr Taylor has secondary infections that are most dangerous at this time. It is absolutely imperative these are not complicated by a visit from you.'

'Come on, Dorje, all I want to do is look round the door and check on him. Where is he anyway? In a room near mine?'

'No, it's lower . . .' Dorje began, then quickly stopped himself. He inhaled, giving a small smile. 'Mr Matthews, you have been specifically asked not to interfere with the work of our physicians.'

'But all I want to do is see my friend! Surely you understand that, Dorje. I'm worried about him.'

There was a pause before the monk stood up and paced towards the open window. He peered through it for a moment as if inspecting something in the distance, despite the fact that it was already dark outside. As Luca's eyes bored into him he slowly turned back again, squaring off his chair with the table.

'You must understand that I am only a simple guide here at Geltang. It is not for me to make decisions on such matters and I am only passing on what I have been told. I do not want you to feel worried, Mr Matthews, but please understand – seeing Mr Taylor is quite impossible at this time. Now, why don't you try some of this tea from Samye Monastery? As I understand it, tea is something of a fascination with the British, is it not? Was it not one of your countrymen who said, "why have bread and water when they can so easily be tea and toast?"'

Dorje smiled amiably while Luca eyed him across the table,

wondering if Dorje really was the simple guide he claimed to be. There was something authoritative about the way he spoke, something that suggested he was far more adept at steering conversations than he let on. Luca studied him for a moment then his expression suddenly softened. He stood up, scraping back the legs of his chair on the stone floor.

'You know what, Dorje, you're right,' he said. 'I should just let the doctors get on with their job.'

Dorje raised an eyebrow and looked into his eyes.

'Well, yes,' he said. 'I am relieved to hear you say so. Your companion's welfare is really the most important thing now.'

'And we shouldn't jeopardise that by visiting him,' Luca continued.

'Quite so.'

'Well then, why don't we call it a night? Perhaps tomorrow, he'll be well enough for a visit.'

Dorje nodded approvingly, obviously feeling better for the sudden lift in the atmosphere. He gave Luca a nod and was turning to leave when he suddenly halted.

'But what about the tea?'

Luca smiled tightly. 'Why don't we save that for tomorrow, eh?'

Chapter 38

With a sudden burst of energy, Luca strode over to the open window of his room and looked down along the length of the outside wall.

'OK,' he whispered to himself, trying to steady his nerves. 'Piece of piss.'

The moon had risen above the far mountains and by its pale light he could see the many levels of the monastery stacked under him, the heavy stone walls disappearing into the darkness below. Dragging his sweaty palms across his trousers, he took another deep breath. Christ, it was a long way down.

He glanced back at the squat wooden door of his room. Dorje had left nearly two hours ago, locking it from the outside. Since then Luca had been lying on his bed, waiting for the sounds of the monastery to fade. Now everything was silent. It was the perfect time to break out.

After exhaling a few times in quick succession, he sat down on the windowsill and swung his legs round until they dangled over the outside edge. He could feel the cool night air on his face and his heart beat pulsed through the vein in his neck.

It was just a few simple moves. He could do this.

Sucking in his breath, he swivelled his body round and dangled from the edge of the windowsill, scraping the tips of his boots down until he could feel an indentation in the stone wall beneath. A sharp pain shot through from his lower back but he gritted his teeth and ignored it, extending his arms to slide lower down the wall.

Gripping tight with his right arm, he swung his left down, using his fingertips to hang on to a small fissure in the block of stone by his head. Then he leaned out, arching from his hips, so he could look down between his legs at the frame of the window directly beneath. It was just a few inches further.

Slowly releasing the grip of his right hand, Luca felt his body start to slide. With well-practised precision, his foot connected with the sill below and he jolted to a halt.

He exhaled again. Just a couple of moves, but in the dark, and over such a long drop, they'd been difficult. A few seconds later, he kicked open the shutter of the room below and swung himself in through the open window.

It was some kind of storeroom. There were row upon row of receptacles, each with labels inscribed with neat Tibetan writing. Luca reached out to touch one and realised that his hands were trembling. He clenched his fists, squeezing the shakes out of them.

This was the way it always was with free climbing.

He moved towards the door, feeling a new excitement build in him as the wave of adrenaline passed. He was finally free from Dorje and able to explore the monastery unhindered. Since they had first arrived, he was sure their routes through the miles of passageways had been very carefully chosen. Certain corridors had been deliberately avoided; certain doors closed ahead of his arrival. Dorje had taken great pains to shepherd him through the monastery, ensuring that he saw as little of it as possible.

Now he had the chance to see it all for himself. But first he had to find Bill – and Dorje had let it slip that he was somewhere in the lower levels.

Stepping out into the corridor, he half-expected to see Dorje's figure materialise out of the darkness, but everything remained still. Luca swivelled his head from side to side, wondering which way to go. At the far end of the corridor, a faint light emanated from a flickering yak-butter candle.

Luca patted the pocket of his trousers, feeling for some wedges of sliced chocolate. Lying on his bed in the darkness, he had decided that the real danger with breaking out of his room was getting lost in the maze of catacombs that presumably lay below the monastery's main levels. His GPS had been left in the cave with most of his other climbing gear, but even if he did have it, with such thick walls it would have been useless anyway. Instead, he'd remembered something from his schooldays: Theseus and the Minotaur. He didn't have a ball of string, but he could use pieces from the two crumbled chocolate bars they'd had left to mark each stairway he used or door he opened. That was if the rats didn't get to them before he returned.

Luca moved off swiftly, descending a staircase just in front of him that led down to the next level. He moved as fast as his bulky climbing boots would allow, stopping when he remembered to tuck one of the bits of chocolate into the top rung of the stairs.

He shook his head. The plan was ridiculous. It felt like something out of Hansel and Gretel.

Below was another corridor, identical to the previous one. He edged across the stone floor, feeling weighed down by the oppressive stillness of the monastery. The only sound was the rise and fall of his own breath. On he went, down more staircases and corridors, the smell of the dripping candles heavy on everything he passed.

A few levels lower down, the corridor he was following came to a dead end. He stopped, studying the wooden door ahead of him. It was much larger than the others and had been ornately carved. Luca turned the handle with a loud click and pulled his lighter from his pocket.

As he opened the door, Luca's eyes narrowed in surprise. He could see the roof of the chamber high above him. Directly in front was one long, continuous row of bookshelves, stretching off for as far as he could see. The flickering light picked out the spines of countless books. He paced alongside them, following them deeper into the room.

He turned left at the end of the shelves, the flame of the lighter revealing random glimpses of the room beyond. Writing desks were neatly spaced out across it, and behind them stood towering columns of paper set in wooden boxes. Each contained hundreds of old parchments stacked on top of each other, reaching towards the ceiling like crooked stalagmites. Luca waved his lighter higher. The columns led back as far as he could see.

Approaching the nearest, he picked out a few loose pages at random. They were covered with dense Tibetan writing. These must be prayer parchments, like the ones he'd seen in the market stalls in Lhasa. Sweeping the lighter around in a slow arc, he wondered how on earth they knew which one was which.

'Just like Cambridge,' he muttered under his breath.

Retreating along the line of the bookshelves, he then went out of the door and down another level, then another. He left bits of chocolate on the top tread of each stairway. Now he stood halfway down the next, finally realising how idiotic he had been to think he would be able to find Bill in such a gigantic place. It could take weeks. As he stood there, wondering whether to retrace his steps, he noticed a musty, almost chemical smell. He sniffed, wondering what on earth it could be.

He stood in the heavy silence, hairs rising on the back of his neck. Something other than the smell had changed, he could feel it. There was a low reverberation in the air, a noise so faint it seemed to fade into the walls of the monastery. He took a few steps forward, his heart beginning to beat faster.

Soon it was a deep, rumbling sound, pitched on so many levels that it seemed to roll up and down in a strange melody. It was a few minutes before Luca even realised it was made by humans. Ahead of him, light flickered under a wide, gilded doorway and Luca found himself being drawn towards it, mesmerised by the dancing shadows. The smell was stronger now, a bitter odour that clung to the air.

At the base of the doorway, tens of pairs of felt slippers lay fanned out across the floor as if their owners had just stepped out of them. Luca kneeled beside them, pressing his head to the cold floor as he tried to see under the crack in the door.

The first thing to hit him was the smell. As the air circulated under the door it wafted across his face, burning his throat and making his chest suddenly tighten. Inside, he could see a cavernous room lit by immense flaming candelabras arranged at intervals along the vaulted walls. At the far end of the room was a line of seated monks.

He couldn't see all of them, just the first few, their heads swaying in drifting circular motions as they continued an endless chant. Further towards the left, he could see the doorway to another chamber. It was open, and a light was shining from it.

Luca moved his head slightly, trying to get a better view, and saw a thin figure being escorted to this next chamber by two strangely clad silhouettes. The figure between them could barely stand. As Luca pressed his head harder to the ground, trying to see who it was, he caught a glimpse of a monk, eyes rolling and face completely drained of colour, before the inner doors were slammed shut and he disappeared from view.

Luca lay there, blinking his eyes and trying to make some sense of it all. A headache had spread across his forehead and he was finding it hard to think. The tightness in his chest was getting worse and he could taste the chemical taint in his mouth.

Why was a drugged monk being led into some strange ante-chamber? What were they doing in there?

Gripped by a sudden fear, he raised himself to his feet but the blood rushed to his head. He widened his stance, trying to keep his balance, feeling disorientated and sick.

There was the sound of footsteps on the other side of the door and then a scraping as heavy metal bolts were being drawn back. The ceremony had finished. The monks were leaving.

Luca staggered off down the corridor, trying to break into a run, but his legs felt clumsy and slow. After a hundred yards he rounded the corner, looking for the piece of chocolate on the staircase he had come down. It wasn't there.

How could he have turned the wrong way?

Ahead of him the corridor branched off into two narrower passageways and he stopped, wondering which to choose. To his left, a large metal chain was wrapped over a circular wooden wheel and bolted to the wall. He moved closer to one of the flaming candles and tried to think, but the sizzling noise of the wick burning through the candle was growing impossibly loud. Luca stared at the dancing yellow flame as a long plume of black smoke belched out on to the wall above.

As he stared at the light, his jaw slack and his eyes wide open, his mind started to fill with strange, swirling images. It was that smell . . . It was making him feel faint. His eyelids were getting heavier.

He heard footsteps, then voices. They were drawing closer. Light from around the corner appeared on the wall. Luca shook his head, trying to snap himself out of it, when his eyes came to rest on the metal chain reaching down to the floor. He looked more closely. It was a trapdoor, cut into the stone floor below.

With a dull metal clank from the chain, he heaved open the trapdoor and shuffled down the wooden ladder, drawing his lighter from his pocket but not sparking it.

Beneath, there was absolute darkness.

A moment later there was a padding sound above him as a procession of felt slippers walked over the timbers of the trapdoor, then eventually silence. Luca waited a moment longer, listening to the sound of his own strained breathing, before finally rolling his thumb down the flint of the lighter.

As the flame sparked, the outline of a terrifying figure exploded out of the darkness. Luca jumped back, pressing himself against the wall, and accidentally let his thumb off the gas, sending the space ahead into pitch blackness. It took a moment for him to steady his nerves and realise that the figure was nothing more than a painting on the wall of the narrow tunnel he now found himself in.

With the lighter held high above his head, he took in the picture. It was of some strange god with blue skin and flaming orange hair. Its lips were pulled back, snarling ferociously with great incisor teeth and yellow eyes that stared accusingly ahead. In its hands were dozens of naked human figures, which were being crushed and burnt in the fires all about its hideous body.

The figure was part of a mural that stretched the entire length of the corridor, from floor to ceiling, reaching back into the darkness. Luca slowly edged his way along, eyes transfixed by the scenes before him. There was just an overwhelming array of colour and form.

'What is this place?' he whispered.

In a deep alcove off the main stem of the tunnel, his lighter picked up another figure. It was statue of the Buddha, about four feet high and raised on a plinth. As he slowly approached, the surface of the statue seemed to shimmer in the light. He moved closer still, reaching out his hand and letting his fingertips brush across its hard surface.

The entire statue was encrusted with thousands of tiny gems. Even through the haze of his headache Luca grasped the significance of what he was seeing, and for a long moment just let his hand linger on the cool brittleness of the stones. As he moved the lighter in front of the statue's eyes, two huge diamonds danced and flashed before him.

Finally he tore his gaze away, looking further down the corridor. He could see other alcoves set back from the tunnel. In the closest, another statue was shining in the darkness. How many more were there? And what other treasures were to be found, sealed away in this vault?

A sense of wonderment spread over him. Surely this was what the fortune hunters had been searching for all those years – the hidden treasure that the professor had said was just a myth.

Studded into the plinth of the statue were long lines of metal nuggets, each no bigger than a human finger. There were hundreds of them. He picked one up at random, turning it over in his hand. The metal was coarse and dull, and at one end he could see a circular mark had been branded into it, with eight points merging into a central triangle.

He had seen that mark before – in the *thangka* Jack had given him. It was the exact same symbol the priest had held in his open hand.

Running his own hand over the studded surface, Luca finally understood what these were. They were seals, used to brand letters with the official mark of Geltang. They didn't look valuable, but they would at last be some kind of tangible proof that the place actually existed when they returned to the outside world. Plucking one from the lowest part of the plinth, he slipped it into his pocket.

As Luca looked up again and into the white diamonds of the statue's eyes, he heard a loud groaning. He froze. The sound was close, hidden somewhere just beyond the statue.

Then it came again.

Waving the lighter from side to side, Luca tried to peer further into the darkness. The flame blew sideways, struggling to stay lit.

'Who's there?'

Nothing.

'Answer me!'

He shuffled forward, passing round the front of the statue. The alcove opened up into a dark well and on the far side was the grey profile of a human figure, its outline vague against the stone wall. Luca stopped dead, feeling his insides turn to water.

The figure was contorted into the lotus position, head bent low, chin almost touching its chest. The legs were bent across each other and hands folded back, palms facing upwards. Tight leather straps ran right around its body, crisscrossing over the thighs then back across the shoulders, forcing it to remain unnaturally rigid.

'Holy shit,' Luca breathed.

At the sound of his voice, the figure's head suddenly jolted upwards, revealing pale eyes that glowed in the half-light. The apparition wailed, a pitiful, strangled sound that sent Luca leaping backwards in fright. He bumped into the far wall, nearly toppling the statue. Somewhere in the confusion, his thumb slipped from the lighter wheel, plunging him into darkness once again.

He ran back, hemmed in on both sides by the tight walls of the tunnel, his hands brushing against them. Then it came again – the howl from the darkness. He fumbled with the lighter, and a few sparks flashed before the flame finally caught. Hurling himself up the ladder, Luca used his shoulder to barge open the heavy trapdoor into the corridor above.

For a second he stopped there, his hands on his knees, staring down into the black void as he tried to catch his breath.

'Don't panic,' he said to himself, trying to steady his breathing. 'Just don't panic . . .'

Then he shook his head. Screw that. This was exactly the time to panic.

Sprinting off down the corridor, he reached the gilded door of the ante-chamber from where they had taken the monk. It was shut, with no light coming from underneath. Ahead was another stairway. Luca pounded noisily up the steps, taking three at a time. Reaching the top, he bent down and fumbled across the tread.

The piece of chocolate was there! He was on the right track. Feeling a new surge of energy, he started running again, the sound of his boots fading against the heavy stone walls.

On the lower level by the trapdoor, in a corner hidden from the light of the candle, a figure stood motionless. It listened, senses well attuned to the dark. Concealed under the hood of blue monastic robes, clouded pupils stared out sightlessly, instinctively following the noise of Luca's retreat along the level above.

Then, without a sound, the figure turned, fading back into the shadows.

Chapter 39

At the base of an enormous cliff, Captain Zhu stood with a thick-weave blanket wrapped around his shoulders. It was early-morning and a heavy mist hung in the cold air. He had taken the blanket off one of the yaks and the lingering smell seemed to seep through every pore of his skin, worsening his already foul mood.

Five hundred yards from where he stood, the patrol's tents were arranged in a semi-circle around a low fire. Thin wisps of smoke smouldered up from the wood and wet heather crackling feebly. The whole camp was still. It was their third day in the same position.

Zhu stared at the cliff-face, the same thoughts circling over and over in his mind. Something wasn't right. He could feel it.

When they had first begun interrogating the villagers, none of them had said a word. But as the women were forced to stand on the banks of the stream in the sweltering heat of the midday sun, the weaker of them soon collapsed. One woman, skeletal from illness, eventually pointed to the cliff-face as she sagged to her knees, insisting that was the way the Westerners had gone.

Every day, Zhu had walked underneath the exact same spot, wondering how they could have climbed it. The rock was sheer, reaching up hundreds of feet into the sky. Only the summit was lost in a thick belt of cloud that seemed to hang over the mountainside interminably. He shook his head, eyes slowly tracing up and down the overhanging rock. He was missing something, he was sure of it. There had to be an easier way.

His eyes followed the line of a deep-set crack that ran from the summit right down to the base. There was something about it that drew his attention. He stood motionless for several minutes, just staring at it with his eyes blurring in and out of focus. Eventually he turned away from the cliff and lit a cigarette, drawing the smoke deep into his lungs in frustration.

Why were the Westerners here exactly? What was so special about *this* place? The border and the route to India were over eighty kilometres south of Menkom.

Perhaps he'd been wrong and they weren't trying to get the boy across the border after all. What if India had never been their destination and there was something here, something beyond these mountains, that they were trying to reach? That was the only possible explanation. Unless . . . unless Falkus had been leading him astray from the very beginning and they'd been wasting their time staring up at that cliff-face.

Zhu turned suddenly, stalking across the scrub and heather back to camp.

Emerging from the fly-sheet of his tent, René stepped out unsteadily into the fresh air. He looked across the valley, enjoying the misty quiet of the morning before yawning heavily. His hand went down the front of his trousers, rearranging himself, as he turned back to the inners of his tent and pulled on a thick knitted jumper that was fractionally too short for him, exposing a patch of hairy midriff.

As René took in the glorious mountain panorama, he caught sight of Zhu striding purposefully towards him. He looked over his shoulder to see if there was anyone else at camp, but everything was still. The captain obviously wanted him.

'Oh, shit.'

René shook his head and moved slowly towards the fire, poking one of his tea bags into the bottom of a plastic cup. He couldn't stand it when there were only the two of them in camp. Everything about the captain made his skin crawl.

Each morning the routine was always the same. While two pairs of soldiers scouted in each direction along the cliffs, the others usually left before dawn and set up target practice in one of the fields below the village. René would lie in his sleeping bag, listening to the crack of their QBZ-95 rifles echo across the valley, the sound muted by the damp heather. They would come back a few hours later, tossing the splintered wooden targets on the fire, each one with a fist-sized chunk blown out of the centre by the tight grouping of 5.56mm rounds.

The only other person who stayed in camp was Chen, but he seemed to spend the majority of his time inside his tent, fly-sheet zipped shut, tapping away on a Panasonic Toughbook CF-30 laptop. The computer was lightweight with a magnesium alloy cover and a waterproof screen – standard issue for the elite patrols in the field. Chen had it hooked up to an Inmarsat BGAN system, folding open the halves of the satellite dish like an upended briefcase on a rock by his tent. Above the dish, a long string of solar panels dangled from the top of his tent, the sheets of dull blue silicon absorbing what little energy there was from the clouded sky. Occasionally, Chen's broad face would emerge and he would minutely adjust the solar panels to better catch the sun before sinking back inside his tent for the remainder of the afternoon.

This often left René and Zhu alone by the fire, and despite the open space René still felt flashes of the same claustrophobia he had suffered in the police cell. But this morning was different. He could tell by Zhu's stride that he wasn't prepared to wait any longer. Something was about to give.

The captain arrived by the fire, his eyes as black and lifeless as a shark. 'They were never heading for the Indian border, were they?'

René looked up in surprise.

'What? No, I never said they were. They were heading back to Makalu to do some climbing.'

'So why stop here? Why *didn't* they head towards Makalu?'

The pitch of Zhu's voice had risen alarmingly.

'Look, I know as much as you do,' René said defensively. 'They told the yak herders to come this way instead and Menkom's the last place they were seen. That's all I know.'

As he said the village's name, René's eyes instinctively switched up the valley towards the blackened houses on the far ridge. Husks were all that remained; broken beams, twisted and collapsed, black from ash. They had seen smoke rising from them for three days now, while the villagers limped their way back along the path to find what shelter they could in the lower fields.

'That's all I know,' he repeated, pouring some boiling water into his cup and trying to avoid eye contact.

'We'll see,' Zhu said quietly. 'We'll see how much you really know.'

Over René's shoulder, Zhu noticed two soldiers making their way back along the cliff edge from their patrol. As they came closer, he recognised the sergeant from the SOF group and Xie, that idiot private they had brought with them from Lhasa.

'If you don't provide us with answers then all you are is dead weight,' Zhu continued, his eyes running over René's bulbous stomach. 'And I have no use for dead weight. It gets cut away.'

The word 'cut' came out in a hiss. As Zhu signalled to the soldiers, René's mind started reeling with fear. What did he mean, 'cut away'? He felt his mouth go dry as the soldiers started hurrying towards them. He had seen enough already to realise that Captain Zhu had neither morals nor conscience. Ever since Zhu had first walked into his restaurant, René had been living with the terrifying realisation that this man could do whatever he wanted to him and nobody on earth would be able to stop him.

Zhu gave a few curt orders in Mandarin and without warning the two soldiers rushed towards René, grabbing him by the front of his woollen jumper. Xie was first, his ruddy cheeks and square neck only inches from his face, but René's eyes were immediately drawn past him to the shoulder strap of the sergeant's rucksack. Taped across the webbing, he could see the outline of a large survival knife, its metal handle faded and scratched from use. Each soldier had one and despite only being able to see an impression of the blade through the sheath, he knew enough about the sergeant to bet that it was razor-sharp.

René felt his stomach clench tight.

'You have until tomorrow morning to find out where they went,' he heard Zhu say from behind him. 'After that, you are of no further use to me.'

Xie shunted René forward so that he stumbled, tripping over one of the guy ropes. A moment later he was dragged out of the camp towards the long line of the cliff edge.

Zhu ignored the Westerner's shouts, his mind already elsewhere. Time was ticking away and he still had no results. One month. That's what he had said to the Director General of the PSB. One month. Yet that time was already nearly up and he knew that Beijing would be waiting impatiently for his next report.

There was a rustling of fabric and Chen's massive frame slowly unfolded itself from his tent. Reaching back inside, he grabbed his laptop, disconnecting one of the wires as he pulled it out into the open.

'Sir, I have found something that might be of interest.'

Zhu's eyes turned towards him.

'I've just downloaded a new email that concerns a report from Cambridge, England.'

Zhu remained silent, an air of hostility surrounding his entire body. Chen cleared his throat, looking back to the computer screen as if for support.

'The report was from four weeks ago but I am afraid I hadn't seen it as my security clearance was temporarily revoked . . . after the incident . . . with the boy.'

Zhu waited, his patience straining.

'I have been going back through all my files and found that the report concerns one of the men we are looking for – Luca Matthews. He purportedly spoke to an old informant about something called a *beyul*. The report was filed by a . . .' he paused, double-checking the screen '. . . a Professor Tang.'

Zhu stared at him, his eyes suddenly alive.

'Read the report again.'

'Yes, sir.'

He read the brief in full, including dates and times.

'I've checked twice, sir, and couldn't find any reference to the word *beyul* in any of our files.'

'That's because it's classified,' Zhu snapped distractedly. He turned back towards the cliff, feeling a sudden surge of excitement. He'd been right all along. There *was* something up there – but could it really be one of the fabled *beyuls*? Surely the last of them had been destroyed over thirty years ago? The Cultural Revolution had put paid to all that. They'd combed every river gorge, every mountain summit.

Could there really be one left?

'Get Beijing on the line immediately. I want full satellite imagery for everything above this cliff-face. Get them to divert a satellite if necessary. And I want full-spectrum coverage to cut straight through this cloud.'

'Yes, sir.'

'And Lieutenant, ensure that no one in the bureau hears of this. Instruct the technician to delete all reference to the search once it has been emailed to you.'

Chen looked momentarily puzzled, but then quickly turned back to his tent.

After a moment, Zhu heard him rummaging through the mess of clothing and cables to retrieve one of their two GSM 900 satellite phones.

He stood for a moment, staring up at the sheer side of mountain, his eyes tracing up and down the great lines of the rock. If there really was a *beyul* up there, he was sure that's where the Gelugpas would have hidden the boy. It made perfect sense. But the discovery had to remain his, and his alone. He wasn't about to let anyone else at the bureau claim credit for such a monumental finding. The *beyul* would be his and that cliff was now the only thing standing between him and the final hiding place of the Panchen Lama.

Come tomorrow morning, he would start to send the soldiers up there two at a time, whether they could climb or not.

Chapter 40

There was no path so René and the two soldiers were forced to pick their way over the shrubs and bracken that clung to the mountain slopes, tripping on roots or tearing the lower parts of their trousers on the ragged thorn bushes. It was slow going. Ahead of them, the towering façade of the rock-face continued unbroken for as far as they could see.

They had been walking for six hours without rest. René was continuing with dogged determination, but could feel his thighs getting shaky with the effort. He muttered to himself, channelling his hatred on to the rapist private a few hundred yards in front. He could see the thickset neck and shuffling walk as Xie followed the SOF sergeant like a lap dog.

René stopped suddenly and peered down at some strange flowers growing by the side of a large boulder. The flowers looked like prunes, black in colour and wrinkled on top. Short, bristly hairs stuck out in all directions.

'*Mandragora caulescens,*' he muttered, gently rubbing his hand over the petals. He had spent almost an entire month trying to find this particular species when he had first arrived in Tibet over eight years ago. And now here it was, right in front of him. If only the circumstances were different.

He looked up to find that the sergeant had stopped and was watching him closely. René stood up and continued walking, coming to a halt just in front of the other two men. He reached into the pocket of his corduroy trousers and pulled out a squashed packet of cigarettes. He was playing for time, thankful for the rest. Folding open the pack, he offered one to the sergeant, who shook his head impatiently. He then deliberately passed over Xie, taking one for himself, and with his other hand, reached back into his pocket for the lighter.

Xie's quick eyes moved from the pack to René's face. He lunged forward, trying to snatch them from René's grasp, but missed. He went to try again but the sergeant's hand shot out, stopping him in his tracks. The sergeant then whispered something in Mandarin and Xie quickly lowered his eyes to the ground. With a slow shake of his head, the sergeant moved off again in the direction they were headed.

'Guess you're not so matey with the boss after all,' René said. Xie's expression hardened as he caught the tone of the Westerner's voice and his eyes followed the line of Renés mocking smile.

As René was about to walk off, Xie suddenly made a soft moaning sound. It was quiet enough for the sergeant not to hear and, as René stared quizzically at him, Xie closed his eyes and licked his lips in a horrible parody of pleasure. He moaned again, high-pitched, like a girl.

'You son of a bitch!' René hissed. 'She was just a child . . .'

Xie gave a leering smile and then swaggered off, content that the Westerner had understood. For a moment René just stared after him, his cheeks flushing red while his titanic body seemed to swell, belly clenching in and barrel chest lifting. Then his huge frame listed forward and he staggered into a run, reaching full speed in just a few strides.

With his shoulder hunched, he crashed into Xie's back at full force, the impact resounding with a dull thump. Xie was thrown forward, his body twisting horizontally in mid-air before landing heavily on his chest and face. René came crashing down beside him on the wet heather but used his hands to break his fall, rolling away and panting from the effort.

Xie lay on the ground, arms flailing as he tried to recover from the shock of the impact and raise himself on to all fours. A strangled wheezing came from his chest and he lifted his head, panicked eyes staring directly at René. He was so badly winded that for a few seconds the only sound was his laboured gasping for air.

René watched him, a broad smile spreading over his face until, suddenly, his massive head jolted to one side and he dropped to the ground with a thud.

The sergeant stood over him, rifle butt clasped in his hands. He stared down expressionlessly and then slowly shook his head as René lolled on to his back, unconscious.

René stumbled on, feeling as if the pain would crack his head in two. They were on their way back to camp. He moved as fast as he could, but the effort was almost unbearable.

Xie walked twenty or so paces behind him in silence, staring like a petulant child at the back of René's shoulders. Further back still was the sergeant. His rifle was held in his hands rather than slung over his shoulder and he was watching them both carefully. The safety was on, but René had heard the metallic crack of the bolt being pulled back. A round was now loaded in the chamber of his rifle.

As they finally crested the brow of a hill to look down on the green, rip-stop nylon tents of the campsite, René immediately sensed something was amiss. The soldier's clockwork routine had changed – everyone was in camp and they seemed to be busy. Men were running from tent to tent with a purposeful air about them.

As they drew closer, René could see three of the soldiers were packing rucksacks. High-calorific ration packs and aluminium cooking pots had already been laid out on the grass by the main tent. Two other men were measuring coils of rope, paying them out in metre sections as they counted. Nearer to the fire, the remaining soldiers had spread out nylon covers. On top of them were the entire patrol's rifles. Each had been recently oiled and hardened plastic caps had been fixed over the sights to protect them from the drizzling rain, while magazines of ammunition lay stacked in piles by each stock.

Their small group walked into the centre of camp and stopped by the fire. Running his eyes anxiously over the weapons on the ground, René looked up just as Captain Zhu approached the fire. The yak's blanket was still wrapped around his shoulders and he smoked a cigarette, but for the first time since they had set off from Lhasa, he looked truly alive.

The bastard had somehow found the route up the cliff-face. René was sure of it.

'You've been busy,' he remarked, trying to prompt Zhu into conversation.

Zhu paused for a moment in front of him, noting the large swelling on René's forehead and the sullen looks from the private. Then he turned and barked an order across the campsite. A moment later Chen appeared, his laptop in his hands.

As Chen pressed the 'on' button and they waited for the computer to boot up, Zhu's eyes switched back to René once again and he allowed himself the smallest smiles. The stupid Westerner and his games were irrelevant now. He had found the route up the rock-face all by himself.

Only one hour ago, he had been smoking a cigarette and staring absent-mindedly at the mountain, his mind on the report he was going to have to send back to Beijing. As his eyes had blurred in and out of focus, it had suddenly occurred to him that the giant crack running down the face was in fact, a ledge. At first, he had thought he was imagining it and had blinked over and over again, trying to switch his focus. But after staring for several minutes, the ledge became clearer and clearer, until he could scarcely believe he had missed it in the first place.

That's how the Westerners had done it. And in only a few hours time, he would be on their trail once again.

Chen swivelled the screen of his laptop on its central stem and starting explaining the detailed satellite map they had been sent. They spoke for several minutes, with Zhu nodding occasionally, before Chen produced a folded topographical map which he used to cross-reference with the image on the screen. As they spoke, René watched in silence from behind the fire, his eyes following their every move.

A moment later, Chen carefully placed the map in between the two halves of the laptop and closed it shut. He then returned them both to a plastic pelican case lying by the entrance to his tent and settled back by the fire to resume his conversation with the captain. René got up from where he was sitting and quickly walked round the back of one of the tents. He was right. He was sure of it. They had found a way up.

From the moment he'd been hauled into the police cells, he had realised that there must be more to this than he had ever suspected. But what were the Chinese looking for, and why were they so desperate to find Bill and Luca? René let his fingers trace over the swelling on his head distractedly. What the hell were those boys up to? Had they been lying to him that night at the restaurant? Whatever the answer, one thing was for sure – they were in way over their heads.

In Tibet, you look after just one person – yourself. That's what his friend had said but if he didn't do something, Zhu would eventually track those boys down. And if that happened, they'd be lucky to escape with their lives.

He had to do something. But how could he stop the captain?

René suddenly turned, walking back along the line of tents. He looked up, checking that no one was watching, then quickly knelt down by the fly-sheet of Chen's tent. A few moments later he straightened up and with his hands casually tucked into his pockets, he stepped over the guy line of the tent in front and straight into three soldiers standing in a row.

Xie was in the middle, arms folded across his chest, while two SOF soldiers stood either side of him. They looked young, but fit and well-built. René moved out of their way, gesturing for them to pass, but none of them moved. He wondered whether they had seen him in Chen's tent, but looking into Xie's eyes, he realised they were there for a different purpose entirely.

Slowly bringing himself to his full height, René began folding up his shirtsleeves.

'Go on then, you son of a bitch,' he said, his eyes settling on Xie. 'Let's settle this.'

Xie's eyes flicked to either side of him, checking that the other soldiers were right on his shoulder. Then he edged forward, inch by inch, his tongue shooting out over dry lips. Despite being three to one, he felt nervous. The Westerner somehow looked even larger than normal, the bulbous stomach and thick forearms swelling with rage. The westerner was ready for him.

With a sudden lunge, Xie swung his right arm towards the side of René's head. The blow was clumsy and swung wide. René let it glance off his shoulder, then with a quick step forward, jabbed his fist out, straight into the soft flesh of Xie's throat. With a strangled gurgling, Xie sank to his knees, hands clutching his neck. René followed through with a heavy right hook that crashed into the side of Xie's temple, sending him sprawling into the mud.

With his fists raised like a prize fighter, René looked at the two remaining soldiers, wondering whether they would engage. He knew Xie was nothing to do with their unit and hoped their loyalty wouldn't stretch that far. Both looked unfazed by the sight of Xie squirming in the mud, but they eyed René carefully, both of them ready to strike.

Just as he was starting to relax, the soldier closest to him swayed to the right. With explosive speed he hammer-kicked down on René's thigh, striking with the heel of his boot. René howled in pain as the soldier then swivelled on the ball of his left foot, sweeping his leg round in a side kick, which connected deep into René's ribs.

René staggered back, his arms wide as he tried to keep himself from falling. The second soldier sprang forward, throwing a swift one-two punch at his face and chest. As René tried to duck, the second punch connected with the crown of his head, spinning him off balance and flat on to his back.

Lying in the mud, René had his arms raised to protect his face. Both soldiers paused and, slowly unclenching their fists, turned away from him, satisfied that he had been taught enough of a lesson. With a hand clamped to the top of his head, René shut his eyes. He was groaning softly when he suddenly heard a terrible screeching. His eyes flicked open to see Xie stumbling towards him with a survival knife swinging from his right hand. The blade was dull silver, with a cruel serrated edge running along its spine.

As the two soldiers swung round and tried to grab the knife from his grasp, Xie leaped forward with both hands on the hilt, plunging it into the top of René's right thigh. It cut down into the soft muscle, tearing the flesh open with a spray of blood. René screamed, clutching his leg and pressing both hands down across the wound. His breath came in short, erratic bursts as he stared at his own leg, transfixed by the sight of the knife still buried within it.

With a violent jerk, the soldiers yanked Xie backwards, pulling him off René and on to his knees. René's scream had attracted others. They now they stood in a semi-circle around where he lay, watching. Chen pushed his way to the front.

'Get the field dressings!' he barked in Mandarin, staring down at René's leg. 'I want him patched up immediately.'

The line of soldiers suddenly parted as Zhu stepped into the middle of the fray. René gazed up at him hopelessly while Xie lowered his head in disgrace.

'Did you hear what I said?' Chen shouted, rounding on the nearest soldiers to him.

'Wait,' Zhu said, eyes calmly passing from René to Xie.

He drew a nickel-plated pistol from the holster at his waist. It was a small, delicate weapon. Zhu held it close to his side, resting the barrel against his thigh so that it was almost invisible against the folds of his trousers. Standing over René, he examined the knife in his leg with mild interest.

'I have found the route up the cliff-face and have the exact GPS point for the monastery,' he said in English. 'Now, you're nothing more than dead weight.'

Raising the pistol higher, he suddenly swung round, whipping it across Xie's face. The blow knocked the soldier backwards, the sights from the pistol cutting into the flesh of his left cheek.

'Act without my orders again and you will be shot,' said Zhu, his black eyes never leaving René for a second. 'Lieutenant, ensure that the Westerner is left exactly where he is. If he's still alive by the time we return, then he will face charges and be taken to Drapchi. If he bleeds to death in the meantime . . .'

Zhu paused, the corners of his mouth curling slightly.

'. . . so be it.'

Chapter 41

Luca followed two junior monks as they swept down endless flights of wooden ladders, moving lower into the foundations of the monastery.

'What's going on?' he demanded. 'Where is Dorje?'

One of the monks briefly turned, raising his finger to his lips, then continued climbing in silence. Luca's shoulders hunched in frustration, but he followed on regardless.

They passed level after level, gradually veering further back into the mountain and away from the natural light of the windows. Corridors had been tunnelled directly into the rock like mineshafts, lit only by a long procession of squat yellow candles. The further down they went, the heavier and hotter the air became.

Luca noticed that the ladders were no longer worn and bowed at the centre. They felt rigid and unused, as if they hadn't been used in centuries. The ceiling of the tunnel became lower still and, being nearly a head taller than his two guides, Luca was the only one forced to angle his neck to one side.

The guides hurried on, while Luca felt a growing sense of dread build within him. Where was he being led? He'd already seen what these monks were capable of the previous night – a tormented soul, bound by leather straps in the darkness. For how long had that poor man been rotting down there? Luca could still picture his colourless face. And those eyes . . . They had just stared at him through the darkness with such desperate sadness.

Who was he? The last person to stumble accidentally on this secret monastery?

Luca felt the muscles on his arms tense involuntarily as he stared at the backs of his two guides. The only consolation was that they were little more than kids. He knew he could overpower them both if he needed to, but for now it was worth the gamble of following and obeying – more than anything, he desperately needed some answers.

The tunnel opened out into a high chamber where two pillars had been carved out of the natural rock, stretching twenty feet above their heads. Both were covered in gilded swastikas from top to bottom, covering the entire height of the pillar. As one of the guides reached across and picked up a burning torch from its stand, the patterns caught in the flickering light.

Using the base of the torch, the monk rapped twice on a door to the far side of the chamber. There was the sound of heavy metal runners being pulled back and, with a rush of air, the door creaked open on its hinges.

'What's in there?' Luca whispered, feeling the pulse in his neck quicken. He threw a glance over his shoulder back the way they had come, wondering if he should make a break for it. Perhaps he had been foolish to have trusted the guides this far.

A young face appeared at the door and a figure stepped out towards them. It was a boy – about fourteen years old, but tall for his age. He moved awkwardly, with a hesitant shuffling of his feet. As he came closer, Luca realised there was nothing to fear from him. His brown eyes were timid and gentle, and he was smiling apprehensively.

'Please,' he said in a thick accent, sweeping his hand low and gesturing Luca inside.

'What's in there?' Luca asked. He could see light glimmering beyond the door.

'Please,' the boy repeated, his English clearly limited to no more than a few words.

Retreating inside, he gestured for Luca to follow once again. Luca hesitated for a moment longer, fighting his natural instinct to flee, then ducked his head under the low doorway.

It was a large room, bright with colour and heat, and dazzling to the senses. Hundreds of miniature candles had been placed in long lines in alcoves along the walls. Wax welled from their sides, dripping on to the floor with an irregular beat.

Along the uninterrupted back wall, huge golden prayer wheels were lined up like sentinels. The cylinders towered towards the ceiling, the gold looking old and battered from use, while the sacred words etched into their sides were rubbed almost clean. On the far side of the room a large recess had been carved into the wall and was covered by a wide, translucent screen. At the centre of this was an enormous picture of the Buddha with piercing blue eyes. Despite the serene countenance of the face, there was something about those eyes that Luca found unnerving. They seemed to stare down at him wherever he positioned himself in the room.

Dorje stood to one side of the screen, his hands clasped behind his back.

'You are in the presence of His Holiness the seventh Abbot of Geltang Monastery and High Lama of the Blue Order,' Dorje intoned. His expression was deadly serious as he raised a finger towards Luca. 'Do not presume to speak unless spoken to.'

Luca turned as the door behind him was slammed shut, the metal runners scraping noisily across the wood. He looked back towards the screen and could just pick out the outline of a figure seated on the ground behind. It was leaning forward, whispering to Dorje.

'What were you searching for last night?' he passed on, turning towards Luca.

'Hey, wait a second! I saw stuff last night that . . .'

'What were you searching for?' Dorje repeated, his voice firmer.

Luca stared back for a moment, eyes boring into the monk.

'I was looking for Bill. You satisfied?'

Luca took a step closer to the screen and suddenly registered movement, a shifting of the shadows just visible under the doors at the far end of the room. There were other people there, watching him. The Abbot's guards?

He stopped about ten feet away from the screen.

'Look, you haven't allowed me to see him in all this time. And since he was barely breathing by the time we got here, I broke out last night to check whether he was all right.'

'That is all you were looking for?' Dorje asked.

'What? That's not enough for you?' Luca snapped. 'I don't give a damn what's going on at this monastery. I've got a right to see Bill.'

Whispering came from behind the screen and Dorje angled his head to listen then straightened up once again.

'His Holiness understands your concern for your companion's welfare and, once this meeting is concluded, has instructed me to take you to see him directly.'

'Finally. Thank you,' Luca said, hiding his surprise.

'His Holiness also said that he is most relieved to hear your reason for venturing into the monastery alone. But again he asks – is this *all* you were searching for?'

Luca put his hands in his pockets, his fingers curling round the small lead seal he had taken. He inhaled deeply, the heat and billowing smoke from the candles searing his lungs.

'Let's stop these games, Dorje. I know that this is one of the sacred *beyuls*. And last night I saw the treasure that you guys have been keeping secret. I know all about it.'

Dorje remained very still, listening to every word he said.

'I saw the statues, the gems . . . everything,' Luca continued. 'I know people have been trying to find this treasure for years, but you guys have got to understand something – we're not here for any of that. We came to Tibet to climb the pyramid mountain. That's all we were ever interested in and all we came to do. The only reason we're even here now is because Bill got injured.'

He shrugged his shoulders.

'If you are hiding treasure from the Chinese, then that's your business. We're climbers, Dorje. We like mountains. It's that simple – snow and ice.'

Dorje nodded slowly, then added, 'And how could you guarantee that you will not tell others the secret of this monastery, when you return to the outside world?'

Luca hesitated a moment. 'I guess you would just have to trust us,' he said finally.

Dorje nodded again. 'Trust,' he repeated, drawing the word out. 'That is indeed a lot to ask. Especially when we have already seen what you do with our trust. Can we really allow you to leave, trusting to your word alone?'

'Allow me to leave?' Luca repeated in surprise.

He saw movement again behind the doors. It was slight, a person shifting from one foot to the other, but it was definitely there. He tried to see more clearly, but the flames of the candles were too bright. There was a sense of menace to those shadows under the door, as if they were poised to leap out at him.

For a moment Luca just stared at Dorje in silence, then he reached into his trouser pocket and pulled out the seal.

'Perhaps this will help,' he said, offering it on the palm of his hand. 'I took this last night. I'm sorry, but there were hundreds of them and I thought you wouldn't notice.'

As Dorje craned his neck to see more clearly, a faint smile passed across his lips.

'Perhaps we can learn to trust you, Mr Matthews,' he said, the smile widening a little further. 'Perhaps we can.'

He made a subtle movement with his right hand and a moment later the silhouettes lurking behind the far doors seemed to melt away completely. Luca felt the tension in the room lift, but his own expression remained unchanged. He had seen so much last night and they still had not answered a single one of his questions.

'You talk about trust,' he said, raising his chin defiantly, 'yet you've got people tied up in the darkness. What the hell kind of a monastery is this?'

'A very special one,' Dorje replied evenly. 'I am sure what you saw last night was indeed frightening, but I can assure you that you have nothing to fear from us. The devotees you saw form an extreme part of our sect that we call the "Perfect Life".'

'The Perfect Life? Dorje, they were bound up like criminals!'

Dorje shifted out of his formal stance, his features relaxing.

'Please, Mr Matthews, allow me to explain. As you may be aware, in our belief when a person dies they move round the Wheel of Life. If it has been good life, they move a step closer to the state of total enlightenment or what we call Nirvana. Ultimately this is what we all hope to attain, but for many it can takes tens, hundreds, even thousands of lifetimes. The devotees you witnessed last night have chosen the hard and lonely path. They have decided to dedicate every hour of every day in this existence to meditation, in the hope that they will move directly into Nirvana and achieve enlightenment in a single lifetime.'

'But why are they bound in leather straps?'

'So that even in sleep they may maintain the perfect state of meditation. No one forces them to be there. They choose this path freely.'

Luca remained silent, amazed that a person would actually choose to endure such endless years of suffering.

'Incredible to you, I know,' Dorje said, catching the look in his eye. 'But to us belief is everything. Our religion permeates every facet of our lives. And we will do anything to safeguard it.'

He walked forward, stopping just in front of Luca.

'I must apologise if you feel us to be excessively secretive, but we are only cautious because so much of what we once had has been destroyed. When the Chinese came, almost everything was taken from us during the Cultural Revolution – monastery after monastery was simply burned to the ground. Even the Jokhang, our most holy temple, was turned into a pigsty, while the sacred Mani stones were used to build a soldiers' latrine. Thousands upon thousands of our brothers were imprisoned, and many of them died for refusing to recant their belief.'

A deep frown had appeared across Dorje's forehead and his eyes were clouded by bitter memories.

'One by one the twenty-one *beyuls* across our land were discovered and lost to the horror. All of them were lost. All except this single monastery in which you now stand. Our High Lamas then made the decision to bring everything precious that remained to Geltang for safe-keeping, including the treasure that you saw last night. Our blue order was thus created, with the express purpose of preserving our heritage. Now, after so many years of retreat from the world, we are all but forgotten – and happy for this to be so. The only sign that we even exist is the blue in the prayer flags you see over the busy streets of Lhasa.

So, Mr Matthews, if you find us secretive it is because we have been hunted to the very brink of extinction. Geltang is the last *beyul* we have. The very last. Should the Chinese ever discover the route to our gates, we would have nowhere left to hide.'

He moved forward, placing a hand on Luca's shoulder and staring directly into his eyes.

'I hope you can forgive us now for questioning your motives.'

Luca's shoulders slumped and he nodded slowly.

'There's nothing to forgive. I'm sorry I said what I said, but I just saw those things and presumed . . .' He paused. 'Thank you for taking us in, when you had so much to risk.'

As Dorje smiled warmly, Luca turned to address the screen in front of him.

'You've got nothing to fear from us,' he said, seeing the silhouette bend forward attentively. 'We won't tell anyone about this place. No matter what happens. I give you my word.'

Dorje moved closer to the screen, and Luca waited patiently as he whispered to the Abbot beyond.

'His Holiness is most pleased that we have reached such an agreement. He thanks you for your trust.'

Dorje bowed, then signalled towards the door by which Luca had arrived. The young aide drew back the bolts.

'Young Norbu will return you to your quarters, and later this evening I shall take you to visit Mr Taylor.'

'Thank you, Dorje,' Luca said, and with a nod towards the screen, followed Norbu out of the room. Dorje waited until the door had closed once again before turning back to the hidden figure.

'Do you think he suspects the truth?' he asked.

The outline behind the screen leaned forward. When he spoke, his voice was slow and deliberate.

'I believe not.'

'So, do you wish that we now let them leave?'

The figure slowly got to his feet, gathering his robes closer to his body.

'I do not yet understand why they are here, but I know that they have been sent for a reason. Until such time as this becomes clear to me, they will remain within our walls.'

Dorje bowed low as the figure withdrew into an unseen annexe behind the screen. Then he walked towards the door of the chamber, his brow furrowed with concern once more. The Abbot was taking a terrible risk. It could only be a matter of time before the Westerners discovered the truth.

Chapter 42

Shara swept down the corridor, the boy clasped in her arms. Every so often she paused to shift his weight from one arm to the other causing his head to loll against her chest. At the movement, a soft murmur escaped his lips and his eyes shut tight from pain.

A wide cut ran over the top of the boy's knee. With her spare hand, Shara pressed down against it causing a thin trickle of blood to fan out over her fingers and down the length of his calf.

'We're nearly there, Babu,' she breathed into the mop of tousled hair. 'It was just an accident. That's all. Remember, we've got to stay as quiet as a mouse, OK?'

At the entrance to the medical quarter she stopped, craning her neck to see beyond the open door. It looked empty. Then, just as she was about to enter, she caught sight of one of Rega's aides in the far end of the room, half hidden by the lines of shelving. He held a vial of clear liquid up to the light, his face so close as to almost be touching the glass. As Shara quickly swivelled away and back into the shadow of the corridor, his eyes instinctively flicked towards the door to where she had been.

Shara hurried back, passed the lines of doors studded into either side of the corridor. Behind her, there was the soft chink of glass being set down, then footsteps. With a quick glance over her shoulder, she drew back the bolt of the door nearest to her and quickly eased herself inside, Babu still hugged to her chest. The room was small with two beds neatly arranged a few feet apart. One of them was covered in a mound of sheets. The top half of Bill's body poked out from the folds.

Shara stayed by the door for several seconds, eyes fixed on Bill. His head was turned away from them and one arm hung limply over the edge of the bed. The sheets moved up and down in a constant rhythm. He was either asleep, or more likely, unconscious.

Tipping Babu onto the empty bed, she motioned for him to be silent, then started hunting through the wooden cupboard to the right of the door. Medical supplies were carefully stacked within.

A moment later, she turned back with a roll of gauze tucked under her arm, a needle and thread and a small, half-full bottle of clear liquid. Sloshing the liquid onto the gauze, she raised it towards the open cut on Babu's knee.

'This is going to sting,' she whispered. 'But don't make a sound.'

Reaching up to his neck, she slipped the string of jade prayer beads over his head and pressed them into his hand.

'Squeeze on these when it hurts.'

Babu inhaled deeply, his fist tightening round the beads as she carefully stroked the gauze over his knee, cleaning away the blood.

'Brave boy,' Shara breathed. 'I'm going to have to put a couple of stitches in. It will hurt but not for long. Do you think you can keep silent for a while longer?'

Babu nodded, but his brown eyes widened as he saw Shara hold the needle up to the light and thread the cotton through. He gripped the beads in his hands tighter.

With an encouraging squeeze on his shoulder, Shara bent forward, her hair spilling across her face. As the tip of the needle pierced the skin, Babu's whole leg stiffened and he let out a yell, before quickly clapping his hand across his mouth. Shara shot a nervous glance at the door, before continuing to sew, her mouth pursed in concentration.

The thread was just being tugged through a second time, when there was a rustling from the opposite bed. She turned to see Bill staring straight at her, his face pale with dark lines of bruising running over the bridge of his nose.

'Shara?' he said, his voice husky. 'What are you doing here?'

'This little boy hurt his leg,' she said, biting through the last bit of thread. 'He fell down some stairs and cut himself. It's nothing. Why don't you just go back to sleep?'

Bill pulled himself up onto the pillows, grimacing as his legs dragged over the sheets. Thick belts of gauze had been wound around his calves and the lower part of his thighs.

'Sleep?' he asked, his expression hardening. 'What the hell do you mean "sleep"? Why hasn't anyone come and seen me? There's just been these two monks, and neither of them speak a word of English. What's going on?'

Shara sighed and, gently patting Babu's shoulder, stood up. Her eyes traced over Bill's face, at the line of swollen black where he had fallen on to the stone step. His right eye was almost entirely closed, blotched yellow and mauve in ugly bruising, whilst across his thickset jaw, a few days' worth of stubble had developed into a full beard.

'I'm sorry, Bill. I know you've been left in the dark. But I've got to get Babu back to the Abbot's quarters. He really shouldn't be here at all. I'll come back and explain everything . . .'

'No, Shara,' Bill said, his voice rising to almost a shout. Shara raised her hands, palms upwards, pleading for him to calm down. The frown on Bill's face deepened and, as he leant forward to speak, a wave of pain shot up from his injured legs. His jaw clenched and he shut his eyes, fighting back the pain. Eventually he opened his eyes again.

'We saved your life out there in the storm. The least you could do is give me an explanation.'

Shara remained still for a moment, lost in thought. Then she nodded slowly. 'OK. You're right. But I can only tell you a few things – as much as I'm allowed.'

'You were planning on ditching us all along, weren't you? Right from the very beginning.'

'I'm sorry, Bill. Really I am. But you and Luca were my only chance of getting up the cliff-face. With the guide ill in Menkom, I didn't have any choice.'

She reached across, resting her hand on Bill's forearm. 'I am sorry for getting you involved in all this. It was never supposed to happen this way.'

He stared down at her hand for a moment, then moved his arm away.

'And where the hell is Luca? When can I see him?'

'Soon, I hope.'

'Soon? What does that mean?'

Shara looked back towards the door, as if expecting it to open at any moment.

'It's . . . it's complicated,' she said finally. 'That's all. You're going to have to trust me on this.'

'I don't give a shit how complicated it is,' Bill snapped, his voice rising again. He blinked slowly, feeling his head spin from the effort. 'I have a family to get back to, Shara. You understand me? A family. Luca and I are getting out of here the moment I'm on my feet again.'

Bill grabbed her wrist, yanking her body round to face him.

'Do you understand,' he said, the temper rising even further. As he spoke, he looked across to the other bed to where Babu was still sitting, his eyes moving between them both. Tears were spilling down his cheeks and he looked terrified by Bill's sudden anger.

Bill let go of Shara's wrist and slowly sank back on to his pillow.

'I'm sorry,' he whispered. 'I didn't mean to shout. I've just been going crazy, lying here thinking about it all.'

Shara moved closer to Babu and placing her hand on the back of his neck, gave him a reassuring smile.

'I know I misled you,' she said, speaking over her shoulder, 'but I had important reasons, and I'm asking you to give me the benefit of the doubt. You talk about owing things – well, we've taken you in and are tending to your wounds. All I ask is that you now show a little patience.'

She pulled a strand of black hair back from her face. When she turned back to Bill she suddenly looked very tired.

'You have no idea what it cost me to bring you here. You were never meant to see Geltang and now that you have . . . it's something that can't just be undone.'

Bill was still staring at Babu, his expression softening as he thought back to his own son, Hal.

'Can you tell him I'm sorry for shouting,' he said. Then, raising his hand to his face, he let his fingertips run over the top of his broken nose and across his split lip. He gave a ghost of a smile. 'I'm not surprised I scared him. I probably look terrifying.'

Shara whispered a few sentences in Tibetan, her fingers curling through Babu's hair.

'Don't worry. He may only be a boy,' she said to Bill, 'but Babu's tougher than he looks. We travelled the whole way across Tibet together.'

As she spoke, Bill reached forward and grabbed his small diary off the bedside table. A few of his other possessions were there, including a crumpled picture of Cathy and the kids. Ripping a blank page from the spine, he started folding the page in half.

'Yeah, well, I shouldn't have lost my temper. I'm sorry.'

'You've been through a lot,' Shara answered. 'We all have.'

Bill was silent for a moment, then leaned forward again, wincing slightly from the effort and opened the palm of his hand to reveal a small paper frog.

'Ribbit,' he said softly. As Shara passed the frog across to Babu and he held it aloft, his expression slowly changed from fear to curiosity. He pulled down on the head, marvelling at the way the legs moved. After a moment, Babu's nose wrinkled as the beginnings of a smile passed across his face.

'Ribbit,' he repeated, his smile widening a little more.

Bill went to speak when the door bolts were suddenly shot back. A broad-set monk dipped his head and entered the room. His eyes carefully passed over each of them in turn, before he folded his arms across his chest, the bare muscles flexing in his upper arm. A long, jagged scar ran down from the crown of his head.

'Drang,' Shara said, her jaw clenching with frustration. He didn't respond but stood impassively to one side of the door. As Shara signalled for Babu to remain quiet, a second figure swept into the room. Even before he had thrown back the cowl of his robe, Shara recognised the unmistakable silhouette of Rega.

'Tashi delek, Venerable Father,' Shara said, dropping into a low bow. 'We are honoured by your presence.'

Rega didn't answer. His head was inclined to one side and his nostrils flared wide, taking in the sharp smell of disinfectant in the room.

'Father?' Shara prompted and his head suddenly jerked towards her.

'I was told there was some commotion coming from this room,' Rega said eventually. 'What is happening here?'

Shara looked towards Bill, who was staring at her and the old monk, trying to understand what they were saying.

'I just came to check on the patient,' Shara answered quickly. 'But I need to deal with an urgent matter. If you will excuse me . . .' She trailed off as Rega became distracted, his head tilting to where Babu was sitting on the other bed.

The old monk moved closer as Babu shrank back into the pillows, his prayer beads clacking nervously in his hand. 'Shara?' he said, his voice high-pitched and scared.

Rega's nostrils flared again. 'So finally, I meet the child. Governor Depon's son.'

He reached out a hand, the fingers long and delicate. 'Come closer, child.'

Shara gave a strained smile.

'With due respect, His Holiness the Abbot has instructed that he should not socialise with other members of our order. I will take him back to his quarters.'

'Yet he is here with the Westerner? And I only ask the chance to meet a boy so special that he does not even pass our initiations.' Rega's lips pulled back to reveal worn teeth as he attempted a smile. 'The only way for me to see is through touch. Surely you would not begrudge an old blind man?'

Shara hesitated for a second, glancing to where Drang was standing by the door. He looked preoccupied, staring at the jade beads Babu was holding in his hands. His head finally tilted up, to meet her gaze, then he moved a step to his right, covering the door.

Shara helped Babu on to the ground and as Rega approached he stood rigid, hands outstretched.

'Hold still while our father greets you,' Shara said, hearing the tension in her own voice.

Rega's bony hands traced across Babu's cheeks, sweeping over the top of his forehead and down under his chin. As his fingers passed over Babu's closed eyes, the prayer beads in his hand fell to the floor with a clatter. Eventually, Rega straightened, flexing his fingers.

'You say you are the son of the governor, but I can tell you were born on the plateau. Tell me, child, when did you move to Lhasa?'

'Really Father, he is just a child,' Shara protested. 'He is surely too young to answer such questions.'

'Too young or unable?' Rega said. 'Many irregularities have occurred recently and it is for me to decide what . . .'

He was interrupted by clattering footsteps. A young monk appeared at the doorway, his eyes frantic. He bowed quickly at the room, and then leaned forward again, supporting hands on his knees as he tried to catch his breath.

'Father, I must speak with you.'

Rega swivelled round, his jaw clenched.

'Wait, impertinent child,' he hissed, raising a finger, 'I am engaged with other matters.'

'Father you must listen! Something terrible has happened.'

Rega hesitated for a second, then with a sweep of his hand, signalled for Drang to follow him. He stalked out of the door, his robe billowing behind him. As his steps disappeared down the corridor, Bill propped himself further up in the bed.

'What on earth was all that about?'

'I'll explain later,' Shara said quickly, scooping Babu up from the ground. 'I'm sorry, Bill, but it was stupid of me to have brought him here. I'll come back, I promise.'

As she carried Babu to the door, he started squirming in her arms, his eyes locked down towards the floor.

'Shara, wait!' he said, pointing over her shoulder.

'Not now,' Shara said distractedly. 'We've got to go.'

With Babu still trying to break free of her grip, she swept out the door and into the corridor beyond, leaving Bill alone in the sudden quiet of his chamber.

Two hours later, the bolts on the door to Bill's room were softly drawn back.

As the door inched open, the gentle draught of air made Bill stir in his sleep, but not wake. Drang stepped silently into the room. His eyes remained fixed on Bill's face, the scar on his face glinting in the light. He moved further into the room, his felt boots padding over the stone floor.

With his eyes still on the bed, he crouched down, his hands feeling across the stone floor. Eventually his fingertips connected with the beads he was looking for and with another quick glance at Bill's sleeping form, he retreated back towards the door.

In the corridor outside, he lifted the prayer beads towards the nearest lamp, so that it cast a dim light across the silver clasp and the ornate symbol embossed across it. He was right to have come back.

He had seen that symbol before.

Chapter 43

'Keep it tight.'

The words drifted up the cliff-face to where Chen stood, his stance wide and his arms flexing as he hauled on the rope. He grunted from the effort, his powerful shoulders swinging forward with each great heave. A moment later Zhu appeared, his gloved hands clinging to the rock while the rope snapped taut at his waist.

As Chen watched him worm his way on to the ledge, he stared into the captain's face, at the black eyes and thin, pursed lips. Zhu was sheet-white, his cheeks devoid of the slightest hint of colour. He looked as if he were about to be sick.

Coiling in the slack, Chen wiped his forehead on the sleeve of his heavy winter jacket. He had practically pulled the captain up the entire cliff-face and, despite their difference in size, it was heavy work. As they went higher, it had slowly dawned on him that Zhu was more or less a dead weight, his eyes moving nervously in a constant rhythm from the rock to the rope and back again.

It was almost unbelievable, but there was only one explanation – Zhu was scared of heights.

'Are you OK, sir?'

For a moment Zhu didn't answer. He simply moved past Chen to the back of the ledge, pressing his shoulders against the rock.

'How much further?' he murmured.

Chen looked up, watching the other soldiers climbing in pairs along the line of the ledge. They were getting close to the top, maybe a hundred metres more to go.

'Another twenty minutes. No more.'

Zhu nodded. He was trying to steady his breathing and tiny beads of sweat had collected on his upper lip.

Chen watched him curiously for a moment. It was hard to believe this was the same man who had so casually ordered the execution of the monk in Drapchi or the rape of the little girl in Lhasa headquarters.

Zhu caught his gaze and his expression hardened.

'Don't you ever say a word about this,' he hissed.

'No, sir.'

Chen turned away, staring down into the valley below. Blurred from the height, he could see the single tent. It was all that remained of their campsite and in it, he knew, the Westerner would be either dead or dying.

All night they had heard his desperate whimpering. It was soft, little more than a murmur, but Chen had been unable to sleep through it. It had echoed round the campsite, the undercurrent of another's suffering silencing everyone at dinner. Only Zhu had eaten heartily, spooning out extra portions of noodles and, unusually, making idle conversation with the men.

From the sheer amount of blood lost, Chen was almost certain the knife had severed the Westerner's femoral artery. By now, he must surely have bled to death. Many years ago he had seen a construction worker injured in the same way. A crane had malfunctioned and a strand of the wire cabling had sliced his artery in two. Blood had pumped ceaselessly on to the dusty ground, the life seeping from the man with terrifying ease.

Zhu had surely known that. He had known that such a knife wound, left untreated, would inevitably lead to a slow and painful death.

Chen had come across many ruthless men at the Bureau. While

out in the field, they chose between life or death, using torture whenever it served their purpose. It was how the Bureau operated.

From their first meeting at Drapchi, Chen had thought Zhu was the same as the others. The ruthlessness he displayed was simply part of the job. But last night something had switched inside him and Chen had finally seen things the way they really were. Expedience was only one part of the equation for Zhu. What really drove him was pleasure.

He had decided to let the Westerner bleed to death when, at any stage, he could have put a bullet in the back of his head and been done with it. But for Zhu violence was not merely a means to an end. Violence *was* the end. He was a sadist, Chen realised. A man made genuinely happier by the suffering of others.

When they had struck camp in the morning, no one had approached the Westerner's tent. There was only silence from within and the soldiers had left it standing, like a tombstone to mark his unburied body.

Back on the ledge behind him, Chen heard the sound of coughing. He turned to see Zhu still standing with his shoulders pressed against the rock.

'What's the route from the summit?' he asked, his face ashen.

Chen reached behind him automatically to touch the back of his rucksack, where he knew his laptop was sitting protected by its hardened casing.

'We head south, sir. Nearly five kilometres across the glacier floor. I think it's due east after that, but I shall check.'

'Then get moving,' Zhu said, waving his hand impatiently. 'I want to reach the monastery before nightfall.'

Chen nodded his head, and without another word started up the ledge once more, paying out the rope as he went.

Four hours later Zhu held open the corner of his tent with his gloved right hand, blinking as the afternoon light reflected off the snow. He cursed as the icy wind sent the smoke from his cigarette twisting away behind him.

They had made it across the flat ground of the glacier with ease, but now a new obstacle stood in their way.

Reaching behind him for his Leica Ultravid 20 binoculars, he adjusted the focus and stared ahead at the problem: the piles of rock stacked in front of their new campsite. The scene was apocalyptic, as if half the mountain had somehow collapsed during the night, leaving debris strewn in every direction. Finding a route through that would be difficult. It would also be highly dangerous.

With his spare hand, Zhu stubbed his cigarette out in the pristine white snow. Perhaps they had made a mistake. Perhaps there was no route through here after all.

His attention was drawn to the SOF sergeant walking between each tent, checking on the men. His head was angled to one side as he tried to shelter his face from the worst of the wind. With each pace his boots punched through the crust of snow, so that he sank down into the powder beneath. He trudged past the line of tents slowly, tightening the guy ropes and double-checking that everything had been properly stowed away.

Eventually, he made it to Zhu's tent and saluted.

'Everything all right, sir?'

Zhu nodded distractedly.

'Send out two men to find a route through the rocks,' he said. 'And get Lieutenant Chen to report here immediately with the satellite mapping.'

The sergeant hesitated for a second, shifting uncomfortably from one leg to the other.

'With all due respect, sir, the sun will be down in no more than an hour. The weather's worsening. I thought perhaps we might send out scouts tomorrow morning instead.'

'Send them now,' Zhu ordered. He began folding shut the fly-sheet of his tent, then paused. 'And make sure one of them is that idiot private.'

The sergeant saluted then continued back along the line of tents, squatting down by Chen's. He banged on the tent frame before reaching forward and pulling open the zipper. The lieutenant was there, sitting with his back to the entrance.

'Sir, the captain wants you to bring the satellite imagery to his tent.'

Chen didn't turn, instead only raising his right hand in response. The sergeant nodded briefly, then straightened up, walking back to his own tent, grateful to be out of the cold.

Chen remained absolutely still, letting the open tent door flap in the wind. He had been in the exact same position for nearly an hour, staring down at the rucksack by his feet. Eventually, he closed his eyes, feeling the nervous weight press down on his chest, stifling his breathing.

He had no choice. He was going to have to tell the captain.

After they had first made camp, Chen had unfolded his laptop and pressed the start button. Nothing happened. He had rubbed his hands over the cold metal before pushing the button again, craning his head down to listen for the soft whir of the hard drive booting up. Nothing. With a growing sense of dread, he'd swivelled the computer over in his hands and immediately realised what was wrong.

The battery was missing. Someone had deliberately removed it.

He'd immediately looked in the case for the spare, but it had been taken too. Then he realised something else was missing. The map. He had carefully folded it inside the screen of the laptop.

Falkus . . . It had to be him. Chen had left the pelican case with all the communication equipment by the entrance to his tent the previous evening. Even the small rectangular batteries for the GSM 900 satellite phones had been pulled out from the protective foam casing and were gone.

Chen had frantically tried to find a way of rewiring the solar panels to link directly into the power adaptor. He knew it wouldn't work, but tried anyway, cutting back the plastic coating on the wires with the razor edge of his survival knife and twisting the metal fibres together. The panels only had the power to trickle charge the batteries and without a single flicker of power he had eventually given up, leaving a tangled heap of wires at his feet.

There was no other choice. He was going to have to tell the captain he no longer had the map.

Chen inhaled slowly, steadying his breathing. When they had studied the maps together at Menkom, he remembered the monastery as being due east from the cliff edge. But due east led them straight into this impassable avalanche of rocks, and even if they did manage to find a way through, the gulley behind looked impossibly steep. Had he made a mistake? Was the monastery really on another bearing altogether?

If only he had the damn maps!

Eventually Chen rocked forward on to his knees. He slowly manoeuvred his massive frame round inside the tent and laced up his snow-covered boots.

As he stepped out into the wind, he shivered from the sudden change in temperature. His right hand instinctively went up to the top pocket of his winter jacket, resting on the photos of his family that he knew were carefully tucked inside. Tilting his chin up defiantly, he took a deep breath.

He was an officer of the PSB, not some common villager. Zhu would have to treat him by the book.

He trudged forward purposefully, passing the line of tents, but as he drew closer to Zhu's, his pace slowed further with every stride. The wind tugged at his hair. Once again he felt a shiver run down his spine.

This time, however, it had nothing to do with the cold.

Chapter 44

Rega sat in the dark of his chambers, thumbing through the string of jade prayer beads. They passed over the back of his hand with an endless clack, clack, clack.

In the far corner, a small fire burned in the hearth, but did little to warm the remainder of the room. Drang stood close by, slowly working some heavy leather bellows. With each gust of air the fire crackled to life, the embers flaring white and sending shadows dancing on the high, vaulted ceiling.

Placing the bellows back on their stand, Drang sat back down at a small table and continued to thumb through a giant leather-bound book, his ugly face creased in concentration. The book was filled with ornate designs, some sketched in black ink, others outlined in ornate gold leaf. The pages crackled as he turned them. Rega's head twitched towards him with impatience.

'Well?'

'Not yet, Father,' said Drang, flicking over another page, and studying the next symbol.

A blackened metal kettle hung from a chain above the centre of the fire, slowly twisting in the heat. As it turned, some of the water boiled over the edges, sloshing onto the coals with a hiss.

A muscle twitched in Rega's face. Since the messenger had told him that Menkom was burning, the old memories had begun to resurface again.

Five decades had passed, but he remembered that night in every detail; the intoxicating heat of the burning rooftops, the panic as he stumbled blind through rhododendron bushes, headlong into the night. Despite so many years and the peace he had found at Geltang, the same feeling of absolute terror washed over him. And only now, with the threat before him once again, did he finally realise that the terror had never left. It had always been with him, behind every waking thought and deed.

And now the Chinese were here again. The messenger had reported towers of smoke rising into the sky from the village at the bottom of the cliff-face, before spotting a small military encampment in the valley directly below. It could be no mere coincidence. The Westerners had led them there, straight to their gates.

The single consolation was that they still had to discover the way up the rock face and then pass through the Kooms, and without the Kalak Tantra, surely that was not possible?

But the Chinese weren't the only threat. The Westerners were already within their walls. And now it appeared that the Abbot had welcomed them with open arms, allowing them to wander through the monastery at will and discover its secrets. This had to stop. The old fool's misplaced belief in them would be the ruin of them all.

Surely now, with the enemy pressing in on them, the Abbot would finally see sense? He would understand the need for action.

Action. Rega's lips moved as he mulled the word over in his mind. That is what they truly needed – action.

For years now he had believed that Geltang itself had to change. It had to evolve and understand the true nature of the modern world and fight for what it held dear. Every other religion had shed blood for its belief, yet still they persisted in their passive ways. Even as their lights were snuffed out one by one by the Chinese.

Tibet had always been in the balance, the Chinese only maintaining control through fear and isolation. In every village and town, the hatred ran deep; a tinderbox requiring only the slightest spark. For fifty years, Beijing had sat like a cancerous plague across their land, robbing every last vestige of pride and identity from their people.

And while the people suffered, while their monasteries were razed to the ground and their leader fled into exile, Geltang had done nothing but remain hidden, sulking in the shadows of the Himalayas. Decades of inaction had left them unsure and fragmented, the Abbot nothing more than a slave to the old ways.

Yet the truth was plain to see. They were the single power that could unify the tribes of Tibet. Under Geltang, there could be a call to arms, a focus for the revolution. The treasure that they had held for so long would give them the legitimacy they required. Now, they just had to fight.

Rega had already convened the Council of Elders. They would meet in just a few hours to discuss the burning of Menkom and the approach of the Chinese. With such a threat on their doorstep, surely they would now understand the truth. They could not sit by and listen to the Abbot procrastinate while the very last of their sacred *beyuls* was under threat.

'That's it!' Drang's voice cut through Rega's daydream. Scraping back his chair, he padded towards his master with the book open in his hands, his scarred face lit with triumph.

'The clasp,' Drang took the beads from Rega's hands and examined the seal engraved on the silver, comparing it with the one on the page. 'It's the sign of Tashilhunpo. I knew I had seen it before.'

Rega's old spine straightened in shock, his mind whirring. The meaning was unmistakeable.

From the night of his arrival, Rega had suspected something was amiss, but he had never suspected anything so incredible. Could it really be possible? Could it really have happened at the monastery without him knowing?

The more he thought about it, the more it made sense. Why else would a boy have been brought to Geltang in such haste and secrecy? Why else would he be the only one exempt from the initiations? There was only one possible explanation.

The new reincarnation of the Panchen Lama was within these walls. The rightful ruler of Tibet was here amongst them!

Rega stood up from the chair in a flurry of robes. Drang went to support his arm, but Rega brushed past him, sweeping out of his chambers and along the corridor. He had to convene the council immediately.

The boy was the key to it all. Everything hinged on him. If he found a way to control him, he would be armed with Geltang's sacred treasure and the rightful leader of Tibet – the Panchen Lama himself.

Chapter 45

'The Abbot will deliberate!'

Rega swept out of the council chamber and into the corridor, repeating the same sentence again in disgust. His head moved from side to side in a nervous twitch and he pulled the ornate prayer beads Drang had taken from Babu from the folds of his robe, rattling them over his knuckles as he walked.

'Deliberate!' he said again, his voice raised in frustration.

Two novices were about to shut the doors of the council chamber when Dorje suddenly bustled through them into the corridor.

'Wait!' he called, gathering his robes and hurrying forward. 'Please, Rega, you must listen.'

Rega raised one hand in refusal, continuing at the same pace.

'I have heard enough,' he said, the words drifting back to Dorje across his shoulder. 'I inform the Council of the proximity of the Chinese and what does the Abbot decree? He asks for time to deliberate!'

He spat out the last word as Dorje finally caught up with him, reaching forward to grab on to Rega's arm.

'The Abbot needs time to make the right decision,' he explained, cheeks flushed. 'There still remain two formidable obstacles between us and the Chinese. There is time left.'

Rega squeezed the beads in his fist, the knuckles whitening. For over two hours the arguments had been batted back and forth in the

Council, with many of the elders inclining to his point of view. The enemy was at the gates. This was finally the time for a new beginning, for their defiance to be spread across the rest of Tibet.

Then, from behind the screen concealing the Abbot, a scroll had been passed forward. The Abbot had written that he wanted more time to consider what must be done.

Rega's voice dropped to a hiss as he swivelled round to face Dorje.

'Now is the time to act. Now! And if the Abbot has not got the courage to do what needs to be done, then . . .'

His voice trailed into silence as Dorje stared at him, at the jutting chin and pale skin that looked ghostly even in the daylight.

'You mustn't even talk this way,' Dorje said, dropping his voice to a whisper. 'You may not agree with the Abbot's path, but that does not give you the right to question him or to act without his permission. He is still our Abbot.'

Rega nodded slowly. 'Yes. He is indeed.'

A novice approached from the far end of the corridor, a large lantern held above his head. As he passed each of the yak-butter candles along the corridor, he reached inside the glass door of the lantern and fished out a flaming taper with which to light it. Seeing both Rega and Dorje ahead of him, he bowed low before moving silently forward. Both men waited until he was out of earshot before continuing.

'The Abbot values our counsel,' Dorje continued, his tone softening. 'He trusts your judgment but must be allowed time to decide our future, especially given the significance of such news.'

'Trusts our judgment?' Rega repeated, the corners of his thin lips twisting cynically. 'If you think he trusts us so much, why has the identity of that boy remained such a secret?'

'The boy? What has he to do with all of this?' Dorje asked. 'The Abbot's aide was quite specific on the matter. He is the governor's son.'

'Is he?' Rega asked, still smiling.

Dorje thought back to the night the boy had arrived at the monastery and all that the mountain guide had said. He was the third son of Governor Depon and had been spirited away from Lhasa in the middle of the night.

Rega raised the prayer beads in his hands so they dangled an inch away from Dorje's face.

'Do you really think a Governor's son would possess such unique riches? The mark of Shigtase is on them.'

'Shigatse?' Dorje repeated, eyes casting down to the delicate clasps of silver connecting the individual nuggets of worn jade. 'I don't understand what Shigatse . . .'

'Don't be such a trusting fool,' Rega interrupted. 'Wake up to what is really happening.'

With that he strode off down the corridor, leaving Dorje to stare after him in confusion.

Chapter 46

Chen put his hand up against the cold rock and stopped. He looked from side to side, taking in the mass of towering columns, twisted and broken in every direction, and sighed.

They were lost. And had been ever since they had first walked into this God-forsaken maze.

Adjusting his footing, he unclipped the waistband of his battered rucksack and swung it on to the ground. Still holding his rifle in his left hand, he reached up, pulling off his fleece hat and scratching the back of his neck. His fingers ran through his damp hair and he exhaled heavily, watching the moisture in his breath condense in the cold air like cigarette smoke. For the briefest of moments he shut his eyes, blotting out the frustration of the last few hours.

This was Zhu's punishment of him for losing the satellite map, of that much he was sure. There was no other reason why they would have been sent off to find a route through the rocks so late in the day. Tilting his head up towards the leaden sky, Chen watched the light greying out as evening approached. He consoled himself with a single thought – it could have been worse. With Zhu it could always be worse.

Every time they crossed one obstacle another seemed to rise up from the ground, barring the way. Between the huge pillars of rock there were only brief patches of sky visible, making it impossible for him to catch his bearings or get a satellite signal on his GPS. As the afternoon dragged on, particles of snow drifted around them, eddying in the currents of air and settling on their camouflage jackets. The temperature was dropping fast. Night would soon be upon them.

Chen felt a tug at his waist as the climbing rope was yanked tight. A few metres behind, Xie scrambled over a slab of rock and stopped just behind him.

'That way.'

Chen swivelled round in surprise. Up until now, he had never heard the private speak. It had been only his eyes that moved, silently taking it all in. He looked closer at Xie. His square head was pulled back and his shoulders hunched in on themselves, making his body curl forward like a toad's. A fresh scar ran down the side of his face from where he'd been pistol-whipped by Zhu.

'We should go more that way,' Xie continued, his voice breathless and deep.

Chen stood impassively on the rock, considering what to do. He held his rifle loosely in his left hand and the rope was coiled diagonally across his massive shoulders, making him look more like a professional mountaineer than a soldier. Xie's eyes narrowed as he took in every detail then he shifted his own position, widening his feet a little and trying to strike a similar pose.

'No. We keep to this line,' Chen said, gesturing confidently ahead. He wasn't about to lose face to such a mindless thug.

Xie gritted his teeth but didn't answer, eyes darting forward to where Chen was pointing. There was nothing to be seen, only the same broken rocks, the endless looming pillars. They were going the wrong way, he was sure of it. He shivered slightly, the sweat collecting across his lower back and pasting his shirt to his skin.

After a moment's pause they continued forward, Chen leading and Xie trailing behind.

High above them the sky slowly lost the last of its colour. As each minute passed the wind seemed to increase. It funnelled through the gaps in the rocks with a hollow whistling sound, picking up the loose snow and flurrying it all around them. Spindrift frosted every part of their clothing, lacing the hoods of their jackets and sticking to their exposed cheeks. Xie dragged his sleeve across his face irritably, trying to wipe the snow from his eyes and see the way forward.

They came to another fallen slab. For a moment Chen paused, craning his head to one side to check the route. Xie hovered just behind him, hands clenching into fists in frustration. His tongue darted across his lips as started to speak, but he held himself in check. He slowly raised his hand, pointing to the left but Chen ignored him, moving forward again in line with the direction of the rocks – to the right.

For another hour they continued in this way before Chen finally stopped. He rested his hands on his knees, trying to catch his breath, and slowly shook his head. It was hopeless. He couldn't make head nor tail of this damn labyrinth. Xie was just behind, impatiently rocking from one foot to the next.

'The terrain looks like it is worsening,' Chen said, without making eye contact. 'The best climber should be at the back.'

He gestured for them to switch positions and, as Xie stepped forward over the coils of climbing rope, a crooked smile spread across his face. He immediately set off, turning sharp left.

He moved fast, hurrying from one rock to the next, picking his way through the fallen slabs. His eyes scanned the dark shadows on the ground, his confidence growing with each new bound. Letting the rope trail out between them, he forced his way on to one of the higher outcrops of rock and twisted his thick neck from side to side, trying to see the way ahead. Then he was off again, worming his way over the next obstacle without looking back to check if Chen was still following.

After a while, they came up to a large, tabular boulder and Xie swiftly levered himself on top. Straightening up he started walking across to the other side. Chen was a few metres behind when he suddenly stopped. To the left of his hand he noticed a small triangular mark that had been etched into the rock. It looked to be man-made. He peered closer, wondering what it could be.

As his finger traced the lines of the mark, he slowly became aware of the sound of rushing water. He hadn't heard it before over the noise of his own breathing but it was definitely there, bubbling away in the distance. Chen was looking about him, wondering where it was coming from, when the rope impatiently tugged at his waist. Xie, standing on the far edge of the boulder, was ready to drop down the other side.

Chen stopped dead in his tracks. Water! They must be standing on top of an underground river.

'Wait,' he shouted, advancing quickly across the top of the rock, but Xie turned away, ignoring him. He had followed the lieutenant for hour after hour in the wrong direction. This was the way ahead, he was sure of it.

'I said, wait!' Chen bellowed, moving faster, but Xie simply slithered down the far side of the boulder. He took another pace forward when the rock beneath his feet suddenly shifted, breaking off and falling into the darkness below with a dull hiss. Xie's whole body jerked downwards, his chest smashing into the boulder in front and almost winding him.

Xie screamed, his hands clawing over the smooth rock facing him while his legs kicked out helplessly into thin air. The climbing rope was tight at his waist – the only thing preventing him from slipping into the blackness below.

A few metres away, Chen was yanked off his feet, landing heavily on his elbows. He groaned in pain, but his hands instinctively tightened around the rope in front, trying to resist its pull. Swivelling round, he managed to dig his heels in, but as the rope jarred, he felt himself slide forward again, the drop on the far side looming closer with each inch.

Xie screamed again, a high-pitched note stretched by terror as he frantically jerked his body up and down, trying to pull himself free from the hole. The sound of gushing water was all around him now.

He could feel the sudden chill of the river drawing up from the gaps between the rocks. It was somewhere in the darkness just below his feet, rushing over the stone in an underground torrent.

Xie reached forward, grabbing on to the rope and pulling down on it with all his strength, trying to lever his body upwards. He kicked again and again, desperately trying to worm his way out while his shoulders spasmed from the strain. As he slumped back and the rope burned through his hands, his scream faded into a frantic, breathless whimper.

'Stop pulling the rope!' Chen screamed, his feet now only a couple of inches from the edge. His whole body was rigid, trying to resist its immense pull, but each time Xie jerked downwards, the rope would bounce from the strain, yanking him closer.

'Please . . . please,' Xie whimpered, his cries muffled by his camouflage jacket which had bunched up past his neck and was now covering his mouth. Only his eyes were visible above the collar, pupils wide as they stared pleadingly at the top of the boulder. He jerked forward again, trying to break free.

'Don't pull the rope!' Chen roared again, but there was no response.

Xie felt the tip of his right boot connect with the rushing water below. As it dipped only an inch below the streaming surface, the river grabbed hold of it, wrenching it along with the fast-moving current. Xie's whole body twisted from the force, pulling him a few more precious inches further down the hole and into the blackness of the river. He could feel the icy water surging up his leg as if reaching up to claim him.

Chen teetered on the very edge of the boulder, every muscle in his back and thighs fighting. He could now see the top half of Xie's head poking out from between the line of rocks below. Turning his own head a few inches to the side, he stared down at the instep of his own boot. It was wedged into a crack no more than a couple of millimetres deep. It was all that was stopping him from being flung into the same chasm as Xie.

Chen murmured a silent prayer, willing his grip to hold. He could see the rubber on the sole of his boot buckling to one side from the pressure.

There was another jolt on the rope as Xie's other leg dipped down into the water.

Chen couldn't hold it. He was going to be dragged down too.

On the shoulder strap of his webbing was his survival knife. With one fluid movement, he reached up and unclipped it from its sheath. His hand curled round the cold metal of the handle, while the steel blade gleamed in the darkness.

At the sudden movement of the knife, Xie froze.

'Please . . .' he whimpered, staring into Chen's eyes. His arms had stopped flailing and hung pathetically by his sides. Underneath the line of the rocks, his legs were bent back on themselves, knees skimming the surface of the rushing water.

Chen held his gaze for the briefest moment. Then, bringing down the knife, he pressed it against the rope. The line was under such pressure it felt as rigid as steel. He had to saw down on it, drawing the blade back and forth with sharp jerks of his wrist.

'Plea—'

Xie did not have time to finish the word before the blade finally cut through and the fibres of the rope tore in two. Immediately he was sucked down into the heaving mass of icy water with just the frayed end of the rope trailing behind him like an umbilical cord. The raging noise of the river was all around him, the cold driving the breath from his lungs as if his whole chest had imploded. Then there was a crack as his neck struck against stone and everything went black.

Chen stared at the empty space beneath the rock for a few moments. Then slowly raising himself to his feet, he slid the survival knife back into its sheath. He remembered the overwhelming sickness he had felt when shooting that boy all those weeks ago. How he had spent the time since trying to banish the terrible guilt.

There was none of that now. No pity, no remorse. For a moment he wondered whether he had lost all feeling; whether this mission had finally got to him, making him as ruthless as the others. But somewhere deep within him, he already knew that wasn't the truth. The fact remained that Xie had been nothing more than a rapist and a thug. If he hadn't panicked and pulled on the rope, he would still have been alive now.

'So long,' Chen muttered under his breath. He turned, walking back along the boulder towards the marking he had seen on the way up. That was the key to finding their way out of this maze, he was sure of it.

Chapter 47

'Please, Mr Matthews, we must hurry.'

Dorje padded down the corridor with Luca following a few feet behind. The monk's arms swung briskly by his sides, the hem of his robe wafting behind. He glanced over his shoulder, checking on Luca's progress, then swept down yet another staircase.

'I have been instructed by His Holiness the Abbot to take you to see Miss Shara immediately,' he said, eyes fixed ahead in search of the correct door.

'Shara?' Luca said, hurrying forward. 'But you said we were going to see Bill. What's going on, Dorje? The Abbot gave me his word on this.'

'Plans change!' Dorje exclaimed, raising his hands into the air. 'You will get your wish, Mr Matthews, but not everything in this monastery revolves around you.'

Luca stared at the perfectly shaved back of Dorje's head, wondering what had made him so agitated. He had only ever seen Dorje meander through the monastery, his pace infuriatingly slow, yet today he was striding forward as if his life depended on it. The habitual sense of calm had vanished, and for the first time since Luca had met him, Dorje looked decidedly flustered. Luca paced behind him, wondering what could have rattled the monk so badly.

Eventually the corridor came to an end with a large wooden door barring their way. It was ornately carved and, after a moment, Luca recognised it as the same door he'd found on the night he'd broken out of his room. It led to the chamber filled with books and piles of parchments – the one he'd guessed was the monastery library.

Dorje strained to get the heavy door open, waving away Luca's attempt to help before he finally succeeded in drawing it back on its hinges. In front of them stood the same long line of bookshelves. This time, however, the room was brightly lit by the line of iron candelabra that stretched back along its immense vaulted ceiling.

In the light, Luca could now see just how vast the room was. It must have occupied a huge proportion of the monastery. But despite its obvious size, the main part of the chamber was concealed beyond the line of the bookshelves.

'Wait here, Mr Matthews,' Dorje said sternly, and quickly paced forward. At the end of the shelves, he turned left into the main chamber and disappeared from view. Luca was leaning against the wall watching him go, when he heard a soft murmuring sound. It was faint, almost imperceptible. He listened harder. It sounded as if someone was murmuring an unintelligible stream of words. Then he realised – it wasn't just one person speaking, there was a whole cross-current of voices.

The noise was coming from somewhere past the endless line of books. His eyes traced across them, at the spines running back in a crooked sea of colour. Most were weighty tomes, inches thick, with decrepit old covers that had long since seen better days.

What *was* that noise?

Luca guessed the top of the shelving was about twelve feet high. With the toe of his boot pressing down on the first row of books, he suddenly sprang upwards, reaching his right arm up and over the top. His fingers gripped the dusty wooden surface before he swung his left arm over as well and pulled himself higher. The top of his head slowly craned above the line of the shelving and he was able to look down into the room behind.

About thirty monks were seated at individual writing desks spaced neatly in rows across the central part of the room. Each of them sat with a huge book open in front of them and an old-fashioned quill pen in their hands. Some were at the beginning of their volume while others were on the final few pages, but all of them had their eyes half-closed and were rocking back and forth in their seat, their pens scratching across the pages in continual movement.

As their pens moved so did their lips, working in time with the soft undercurrent of murmuring. They were all saying different things, each one reciting his own endless monologue. Luca pulled himself a little higher, staring down at the monk closest to him. His pen moved in a constant flow, only stopping for a second as his left arm whipped across the desk and turned the page to begin once again. There were no spaces in the writing, no gaps or punctuation. The words were coming out as if melded together by memory.

Luca could feel his muscles straining, but knew he could hold the position for a little longer and resisted the gentle tremor in his forearms. His eyes passed from monk to monk, watching their heads sway up and down. It was as if they were all in some kind of trance. For the entire time he had been watching, not a single one of them had paused to draw breath.

What were they writing? And how could they keep going without a moment's hesitation?

As he was about to lower himself back down, he suddenly caught sight of Dorje standing over one of the desks. For a moment he saw Shara's long black hair swaying in time with the others, then Dorje placed his hand on her shoulder and she seemed to break out of the spell. She stared up at him, confused, then slowly put down her pen and took the scroll that he was offering. She read it in front of him then briskly stood up, following him along the line of desks and out towards the bookshelves.

As Luca landed on the floor, he saw them both turn the corner and approach.

'We must talk in private,' Shara said, without further greeting. Luca looked from her to Dorje as she led him by the arm into the corridor outside.

'I will take him to see Bill,' she said to the monk.

After a moment's hesitation, Dorje nodded his consent. 'Very well, but be sure to keep me informed.'

As Dorje hurried off, Shara looked about her. Opening a small door just a few metres to their left, she beckoned Luca inside. It was a store-room filled with urns of blue ink stacked against the far wall. A multi-tude of books were piled in high, tapering columns reaching all the way up to the low ceiling.

Shara drew level with him, her face so close he could smell her freshly washed hair.

'Something terrible has happened,' she whispered, her green eyes staring directly at him. Luca felt his mouth go dry, his thoughts imme-diately turning to Bill. Had something else happened to him? He went to speak, but Shara reached out, grabbing on to his arm.

'We were followed by Chinese soldiers,' she said. 'They have just been sighted just below the cliff-face and are trying to reach Geltang.'

'Chinese soldiers?' asked Luca, his forehead creasing in confusion. 'What the hell would they want with us?'

'It's not you they're after. Listen, Luca, the Abbot wants to know if you will help us. And, in doing so, he is putting an enormous amount of faith in you.'

She took her hand off his arm and inhaled deeply.

'Can we trust you, Luca?'

'Sure,' he said, his gaze breaking from hers and moving down past her lips. He nodded distractedly, trying to dismiss a sudden urge to lean forward and kiss her.

'No. You need to think about your answer. What you decide now could alter everything.'

He shut his eyes for a moment, trying to steady his pulse and focus on what she was saying. 'I promise you, Shara, you can depend on me. I meant what I said to the Abbot.'

Shara seemed to steady herself, rubbing her wrists distractedly. In one hand she still held the scroll Dorje had given her. Luca could see her forefinger was stained with blue ink from the hours she had spent at her desk. No wonder this woman was getting under his skin – she was just so damn mysterious. There was always such urgency to the way she spoke, each sentence whispered, each question only ever partially-explained.

'OK,' Shara said, glancing back towards the door. 'For reasons that I can't go into right now, we need to get a nine-year-old boy called Babu out of this monastery. That's why the Chinese are here. It's who they're looking for.'

'A nine-year-old boy?' Luca repeated, his voice rising in surprise. 'What the hell do the Chinese want with a little boy?'

'He's not just a boy.' Shara paused, glancing down. Every instinct screamed to her to keep his identity secret, but the Abbot had specifically instructed her to tell Bill and Luca. It was *their* help that was now needed.

'Babu's full name is Babugedhun Choekyi Nyima. He is the next reincarnation of His Holiness the eleventh Panchen Lama.'

Luca's eyes widened.

'Holy shit,' he said, shaking his head. 'But that's impossible. There were posters of him all over Lhasa. The Panchen Lama was this pale, older-looking guy.'

'That's the candidate the Chinese are preparing to install at the Linka Festival. And that is precisely why Babu is in such danger. They need to get rid of him before the festival takes place because if Babu's true identity ever became known, the whole inauguration would become a farce.'

Shara's hand tightened around the scroll, scrunching it in the middle. As she continued, Luca could hear a new edge to her voice, a hardness that he had heard once before at Menkom.

'What few foreigners understand is that the Chinese only hold on to this country by their fingertips. If you'd ever been in Lhasa after one of the uprisings, you'd have seen how deep the tensions run. And if it ever became public knowledge that they had tried to assassinate the rightful heir to Tibet . . .'

She paused, trying to imagine the chaos that would ensue. Uprisings would spread throughout the land, rippling out along the spine of the Himalayas as the local tribes rose up against the military garrisons in each town. Every police station would burn, every Chinese shop window would be smashed. It had happened in the past on a smaller scale. This time, it would be unstoppable.

'It would get very bloody,' Shara said eventually. 'They have already tried to kill Babu once, but we managed to get to him first. And now, with the Dalai Lama in permanent exile, the stakes are too high for the Chinese just to let him be. They won't rest until he's dead.'

'Dead?' Luca shook his head. 'Jesus, I had no idea. The poor kid must be terrified.'

'The only people to know of his identity are you, me and the Abbot. Dorje has only just been informed this morning.'

'But Dorje's just a guide here at Geltang. Why would he know?'

'Dorje is a great deal more than he seems. He is one of the High Lamas here at Geltang and along with Rega, second only to his Holiness the Abbot.'

Luca stared past her thoughtfully.

'All this time and he told me he was just an interpreter,' he said, remembering how Dorje skillfully seemed to dodge every enquiry. Throughout their many hours touring the monastery and eating together, Luca had wondered if he was telling him the truth, but there had always been so many other unanswered questions. 'But, Shara, there's something I don't understand. The Chinese have still got to find a route up the rock-face and through the Kooms. Surely Geltang's got to be the safest place for the boy right now?'

Shara shook her head. 'There are other elements at work. He's safe in the Abbot's quarters for now, but we have to move him to another location, and to do that, we need mountaineers. The Abbot thought you and Bill would be willing to guide us.'

Luca stared at her quizzically.

'Bill? Bill's not going to be well enough. The last I saw him, he couldn't even stand.'

'I've checked on him many times and saw him yesterday. He is over the worst of the fever now. He hasn't got all his strength but he can definitely walk.'

Luca's eyes narrowed in frustration. 'You saw him yesterday? So why haven't I been allowed in?'

'I'm taking you to him now,' Shara replied evenly. 'The Abbot had to know whether he could trust you before letting you see each other. Please understand that it was for your own good. But the question still stands, Luca. Will you help us or not?'

Luca stared down at the floor, trying to process everything she had told him. He felt the same suspicions resurfacing and wondered whether Shara was telling him the whole truth or, as with the route up the rock-face, whether this was only part of the story once again. He wanted so much to trust her, but there was still so much that didn't make sense, so much that needed answering.

As he was about to speak, an image came to him of the Abbot, his ghostly silhouette visible behind the giant screen. The Abbot had obviously placed a huge amount of trust in him, and for each of his suspicions there had been a perfectly reasonable explanation. Perhaps now was the time to finally take something on faith and trust what Shara was telling him.

Luca raised himself to his full height without a twinge from his back. A new energy seemed to flood through him at the prospect of this new adventure.

'Yeah, I'll do it. But if the four of us are heading out into the mountains we're going to need some more supplies. Only Bill's rucksack made it out of the cave and there's not much: an MRS stove, fifty metres of rope, some hardware.'

'I've spoken to Dorje about it. He's already organised supplies and extra clothing.'

'OK,' said Luca, his mind racing. 'I'll have to sort through them. When do we leave?'

'Tomorrow morning at first light,' Shara said, suddenly feeling caught up by Luca's enthusiasm. Maybe the Abbot had been right all along. Maybe they really could depend on these men.

'Wait a second,' Luca said. 'You haven't even told me where we're going.'

Shara didn't answer for a moment, then a smile seemed to play across her lips.

'You're finally getting what you wished for,' she said. 'We're heading for the pyramid mountain.'

Chapter 48

Four figures moved silently along the corridors of the monastery. They brushed past the countless doors, occasionally cutting through a faint beam of light from an outside window as the late-afternoon sun spilled in from the far mountain ridge.

It was dusk and time for personal reflection. All the monks were in their cells, deep in meditation, leaving every corridor deserted, every door closed. It was the perfect time to act.

Rega moved fast, his left hand dragging against the wall, guided by every contour and imperfection. He turned sharply down a flight of stairs, then into a corridor which tunnelled directly back into the mountain. As the natural light began to fade, one of the three figures following in his wake paused to pull a nearby torch from the wall. The flame leaped up as he held it high, illuminating Drang's scarred face.

Eventually they came to the entrance to the Abbot's quarters and paused. Despite the urgency of their mission, everyone but Rega stared up in wonder at the mighty pillars flanking the door, amazed by the golden swastikas dancing in the firelight.

'Hide yourselves,' he whispered, grabbing the torch from Drang's hand. The others retreated a few paces, fading out of the circle of light.

Rega swung the base of the torch against the heavy door. A moment later a small wooden shutter was pulled back to reveal a pair of large brown eyes set in a young face.

'Venerable Father,' Norbu said in greeting, his voice high and wispy, 'The meeting of the full moon is not for another three days.'

'I have urgent information for His Holiness. Make way.'

Norbu blinked several times in quick succession.

'But, Father,' he stuttered, 'the law decrees that information must be passed in writing unless His Holiness ordains otherwise.' Norbu's eyes stared through the hatch, studying Rega's wizened face. 'I have been instructed to allow no visitors.'

Rega moved closer still so that Norbu could smell the sour aroma of his breath. 'How dare you quote the law to me, boy?'

'I apologise, Father, but I am only passing on . . .'

'Silence,' Rega hissed. 'Open the door.'

Norbu looked imploringly at him, the strain of this conversation making his cheeks flush red.

'But, Father, please understand, I am not allowed . . . I was expressly told so.'

Rega inhaled deeply, stepping back from the door. His voice softened. 'Well, in that case, I will have to trust you with what needs to be said. After all, the Abbot does speak most highly of you, young Norbu.'

The boy smiled nervously, tilting his head to one side so that his ear was pressed against the opening.

'But what I tell you is of the utmost secrecy,' Rega continued, breathing the words. 'Our Abbot is in grave danger. We must warn him together.'

Norbu's eyes widened in alarm. It took several seconds for him to fight his stammer.

'Danger? But . . . who . . . who would harm His Holiness?'

'There have been many murmurs of discontent while the Abbot follows the last stage of his path and many have become disenchanted with his rule. You must let me in so that I can warn him of the danger he faces.'

Norbu blinked, hesitating once again.

'But if there is danger, I shouldn't let anyone in . . . and His Holiness specifically said . . . said . . . that . . .'

Rega smiled, bringing the torch higher towards his own face.

'Look at me,' he said gently. 'I am just an old, blind man. What possible danger could I be? Now open the door, young Norbu, and let us warn him together.'

There was a moment's pause before Rega heard the heavy metal runners grating. The door opened an inch and Norbu's head peered out cautiously.

'Please, Father, come in quickly,' he whispered. 'I shall inform His Holiness you are here.'

As Rega stepped across the threshold he lashed out, shoving Norbu back with surprising strength. At the same moment three figures came crashing in behind him, Drang at their head. His sinewy right arm grabbed Norbu by the throat and wheeled him round, dragging him back into the main chamber. Norbu's arms flailed pathetically as he squirmed in the iron grip, eyes bulging from the pressure on his windpipe. A few paces farther in and Drang flung him down on to the stone floor.

'Simple fool,' he sneered.

Rega now stood beneath the vast screen illustrated with a picture of the Buddha and lit by a small row of lamps at its base. The crystal-blue eyes shone in the candlelight, staring out into the room with an otherworldly calm. With a sweep of his hand, he signalled for two of his aides to begin searching the maze of rooms at the opposite end of the central chamber.

Rega's head turned towards Drang.

'Tear it down,' he said.

Drang gave the fabric of the screen a mighty wrench, pulling the entire thing from its fixings. The great cloth buckled, slowly collapsing in on itself, before dropping to the floor, snuffing out the lamps at its base.

Behind it, a figure was seated in the lotus position. Its eyes remained closed as Rega stepped over the fallen screen.

'Your rule is finished,' he whispered. 'I am taking over the monastery.'

The eyes flickered open, staring at Rega as if he were a figment of his imagination. The Abbot had a broad oval face, etched with lines of old age. His hair was cropped short, fading into baldness towards the crown, while his eyes stared out from beneath heavy black eyebrows. Ornate gold robes were wrapped around his body in tight folds, while his hands lay clasped on his lap. From the warm light of the room a gentleness seemed to radiate from his entire body, making it seem as if he were about to break into a broad smile at any moment.

'You have left me no choice,' Rega continued. 'Hand over the boy. It is time for him to become known.'

The Abbot slowly raised his right hand, signalling to a large metal rod placed on a stand just before him. Its stem was made from unpolished gold with a string of jade beads hanging from one end. The seal of Geltang was etched into the other.

'Then take the *Dharmachakra*,' the Abbot said. 'If it is what you most truly desire, take our Wheel of Law, and take my place as Abbot. But do not ask me for the boy. Show compassion for his innocence.'

'His innocence is immaterial!' Rega snapped. 'He must take his place as rightful leader of Tibet. I cannot stand by any longer while you hide him from the outside world. I will do what you should have done and install him in Shigatse, his rightful place.'

The Abbot remained impassive, a look of deep contemplation on his face.

'You seek only to use him to fulfil your vision for our country,' he said finally, his voice soft and free from any hint of recrimination. 'You fail to understand that if we use the Chinese ways, if we succumb to the expedience of violence, we will become nothing more than a reflection of our enemies, a shadow of the same. Our path on the Wheel of Life will reverse, tainting all we have worked so long to protect.'

The Abbot's eyes slowly focused on Rega.

'Take my place, old friend. Become Geltang's next Abbot, but I beg you to reconsider the path you intend to follow.'

Rega seemed lost in thought, his hands bunching into fists at his side.

'This time, I will not stand by while our rooftops burn,' he said, his voice harsh with emotion. 'With the treasure and the boy, I finally have the power to overthrow the Chinese. Make no mistake, Abbot, the revolution will start from these very walls. From here, we will finally fight for our own country!'

The Abbot exhaled a long, slow breath. 'We might win our country, but we will lose our faith.'

From the far corner of the room one of Rega's aides suddenly appeared. He took a couple of steps forward then paused.

'The boy is not here.'

Rega swivelled round to face the Abbot again, anger rising within him.

'Where have you hidden him?' he demanded. 'Tell me where he is or I will tear this monastery apart!'

There was silence in the chamber as the Abbot stared directly ahead, his expression unchanged.

'You will not find him,' he said quietly. 'He has already gone from here.'

'We shall see,' Rega replied. Then, signalling to Drang, 'Take the Abbot away. His enlightenment can only be hastened by joining the Perfect Life. Prepare the straps for his body and take his robes of office from him.'

Drang moved forward, his hands hesitating for the briefest of moments before hauling the Abbot to his feet. The old man's legs struggled to find the ground as he was pulled across his own chamber.

As the procession swept out of the door, they passed Norbu lying on the floor. He stared up at them, eyes clouded by fear and confusion.

'And what of him?' Drang asked.

'He is of no consequence. Throw the halfwit in with the other novices.' Rega swept forward again. 'Sound the assembly. I want every monk in this order before me within the hour.'

He had to win over the rest of the monks before Geltang would be truly his. Then he would find that precious boy.

Chapter 49

Luca raced down the stone steps of the monastery with Babu hugged under his right arm. The boy's head jostled up and down to the same rhythm as the rucksack slung across his back as Luca took two stairs at a time, running headlong into the night.

Trying to keep up, Shara hurried down behind them with Bill gripping on to her shoulder for support. He grimaced, jaw clenching in pain as the fabric of his trousers chafed against the newly healed scars. But none of them stopped for a second. They had to get away from Geltang and into the safety of the mountains.

Luca reached the end of the stairway and continued at full tilt, his stride opening up as he broke into a full sprint on the gravel pathway. He followed the path down, winding towards the lowest reaches of the valley before he slowed and finally stopped. Sliding Babu down on to his feet, he bent forward, winded from the effort, and stared back at the towering façade of Geltang monastery. Grey in the moonlight, it loomed over them like a colossal tombstone.

There was a clattering of feet as Bill and Shara arrived, breathing hard.

'Everyone OK?' Luca asked. Both of them nodded, trying to catch their breath. 'I think we can rest for a moment. We should be far enough away.'

While Shara and Babu sat down on a nearby boulder, Bill limped towards Luca, rubbing his hands gingerly down the back of his thigh. He could feel a small damp patch just above his knee where the scar had broken and a watery mix of blood and pus had oozed on to his trousers.

'That wasn't such a smart idea,' he said, wincing from the dull throbbing in his legs.

'Sorry, mate, I thought I saw someone coming towards us across the courtyard. I just ran.'

Bill nodded.

'I saw them too.'

Bill stared across at Luca from under the brow of his fleece hat. It was pulled low over his forehead, casting a deep shadow across his eyes. A thick beard now covered his jawline and his cheeks looked uncharacteristically hollow from the weight he had lost over the last week. Despite claiming to feel stronger, he still looked gaunt and tired.

Luca stared up into the night sky, distracted by a thick swathe of cloud that had drifted across the full moon. Reaching down into his rucksack, he pulled his head-torch from the side pouch. A moment later his face was bathed in a stark neon light which picked up the curls of vapour from his breath.

'You think it's safe to use these?' he whispered.

Bill stared across at him, squinting under the glare.

'Unless you want to fall down the side of the mountain, I don't think we have much of a choice. There's too much cloud tonight.'

Bill released his grip on his thigh, straightening his back.

'I'm worried,' he said, staring at Luca.

'About your legs?'

'No, not me. Them.'

With a nod of his head, he gestured towards Shara and Babu resting on a rock ten feet away. Shara was holding a leather water bottle, gently pouring the liquid into Babu's open mouth. The child swallowed, then wiped his face with his sleeve. His small frame seemed to be engulfed by the heavy sheepskin jacket he was wearing, with only his little felt boots protruding underneath.

'You heard what Shara said,' Luca whispered, following Bill's gaze. 'We just have to get them to this shrine.'

'Yeah, but why us?'

'Because no one's been there for nearly a hundred years and the shrine's apparently halfway up the mountain. No one knows how bad the route's going to be.'

Bill turned his back to Shara and Babu, lowering his voice further.

'Jesus, Luca. Don't you think things through? I'm not talking about the route. I mean why did the Abbot want *us* to go and not someone else from the monastery? If the boy's so important, why hand him to a couple of strangers?'

'I have thought it through,' Luca answered defensively. 'Geltang's full of monks, not mountaineers. Can you imagine Dorje traversing mountain passes in the middle of the bloody night!'

Bill exhaled heavily, sending a wash of vapour through the glow of the head-torch. Behind them Shara was standing up, getting ready to leave again. She pulled tight the hood of Babu's jacket so that curls of hair stuck out across his cheeks. Bill watched them for a moment, then reached up to scratch his beard.

'I know you gave Shara your word, but Chinese soldiers? This is dangerous shit, Luca. We shouldn't even be here.'

Luca didn't answer but stared down at his hands, lost in thought. His fingers were swollen and calloused from years spent climbing and his thumb worked across the pads of hardened skin on his palms. He'd never come across soldiers before on any of his expeditions. Nor, for that matter, had he ever held a gun. But guns or not, soldiers weren't mountaineers. If they spotted any sign of trouble, all they had to do to remain safe was climb deeper into the Himalayas. They had over a week's worth of food that Dorje had given them and enough fuel left over in Bill's MSR stove for even longer.

Luca smiled slowly as he remembered something Dorje had told him while they were sorting through the equipment.

'You know, I'm not exactly one for karma,' he told Bill, 'but you've got to admit, it's strange how things work out. All this time looking for the pyramid mountain and here we are, hiking through the middle of the night to get to it.'

'Yeah.' Bill looked up, catching the expression on his face. 'Wait a second. This is about more than getting to the shrine, isn't it? You're thinking that after we dump Shara and the kid, we'll go for the summit.'

Luca raised his hands, his smile widening innocently.

'The way I see it, if the Abbot wants us to kick our heels at the shrine for a week, then why the hell *not* go for the summit while we're there?'

Bill's expression hardened and he reached out, gripping Luca hard by his wrist.

'Because I have to get home, that's why,' he said. 'All I've been thinking about lying on that bed has been getting back to Cathy and the kids. And right now that's pretty much all I care about. We deliver the boy, then we head back down the mountain to the village.'

He paused for a second, his voice dropping lower.

'I'm serious Luca. That's what we agreed and that's what we are going to do.'

Shara came over to where they stood. She pulled her hair back from her face, tying it round in a knot behind her head, and looked at them both questioningly.

'Whatever you guys are discussing, it can wait. We need to get moving.' She turned to Bill. 'How are the legs holding up?'

'OK, but I think Babu and I are going to be the ones bringing up the rear.'

Shara smiled. 'Well, I don't think he'd be too unhappy with that. I think you've got yourself a fan.'

Babu joined them on the pathway, looking up at Bill from under the furry lining of his hood.

'Ribbit,' he said, and his nose wrinkled into a smile.

Luca walked swiftly along the path, twisting as it zig-zagged up the other side of the valley. He drew the night air deep into his lungs, enjoying the burn in his thighs as he worked his way higher with each step. Despite everything, it felt good finally to be out of the monastery and climbing once again.

Thirty feet behind him on the trail he could see the glow of Bill's head-torch and the faint silhouettes of Shara and Babu beyond. They were moving surprisingly well.

Less than an hour after they had set off, he came to the top of the same snow gulley they had climbed on their way to the monastery. He paused, staring down into the long drag of snow as it faded into the darkness. It was deeper now, with the top layer frozen from the cooler night air. Checking his bearings, Luca realised that the gulley was south-facing and would be most affected by any change in temperature. In the heat of the midday sun, the entire thing would be little more than heavy slush.

Shara joined him, standing by his side with the *Kalak Tantra* open in her hands. Using the light from his head-torch, she stared down at the densely packed script, her finger tracing one particular line. Luca craned his neck, intrigued by the book's black pages and white angular text.

'From here we bear west,' she said, looking up into the night. Luca raised his hand, pointing towards the looming shadow of a steep cliff curving round in a semi-circle.

'Looks steep,' he said. 'You sure about this?'

'I think so. We traverse above the cliff for another five or six hours, then drop down the other side. From there, we should be able to see the base of the pyramid mountain.'

Luca nodded, then shook his head as Shara's brow furrowed again while she tried to decipher the next paragraph of the book.

'Doesn't anyone round here know how to draw a map?' he asked.

She looked up from the page.

'Anyone can read a map. We prefer it this way.'

Closing the book, she placed it back in the canvas bag over her shoulder.

'We should hurry. The Chinese could be closer than we think.'

Chapter 50

Trumpets sounded, silencing the restless hum of monks.

The entire order of Geltang sat shoulder to shoulder on the padded floor of the Great Temple. Their blue robes blended into a single, shifting form as they looked up expectantly to the central dais which bore the Abbot's vast marble throne. The service was about to begin.

Towards the rear of the temple two novices held the giant wooden doors ajar, allowing the evening breeze to circulate, but it did little to cool the mass of heaving bodies. Hundreds of monks were seated, line after line, in perfect symmetry. Each held their prayer wheel in their right hand, some staring anxiously towards the stage while others rocked back and forth, already murmuring the evening *sutra*. They all knew that the entire order of Geltang only came together on the most portentous occasions. Something significant was about to happen and the atmosphere was charged with expectation.

A hush spread across the monks as all eyes turned towards a single figure striding in through the temple doors. His robes were light gold in colour, ornately stitched around the cuffs and interlaced with rich blue patterns woven subtly into the fabric.

The congregation rose to their feet as the figure mounted the dais and bowed before the great statue of the Buddha. Its face was masked by a large curving blue hat trimmed with fur. In its right hand, the figure held the long golden rod of the *Dharmachakra* – the ultimate symbol of authority in Geltang Monastery.

With its free hand, the figure reached down into the golden urn at the statue's base, withdrawing a fistful of chalky *tsampa* flour and flinging it into the air. It hung briefly in the candlelight, then gently drifted to the ground as the figure turned towards the sea of upturned faces.

As one the monks leaned forward. Many had never even seen the Abbot in the flesh before. They had only heard the rumours and seen his likeness drawn in the prayer halls. The Abbot was as much a part of Geltang as its bricks and mortar, an unseen presence, cloistered away from all but the most enlightened amongst them. Now the living legend was finally showing himself.

The hat came off and Rega's familiar face was revealed to the crowd. Despite the warming light of the candles, his skin was the colour of stone, his dead eyes fixed ahead to the middle distance.

A gasp of astonishment rippled through the crowd of seated monks. Rega drew himself to his full height, his old back unbending and his bony shoulders straightening. He raised the Wheel of Law above his head, its metal glinting.

'I hold the *Dharmachakra*,' he shouted, his voice wavering from the effort. 'And with its vested powers, I now command the monastery.'

Some of the monks recoiled as if they had been physically assailed by this news. Murmurs of surprise and alarm were clearly audible as the same questions were asked again and again. Where was the Abbot? How could their sacred leader be so summarily replaced?

'I speak for the Council,' Rega barked above the noise. 'The Abbot has stepped down from his duties. I am your leader now.'

Confusion mounted amongst the monks. Most turned, bewildered, to ask questions of their neighbours. Some younger monks stood up in confusion, demanding answers.

Towards the front of the temple, seated by one of the high wooden columns near the dais, was Norbu. He stared in disbelief at the crowd.

He had not understood what was happening until he saw Rega hold the *Dharmachakra* aloft, brandishing it in his hand like a prize. Suddenly, his eyes fogged with tears and he sank to his knees, his face buried in his hands.

He had betrayed the Abbot. He had unbolted the door when he had been told not to, tricked by Rega and his men. His only consolation was that the Westerners had changed their plans and arrived in time to rescue the boy.

Rega was pacing from side to side on the dais, displaying the *Dharmachakra* to all the monks gathered in the temple. Norbu stared up at him helplessly, eyes still shining with tears.

Rega raised his hands.

'Silence!' he shouted, the veins of his neck bulging. 'Silence, I say!'

Gradually, the murmuring faded away as each monk obeyed and stared up at him.

'I come before you as your Abbot bearing grave news. Chinese soldiers have discovered the route to Geltang. They approach even as I speak.'

There was stunned silence for a moment as the weight of this news slowly sank in. The impossible had happened; their greatest fears had become reality.

Slowly, a new clamour rang out as the monks began to panic. It reverberated against the closed acoustics of the temple roof, pierced by sudden shrieks of shock and fear. Rega tried to speak, but his voice was drowned out by the turmoil. After several attempts he signalled to three men standing alongside the dais. Raising their silver trumpets, they blew a high-pitched wavering note that finally cut through the noise.

In the brief moment of silence that followed, Rega shouted to make himself heard.

'The Chinese are coming, my brothers! They seek to destroy our treasure. I know what will happen if they reach our gates. Fires will burn . . . everything will be lost.'

The noise began to swell once again.

'But we can defeat them! All is not lost if we only have the courage to show our strength and resist. They are but a few soldiers and we are many. We can overcome them and protect ourselves. As your Abbot now, I order you to fight!'

When he shouted the last word, the crowd erupted. While many of the older monks stood aghast at this call to arms, stunned by the shattering implications of what Rega was saying, around the periphery of the temple novices surged towards the dais, shouting with excitement and determination.

Norbu was shunted forward in the commotion and tripped, falling down to his knees on the floor. He stared up through the sea of legs surrounding him, bewildered by it all. Then suddenly he realised what must be done. He must get back to the real Abbot. He would free him from his quarters and return him to his rightful place.

Norbu set off, fighting his way through the crowd. He felt his awkwardness melt away in the face of his self-appointed task. He pushed his way through the press of monks, fighting his way through to the temple doors.

Despite all the confusion, that single movement going against the grain caught the eye of Drang who was standing on the far corner of the dais, his head raised above the crowd. Quickly realising what Norbu intended, he leaped into the throng after him, shouldering monks out of his way as he gave chase.

Norbu managed to work his way round the back of the line of pillars, to where the temple was less densely packed. He had turned right, towards the doors, when he suddenly caught sight of Drang scything his way through the crowd towards him. Norbu froze in terror. He blinked, hypnotised by the brutal energy in Drang's eyes. The scar running down his shaved head seemed to distort the whole left side of his face, making him look truly monstrous.

Finally, Norbu managed to drag himself out through the temple doors. The air outside was cool with the last of the evening light fading fast. Bounding down the stone steps of the temple, he sprinted across the courtyard and pressed his body flat against the stone wall on the far side, melting back into the shadow cast by the eaves of the building.

Suddenly the doors of the temple were flung back and Drang came crashing down the steps. He paused, head sweeping from side to side as he tried to see in the gathering darkness. Retreating a couple of paces, he snatched one of the torches by the temple door and raised it above his head. He then walked out into the centre of the courtyard, searched frantically for the boy, the flames from the torch flattening as he moved.

Just a few feet away, Norbu could see one of the doors to the interior of the monastery. He could feel the air grating in his lungs as his chest heaved up and down, and sweat ran freely into his eyes. Pushing off against the wall, he lunged forward and made it through the door of the monastery. Behind him he heard Drang roar, then the sound of feet clattering in pursuit.

Norbu raced along the corridor. Wells of light flashed by as he sprinted past doorway after doorway. He came across a wooden ladder leading to a lower level and hammered down it. As he came to the last rung, his feet seemed to overtake him and suddenly he pitched forward, crashing down on the stone floor in a sprawling heap.

With a moan, he dragged himself into a sitting position so that his back was leaning against one of the many wooden doors. As he stared down at the scuffed and bleeding palms of his hands, he could hear the sound of Drang's footsteps on the level above. He was close. Just above the ladder. Norbu quickly reached up and pulled down the latch, collapsing back inside the darkened room behind.

Drang came quickly down the steps. He paused at the bottom, craning his neck from right to left. Then he put his shoulder to the door, sending it flying back on its hinges. With his torch held out in front of him, he stepped into the darkness of the room, bolting the door shut behind him.

Shelving was arranged in several well-ordered lines before the door, filled with jars, boxes and crates. Drang moved stealthily down each row in turn, the sinewy muscles of his right arm visible in the torch-light, eyes darting ceaselessly from one object to the next.

Rounding the last line of shelves, he paused.

'I've got you now,' he whispered.

There was a whooshing sound as his torch suddenly flared into a fountain of flames. Fire rained down over his neck and the bare flesh of his arm, as the shoulder of his robe burst into flame. He dropped to the floor, screaming in surprise and pain as his hands raised instinctively to protect his face. He twisted round, the flames leaping higher with each move he made, eating through the dry fabric of his clothes and into his muscle and flesh.

With a horrible gurgling sound, Drang's hands clawed at his clothing, trying to pull it free from his body, as the flames seemed to jump from one part of his body to the next. He screamed again, his fingernails digging deep into his own flesh as he tore the last of his robe from his shoulders. In the far corner of the room, the bolts on the door were quickly drawn back.

Norbu emerged from the storeroom, trembling with shock. His mind was numb, the enormity of what he had done threatening to paralyse him. The half-empty vial of candle oil he was holding slipped from his grasp, smashing on the flagstones.

Across the calm of the monastery, the sound of trumpets struck up once again. It was a brief wavering sound, fading almost as soon as it began.

Norbu started running down the corridor again. The Abbot was the only one who could stop Rega now.

Chapter 51

Smoke rose from the crooked line of pencil flares, glowing orange in the darkness. Chen worked slowly, double-checking each marking. Every twenty yards or so he would reach into a small canvas sack and strike the base of a flare on a nearby rock, triggering it to life. Sparks shot up into the night sky, bathing the vast slabs of rocks in their blood-red glow before settling into a long, steady flame.

For three hours he had been moving from rock to rock, searching for the next marking and leading the way through the Kooms. The entire SOF unit followed silently in his wake. They moved with their rifles slung across their backs, keeping their hands free for balance. Despite their training and experience in mountain warfare, none of them had ever experienced such relentless terrain.

Eventually Chen came to a huge boulder separated from the rest. He reached inside his bag, thumbed off the safety and sparked another flare. In front of him, a wide tract of deep snow was suddenly illuminated, sloping up into a gulley. He reached up to wipe the sweat from his forehead. Finally they were through.

In the main sweep of the gulley the snow was even deeper, forcing him to rock his body forward as he tried to move forward. To his left was a towering cliff, possibly two hundred metres high. Jagged buttresses were lined in vertical towers along it, sweeping round to where they finally joined with the snow gulley ahead.

Chen tilted his head up, letting his eyes trace the sides of the cliff. The scale of them was simply awesome. The mountain seemed to loom over him with an air of silent menace.

Suddenly he caught sight of a light. It shimmered somewhere high up towards the top of the cliff. He tried to focus on it, but the light blurred back into the darkness. He waited, eyes straining against the dark, but there was nothing. Then, just as he was about to turn back to the other soldiers, he saw it again – but this time there were two.

'Sir, you need to see this.'

Zhu came to a halt, his eyes following the line of Chen's pointing finger. Reaching into the front pouch of his webbing, he pulled out his Leica binoculars, swivelling the focus wheel impatiently. After a moment, he lowered them again.

'It must be the Westerners,' he said, then continued matter-of-factly. 'Take three men and lead them up the cliff in front. You'll need to move fast to cut them off.'

'Climb that? At night?'

Chen heard the shock in his own voice. He stared in disbelief at the towering cliff-face in front of them. Even during the day it would have been a formidable climb.

'Capturing the Westerners should be your only concern, Lieutenant. You have ropes and harnesses. I suggest you use them.'

'But, Captain, if we were only to traverse round up the gulley . . .' Chen trailed off as he stared into Zhu's black eyes, made blacker by the darkness. He knew there was no point in arguing. The captain would never back down.

Ten minutes later he stood at the base of the cliff with three of the SOF soldiers as the remainder busied themselves establishing a new camp on the edge of the snowline. As he explained the mission he looked into their faces, suddenly realising how young they all were. At most they were in their early-twenties. In the moonlight, he could see their frightened expressions. Fighting men was one thing. Fighting nature was something else.

Roped together in two separate pairs they set off, rifles slung across their backs. They climbed without gloves, the rock ice-cold to the touch, with pockets of drifted snow collected in the deep cracks. But the granite itself was solid, making their footing more stable and their handholds secure.

Above them the clouds began to disperse, scattering in thin wisps across the sky and allowing a wash of silvery moonlight. Climbing slowly, they could just make out the route ahead. Both pairs followed the edge of one of the main buttresses, pressing their right shoulder against the cliff-face as they clawed their way higher. With no bolts or friends to jam into the cracks for security, the two leading climbers fed the rope over outcrops of rock that they passed, hoping it would snag if one of them fell.

Chen stopped to catch his breath and stared down between his legs, watching the soldier below him force his way higher up the face. He could hear the laboured sound of the man's breath and see the absolute concentration in his eyes. Chen pulled up some slack, looping it over a spur by his head, then turned and began climbing again.

They had chanced upon a good route and with each minute drew closer to the summit. Chen's confidence began to soar as he saw the twinkling of stars beyond the top of the ridge. They were close now. No more than fifty feet.

From somewhere lower down he heard a scraping sound, then a long, panicked yell. Chen turned to see the lead climber from the other pair slipping down the cliff. His arms flailed desperately and his body twisted round like a spinning top, gaining momentum as he fell. For a split second, the rope between the two climbers caught on a spur, then the sheer force of the fall ripped it free, yanking the second climber from the face also. There was a long, petrified scream.

Chen watched both bodies fall the length of the cliff before thudding into the rock at its base. One of the rifles went off with the force of the impact, sending a booming echo across the entire mountainside as the bullet ricocheted off into some unseen distance. A silence followed that seemed to drag on and on.

Chen felt a pulse thundering in his neck. He could feel his hands shaking as he instinctively tried to tighten his grip on the rock. His eyes switched from where the two men had fallen and connected with the soldier beneath him, attached to his rope. They stared at each other, the same fear imprinted on both faces. Then, as one, they scrambled upward again, panic and adrenaline flooding their tired muscles.

They had to get off this terrible cliff-face.

'What the hell was that?' Bill said, looking in alarm towards Luca.

Luca was staring down into a long vertical crack in the ground. He adjusted the beam of his head-torch to see into its depths, scanning the light over the sheer sides. In the darkness, he had almost walked straight into it.

At the sudden sound he looked up, swinging the beam of his torch over Bill. No avalanche or rock fall could have made that sound. That was something else. Flinging his rucksack to the ground and unbuckling the top flap, he pulled out the climbing rope.

'Tie me off,' he muttered to Bill, uncoiling the rope into a pile on the ground. He ran the few paces to the edge of the cliff, then flung one end over. A few feet behind him, Bill jammed tight a quick-release knot around a nearby boulder, before feeding the rope over his back and gripping it tight with both hands.

'OK,' he whispered to Luca, widening his stance to take the strain.

Luca switched off his head-torch then edged his feet out over the cliff and sank his weight into the rope. Without using a harness, he gripped tight with his hands, walking back a few paces so that he could lean right out over the cliff's sheer side.

His eyes scanned across its great flanks, searching the darkness. Then, thirty feet to the right of where he was standing, he caught sight of a figure. It was grey in the moonlight, merging with the colour of the rock, but its quick movement had caught his eye. It was climbing fast and was now just below the crest of the cliff.

'That's not possible,' he muttered, the words dropping involuntarily from his mouth.

It was the Chinese soldiers. It had to be. But how had they found them so fast?

Signalling to Bill to haul him in, Luca made it back to the flat ground, his mind racing.

'Soldiers,' he breathed, staring from Shara to the boy. 'Fucking soldiers! They're climbing the cliff-face.'

Shara instinctively grabbed hold of Babu, her fingers kneading the collar of his jacket.

'We've got to run,' she said, voice rising in panic. She pulled Babu forward by his arm, turning back towards the monastery.

'No, wait!' Bill shouted, raising his hand. 'It's too dangerous. You'll fall.'

Shara paused, fighting her natural inclination to flee. She stood with her legs shoulder-width apart, eyes wild in the darkness. Her hands gripped Babu more tightly.

'I'm not going to let them take him,' she hissed. 'I swear, they will not take this boy.'

Babu looked up at her, alarmed by the sudden vehemence of her tone and the feeling of her nails biting through his sheepskin jacket. He stood silently, overwhelmed by fear.

'What the hell do we do?' Bill asked, breathing hard.

Luca was staring back at the cliff edge. The Chinese would be over it in less than a minute.

'Luca, what do we do,' Bill repeated. With a burst of determination, Luca sprinted over to where Shara and Babu stood. Grabbing them both by the arms, he pulled them towards the deep crack in the ground.

'We'll lower you down there. You can hide from them and use the rope to climb out when we're gone.'

'But what about you?' Shara asked.

'You worry about the boy,' he snapped, pulling the rope in from the cliff-face and feeding it down into the crack. He turned to face Shara, grabbing on to her shoulders so hard that his face was only a few inches from hers.

'You take care of Babu,' he whispered. 'I promise we'll be back. Just stay quiet, whatever you do.'

Before Shara could protest, Bill had grabbed hold of Babu and was raising him on to her chest. Babu looped his arms behind her neck, clinging to her so that his head was pressed tight under her chin. With a final, questioning look at Luca, Shara gripped on to the rope and stepped backwards into the darkness beneath her.

While Luca lay flat on the ground, his arm outstretched, shining the torch as far down as he could to guide her, Shara's felt boots edged down the sheer wall of rock, her arms shaking from the strain. Her feet suddenly pedalled out into mid-air and she hung from the rope, twisting her head to try and see below.

Luca's torch flashed underneath her. The ground was close. Releasing her grip, she leaped back from the rope, landing heavily on the ground. For a moment she remained motionless, trying to get her bearings.

'OK,' she shouted, her voice echoing up the closed rock walls. In the single beam of the light they could see her staring up at them, the same look of uncertainty in her eyes. Without another word, Luca pulled the torch away, pitching the crack into absolute darkness. They heard Babu cry out before the sound was quickly muffled by Shara's gloved hand.

Luca began moving forward with his head bent low, swinging the beam of the torch from side to side across the broken ground.

'What the hell are you doing?' Bill whispered.

'Trying to stop those bastards,' he said and, squatting down on the ground, picked up two rocks lying by the edge of the crack. They were each the size of a man's head. Holding one under each arm, he ran to the edge of the cliff to where he had seen the soldiers climbing.

Dropping one by his feet, he sent the other hurtling down the rock-face. It clattered down, splintering with each turn, before the pieces spun off, away from the cliff.

Luca had just picked up the next one when, out of the corner of his eye, he saw an arm appear over the edge of the cliff, just a few feet to his right. He swivelled round as a massive Chinese soldier pulled himself over the lip and rolled onto his back on the ground beside him. The soldier was panting hard, his face bathed in sweat.

Luca stared down, a terrible rage rising within him. He felt his cheeks flush with heat and adrenaline pump into his chest. He was not going to let them take the boy.

With an animal sound, he raised the rock above his head with both hands, ready to crash it down on the soldier's face. Dazed by the glare of the head-torch, the soldier made no attempt to move, staring up in mute horror as Luca towered above him.

'Luca!'

Bill screamed his name with all his strength.

Luca stopped, fists white from the tightness of his grip. He hesitated, then slowly turned towards Bill.

'Don't do it, Luca,' he shouted.

From behind there was a loud metallic click. A second soldier had crawled over the edge of the cliff a few metres further to the right. He was breathing hard like the one before him but this time there was a rifle in his hands. It was pointing directly at Luca.

The soldier slowly clambered to his feet, the muzzle of his rifle dipping in the process. He stepped closer, catching his breath, before shouting an order in Mandarin. Luca didn't understand but let the rock fall from his grasp and stepped back a pace.

The first soldier dragged himself up and swung his own rifle off his shoulder, loading a round into the chamber. His brown eyes were round with shock, and Luca could see his chest still rising and falling in double-time. A moment later both soldiers stepped forward, their rifles trained on Luca's chest.

A few paces further back, Bill already had his hands up. His eyes remained fixed on the ground where the coil of rope was still wrapped around the rock, feeding down into the gap below. The soldiers would see it. They would discover Shara and Babu. Using the toe of his boot, he dug his foot into the loop of the quick-release knot and pulled. Just as the rope whizzed round the boulder, he stepped forward, waving his hands to distract them.

'What do you want with us?' he shouted.

Both soldiers instinctively swivelled towards him, fingers curling around the triggers.

'Stay back,' Chen said in a thick Chinese accent. He advanced a pace while the other man remained at a distance, covering them.

'Where boy?' Chen asked.

Luca remained silent. Chen's eyes darted between them.

'Where boy?' he repeated, jerking his rifle towards Luca's chest.

'There is no boy,' Luca said angrily. 'We're climbers.'

Chen stared into his eyes for several seconds. Then he slowly took in their surroundings, eyes scanning every inch of the ground. He walked in a semi-circle around them, taking in the two rucksacks lying at their feet and the flat ground above the cliff. There was no other place to hide.

'Then you tell Captain,' he said, signalling with a nod towards the cliff edge.

He turned and barked an order in Mandarin to the second soldier who immediately threw off his rucksack and pulled out a second, longer rope. He moved forward, looping it around the same heavy boulder Bill had used on the edge of the crack.

Bill and Luca exchanged glances but the soldier continued tying off the rope, oblivious to what lay just beneath him in the shadows. He drew up next to the cliff edge, throwing the coils over.

'If we're going to abseil off there, we're going to need more than one rope,' Bill said, gesturing to the rucksack at his feet.

Chen stared at him for a moment, then nodded his consent. As

Bill folded back the top of the rucksack, he saw the big soldier's grip tighten on the rifle. The solders were taking no chances.

'Easy,' Bill said, moving with exaggerated slowness. 'Easy. We're not going to cause any trouble.'

He handed their rope over to the soldier, then moved back a few paces so that he was shoulder to shoulder with Luca.

'Take it easy, Luca,' he whispered. 'Don't do anything stupid.'

Luca stared directly ahead, watching every movement the soldiers made.

'They're trapped in there,' he breathed, glancing sidelong towards the crack. 'We've got to think of something. And fast.'

Chapter 52

Norbu sprinted down the corridor, the clatter of his sandals echoing noisily behind him. In one hand he held a burning torch which trailed black smoke. His breath came in long choking sobs.

He had killed Drang. Killed another human being!

The full horror of what he had done welled up inside him, choking him with guilt. He would be expelled from the order, left to wander in the wilderness as Geltang's gates were slammed shut behind him.

He gasped, only managing to half-fill his lungs in panic. He could feel hysteria growing inside him with each door he passed and stairway he descended. His vision started to close in, becoming a circular tunnel of light surrounded by inky blackness. It was dizzying. His shoulder crashed into the wall beside him, sending him staggering off balance, but still his legs continued pounding over the flagstones. They felt numb and detached, as if they belonged to another person entirely.

He had to get to him, to tell him what he had done.

'Abbot!' he cried out. 'Please . . . Abbot!'

The Perfect Life. That's what Rega had said.

Just ahead he saw the chain and the trapdoor. With a frantic straining of his arms, he pulled up the heavy wooden door and scampered down the steps, letting the door slam shut behind him. The air below was still; the only sound his own panicked breathing. Norbu waved the torch ahead of him as he edged down the tunnel, directing its orange glow across the murals. Terrible images leaped out at him, with open mouths and fangs, clawing to touch him.

'A . . . A . . . Abbot . . .' Norbu stammered, eyes wide with fear. 'Abbot!'

'My child, I am here.'

At the sound of the Abbot's voice, Norbu swivelled his head to face the end of the tunnel. He lunged forward, swinging the torch from side to side, hunting in the darkness. There was a statue shimmering up ahead and Norbu raced towards it, nearly toppling it from its plinth.

Behind it a figure was seated in an alcove, bound by leather straps. As the flames of the torch leaped higher, a mop of hair fell back to reveal pale, unfocused eyes. The apparition's face remained set for a moment, then slowly creased into an expression of infinite pain. The whole face was hollow, tortured; it was as if he was staring straight into the naked soul of the man. Norbu screamed, falling back against the statue and waving the torch frantically to ward off the sight.

'Here, child,' the Abbot called, louder now. '*I am here.*'

Norbu twisted round and raced back along the tunnel. More statues, more recesses. As he hurried past them, the light revealed yet more figures, trussed up in the darkness. They looked up one by one, their eyes staring vacantly at the sudden disturbance to their endless days.

The Abbot was in the last but one alcove. Straps had been bound across his body with the buckles pulled unnaturally tight, forcing his back into a painful arch. His hands were tied with rope in front of him, with the remaining coils looped round his ankles to prevent him moving his legs. Despite it all, his expression was calm. He looked up at Norbu, his forehead creasing in concern.

'My dear child, calm yourself,' he said, his voice steady and soothing. 'Whatever has happened, we will make amends.'

Norbu crashed down on to his knees, letting the torch drop by his side so that sparks were dashed across the stone floor. He put his head on to the Abbot's chest and wept openly.

'I have . . . killed a man!' he choked out, the strength of his emotions nearly winding him. 'I . . . didn't mean to . . . but he kept on . . .'

The Abbot waited, ignoring the pain caused by the boy's weight leaning against him. Norbu drew in one shuddering breath, then another, and gradually his crying eased. He raised his head, eyes red from tears, and the Abbot smiled.

'Come, untie me, young Norbu,' he said. 'We must not let the fear take control of us. We must detach ourselves from such emotion and believe that all will be well.'

Norbu nodded hesitantly then reached up to the Abbot's shoulder, unclipping the first of the leather straps with shaking hands. He unwound them from the Abbot's frail body, looping them back over themselves with each turn. Eventually, the Abbot's body was released and he exhaled slowly, letting his shoulders fall back into their natural position. Then he reached forward himself, using the torch flame to eat through the thick woven rope around his ankles. It smouldered and blackened before finally pulling apart. With a final kick, the Abbot freed himself and got stiffly to his feet, using Norbu for support.

'Well done indeed,' he said, his arm draped over his aide's shoulder. 'Only in the most adverse situations do we ever truly know ourselves. And you have shown great courage.'

Norbu bit his lip, the horror beginning to drain from his face.

'Now, do you have the strength to help an old man one last time?' the Abbot continued. 'We must find Dorje and the rest of the elders. Once they hear me speak, we will restore order to Geltang and quell this panic Rega has created.'

The Abbot hobbled forward with Norbu at his side, their shoulders pressed together in the tight confines of the corridor. With their combined strength, they heaved open the trapdoor and slowly clambered out into the brightly lit corridor above.

'Rega has the entire order in the Great Temple. I saw him there myself,' Norbu explained. 'He has the *Dharmachakra* and was . . .'

His voice faded into silence and his expression suddenly froze. He was staring over the Abbot's shoulder.

'What is it, my child?' the Abbot asked, turning to follow the direction of his gaze.

From the shadows behind the last torch a nightmare figure emerged, striding towards them. The entire top half of its body was naked, revealing brawny slab-like muscles across its abdomen. The skin was red and shining, flaked in patches that stretched across the shoulders and thickset neck. Then, as it stepped further into the light, the hideous face of Drang emerged.

Both the Abbot and Norbu froze, paralysed by what they saw. The entire right side of his face was charred black, with raw flesh striped across the neckline. His right eye looked too big for the socket as the delicate skin around it had burned away. From within the exposed orbit, the damaged eye stared at them with violent hatred.

With a mighty swing of his arm, Drang knocked Norbu clean off his feet. The boy's body arched in mid-air, before crashing down on top the flagstones with a sickening slap. He lay absolutely still as Drang swung back towards the Abbot, his singed flesh only inches from the old man's face.

'Rega will punish you for this,' he seethed, and before the Abbot could even speak, he had grabbed him by the shoulder of his robes, dragging him back along the corridor to the Great Temple and the judgement that awaited him.

Chapter 53

Luca pulled the abseiling rope from his harness and turned around to find four more soldiers standing at the base of the cliff. Two of them had their rifles trained on him, covering him from a distance, while the others dragged a body through the snow by the shoulder straps of its webbing. They were heading for a small semi-circle of tents at the edge of the Kooms.

The heels of the dead soldier's boots ploughed grooves in the deep snow and Luca followed, trying to stop himself from staring at the man's face. His neck lolled unnaturally to one side and the entire top section of his head had caved in from the impact of a fall. As they approached the first of the tents, the body was carefully laid next to another, before the soldiers swiftly assembled two collapsible shovels and began piling snow over them both.

Bill and Luca were shunted forward towards the centre of the camp-site. A single figure was standing there, waiting, the epaulettes on his shoulder glimmering gold in the moonlight.

As the big soldier from the cliff approached him, the figure listened carefully to what he was saying. Then he reached into his trouser pocket and the sudden flare of a cigarette lighter briefly illuminated the man's face. It was ashen, with black eyes that stared at them without a trace of emotion.

The figure came closer, halting in the snow just in front of Bill and Luca. As he drew the smoke into his lungs, the tip of the cigarette glowed in the darkness.

'I offer you one chance. Give me the boy and I will release the pair of you.'

The man's voice was light, almost conversational. Both Bill and Luca remained silent.

'The boy,' the figure repeated.

Zhu waited a moment longer for them to answer then turned to Chen, standing just to his right.

'Make them understand,' he said in Mandarin.

Chen inhaled slowly, wishing the captain had chosen another of the soldiers standing nearby. An image of the Westerner standing over him with a rock raised above his head flashed through his mind. Would the captain have hesitated like that? Would the captain have spared his life?

Chen stepped forward, halting just in front of Luca. The Westerner was staring up at him, eyes shining with a mixture of arrogance and defiance. From that single look Chen sensed that he would not back down, that he wouldn't be intimidated by a few simple punches or threats. This was going to go all the way.

He hesitated, his hands balling into fists.

'What are you waiting for?' Zhu snapped from behind him.

With a sudden twist of his body, Chen brought his hand whipping across Luca's face. There was a dull slap as Luca's head jerked backwards with the force of the blow.

'What the hell are you doing?' Bill shouted, clambering to his feet. Immediately one of the soldiers behind him grabbed him by his shoulders while another rammed the butt of his rifle into the back of his knees, collapsing him into the snow. Bill clenched his jaw in pain as the scars across his thigh split open once again.

'We're British Nationals,' he said, grimacing. 'You've no right to do this.'

Zhu didn't respond, signalling instead for Chen to continue. With a quick jab of his arm, Chen sent his fist crashing into the bridge of Luca's nose. There was a sharp crack and Luca's head snapped backwards again. He groaned in pain then slowly raised his head again, spitting out a thick string of blood into the snow in front of him.

'The boy,' Zhu repeated. 'I want the boy.'

Luca stared up at him, blood oozing out between his teeth.

'Fucking coward,' he said, spitting the words out.

Zhu inhaled on his cigarette, his expression unchanged. Then, with a brief nod, he motioned once again. Inhaling deeply, Chen raised himself to his full height and tilting his body forward lashed out with both fists, thudding them down on to Luca's head and chest. He did it again, and again. The blows became faster, his huge fists hammering down indiscriminately as his arms swung in wide, powerful arcs. The constant fear he had been living with since he had first met captain Zhu, boiled over into a terrible consuming rage. His eyes were half-shut and his body heaved from the effort, until sweat ran from his temples and the skin across his knuckles tore open. If only the Westerner would say something, he could stop. All he had to do was talk.

'Talk!' Chen bellowed in Mandarin. 'Just fucking talk!'

Bill tried to get to his feet, his right hand reaching up to grab hold of Chen, but before he had even got off one knee, the two soldiers behind had wrestled him back down to the ground. He shouted in defiance, wrenching his shoulders from side to side and hitting out with his elbows as he tried to break free. Despite the soldiers' combined strength, they struggled to hold him back until two more of their number stepped forward to help. Their hands gripped tight, bunching the fabric of Bill's jacket in their fists, until all he could do was stare in horror at the terrible beating.

As Chen raised his fist once more, Luca simply collapsed back on to the snow, his body limp. Two of the soldiers holding Bill moved forward to prop Luca up on to his knees, but his whole body sagged and his head lolled forward. Bill reached out an arm to steady him.

'Jesus Christ,' he murmured, taking in the terrible damage to Luca's face. The skin above his right eye had split, weeping blood down his cheek and neck. The other cheek was already swelling, the eye above it starting to close. Bill turned to stare directly at Chen.

'You animal,' he hissed.

Chen stepped backwards. With his hands still clenched into fists, he stared down at the Westerner's face. He watched the blood slowly well up above the eye, before dripping down onto his cheek and a wave of guilt broke over him. All the energy seemed to drain from his body and his shoulders sagged with self-disgust. He had nearly beaten the Westerner to death with his bare hands.

Zhu stepped closer, leaning over Luca. He stubbed the cigarette out, pressing it down into the snow with the toe of his boot.

'There are only a few hours left till dawn and my patience is running out. I am going to ask you for the last time: where is the boy?'

Luca blinked, the pounding at his temples searing right across his forehead. The figure before him swam in and out of focus and he could hear the sound of his own breathing. Eventually he shook his head, murmuring a single word.

'No.'

There was silence as the word resonated through the still air. Chen shut his eyes, leaning his head back towards the sky. He knew what was coming. He wanted to reach across and grab hold of the Westerner, tell him to say something! Say anything! They had no idea who they were dealing with.

Zhu unclipped the pistol from the side of his belt. With a sharp click he pulled back the slider, chambering the first round and pushing off the safety. Then he slowly raised the pistol level with Bill's head, the sights hovering just an inch from the end of his nose.

'If you don't care for your own life,' Zhu said, only his eyes moving towards Luca, 'then perhaps you will value your friend's more highly.'

'Tell, tell!' Chen shouted, the words bursting from him. 'He kill you.'

Luca looked from the pistol to Bill's face and back again. The pain pulsing across his temples suddenly faded and every sound around the campsite seemed to amplify. The slightest movement registered in his brain, from the fidgeting of the men in the semi-circle around them, to the pleading eyes of the big soldier in front. He could see the officer's knuckles tightening around the pistol grip and the hatred in his cold eyes. Every movement seemed to slow in that single instant, stretching out in terrible suspense.

'OK,' he whispered. 'I'll tell you what you want to know.'

Zhu didn't respond but held the pistol level, waiting for him to continue.

'There's a monastery a few hours from here, over the mountain,' Luca said, his voice distorted by the blood in his mouth. 'The boy is being held there by the monks.'

'It is as I thought,' Zhu said. 'Do you know the way to the monastery from here?'

Luca looked across at Bill's face. He was frozen still, his eyes screwed shut. His lips were moving in silent prayer.

'I know the way.'

'Then I don't need you both,' Zhu said, and his hand suddenly jerked upwards. There was a deafening crack from the pistol and a flash of light as Bill was flung back behind them on to the snow. He lay flat, arms stretched out past his head, and remained perfectly still.

Luca stared, his mind reeling, stunned by the noise of the explosion. It resonated through every fibre of his body, deafening him. A thin spray of blood was wet upon his face and he stared in mute horror at the empty space where Bill had just been. He couldn't bring himself to turn around. Shock held him perfectly still, his mind detached by complete disbelief.

Suddenly he began to shake, the horror rising up from his chest in choking, gasping waves. It wasn't possible. It just wasn't possible that Bill could be dead. He forced himself to turn around, his eyes passing over the prostrate form in the snow behind him. A patch of black blood was fanning out from under the head.

Luca was dimly aware of the other soldiers moving behind him. They had turned their heads away from the scene, staring silently up to the far mountain as if trying not to register what they saw.

'We leave at first light,' Zhu commanded, his voice matter-of-fact as he addressed the men. 'We will get the Westerner to lead us there. When we reach the monastery, it is imperative that the boy is taken alive.'

Zhu stared down at Luca's grief-stricken face.

'And take his boots. That should ensure he doesn't try to leave us during the night.'

With that he turned back towards his own tent. The remaining soldiers slowly dispersed, one of them running a knife down the laces of Luca's boot and pulling them from his feet so that he knelt in his socks in the snow. Despite the icy cold, he didn't even notice.

In only a few moments he was alone with the body of his friend. Finally the tears came. He wept in choked bursts, his right hand clutching on to Bill's chest. It was still warm, but as he stayed in the same position, limbs locked by the confusion and grief, he could feel the body heat slowly drain away.

He had no idea how much time had passed before he was lifted to his feet. He felt his arm being pulled over the big soldier's wide back as he was helped across the open patch of snow to a tent.

Chen gently lowered him inside, pulling his own sleeping bag across Luca's legs. Without a word, Luca curled up into the foetal position, eyes staring blankly at the dark wall of the tent. An image of Bill's face was all that he could see. He imagined the soft eddies of snow gently collecting in the damaged eye sockets as the very last vestiges of heat drained from his body. How could Bill be gone? How could such life and strength be so easily snuffed out?

A terrible cramping spread across his stomach. He groaned, pulling his hands down to his waist and pressing them against his abdomen.

The sickness was laced with self-pity and disgust. Cathy. He would have to be the one to tell Cathy what had happened. He would have to see her disbelieving stare turn to hatred and recrimination as he told her what had happened. He could see it all so clearly now – standing in their kitchen with Hal and Ella playing outside, Cathy's face distorting from grief as she sank down onto her knees on the cold, tiled floor.

The cramping grew worse. Luca groaned softly, pulling his feet up higher and hugging his knees tight with his arms. Cathy. How could he ever face her again?

Outside the tent, Chen straightened up and moved towards the centre of the campsite. He stared at the far line of mountains inhaling deeply. The peaks seemed to trail seamlessly into the night. It was the dark before dawn and an eerie calm presided over everything. He let his hand pass over the breast pocket of his jacket and the photos of his family inside. He tried to picture his son's smiling face, but could see only the faint silhouette of the Westerner lying dead in the snow.

He had always been told that the boy's capture was their only mission, but when they reached the monastery at daybreak tomorrow, what was really going to happen?

Chen inhaled again, feeling the freezing air sear his lungs. He shut his eyes and tried harder to visualise his own boy.

Deep inside, he already knew what Zhu was planning.

Chapter 54

Two heavy climbing boots landed on Luca's chest. He reached up slowly, running his fingers over the worn canvas and hard, rubberised soles. From somewhere in the back of his mind, he recognised them as his own.

Through the triangular opening of the tent door, he saw the broad-set face of the same Chinese soldier who had beaten him.

'Get up,' the soldier whispered, his eyes anxious.

Luca dragged himself upright, his body leaden and unresponsive. He stared at the soldier from puffy, black-ringed eyes, the whole left side of his face swollen and bruised. His mouth hung open, dry blood splattered across his lips as he just sat there, his mind reeling with confusion.

The soldier reached forward with one arm and dragged Luca closer to the opening.

'Get boots on,' he said, keeping his voice low.

Luca reached down automatically, pulling the tongue of the boots wide and jamming them on over his iced up socks. Without laces, the boots flapped open as he crawled outside into the cold night air.

The soldier was standing in front of him, Bill's rucksack in his hands. A few coils from a climbing rope poked out from the half-closed top.

'Go!' he breathed, pointing to the snow gulley. 'Dawn one hour. You leave now.'

Luca blinked, trying to wake himself up. Could this be some kind of trick? He looked past the soldier towards the other tents but the entire campsite was still. They were alone. For a long moment, Luca just stood there, staring into the middle distance. Then the numbness seemed to finally thaw, replaced by an overwhelming desire to escape. With a sudden jerk of his arm, he snatched his rucksack from the soldier's grasp and turned to leave. Then he suddenly stopped.

A few feet ahead of him, Bill's body lay in the snow. His arms were still outstretched and his face angled towards Luca. Luca stared, transfixed. Bill's eyes were dull and glassy. His face looked different, like a carbon copy of the original. It was as if the real Bill had gone, leaving only a likeness behind.

'He dead,' Chen whispered, shaking Luca's shoulder. 'But you have chance for living.'

Luca tore his gaze away, staring direct into Chen's eyes.

'How do you live with such horror?' he asked.

Not waiting for an answer, he turned and sprinted forward without looking back, every ache and bruise forgotten as he powered his way up through the deep snow.

Chen watched the Westerner's outline fade to grey before disappearing into the shadow of the overhanging cliff. He turned, walking back to the campsite with his head held low. Pulling one of the collapsible shovels from the ground, he dug it in the ground and began shovelling snow over Bill's frozen body.

Without completely understanding the Westerner's last words, he had gathered their meaning.

There was only one hour left till dawn. Very soon Zhu would order the raid on the monastery. Right now, he couldn't afford to think.

*   *   *

'Shara!'

Luca's shout drifted out across the black rocks. He stopped, listening for the slightest sound.

'Shara!'

Looking up, he saw the first flecks of dawn rising over the eastern sweep of mountains, bathing the sky in long, blood-red streaks. As each minute passed the light grew in strength, seeping across the sky and burning off the night's gloom.

Luca stared from one rock to the next, desperately trying to make sense of the landscape. Everything looked so damn similar.

'Shara!'

From somewhere to his left, he heard a muffled echo. It was closer to the cliff edge than he had been looking. Sprinting forward, he leaped over a few boulders in his way then changed direction as he heard the noise again. It was clearer now. It could only be Shara.

Luca bellowed her name as he frantically scanned the ground. Finally, he saw it.

'Luca! We're down here!' Shara's voice flooded up through the crack in the rock, bringing tears of relief to his eyes. He scrabbled in his rucksack, pulling out the rope and tying it off around a boulder.

'Tie yourself on,' he shouted.

He began emptying the top half of his rucksack, scattering the contents in a semi-circle around him. Brushing aside the fuel bottles for the MSR stove and a spare pair of gloves, he untangled the long sling filled with their climbing hardware and pulled it free from the pack. Unclipping two pulleys and some carabineers, he uncoiled two stretches of five-millimetre prussic rope, wrapping them onto the main line down to Shara. Attaching the pulleys on to the same rope, he then started heaving backwards on the rope system, slipping the prussic knots forward with each pull. Metre by metre, Shara and Babu were hoisted up.

Shara's hand came over the edge first. Luca turned his body to offset the strain and grabbed on to her wrists, dragging her whole body out from the ground. With Babu still clinging to her neck, she fell forward against him, hugging him tight.

'Luca!' she whispered, her face buried in his shoulder. 'We thought you weren't coming back. It was so dark . . . so cold.'

After a moment she pulled back from him, her eyes passing across his broken face.

'What did they do to you?' she whispered, gently reaching her hand up to his cheek.

He didn't answer, shutting his eyes as the images flashed through his mind. His head tilted down towards the ground as he tried to speak.

'They . . . they shot . . . Bill,' he managed finally, his voice cracking.

Shara's face froze. Then her eyes widened slowly in disbelief, begging him to tell her it was not true.

'Why?' she whispered.

'There was no reason. I'd told them everything they wanted to know.'

Shara's hands moved to her own face and she covered her eyes. Her lips began moving in prayer. She stood with her feet apart, swaying slightly as the words poured out of her. Luca watched her for a moment, then his expression began to change. The terrible grief seemed to crystallise, replaced by something bitter and cold. He reached down to the ground, violently jamming the contents of his rucksack back inside.

'There's no time for this,' he said, without looking at her. 'We've got to get to Geltang before they do.'

He waved one hand, signalling for Babu to come to him, but the boy hesitated. A dark swelling disfigured Luca's face, and his eyes shone with a savage anger. Babu gripped tighter on to Shara's leg before Luca reached forward and ripped him from her, swinging the child up and across his shoulder. Babu struggled under his rigid arm until Shara put her hand on his head, smoothing back his tousled hair.

'It'll be OK,' she said, her voice laced with grief and tears. 'Just trust him.'

Luca set off with his rucksack slung over one shoulder and Babu across the other. He moved fluidly, jogging across the broken terrain with Shara trailing behind him. The tongues of his boots flapped as he ran with the severed laces dragging under the soles, but he didn't once break his stride.

'What do we do?' Shara panted, struggling to keep up. 'Evacuate the monastery?'

Luca didn't seem to hear. Sweat ran down his face as he stared out at the far edge of the cliff, to where the snow gulley rose up to meet it.

'Luca?' Shara shouted, lunging forward to grab on to his arm. Luca's eyes briefly took in the sight of her hand resting on him before he turned away.

'There's no time,' he said, the words punched out in rhythm with his breath.

As they came round the last section of the cliff, Luca drew to a halt. Letting Babu slide from under his arm, he crawled forward across the snow, his bare hands sinking into it, then climbed up the back of the snow cornice. Staring down into the gulley, he could see the camp. The Chinese were still there. There was the sound of distant shouting and a soldier emerged from his tent, standing in the middle of the campsite. A few seconds later more men bundled out, buttoning up their jackets.

This was it. They were on their way.

'Take Babu and get back to the monastery,' Luca said, turning back towards Shara. 'Warn as many monks as you can. Then, for Christ's sake, get the boy out and deeper into the mountains. Get him as far away from here as you can.'

'No. We've got to stick together. We'll make it back and get the monks out together.'

Luca shook his head. 'There's no time. Now do as I say!'

He got to his feet, pushing them towards the path on the far side of the gulley.

'But what are you going to do?' Shara asked.

'Try and buy you some time. Now, please, Shara, go!'

'Luca, you must come . . .'

As she spoke, they heard more shouts and both turned to see the soldiers running out of the campsite and up the snow gulley. They had been seen.

'Go!' Luca shouted and Shara staggered forward, pulling Babu by the arm. She stared at Luca one last time, before dropping out of sight, following the path back towards the monastery. Luca glanced up to see Geltang perched on the distant rocks, its buildings washed red by the glow of the morning sun. He had to do something.

Turning back towards the gulley, he craned his neck over the top of the snow cornice to see three figures ploughing up through the snow towards him. They held their rifles above their heads, surging forward in single file. There were more shouts then others appeared, leaving their tents and following in their comrades' tracks up the steep slope.

Why hadn't they taken a shot at them? Why weren't they firing?

Luca's head turned slowly towards the ground as the answer came to him. The soldiers were scared of triggering an avalanche. The entire gulley was filled with heavy powder, melted into unstable layers by the heat of the midday sun.

An avalanche.

Tearing open his rucksack, Luca pulled out his MSR stove and the reinforced metal fuel bottle. He'd done it as a schoolboy once before, but would this single bottle really have the power to collapse the cornice? He looked at it, the metal cold in his hands, praying it would be enough.

Reaching back into his rucksack, he pulled out his old Nalgene water bottle, unscrewing the top and flinging what was left of his water on to the snow. Decanting the contents of the fuel bottle into it, he raised it to the light, watching the Coleman's white fuel slosh from side to side. Then, with a sharp jab of his pocket-knife, he stabbed a tiny hole through the plastic lid and carefully placed the bottle upright in the snow beside him.

Luca turned, looking down into the gulley. The soldiers were already a third of the way up and moving fast. He could hear their shouts filtering up the side of the mountain.

Wrenching open his jacket, he tore a long strip from the bottom of his T-shirt, cutting the last of the cotton free with his knife. He poured a little more fuel over the cotton, using the blade of the knife to poke it through the hole in the lid of the water bottle. With a sharp twist of his hands, he sealed tight the lid.

He'd been sixteen when, with a few friends, he'd first managed to make a Molotov cocktail from an old whisky bottle and some fuel siphoned from his dad's lawnmower. On the third attempt it had blown the park swings from their foundations, charring the entire metal frame. Pressure . . . that was the secret to making a Molotov cocktail actually explode. He needed to seal the water bottle tight.

Luca stared down at his own shaking hands, the spilled fuel shimmering on his skin. He twisted the lid as tight as he could, then, on his hands and knees, began digging in the snow, stabbing at it with the blade of his pocket-knife. He kept digging, scraping the loose snow away with his bare hands and flinging it in a pile behind him. Soon he was up to his elbow, then his shoulder.

Still he kept digging at the narrow hole. The knuckles of his hands started bleeding, rubbed raw from the snow, and he could feel his chest heaving up and down. Eventually he stopped, sitting back on his knees. He grabbed the water bottle, sloshing the very last dregs of fuel over the wick, and pulled his lighter from his pocket.

The flint caught, sending sparks across his hand, but there was no flame. Desperately he pressed his thumb down, spinning the wheel again and again. At last a tiny blue flame flickered up, no bigger than the nail of his thumb. Luca quickly ran it under the fabric until the fire spread slowly, moving with an almost invisible flame. Then, sliding the bottle down into the hole, he packed handfuls of snow over the opening and stepped back quickly.

Seconds passed. Nothing happened. Luca stood with his hands

clutched in front of his chest, willing the fuel to catch. He heard more shouts and moved to one side, staring down into the gulley.

The first of the line of soldiers was nearing the summit. Luca could see his face clearly now, his cheeks flushed with colour from the effort of wading up through the deep snow. His jacket was unbuttoned, flapping out behind him, and his bare hands were clamped round the grip of his rifle, the finger already resting against the trigger.

The soldier looked up, straight into Luca's eyes. The muzzle of his rifle instinctively swivelled towards him, but then the soldier's eyes flicked towards the huge overhanging snow cornice just to his left. He lowered the rifle, but surged forward with renewed energy. He was almost at the top.

'Shit!' Luca screamed, looking down at the pile of snow. It hadn't worked.

For a moment he glanced towards Geltang, every instinct telling him to follow Shara and run for it. Then, diving forward, he clawed back the snow and reached inside. He pulled the water bottle to the surface, staring down at the improvised wick.

The flame had gone out.

Brushing the snow off, he lit the wick again, the lighter catching easily this time. Slamming the bottle back into the snow, he managed to throw only a single handful over the opening before flinging himself backwards. Just beyond the edge of the snow cornice, he heard a shout. He turned to see the top half of the soldier standing a pace below the ridge. His rifle was raised, pointing at Luca.

It was over.

Chapter 55

'Look at him,' Rega shouted out across the sea of expectant faces. 'The seventh Abbot of Geltang and High Lama of the blue order. Yet he is nothing more than a tired old man!'

Light pierced the Great Temple from tall windows set either side of the gilded doors. The night's torches were still lit but slowly dying as the full light of morning streamed into the crowded chamber.

'Do not be deceived,' Rega continued, his voice straining, 'he is no great leader. He just rots in his chambers, allowing our sacred monastery to go to ruin as he follows his own selfish path. Even now the Chinese approach, yet he does nothing!'

The Abbot was standing in front of the dais wrapped in the coarse, brown clothing of the Perfect Life. The tunic had been ripped open below his chest so that his narrow shoulders were bare, the skin waxen and pale from so many days spent closeted from the daylight. His head was lowered, eyes shut, while Rega ranted just above him.

For nearly an hour the public denunciation had continued, with Rega stirring the crowd into a frenzy. When the Abbot had first been paraded in front of the dais, silence had descended across the Great Temple. Each monk had stared in mute amazement at the filthy old man before them, his clothes in rags and his head bent low. Could this really be their sacred leader?

But as Rega's accusations continued, the untouchable aura that once seemed to surround the Abbot was quickly washed away by the mocking contempt of the novices. They crowded the dais, hanging on Rega's every word and baying for action.

Standing against a side wall, Dorje burned with frustration. He stared out impotently across the sea of sneering faces and the whole incredible scene before him. Why didn't the Abbot say something? Why didn't he deny these ridiculous charges and win back his monastery?

Dorje watched the mass of monks surge forward again. There were over five hundred of them crammed into the temple, shouting and jostling for a better view, while their elders stood, like Dorje, on the periphery. They remained in silence, unable to make themselves heard above the noise and chaos.

Then Dorje understood. It was the same for the Abbot. Even if he tried to protest, no one would have heard him.

A soft breeze blew through the temple. Dorje looked up as the flames of the candles flickered. The gilded doors were being forced back on their hinges, and beyond them two figures had stepped into the light. He saw Shara's long black hair and the boy clutched in her arms.

Dorje moved towards the back of the dais. He jostled against the other monks, fighting his way through, until he could see the trumpeters standing in a line.

'Sound the arrival!' he ordered above the din. The first of the trumpeters stared at him in confusion.

'Do as I say!' Dorje yelled. A moment later, the silver trumpet blasted out a long, shimmering note. The noise of the crowd lessened, as Rega spun round to see what was happening.

'Who ordered you to play?' he thundered, but Dorje had already reached the back of the dais and clambered up on top. He rushed forward across the stage, looking out at the crowd.

'Silence!' he shouted, pointing towards the door. 'Silence for the Panchen Lama – the rightful leader of Tibet.'

Silence fell as all eyes turned to the temple doors where Babu slowly slipped from Shara's grasp. He stood uncertainly by her side, his large brown eyes staring from face to face in the crowd.

'So the boy returns,' Rega whispered, craning his neck round.

A muttering began as Shara led Babu forward by the hand. The monks pressed back and a ragged path was cleared all the way to the dais and the Abbot's marble throne. Babu walked through it, his felt boots taking small, steady steps across the vast temple floor. His heavy sheepskin jacket was bunched up around his shoulders so that his chin was buried in the soft wool while his eyes stared out above, passing slowly from monk to monk.

As they approached, Rega raised a finger.

'This is indeed the new reincarnation of the Panchen Lama,' he shouted. 'He has been within our very walls, yet the Abbot kept him from us. He deceived us all.' Rega stalked forward to the edge of the dais. 'Listen to me, my brothers. I will take the boy and restore him to his rightful place. I will return him to his seat in Shigatse and win back our country!'

There was a cheer from some of the novices as Shara and Babu came to halt in front of them. Shara was staring at Rega, at his gold robes and the *Dharmachakra* raised in his right hand, unable to believe what had happened in her absence. He had taken control of the monastery.

Averting her eyes from his lifeless gaze, she turned to the Abbot, reaching forward and holding on to his arm.

'The Chinese are coming,' she whispered. 'We must evacuate the monastery.'

Before the Abbot could answer, Rega turned back towards the crowd. He had heard what she had said.

'The moment has come, my brothers!' he bellowed. 'The Chinese are finally upon us. It is time to fight!'

At this the Abbot finally raised his hand, trying to shout above the wave of fresh panic and shouting that erupted.

'No! Do not give in to violence. We must evacuate, go deeper into the mountains . . .'

'Fight!' Rega screamed again, punching his arm into the air. 'It is time for Geltang to lead the revolution and defeat the Chinese! We must fight!'

The monks burst into action, surging towards the temple doors. Eyes were wide with elation while fists punched the air, mimicking Rega. Some held heavy brass candlesticks in their hands, while others had broken the low palisade surrounding the dais, using the thick wooden poles as makeshift cudgels. They began stampeding towards the temple doors, a mob ready to lynch anyone in their path.

Rega's voice carried above the din, urging them on with every last breath, while the Abbot shouted in vain, still trying to be heard.

In the space just before the dais, Babu sat down on the floor. He inhaled deeply, tucking one leg across the other in the lotus position, and with his hands gently resting on his knees, began a slow, melodious chant. The words rolled from his lips as his eyes clamped shut, his expression changing to one of complete calm. Amidst the mayhem and confusion, his stillness attracted the attention of those immediately surrounding him.

The Abbot stared down at him, an incredulous smile on his lips. Then he moved forward and lowered himself on to the floor beside him, staring at the boy's face for an instant before shutting his own eyes and picking up the same chant. Their two heads swayed back and forth in unison, the words rolling from their lips in a soft, unbroken flow.

In the semi-circle around the dais the crowd stared at them, caught between the hysteria of the novices and the sudden calmness of the Abbot and the boy. Dorje bustled to the front, joining them on the floor, before Shara quickly followed, settling herself down beside Babu. A few of the elders who were watching also lowered themselves on to the ground, picking up the rhythm of the chant. Then more followed. And still more.

Voice built on voice, merging together to create a steady undercurrent to the panic all around. Up on the dais, Rega jerked his head from side to side.

'What is the meaning of this?' he shouted, trying to understand where the chant was coming from. 'The Chinese approach. You cannot just sit here in prayer!'

Soon a different sort of movement was spreading through the great hall as the remaining monks looked back and saw a growing circle of their brothers seated on the floor. While some just turned to stare at the spectacle, others followed suit. Large swathes of the temple began to fill with seated monks, joined shoulder to shoulder, each swaying in rhythm with the chant.

The noise grew and grew as more monks returned to join their brothers on the floor of the temple, until only a few of the novices were left standing.

The Abbot got to his feet then, signalling to the trumpeter to sound the note again. It blasted out across the temple before wavering into silence. All eyes turned towards him.

'Brothers, this is Geltang,' he said, gesturing to the seated gathering. 'Compassion is our guiding principle. Not violence.'

Gently raising Babu to his feet, he led him to the throne set on the dais. Clambering on to it, he looked tiny in the wide seat of ornately carved stone.

'This is our new leader,' the Abbot announced, turning to face the crowd once again. 'We recognise His Holiness Babugedhun Choekyi Nyima, eleventh Panchen Lama and rightful leader of Tibet.'

A wave of bowing swept through those already seated, while the remaining novices by the temple doors quickly shuffled on to the floor. The Abbot looked at Babu who sat with his hands outstretched, just managing to balance them on the huge armrests of the throne.

'It is for you to decide, Your Holiness. The Chinese approach. Do we evacuate the monastery?'

Rega swung round towards the throne.

'He is but a boy,' he said in disgust. 'How can he decide?'

'Silence!' the Abbot declared, raising a finger. 'You have no place here any more.'

Rega's cheeks flushed with anger and he went to protest, raising the *Dharmachakra* above his head, but the Abbot turned towards the sea of monks before them.

'Silence as His Holiness speaks!' he shouted. The noise in the temple dropped to nothing as each monk stared expectantly at Babu. The young boy's eyes moved from one monk to the next in the endless sea of faces, before he finally spoke, his voice soft and high pitched.

'We must leave,' he said. 'We must go as pilgrims to find sanctuary in the mountains. As your ancestors once did, when Geltang was first made.'

The Abbot nodded before turning back to the monks.

'Take the treasure of Geltang and only what you need to survive,' he ordered. Then, signalling for the temple doors to be opened wide, he stepped down from the throne. In a flurry of robes, every monk in the order got to his feet.

'Now, my brothers, we must hurry.'

Chapter 56

The soldier stood just below the ridge, the sights of his rifle centred on Luca's chest.

'Don't shoot!' Luca shouted, slowly raising his hands above his head. He'd taken a step towards the edge of the gulley when there was a muffled boom and a spray of loose snow shot towards him in a long, sweeping arc. As Luca threw himself back on to the ground, the soldier's finger instinctively squeezed around the trigger.

There was a thunderous crack and a flame leaped from the end of the rifle. The bullet smacked into the snow just behind Luca's shoulder, missing him by inches. The soldier was hugging the stock tighter into his shoulder, quickly taking aim once again, when a crack split the deep snow in front of him. It splintered into further cracks as the towering mass of the snow cornice jolted downwards, sending pressure waves fanning out across the entire width of the gulley.

The soldier rocked backwards, trying to steady his balance. The muzzle of his rifle dipped as the snow all around him started to move. The entire base of the cornice bulged outwards, collapsing under its own weight, and began tumbling down the face of the gulley. Its momentum wrenched snow from the farthest corners of the slope, dragging it down in a series of smaller slides.

The soldier flung himself forwards, his arms outstretched, desperately clawing against the streaming snow. Luca lunged towards him, trying to grab one of his hands, but the avalanche was now rolling downwards with an unstoppable force, and the soldier was swept from his grasp.

With a long rumbling boom, the wave of snow picked up everything in its path, tumbling down with terrifying speed. The snow was wet and heavy, melded together in vast chunks that spun ahead of the main flow like rubble. They bounced past the remaining soldiers, stretched out in single file along the length of the gulley.

As one, the soldiers looked up at the wall of snow crashing down towards them. Some simply stared in bewildered horror while others attempted to turn and run. With frightening ease the avalanche engulfed them all, their bodies disappearing from view within a couple of seconds.

Zhu stared up the gulley, his face frozen with fear. Like Chen, he had heard the sound of the rifle shot and now stood with his binoculars trained, trying to see whether the Westerner had actually been hit. Then they heard the boom of the avalanche starting and watched in horror as the snow began to crash down towards them.

Zhu stood transfixed by the sight. The sheer scale of it was unbelievable, the noise deafening. Suddenly he felt himself being pulled by the arm.

'Follow me!' Chen shouted, yanking him forward with such force that Zhu fought to stay on his feet. Together, they struggled back towards the protection of the Kooms, Chen using his massive body to plough his way through the deep snow and pulling the captain behind him with savage jerks of his arm.

The noise was all around them now as the first tumbling balls of snow ricocheted past them, smacking into the rocks ahead. The massive stone that stood at the entrance to the Kooms was only a few feet from them now. Just a few more paces and they would be there.

Chen pulled Zhu forward again, forcing him round the back of a boulder just as the main flow of the avalanche swept across them. They were ripped apart as snow surged over the top of the rock and around its sides, picking them both up in its flow. The sudden speed was incredible, the snow packing in around them in a moving torrent, knocking the wind from their bodies with brutal force.

Chen could feel himself being hurled forward. There was light, then a sudden blackness, and then all he could feel was the weight of snow packed in around him, in his mouth, ears and nose, choking all the breath from his body. Something smashed into the front of his face and his vision went black.

Eight hundred metres higher up, Luca watched in disbelief as the first columns of the Kooms were knocked down by the force of the avalanche, twisting round in the direction of its flow like pebbles. But as the snow swept further into the maze of rocks it began to slow, losing power and dispersing into long, reaching tentacles. Eventually the last of the avalanche ground to a halt and the mass of snow finally lay still.

An extraordinary silence filled the mountainside.

Luca took in the scene of desolation below him, his mouth hanging open in shock. It was as if the mountain had been scalped. Patches of bare rock were visible in streaks across the face of the gulley. Lower down, at the beginning of the Kooms, the snow lay metres deep. Odd shards of rock managed to pierce through the surface, jutting out at crooked angles, while the remainder lay lost under the vast blanket of snow.

Luca slowly clambered to his feet. He stood alone at the head of the gulley, mesmerised by the sheer power of the avalanche he had unleashed. He had started it deliberately, with the intention of stopping the soldiers from climbing the gulley, but he had never believed it would kill every living thing in its path. He had never imagined such a reckoning.

He had killed them all. Just like that.

A wave of exhaustion spread through him and his whole body sagged. Every bruise and graze seemed to ache at once as the adrenaline he had been feeding off for so long finally ebbed from his veins and he sank down to his knees. His eyes gravitated to where the

Chinese had pitched their camp. It was at the lowest point of the slope where the snow would now be deepest.

At least Bill's body would stay buried. He would remain here, entombed by the mountains he loved, forever shrouded in their frozen snow.

'I'm so sorry,' Luca whispered, as tears ran down his cheeks. 'I'm so sorry I ever got you into this.'

An entire hour passed before he finally turned away from the desolate graveyard and back towards the path and the monastery of Geltang.

Zhu blinked, trying to see in the darkness.

Snow was packed over his face and eyelids, clogging his mouth and throat. His breath came in shallow, wheezing gasps, and the snow in his mouth was making him retch. He twisted his body, trying to break free, then screamed as the movement sent spikes of pain shooting up from his broken ribs.

He didn't feel cold yet. That would come later. His clothes were pasted to his limbs and the layer of snow around his body was slowly beginning to melt from his body heat, drawing the warmth away from his core. His hands were shaking, gloves ripped off by the avalanche and the nail-less fingers of his right hand clawed at the freezing snow, trying to dig himself free.

Jerking forward again, he felt his right leg kick clear of the snow and into the air. He cried out in pain as his ribs flexed from the movement, then, gritting his teeth, tried to force the other leg free. Using every ounce of strength in his thigh, he pulled his knee upwards in desperate jerks but his leg remained locked in position. He tried again, the pain threatening to overwhelm him, before his neck muscles finally relaxed in exhaustion, dropping his head deeper into the snow.

For a moment Zhu's whole body went limp; the fight was just too much, the snow's grip too strong. His eyes were wide, staring blindly into the darkness of the snow as a wave of claustrophobia washed over him. He contemplated nothingness; impassive, black nothingness. Death was close.

Zhu screamed, twisting his whole body round and jerking manically against the imprisoning snow. Madness rose in him, overriding the pain and exhaustion, and he lashed out in all directions, flailing with his limbs. He felt a sudden movement around the ankle and then his other foot broke through the crust of snow. He fought harder, releasing his knee, then the top half of his thigh.

A surge of elation flowed through him. He twisted again and again, pushing out with his hips and punching his arms. Eventually he broke free, raising his hands to his face to paw away the last of the snow. He could breathe; the weight was finally off him.

It took Zhu nearly half an hour to summon the strength to get to his feet. Even then, as his body shook from cold, he realised how lucky he had been to be spat to the top of the avalanche. Only a foot below the surface and yet it had been almost impossible for him to break free.

Now he had to keep moving, to fight off the paralysing cold. The sweat on his lower back had begun to freeze against his body and, without hat or gloves, he could feel the heat draining from him. It wouldn't be long before the cold would overtake him completely.

Zhu looked up and saw the towering rocks ahead of him. He would have to follow their route from here to make it back to the cliff-face.

He stood for a moment longer, his body rigid and aching, listening to the silence of the mountain. Then, from somewhere to his right, he heard the sound of groaning. Crunching his way across the pitted surface of the avalanche, he followed the sound, clutching his hand to his ribs as he walked. The snow was like rubble underfoot, stacked high against the rocks.

As he came closer, he could see the top half of a body slumped forward, head lolling to one side. A soldier was wedged against a low slab of rock, with only his top half exposed. Zhu took another step closer and pulled back the mop of hair. It was Chen. His eyes were half-closed and blood streamed out of his nose in two frozen lines. His jaw was slack and his chest heaved from the effort of breathing.

'I can't feel my legs,' he groaned, trying to focus his eyes on the figure before him. Zhu looked down and saw that his whole pelvis had shifted unnaturally to one side. The avalanche had nearly broken him in two.

Zhu's eyes ran over the shattered body. He could see something in Chen's right hand, a line of photographs that he had pulled from the top pocket of his jacket.

Reaching down, Zhu grabbed on to the sleeve of his jacket with both hands and tugged as hard as he could. Chen felt his body yanked forward, his chin dipping against his chest as Zhu pulled harder and harder.

'Thank you,' he whispered, his eyes finally focusing on the top half of Zhu's head. 'I can make it. I can make it back.'

His hands closed round the pictures in his hands and he shut his eyes. Zhu pulled once again and the sleeve of Chen's jacket slipped from his arm. Zhu twisted it round, peeling it off his massive back and down across the other arm.

As the jacket came free, Zhu staggered back a pace. He swung the warm coat over his own shoulders.

Chen's eyes stared down at the military-issue shirt stretched over his chest. He could see thin traces of his body heat escaping into the icy air.

'You can't . . .' he breathed, his voice barely more than a murmur. 'You can't . . . do this.'

Zhu didn't answer, but finished buttoning up the jacket. Without a word to Chen he turned away, working his way over the snow towards the exposed part of the Kooms. Chen watched him slowly start to clamber his way through, then, in the silence that followed, a broken laugh escaped his lips.

'Scared of heights,' he wheezed. 'You'll never get down the cliff-face.'

He inhaled, mustering the last of his strength.

'You deserve to die out here!' he shouted. 'Just die!'

His head slumped forward against his chest and as the blackness began to well across his vision, he spoke once again.

'We all deserve to die . . .' With one final wheeze, his body went limp and the line of photographs he was holding, gently fluttered to the ground.

Zhu staggered forward, clutching his ribs. As he came down off the last of the avalanche, he turned from side to side, searching for the flares. A few yards ahead of him a dull red glow emanated from a rock. The flame had eaten through almost the entire length of the stick. It had been nearly six hours since they had come this way.

Lurching forward, Zhu searched for the next flare, sweat beading his ashen face. Words came from his mouth in an unintelligible stream, his mind closed off from the world around him.

For hours he continued clambering; the endless rocks, the dull red flares. He pulled his aching body over the next slab of rock, then the next.

Eventually he crawled under an overhanging slab and out into the open bowl of the glacier. As he came into the open space, he wheeled round towards the gulley behind, raising his arms wide.

'You can't hide forever,' he screamed in English. 'I will return with hundreds of men and find you. Do you hear me?'

His face creased with pain as he called out to the mountain: 'And when I return, I will kill every breathing thing!'

Chapter 57

Dorje raised the ornate china teapot a few inches higher and green tea cascaded into the delicate bowls below. Luca sat opposite him on the prayer mat.

Raised on a low platform at one end, the Abbot sat facing them both with his legs folded beneath him. He inhaled the aroma of the tea wafting across the room before his eyes settled on Luca.

They sat in a circular room with a lofty, domed ceiling, like a bell tower. Light poured in from every direction through the narrow windows that had been carved into the walls at regular intervals. They were in the highest point of the entire monastery, but as Luca had climbed the last of the twisting stairs he had settled down on the floor without so much as a glance at the glorious panorama of mountains outside.

The Abbot stared at him, his gaze passing over each part of Luca's face. A long scar ran over the top of his lip and his cheeks were still puffy from the last of the swelling. In the week that had passed since the avalanche, the Westerner's face had healed a great deal. Physically, he was recovering well, but in all that time he had barely uttered a word. The Abbot had been informed that he lay for hours in his cell, staring vacantly at the ceiling and hardly touching his food.

Dorje placed a bowl in Luca's open hand. As Luca set it down in front of him, some of the boiling tea sloshed over the rim and scalded his fingers. He didn't appear to notice. Instead, he returned the Abbot's gaze, his own eyes dull from sleepless nights.

'So what happens now?' he asked.

'That depends to whom you refer,' Dorje answered, before taking a sip of his tea.

'The boy.'

'His Holiness will remain here at Geltang under the direct supervision of our Abbot. He will be instructed in our teachings to the very highest level, until he is ready to take his place in Shigatse.'

'But that means the Chinese will win,' Luca said flatly. 'After all that's happened, after so many people died, you're just going to sit back while they crown their own Panchen Lama.'

Dorje inhaled deeply, then nodded. 'Indeed they will have their victory, but only for now. We cannot risk exposing Babu to the world before he is old enough to know his own mind and his own path. Many would seek to control him, as you saw even within our own walls. You must remember that despite the awesome knowledge and power within Babu, he is still just a boy. We shall wait until he is ready to be known. But rest assured, Mr Matthews, he will be known, and our rightful ruler will be restored.'

'That could be years from now. Decades even.'

Dorje nodded again. 'It could indeed, but fortunately, patience is one of our greatest attributes. We have already waited many decades for our country to be free, and are prepared to wait many more.'

He took another sip of tea and gestured for Luca to do the same. As Luca raised the bowl to his lips, the Abbot's eyes finally left him and turned towards Dorje.

'I believe it is time to tell the Westerner the whole truth about our monastery,' he said in Tibetan, his voice slow and deliberate.

Dorje looked aghast, the bowl tilting in his hands and spilling some tea on to his lap.

'But why, Your Holiness? Why share such knowledge with an outsider?'

The Abbot's eyes traced over Luca's slumped shoulders and the scar running across his lip.

'Because he has given everything for us,' he said. 'After all that has happened, he deserves to know what he has helped save.'

Dorje inhaled deeply, setting his bowl back down in front of him. He hesitated for a second, then as the Abbot nodded again, started to speak.

'Some time ago, Mr Matthews, I told you that Geltang Monastery was a repository of treasure, but the treasure I was referring to had nothing to do with the statues you happened upon in the basement.'

Luca looked up as an image came to him of the Buddha's eyes sparkling in the flame of his lighter.

'But I saw them . . . I saw the diamonds and gems.'

'To some they are significant, true, but to us, they are little more than tokens with which to decorate our holy statues. Geltang was not built to safeguard them. Not at all. Our mountain *beyul*, indeed all our secret *beyuls*, were built for another purpose entirely. But you need to understand something of our history before this story will make sense.'

Dorje stood up, moving over to one of the windows to stare out at the view.

'Over two thousand years ago, an Indian prince called Siddhartha Gautama was the first to attain perfect enlightenment. He became what we call the Supreme Buddha. During his lifetime his teachings, and by that I mean the actual words he spoke, were precisely copied down by scribes and divided into eight sections, or paths as they were called. Each path was then divided again by subject into a further eight.

'This gave rise to a total of sixty-four books. Now, you must remember that these books were not copies or hearsay, they had not been rewritten or revised – they were the actual words spoken by the Supreme Buddha.

The books were then divided and spread amongst our *beyuls* for safe-keeping, housed in our most secure libraries and kept secret from the world.'

Dorje slowly turned away from the window, his expression gradually darkening.

'But, as you know, our *beyuls* were discovered and razed to the ground. One by one they fell, and many of our treasured books were lost. After Benchaan Monastery fell, two complete paths were destroyed by the flames and it was then that a decision was made throughout the five orders to draw all knowledge to Geltang. But the books could not be transported by hand. This was the dark time of the Cultural Revolution and all religious works were either confiscated or burned on sight, their carriers arrested and brutally tortured. We could not afford for any more to be lost.

'So, in all this madness, certain monks were chosen to memorise each of the books by rote. Every word, sentence and paragraph of Buddha was thus preserved in living, walking books. Disguised as peasants or traders, they then made their way past road blocks and patrols, eventually arriving at Geltang to begin the long process of transcribing each of the teachings back on to paper.'

'Books?' Luca repeated. 'That's what all this is about – books?'

'Yes,' Dorje answered softly. 'And now we have nearly all of the surviving texts. The last of the eighth path is all but complete.'

Luca shook his head, picturing the lines of monks he had seen in the library, pens working in a ceaseless flow across the pages. Shara had been there, amongst them.

'That's what she was delivering, wasn't it?'

'I presume you mean Miss Shara? She is indeed a living book – the fifth book of the eighth path, and one of our most treasured works. She is here under most exceptional circumstances. Her brother was meant to deliver the text to us but was caught crossing the border three years ago. We have not heard from him since that day, nor know anything more of his fate. So, after much deliberation, it was discovered that Miss Shara has the same ability as her brother and she volunteered to take his place. As she was travelling across the breadth of Tibet to deliver her book to our sacred monastery, news of an attempt on His Holiness's life was made known to members of the Gelugpa sect. They managed to divert her and she was charged with bringing the boy here. The rest of the story is of course known to you.'

Luca's expression remained blank as he tried to imagine memorising an entire book. The tomes he had seen in the library were inches thick.

'I've been in the library and seen them working,' he said, 'but I can't understand how a person could memorise an entire book.'

'To be sure, it is no small matter, especially given the significance of what they were memorising. But the human mind is capable of so much more than we give it credit for. Even in Western societies you see abundant evidence of all it can do. Take those afflicted by certain types of autism, for instance. They are able to retain and process vast amounts of information.' Dorje paused, thinking back to the early days when he had first arrived at Geltang, disguised as a wandering beggar. 'It was only after many years and countless trials of controlled meditation that some of us were able to access this exact same part of the brain.'

As Dorje fell silent, a beam of sunlight cut through one of the open windows, shining down on to the low table in front of them. The Abbot craned his neck slightly, his eyes crinkling in a soft smile as his gaze moved out to the view of the mountains. After a moment, he gestured for Luca to go to the window for himself. Luca set down his bowl and slowly got to his feet.

Beyond the interlocking valleys the entire pyramid mountain was exposed, its summit free from cloud in a rare moment. Luca's eyes followed the clean lines of its sides until they converged in a sharp, glinting point, as if threatening to pierce a hole in the sky. Despite it all, he was staggered by the mountain's beauty. He could feel the cool air circulating through the open window and inhaled deeply, the emotions he had struggled with during the past week resurfacing with overwhelming force.

There was a soft tinkling sound and Lucaz turned to see the Abbot holding a small, golden bell. The Abbot gestured for Luca to sit before him and, with his right hand outstretched, rested his palm against Luca's forehead. Luca kept his head bent low as the Abbot recited a long blessing before finally removing his hand.

'Time for you to go,' he said in a thick accent.

A sudden fear swept over Luca at the idea of leaving. He had been so engrossed in his own endless remorse that he had blocked out any thought of what would happen when he finally made it home.

Now a chill settled in the pit of his stomach. It wasn't so much having to resume his life and deal with the banality of everything he had left behind – his job, his home, his father's hopes – it was having to face Cathy and explain the terrible tragedy of it all. It was as if he had been living in suspended judgement since Bill had died. But with each day that passed, the images he had first seen in the Chinese soldier's tent had lengthened, hardening into bitter emotions that replayed endlessly in his mind. He would often wake from them feeling physically sick.

How could he possibly go back now? How would they ever understand what had truly happened?

Luca felt the same sickness wash over him and reached out a hand to steady himself. He was suddenly overtaken by a desire to stay here in Geltang, amongst the placid monks and silent mountains. Why should he not stay – fall back into a new life here and leave behind everything he had once known?

'I don't want to go,' he said, his eyes meeting the Abbot's. 'I need some time to work it all out. Begin again.'

The Abbot's expression remained set.

'You must face own life,' he said, pointing a finger at Luca's chest. 'Only once you see own life, can you see others.'

There was the sound of approaching footsteps and Shara arrived at the top of the stairs. She bowed deeply towards the Abbot before her eyes settled on Luca. A flash of concern passed over her face, before she reached out a hand towards him.

'Come,' she said, attempting a smile. 'Everything is ready.'

Luca stood under the blossom trees in the courtyard, watching the petals slowly drift to the ground. Just to the right, the stone steps reached down into the base of the mountain far below. It felt as if a lifetime had passed since they had first staggered across these same flagstones with Bill held in their arms.

Shara had already prepared Luca's rucksack and it was resting on its side by the first of the steps, crammed with provisions and kit. On an enclave in the nearby wall, she was pouring two fist-sized cups of tea.

'So how long will it take you to transcribe the whole book?' Luca asked, still staring at the blossom.

'Two to three years at least,' Shara answered, carefully setting the cups down on the edge of the first step and looking out at the view. Luca moved closer, so that they were side by side. 'Of course, it took me many more years to memorise it in the first place.'

Luca glanced down at the delicate china cups.

'I think I've had enough of that stuff,' he said.

'This one is for me,' Shara said, picking up one of the cups and taking a small sip. 'The other will wait here for you, as is our custom, in case you ever decide to return.'

Luca looked up into her pale green eyes. They shone with a sadness he'd not seen before, and from the way her lips were pressed together, he could tell she was trying to hold back her emotions.

'But the Abbot told me to leave. He doesn't want me back.'

'He told you to face up to your life. When you've done that, you're free to go wherever you choose.' She reached out and took one of his hands between both of hers. 'But whatever happens, Luca, just remember that it was not your fault that Bill died.'

At the mention of his name, Luca turned his eyes away from hers.

The enormity of it all crashed over him again, almost driving the air from his chest.

'Goodbye, Shara,' he whispered, leaning forward to kiss her cheek. His face remained pressed against hers for a moment longer, breathing in her delicate scent. Then he suddenly turned away, squaring his shoulders. He scooped his rucksack off the ground and started down the steps, tilting his face away from her and hiding his eyes.

Shara remained at the head of the stairway, the breeze playing with the long strands of her hair. For a long while she watched his retreating figure, waiting for him to turn his head back towards the monastery. But he kept on walking, until his outline had gradually sunk back into the far mountains and the tea sitting beside her had long since gone cold.

Chapter 58

Rega staggered along the broken pathway, clutching on to Drang's arm. The toes of his sandals caught on the loose stones, tripping him forward, while his spare arm reached out into thin air, fingers splayed wide.

Everything was so unfamiliar. There was no corridor to guide him, no indentations in the stone wall to show him the way. His whole world had been based on familiarity and memory, and now all that had been ripped from him.

The wind streamed across his face and Rega inhaled the cold air deep into his lungs. It smelled bitter and fresh, and he didn't recognise a single part of it. In the monastery he had been able to tell every storeroom from the smell of its countless jars and vials. He could navigate the twists of the library just from the aroma of the dry parchments. Yet here, in the open vastness of the mountains, all that knowledge suddenly counted for nothing.

The wind grew in strength, tugging at his cowl and billowing out his robes.

The moment he was banished from Geltang, and the gates had been bolted shut behind him, Rega had felt a terrible sense of helplessness overcome him.

'We must reach the shelter of the lower valleys,' he said, trying to keep the fear from his voice.

He could feel Drang tugging at his sleeve. They were moving tortuously slowly down the path and he guessed his aide's patience was fast running out. In the mountains, an old blind man could only slow him down.

'You have always been a loyal aide,' Rega said, briefly resting his other hand on Drang's forearm. 'And you shall be rewarded for such service, I give you my word.'

Drang only grunted, his good eye staring down the slope in front of him. Gauze bandages were wrapped tight across his face, and where the skin was visible it shone with a greasy extract used in the treatment of burns. Under the bandages, weeping patches of raw skin clung to the gauze.

'Most loyal,' Rega repeated, fear thick in his voice.

Drang grunted again, pressing him forward. Across the far line of mountain peaks he could see clouds rolling over the sky, blotting out the sun. The wind had already changed direction, bringing in an icy cold front from the higher slopes. A storm was brewing.

Rega stumbled on a rock lying in the centre of the pathway, his hands digging into Drang's arm for support. He pulled himself upright, his breathing laboured, and quickly tried to gather himself to continue. Drang simply watched, his expression unchanged, as Rega staggered forward once more.

For another hour they continued before Drang pulled him to a halt.

'The ground is more dangerous ahead, Father,' he said. 'The path has run out. I need to go ahead and check the way down.'

Rega nodded and very slowly uncurled his hands from Drang's arm. He stood on his own, shifting his weight and reaching out his arms to balance himself. He heard Drang leave a bag at his feet, then the scuffing of his boots across the uneven ground just ahead and some loose pebbles tumbling away down the slope. After that, there was only the noise of the mounting wind.

For over two hours Rega stood where he was, in the vain hope of

Drang returning. Even when he understood that his aide was never coming back, he remained in the same place for want of anywhere else to go. The wind whipped around him, sending ripples across the folds of his robes, but he did not reach down into the bag at his feet and put on one of the heavy jackets they'd been given.

Turning back in the direction they had come, Rega tilted his head up towards the distant walls of Geltang, his expression shadowed with remorse.

'I'm so tired of it all,' he whispered. Then, sitting down on the hard ground, he lowered his head, letting the cold slowly claim him.

Chapter 59

3 *November 2005*

Jack Milton was discussing Phd potential with an undergraduate in his study when there was a knock at his door. It opened a fraction to reveal the left side of Luca's face.

'Jesus, Luca!' he said, jumping up from behind his desk. 'We'll continue this later,' he muttered to the student, waving him up from the armchair and out of the room.

As Luca stepped hesitantly into the office, Jack took him by the shoulders. As soon as he touched him, he could feel just how much weight Luca had lost. His grey eyes looked paler than normal and were ringed with fatigue. Despite his clean clothes, Luca's sunburned face and matted hair made him look weathered and somehow uncivilised, a far cry from the pale academics who normally inhabited Jack's study.

'Why didn't you call?' he demanded. 'We hadn't heard from you in so long, we thought the worst had happened.'

He pulled his nephew forward, hugging him tight in his arms. Eventually, with a couple of awkward pats on his back, Jack stepped away and turned to the window. Behind his reading glasses, Luca could see his eyes were clouded with tears.

'Next time you go on a trip, I'm giving you a bloody satellite phone,' he said, busying himself by making some coffee. Pouring the dregs from the glass pot into the top of the coffee machine again, he packed in some new grounds from a well-thumbed packet and pressed the switch. Soon they were settled into the two armchairs, facing each other.

For over an hour Luca talked. In all that time Jack did not interrupt or ask questions, but sipped his coffee long after it had turned cold. A mixture of disbelief and horror spread across his face as his nephew related every step of the journey. When Luca explained what had happened to Bill, Jack reached up his hands to his face and covered his eyes. His shoulders shook from sobs and for a long time after that they both sat in silence. Eventually Luca got up from his chair and poured his uncle another coffee, resting his hand briefly on his shoulder as he passed him the cup.

When Luca had finished what remained of his story, he reached into his satchel to pull out two battered books, setting them down on the wide armrests of his chair.

'So the Chinese captain was dead when you saw him on the cliff-face?' Jack asked.

Luca nodded. 'He was on a ledge, about ten minutes down from the top, pressed up against the back wall. He must have died of exposure sometime during the night.'

Luca paused for a moment, slowly shaking his head. 'I could see him, Jack. His eyes were frozen open. I could see right into those black eyes.'

'Bastard deserved nothing less,' Jack said vehemently. After another pause, he exhaled deeply and, leaning back in his chair, ran his fingers through his hair. 'So how did you get back to Lhasa?'

Luca almost smiled as an image of René came to mind. He had been there when Luca finally got down off the mountain. Approaching the charred remains of Menkom village, Luca had spotted him in a makeshift chair that was tilted towards the cliff-face, fast asleep in the heat of the midday sun. A towel shaded his face as he slept, while his right leg lay trussed up in bandages, resting on a gnarled wooden tree stump.

He had woken as Luca drew closer across the field, pulling the towel from his face and letting out a shout of laughter. Despite being in obvious pain, he had been tireless in organising yaks with the locals he had befriended, arranging to take them back along the trail to Tingkye, where they had then rejoined a proper road.

'René waited for me that whole time,' Luca said, shaking his head. 'He got me out of Tibet, risking everything once again to smuggle me over the Friendship Bridge into Nepal. All that, and I barely even knew the guy.'

'The kindness of strangers,' Jack said. 'It never ceases to amaze me what human beings are capable of.'

Then he shifted forward in his chair, eyes resting on the two books lying in front of his nephew. Luca followed his gaze, picking up the first and holding it out in front of him.

'I found this in my rucksack when I got back to Lhasa,' he said, unclipping the delicate gilded clasp. 'Shara must have put it there without my knowing.'

As it fell open on Luca's lap, Jack's eyes passed over the white writing set on thick black parchment. The book looked old and well travelled, with angular Tibetan characters stamped across the densely packed pages. Jack's hand reached out, hovering just above it.

'Is that what I think it is?'

'The *Kalak Tantra*,' Luca said, watching the expression on Jack's face change.

'So Sally was wrong. It *does* exist,' he murmured. Jack looked up into Luca's eyes. Aside from everything else, the book corroborated so much of what his nephew had said.

'Shara obviously trusts you,' he said thoughtfully. 'It was a big risk for her to give a foreigner this book. Maybe she is trying to tell you something.'

Luca nodded thoughtfully, but didn't speak. He then shut the book and got up from his chair, returning the *Kalak Tantra* to his satchel. He picked up the other book. It was much smaller: a slim, leather-bound journal, laced together with twine.

'I need you to do something for me, Jack,' he said, handing it over to him. 'Give this to my father. It's my diary and a complete account of what happened. Maybe then he'll understand.'

Jack tried to push it away. 'You give it to him yourself,' he said, a frown appearing on his forehead. 'I know what your father is like, but it would be so much better coming from you.'

Luca shook his head, swinging the satchel over his shoulder.

'I can't. I've got to go and see someone first.'

As he tried to leave, Jack sprang up from his seat.

'OK, I'll take the book to him,' he said, his hand reaching out to grip Luca's arm. 'But you will be all right, won't you, Luca?'

For the first time in their whole meeting, a smile crept across Luca's face. He gently pulled his uncle's hand from his arm.

'Yeah,' he said. 'I think I will. You take care of yourself, Jack.'

With that, he walked out of the dusty study, leaving his uncle staring at the book in his hands.

For a while after that, Jack jumped whenever the phone rang, but it was never Luca. Against his better instincts, he left a few messages on Luca's phone but never received any response. It struck him that, as ever, Luca would let him know when he needed him, but as the weeks passed with still no word, he decided that he should try and track him down.

He discovered that soon after leaving his uncle, Luca had sold his flat, drawing the entire sum of money in a cashier's cheque. He had then gone to Bill's house, spending several hours with Cathy and the kids, before handing over the cheque and leaving once again.

After that, he seemed to vanish.

Some days, Jack sits in his study looking at a satellite map of the Himalayas and thinks he knows where his nephew is. On others, he's not so sure.

But then again, it was always like that with Luca.

Author's Note

The real eleventh Panchen Lama

After the death of the tenth Panchen Lama in 1989, the search for his reincarnation soon became mired in political controversy.

Despite the current Dalai Lama recognising a small boy of only six years old called Gedhun Choekyi Nyima as the rightful successor in 1995, the Chinese authorities immediately arrested the head of the search committee under charges of treason and had the boy and his family removed from Tibet.

A new search committee was then promptly installed who 'chose' Gyancain Norbu as the next Panchen Lama. He still holds this position to this day.

No one has seen or knows the whereabouts of the six-year-old boy, while the Chinese authorities claim to have taken him for 'reasons of his own security'. Even now, no humanitarian groups have been allowed to verify whether he is alive or not.

Although the inauguration of the eleventh Panchen Lama was in 1995, I have decided to set the book in 2005 to make it more current with events as I personally saw them when visiting the country on expedition in 2004.

Acknowledgements

As the book evolved and changed, my thanks must go to so many different people. From the very beginning, sitting around the camp fires in Tibet with Mike Brown and dreaming up the idea of a lost monastery hidden somewhere behind the clouds closing in around us. And to the old woman in the village who took us in and fed us your only chicken. I am always amazed by the kindness of strangers.

To Norbu and the team who helped us hack our way through the rhodendrum forests and got us over those mountain trails, dusty and tired.

To my wife, Robyn, who invested such faith to give me time to write this book, then listened to each new chapter as it was written, always supportive despite the multitude of drafts and new directions.

Then to Kate Weinberg who, more than anyone else, has turned this book into what it is. I can't thank you enough for the endless laps around Holland Park looking for inspiration and the tireless amounts of work and rewrites. You really were amazing. Rosie became the third part of the triangle, patiently offering advice where needed and always steering us back on course. Going to miss our cups of coffee at Café Philies.

To Tif and Luke, as always, with their sound advice and faith – confidence is everything when writing and it was amazing to know you were always there.

My parents for their gentle and constant support in everything I get myself into – especially with the year you guys have had. To Rick and Margie for the space to write and Cirine for reading every single draft. And finally, to Jamie. You made it in!